Big Dogs & Flyboys

A Novel by

SAM MICHEL

SOUTHERN METHODIST UNIVERSITY PRESS

Dallas

9/10

This novel is a work of fiction. Names, characters, places, and incidents are either the product of the author's imagination or are used fictitiously.

Requests for permission to reproduce material from this work should be sent to:
Rights and Permissions
Southern Methodist University Press
PO Box 750415
Dallas, Texas 75275-0415

Cover photo courtesy of the archives of Otto-Lilienthal-Museum (www.lilienthal-museum.de)

Jacket and text design by Tom Dawson

Library of Congress Cataloging-in-Publication Data
Michel, Sam.
Big dogs and flyboys : a novel / by Sam Michel. — 1st ed.
p. cm.
ISBN 978-0-87074-514-0 (acid-free paper)
1. Boys—Fiction. 2. Interracial friendship—Fiction. 3. Flight—Fiction. 4. Burns and scalds—Patients—Fiction. I. Title.

PS3563.I3325B54 2007
813'.54—dc22

2007021254

Printed in the United States of America on acid-free paper

10   9   8   7   6   5   4   3   2   1

Big thanks to Andrew for finding Kathryn. Thanks to Kathryn for passing me on to Gordon and to Lee, and thanks to Gordon and to Lee for recommending these pages to print. My heart as ever to the first Gordon, teacher, inspirer, dear long friend. And a final thanks to my family, Mom and Pop and Brother, to Noy, Benjamin, and Phoebe, intrepid travelers, les amo chicos.

For the General and for Mike, Right Flyers

FLIGHT BECAME ME. A PERSON MIGHT NOT THINK AS MUCH, NOT TO LOOK at me, not now, no, but then, as a kid, in action, certainly back then a person might have seen me and thought, Okay, flight, oh boy, yessir, I guess. In spirit, on the playground, I was hollow boned, the kid with the winged blood, pumped from a feathered heart, the one with the lofted soul whose shape was copied by the genius of Bernoulli. I got picked. I inspired. I ran pretty fast. By height and by weight, I fell somewhere in the upper-middle ranges, in terms of a percentile. Nothing doing with the glands. Doctors, teachers, parents, mirrors—nobody who saw me would have said *disorder*.

I flew, all right. But then I crashed. And then I burned. Let's get this straight. I am the son. The Icarus figure. An update. In the myth of me, I get up there where the sun burns hot, do my crash, have my burn, then happily survive. This is my talent. To survive, happily. I lie here in my gauze and humor while my skin regrows, a healing veteran on the unit. These days, I play a lot of checkers, some chess, watch TV in the lounge and daydream. I close my eyes, go back, and back, and there I see a kid who did not break the bed slats when he hopped and flapped from off the mattress, a kid who soared from swings, from walls, from roofs and lofts and chalk-banked cliffs, a small kid, a light kid, and there I see that kid is me, and there I pony up, unlatch the fat from off my chest and tell myself, *Hello there, meet me, don't I know you, Adam Oney, can it be you, son, all these years now, Adam Oney, flyer?*

1

Sure, back then, I tell you Nature liked me. She embraced me. Early, early on I lay there bawling on the cold linoleum, fallen headfirst from the crib, where I like to think that Nature must have come to me, and whispered in my ear to me, calmingly, entreatingly, enduringly, she must have whispered, *Adam, Adam, try again, boy, you can do it!*

It was a melony thump, according to my mother, a little bawling, and then quiet. She guessed I slept. She had not guessed at blood. A thump, she said, or a whump, in any case a sound too soft to prompt the image in a mother's mind of bleeding. Shock, okay, she said, that I should bawl did not surprise her. That I should cease to bawl did not surprise her. Yet when her soap concluded, and she had clipped her coupons, thawed the milk, signed the checks, and shined the pennies in her loafers, then of course, of course, she said, she was surprised to see my matted scalp and scabby ear when I walked out and made my quiet sign for water.

She told the doctor, "You would have thought it should have sounded something more of like a crack. Like, *crack!* You know? *Sounded like a melon.* I don't think so. But it did. Not just melon either, but a *ripe* one. Do you think that means his head's too soft? And why didn't he cry? I'm thinking, soft or not, there should have been more crying."

In the end, they chalked it up to mystery, why I did not cry; dumb luck, how they figured I had failed sustaining a concussion. Wisely, after fall number six, the two agreed our family should likely not rely on luck and mystery much further, and so it happened that my mother made me up a little pallet, where the photos show me safer in a Dane-sized wire cage.

"Grounded," said my father, first flyer in our household, pilot of our nation's fighting Phantom. Even then, though he only ranked as captain, we were to call him General. According to the photos, the General liked to squat at the door of my cage, poke his finger in so I might grasp a hairy knuckle. This was in the time the General dabbled in varieties of facial hair to compensate his baldness. You see him squatted in his boots, his flight suit, and his shiny jacket, and you can read the mouth beneath that fledgling mustache, meaning to report on my astounding grip. What you might not see are the Winstons and the gin. Hard to see the man whose father left him at birth. Harder still to see his mother's death by Heaven Hill and Sominex, a boyhood given to the custody of friends of second cousins, the General running barefoot through the bayou, an illiterate with ringworm, a towhead posing for the camera in the goatyard with a three-foot-nine-inch catfish. On the other hand, I myself can never wholly see the man who saw so far beyond himself from captain and the bayous. I think it's fair to say you simply see him happy. He looks good, bald. He seems as dry and bone clean as the desert hills to which he chose to have us stationed. He is lean, smooth, and straight. He is tall, long bodied, a man who flies his airship in a slouch to fit his cockpit. He likes a game. He likes me. I think you see me in his eyes, the Adam Oney of the playground, sprightly General of the wild blue yonder.

And me?

The actual me?

Well, I seem plenty happy there to hold the General's finger.

Later, from the days since they decided I was safe enough to sleep uncaged, I recall my happiness extended to the gifts the General made me from the world of playtime aviation. A favorite from that time was *First Flight*, the Wright brothers colorbook. The General sat right on the rug with me, elaborating the miniature history *First Flight* told of Orville and Wilbur bucking the odds at Kitty Hawk. I liked the caps and dunes and the sound of Carolina. I liked that the General did not mind or not if I would keep myself between the lines. /

His job was to be the General. Wing Commander Oney. I was his lieutenant, a pea-green "smoke," the downy-winged ephebe. He sat down with me, though still his voice came up from pretty high above me, and I recall there was a lot of talk up there about your ailerons and flaps, your props, struts, and trim tabs, though I could not give him back the logic when he asked me how the one must be connected to the other. How could I? This was the man with lightning bolts sewn onto his shoulders, the Grim Reaper stepping from the thunderheads, mascot of the General's voodoo squadron: *hahma-hahma-lahma-yahma-hic-hak-hoc!* Logic? Causes and effects? How? A thing was a thing, itself, enough without its other. A kid hears, Mayday, Mayday, Mayday! Roger, he is hearing, out. You got a C66 on your three o'clock, buddy, the pelicans are nesting home to Anahoe, I think old Pap has lit the daylights on the mink farm . . .

Imagine, your daddy buzzed the jungles. He dropped the bombs, strafed the beach, got shot down. He kissed you when he left for work, and his office was the sky, and he called his work a mission. This was the General, leader of men, a man a boy will work so hard to please, he will often lose his view of how to best be pleasing. I remember chewing my tongue a good bit over Orville, really focused on drawing him a mustache in the likeness of the General's. When I told him I was finished, the General held the waxy mess I made up to the sun and told me it was fine, just right, better even than he had expected.

"No lines in flight," he said. "You got the spirit here. We'll worry later how you steer that spirit with the stick and rudder."

As it happened, my trouble in the cockpit bore more strictly on weight and balance than on stick and rudder; the cage my father was to see me grounded by was me, my body, what eats the food here, fills the chair, what swallows its pills, sleeps, wakes, asks for more, and more, and more, only more so. In part, we look to genes. These days I am told I oughtn't wholly blame myself; a person is a person as he's partly told to be a person by genetics. *Face it, your father was a big man, Adam. If I heard you right, you just told me that he had to slouch, sort of scrunch his head down low so he could fit inside his cockpit? Listen, Adam, your mama wasn't any chickadee either. Hardly bird boned. The genes she passed on to you descend from the same line as the genes passed on to her. Tolesrud, am I not mistaken? Well, no offense, but you could stock a football team with a pretty fair-sized interior line using Tolesrud women. Or since it's basketball you like, then think of your mother's people out there playing center, think of your mother as a hefty power forward, maybe, and then ask yourself how you could ever be the fellow in the body playing point.*

Naturally, I am to answer I could never. That's not me, that fellow. Most of what we do here, seems to me, is learn to say which one I am, by saying which one I am not. Easy, once you see poor old Doctor Noggin isn't playing any tricks. He comes in stretched, a little tight around the eyes, possibly excited, though when you look straight into the eye itself you see the man is tired in there, pretty sad at what that eye has given him for seeing. Word around the ward is he has lately married into horses. A second life for Doctor Noggin with a younger lady and a brand new set of younger kids. It's the nurses fill me in. *Doctor Noggin got bucked. Doctor Noggin's old enough to be those kids' grandpa. Oh, well, I don't mean to gossip, I'm just saying, I think it says a lot, a man who knows so much about the human mind to go and get a face-lift.*

"I know exactly what you mean," I tell the doctor. "I never was a shooter. My playing days are over, trust me."

What else should I say? That I spin-dribble? Penetrate? Kick out to our three-point man? When the horn blows, and we take the floor, and the jump ball comes to me, then I ask you, who's the General? Not me. No, sir, not a word from me about the hoops. Not a word about flight. Not for the doc. I like it here, but when I'm up and healed some, I want 0-U-T-T, out. Judging by his questions, I have come to think this doc is thinking desk for me. Phone-work work. Something tappy-tap. Climate controlled. I see him thinking *coverage. Noggin doctors aren't free, you know, it won't be cheap,* he's thinking, *that boy's got some trouble coming with his ticker, he keeps on eating, he'll be looking pretty hard at diabetes.*

No, sir, this doctor's nothing too special. He only means here to remind me that your elevator determines climb and dive; your trim relieves the pressure on your yoke. I am calm enough to see this doctor tints his gray. He has swapped his spectacles for contacts. They scratch, he says, do not agree with him, please excuse him while he fusses with these eyedrops. Poor guy. If he seemed sad in there before, he seems now to be positively weeping. Word is his first wife was a noggin doctor also. The two had a kid, then put the kid in eighteen-hour day care so the mama noggin doctor didn't miss her shut-eye. Word is the kid is grown and gone off east as far as he could go and keep his feet on U.S. terra firma. As for the doctor, I think he blinks too much. The way he looks around my room, it's as if he's wishing for a window maybe more than I am.

"It's natural," he says, "when we're young, Adam, we have our fantasies. Part of growing up is seeing what is real and what is dreaming. It's waking up, Adam. For many people—and I'm thinking here of postadolescents in particular—waking up can be an extremely irritating experience. Could have been a good dream you were having. It's not uncommon for a young man of your age to dream of sex. Nocturnal emissions are not uncommon, nor is the feeling in the morning of helplessness and shame. Some people are deeply confused when they wake. For several terrifying moments, they won't move for fear of learning that they can't. They could be alone, abandoned, some fear they've been taken hostage. For all you know, you could be dead. I'm just talking, Adam. I'm thinking here you might find it helpful, if you could think of growing up that way, needing to get out of bed. There's some truth here, Adam, if you'll give it some thought. Growing up is something not too different from waking."

Duh.

No, duh.

Duh*wee*, I want to tell him, and what of poor dumb us who do not save their dreams for sleep? What of us who nod and nod and tell the General, yes, yes, yes, we understand, and go on sensing man's great leap to flight resides in Homer Oney's mustache?

No, I do not think that I have been much with him, Doctor Noggin. I think my wholly truer self is better saved for our Nurse Sue. Many thanks, Nurse Jill, for the tip on the face-lift; thank you, Nurse Nadeen, for sharing your historical successes with the grapefruit diet. But it's you, Sue, simple Sue, we hit it off, I'd say, now didn't we, we saw each other straight. Good luck, Nurse Nadeen, with that gastric bypass; be kind, Nurse Jill, with how you talk about the frailties of well-meaning people; and please, Doctor, please accept my sympathies regarding the remoteness of your son, I must have seemed a good bit like him to my mother and the General. Genes, is it? Well, maybe I am not so well-evolved to plumb the fancy ethics of genetics. I like waking up. I am happy, fat. I am definitely *alive*. I hurt, all right, and I know I am lucky still to be here, hurting, though with Nurse Sue working at the dressings, I am hopeful to be leaving hurt to bygones. She says if I will bully through the treatment, then I will one day smile up at the sunshine with the best of them, pretty much unscarred.

I said to her, I said, "Sue. I like your name, Sue. I have a friend called Mike. He's my best friend on the planet. We ate Oreos. Have you heard of him? The General took to bringing home the airplane stuff in twos, just for Mike. Two model Phantoms, two T-38s, two B-1s—you name it. It was Mike and me who first discovered that the pits made perfect cliffs for jumping."

I asked Nurse Sue if she had any best friends also, and if she did then what their names were, and what I liked right off was Nurse Sue not insisting only one friend could be best. When it came to names, Nurse Sue knew a trick of how to say her favorite without holding all the rest to rank. Hers were Phoebe and Daisy and Clair and Bingo and Alice and Ruth. She said she didn't know anybody by any of those names, but if she did, she thought it would break her heart if she could find a single reason in the world why not to like one. I liked them all, and though Nurse Sue was all eyes for her swabs and ointments, I could see she liked my Mikes and Joes and Toms and Bobs and wasn't any too surprised to hear I also liked Kareem.

I said, "I like you, too, Sue. I mean you the person."

We went slow. Still do. We have time for names. I'm nowhere near my peak these days, but still I have a big, big body. It's a job to get me turned, and Nurse Sue is determined not to miss a stitch of me; to her the whole entire hide is worth the saving. Barbecue, that was me the papers wrote about, roast pig, a six-foot-seven inch flambé. Sure, it hurts. I hurt. I said so. I entitle myself to an occasional complaint. I don't mean to, but I sweat. After Nurse Sue has unwrapped me, snipped and swabbed, redressed me and rewrapped me, it's as if I've played through overtime in a game-long full-court press, it's as if I've flown the General's umpteenth mission on the delta. I try to settle back into my bed, and though here again I had not meant to, I can feel the wetness on my cheeks and know that I've been crying. I think: *Well, it's as if you lost that ball game at the buzzer; it's as if you torched a village full of children.*

"Tell me if it hurts," says Nurse Sue.

She says, "You know, you're getting better."

I think so also. Way down underneath myself, underneath the blister and the adipose and gristle, it's there again I can feel me, that little fellow floating several galaxies above. It's like the egg again, Nurse Sue, the fabled robin's nest in which I heard the life before the living. The sound that is, that isn't hinged to any visible effect. It's like when I was young, a babe, a toddler, according to my mother, and I fell out of the crib and broke my head. I was calm. I cried some, but not enough to fetch my mother's help. Back then, to economize, my mother bought our milk in bulk and froze it. I ask you, how long does it take to thaw a gallon jug of milk? It was a hot day, and the jug sat on the windowsill, straight on in the sunshine, and my mother said that milk was well to being thawed before I came out asking her for water. And I'll tell you, Sue, I believe that whole entire time I was awake. I believe I was listening, and what I tell myself I heard was Nature—though I'd be just as pleased to call it what you like—a voiced thing, though, like the voice inside that egg, and the voice said I was it, not me; it told me not to worry.

Not to worry!

Your body will break, it said, and this will not be you. Your body will hunger, it said, and this will not be you. Your body will tire, fall sick, age, burn, rot, crumble and be blown away, and this will not be you. Good news, apparently, the message we have seen consistently recorded in the Scriptures near the top of mankind's holy wish list: I, Adam Oney, am untouchable. Please, Nurse Sue, believe me, I am a modern child. I have tried in time to pass off these voices I keep hearing to too much blood in the ear, to the undermoan of gymnasium euphoria, to prop wash. And yet, I seem to understand these sounds, I feel able to recover them as words whose right arrangement stands me eye to eye with meaning. *No*, I hear, *not you. No, not here, not now, not this.* So I ask myself, Well, why then, what else for? Where to? Where from? Who else other can I be?

"It's like this," I said, "before I ever knew one, how come I liked Mike? How come Sue? The General, whatever landed him on Adam?"

WHAT THEY CALLED ME WAS EMERGENT. LATER I WOULD BE ACUTE, THEN Rehabilitative, one step to the next, with periods of slippage and necessary overlap, depending. Helped them to manage their team. The doctor for the skin, the doctor for the head, the therapist, the other therapist, the nurse. Helped them to establish your trajectory, how they could assist each other through the weeks when you were either getting well or dying. I was getting well. They flew me in by chopper. Live as far out from a big town as where we live and they take you into critical by chopper. If you're lucky. If you're critical enough, at least, and lucky; if for instance you have burns of the third degree on twenty, twenty-five percent or better of your body and your local medical community is thinking cardiac arrest, brain damage, massive, maverick sepsis. That was me, airlifted on the whirlybird, Adam Oney as the crow flies through the starry night across the ranging desert, awaited, ready to be cared for, hugely, famously, romantically Emergent.

So I hear. So Sue says. I myself was gone, shocked and doped, the body on autopilot, the mind locked onto reruns of basketball and pizza joints and war, favorite days I could not say enough about with Mike. Good thing we are built to not remember much of what we ever felt. According to Sue, I was hardly through the double doors and there they reamed me with the catheter, stuck me with the six-gauge IV in the groin to monitor my fluids. Tubes in the nose, too, a little nasogastric suction so there wasn't anything for me to throw up of my breakfast, lunch, or dinner on the doctors. Try to think how only that much feels—reamed and stuck—then also how it feels for them to lift your charry self from one bed to another to another to the tank. You moan a lot. You weep. You tell yourself this can't be you. Couldn't be anybody. But it is. It's you, and it is Sue up there above you, somewhere in the sudden light, talking to the paramedics: "What did you give him?"

"Demerol."

"Demerol? You give this boy morphine."

Which is one among the few things I remember. Remember and bless. Bless you, morphine, and bless you, Sue, I do remember.

"I'm Sue," she said. "You've had an accident. I will be your nurse. You'll feel a little pinch here," she was saying, "this next will be a little loud. You'll have some discomfort," she said, "but then you should start feeling better."

I ask her to tell it all to me again, and again, please, there's time, never mind what Doctor Noggin says about that trauma.

"How'd it work?" I said. "What all did I miss?"

I told her not to be afraid, we'd have to trust each other here, same as she told me.

Nurse Sue lifted off the gauze and with the gauze an inch or two of upset, bleedy meat. She trimmed, tweezed, labored in the tank at me for sessions lasting into hours. Loosen the joints, that's it, stretch the muscles, stave off those contractures, get rid of that eschar, look for the granulated stuff, fatty burger, a good, clean bed for grafting. This was called *debridement.*

I said, "Think of it as entertainment. I'm the star. A hero. I want to be amazed at what I've lived through."

So according to Sue, and also to the bits I can remember by myself, I kept coming in and out those first few days of who was who and where I was and what I must have done to make these people in their masks and gloves and needles want to flay me. Strips. Chunks. Bleedy meat. Coming in and out of ordinary sense, I thought those salves and ointments were a kind of crazy glue they slathered onto me so they could rip my skin off.

The stuff dried quick, I thought, and they came back often, and often I was passed into a dream that I was being tortured. I was a fighter pilot, right, held by the yellow enemy, committed to making me talk. Or else I was a fighter pilot held by our own, a white-eyed bunch who meant to draw out anything I might have said while I was hostage of the yellows. They shook me awake. They rolled me to the tank. I was loud. I said I'd tell them anything. I said there wasn't anything to tell. I said I never flew a fighter in my life. I said, *We're gonna bomb you back into the Stone Age. It's a free country. I pay my taxes.* I said, *Ho Chi Minh. F-4s. Big bombs from forty-five at dawn. Plain of Jars, no innocents. I'm going to college. I don't even like Chinese. I'm innocent,* I said, *I'm just the son, you've got me for the General.*

They said I was getting better.

"This looks good," they said.

"Coming along fine."

Men in masks. Women in masks. Skull cap headgear and green scrubs, ignoring me and talking to each other.

"Look here, where it's red? That's what you want to see."

"Better. Good. Nice growth. Much, much better."

I lay in bed after they had left and tried hard not to grow. I closed my eyes and featured rocks and sand and precious metals, blanks of colors I wouldn't match right off with skin. I dreamed I lived six thousand years inside a block of Greenland ice. I waked up enough to think I saw a fellow who his eyelids and his lips and nose were burned completely off so by his face you could not say at all what he was feeling. They wheeled him in a cart. My cart. He was my ally, I was thinking, what did he feel, what could I say to stop them? A tray came, and a spoon of something soft was held up to my mouth.

"Who are you?" I said.

"My name is Sue. I'll be your nurse."

"How long have I been here?"

"A little over forty-eight hours."

"Feels like weeks."

"It will be."

"Is it bad?"

"It's getting better by the minute. You'd better eat."

"I keep wishing I would die."

"You won't die," said Sue. "You're past dying now. One day you'll be happier than most that you are living. Unless you don't eat. You need to eat."

"I'm a good eater," I said. "I've got a history."

"No more," said Sue. "Not that history. Starting now, you've got a brand-new history. And in this one, so far I haven't seen you eat a thing."

True, I did not want to eat. I had a bad smell. Made my stomach flop to see or even think about those places on my body where the burn had gone down through the skin and to the fat and muscle. Looked like dents. Deep pockets gouged out from my legs and back and side flab. Grease fire. Couldn't put me out, I guess. I flared up and melted.

"Melted," I said. "Think of that."

"I think of it every day," said Sue.

"I don't want to grow it back."

"Nobody wants you to."

"I miss my morphine. I want the kind you hear about that has a drip line and a button."

Nurse Sue brought more trays. The oatmeal and the meat loaf, the high-cal chocolate- flavored drinks, the homemade ice cream, hand cranked by the kids down on the children's unit who were well on into rehab.

"I have dreams," I said. "Nightmares. Only worse, because a part of me can see the part that's dreaming, and still I can't wake up to stop it."

"Electrolyte delirium," said Nurse Sue.

"Electrolyte delirium?"

"Food and drink," said Sue. "You need to eat to grow, and you need to eat the things we give you to eat to keep in balance. Your electrolytes are whacked. Please, eat."

I had the dream I would not run. After the torture dreams, I had these dreams in which I wouldn't run, maybe couldn't, wasn't clear. *Run, Adam, or else you'll die.* But I didn't run. And I didn't die. Also if I didn't run then we would lose the game but then I didn't run and still we didn't lose, how come? By not running I was sure to starve and didn't starve; didn't run and didn't drown, didn't run and didn't miss the flight to the enchanted cities. Word spread. I went public. I was interviewed. Radio. TV. I had an agent who informed me there was talk of movies; very soon, I might be issued as a stock. *You don't run, Adam, tell us how you do it. Morphine,* I said, though even in the dream I knew the morphine was behind me.

I slept. I waked up to a plate of vegetarian lasagna. I waked up to the therapist who sized me up for splints. I waked up one day and there was Doctor Noggin from the days before his contacts. He stood at the foot of my bed. By the way the light came off his glasses I could not make out his eyes; by the softness of his voice I could not make out too much what he was saying.

He said, "Adam."

I said, "Who are you?"

He said, "Doctor Feigenbaum. But you may call me Doctor Noggin."

He shrugged and held his palms up.

"It's a joke," he said. "Doctor Noggin. I am called that. To some, this is funny. Do you appreciate the humor?"

He gave the railing at the foot of my bed a little shake, said, Heh, heh, heh, then pulled a chair around to sit down where I couldn't really see him. He had crossed legs and a clipboard—I saw that much—a pen I think he left in his pocket the whole time he was with me.

He said, "Now. Then."

I told Nurse Sue I didn't think I would like him.

She said, "You don't have to. I'll tell you, though, in your case, it's him and the skin doctor both who get the final say on when you leave here."

"Look, though," I said. "I ate my soup."

"Wrong," she said. "I fed you your soup. You just held it in your mouth and swallowed." She gave me the spoon and said, "Would you like to try to eat your pudding?"

I tried, and failed, though less because I could not work my hands, and more because I wasn't hungry.

Why?

It's a question I decided I would put to Doctor Noggin.

"I'm a guy who likes to eat," I said. "So how come I don't want to?"

"That is a difficult question to answer," said Doctor Noggin. "Have you put it to yourself?"

"Sure."

"And?"

"And what?"

"And what did you answer?"

"I don't know, you know, it's why I'm asking."

"Are you certain?"

"Well, I mean, I guess because I got burned is why. I stink, you know? When they take my dressings off, it makes me pretty sick to see those parts I have are missing."

"I see, I see," said Doctor Noggin.

"So you think that's it? That's why I'm not too hot on eating?"

Doctor Noggin tapped his pen against his clipboard and fiddled with his glasses.

"Could be," he said, "could be."

He made himself to leave.

He said, "You might ask yourself, if you still have the question, can those burns still be the answer?"

I told Sue, I said, "I've got the feeling Doctor Noggin's job is just to keep a person asking questions. Seems like, if he could, then he would have me asking back to way before the days when I was falling from my crib. Like until I get back past that cage my folks fixed up for me to sleep in, I'm still getting nowhere."

"Well, you ate your soup tonight," said Sue. "Let's go ahead and call that getting somewhere."

Also, pretty quickly after eating, getting somewhere meant to us that I could walk. *Ambulatory*, the way they say it on the unit. We got me off the bed and propped up on a king-sized, rolling walker.

When we reached the door, I said, "We've got it, folks! NASA, we have ambulation!"

And a crash, collapse, more like, a fall that took us down in quiet stages. First the rocker rolled from under me. Then Sue sort of buckled and we went down on the floor with me on top and big enough so Sue was stuck till someone came along to help us.

"Are you all right?" Sue said. "Don't move. I'm sorry. I'm so sorry. Just be still."

But I was sorry, too. I could be crushing her, I said I thought I could do better, I really was an athlete.

"Relax," Sue said. "Keep quiet. You need to not get too excited."

I rested my head against the floor.

"I played ball," I said. "I flew, you know. Did you know I'm a flyer?"

"I know," said Sue. "We get bios. I know about your father, and your mother. You're an only child, I know that. And now I know you're too big for me to move you."

"Ask me more," I said. "Like anything I might have said when I was in an electrolyte delirium."

"Okay," said Sue. "Who's Mike?"

"He's my friend. The best. One thing about Mike," I said, "is two things," neither one of which I had a chance to say before the orderlies appeared and we were being helped up to our feet. Next thing I'm recarted, tanked, and Sue is sweating over my debridement while I look down at those missing slabs and think again that this cannot be me, nothing more of Mike, not until I'm back in bed, a little doped, a little scared of what my dreams might be if I should get some shut-eye. I could hear Sue's pen against her clipboard, scribbling my progress and my meds.

She said, "So, who's Mike?"

I couldn't say. Didn't even try. Other than my friend, a word I said and could repeat, who was he? Mike. I could not say what he looked like. Weird, I thought, but as I lay there listening, I could not say for sure what Nurse Sue looked like, either. I wondered whether I had ever even seen her face, the whole thing, with her mask off.

"Not yet," Sue said. "I don't think you've seen anybody's face."

"Funny," I said, "I can't make out Mike's face any better than yours, and I saw his a lot."

"You're tired," said Sue. "There's a whole lot else you're going through."

"Still, I'd like to see him."

"You will."

"Sue?"

"Yes?"

"How about I leave my eyes closed here, and you go stand down there at the foot of my bed, and when I say when, then show me what you look like?"

"If you like. No telling, though. You know, highly unprofessional."

I could hear her lay her clipboard on the chair, pull the mask down past her chin.

"Okay," she said, "now open."

"Sue," I said. "Nurse Sue."

"Well?" she said.

"You're pretty, Sue."

I let my head fall back onto my pillow.

"When you were a kid," I said, "did you used to have buck teeth?"

"Horsey teeth," said Sue. "Big overbite."

I heard her put her mask on and move back to her chair.

"I feel all right," I said. "Feels like I could sleep."

"That's good," said Sue. "You sleep. I gave you something extra."

I felt the float come up behind my eyes, a nice, slow tumble through my chest.

"Which way?" I said.

"Which way what?" said Sue.

"That man. The guy with the face burned off. Which way do you have him headed?"

I heard Sue finish up, clip my vitals to the bed.

"That man with his face burned off is seventeen years old," she said. "In three weeks, he'll be dying."

Truth? Mike and I got run down from the tree fort, chased from the hideout in the willow thicket. Didn't take long, either. Here we're introduced, and there the two of us are hunting pill bugs underneath the cinder blocks, wondering to ourselves what happened at that tree fort, why anyone would poke a stick in someone's eye to keep him from a hideout. Seemed to me that sort of meanness in a kid was something not to figure. Still, I kept quiet, thinking maybe if I didn't interrupt him, Mike could get things figured fine; if I listened, I might hear a reason for that meanness and a way to fix it both.

My job was to turn up blocks. Keep mum. I was new here yet, didn't know the rules, seemed as if the General had only just the day before informed us we were leaving Texas. Big news from the man in the tall boots, word down from the straight height and the yondering eye, the wide mouth centered neatly in the goatee grown out from that mustache. Mother, pour the General his libation. Sit, all. Quiet while the General lights himself a Winston, puffs out three fat rings, and raises his glass to toast the good luck owing to his squadron's latest relocation. He would fly. We would drive. Meet him west, he said. We're headed for the Silver State. Promotion. New jet. A wider open sky. Brush country. Fresh air out there, we would see, a place to make a cleaner living.

Right, I thought, *the day before*, it's true, true that time flies, catches up to you, passes by, comes around to find you old enough, in any case, to be in one place while you're thinking of another. There's me, for instance, nine, prying open those pill bugs, marveling at the mess of legs in search of something firmer than the air to walk on, thinking at the same time how it *seemed like only yesterday* that Mother packed up our belongings, wept for good old Lubbock brisket, spoke ungraciously about an Oklahoma country no more flat than ours was, a country, as we drove it, mounting into foothills, mounting into full-on mountains at the continent's divide, a series I saw rising rough and rocky in the moonshine night of range and lime-white basin.

Naturally, the AC broke. The radiator leaked. Mother copped a sunburn on her window arm and slathered it in aloe. I think because I watched her hair stand up and pitch about her head so long I was bound to have that dream of drowning in those weeds that grow down at the bottom of an ocean. To see that hair and Mother's hunched up spine a person would believe we were fairly tearing up the asphalt. Wrong. Us, we were an early American experiment at being Japanese, a failure in economy, decylindered, unaccessorized, a rusted bumper and a rented ball hitched to a poorly loaded four-wheel trailer. More cars passed us going in the same direction we were than were passing in the other. People shouted. One thing people liked to shout was *blinker.* Another thing was *brakes.* Once, we saw a shouter at a station and he took the time out to explain how we could start a fire by the sparks that jumped off from the chain we hadn't bothered fixing snug enough to keep from dragging. Mother showed that man her finger. I think she could not think of what to show the man who showed the thumbs-up sign while steering with a lady bouncing in his lap through Mormon parts at maybe seventy or eighty.

We did not sing. Not "Ninety-Nine Bottles" or "The Ants Go Marching," nothing like the Slug Bug game to pass the time with Mother. To her credit, Mother didn't start her crying till she checked us into our motel and saw the bugs stuck in the aloe. Looked like hair, those bugs, or char, like maybe Mother's arm could be a skinny strip of brisket fetched from falling in a bed of red-hot coals. I offered her to wipe them off. She thanked me, patted my head or stroked my cheek, though when I set to work I know she wasn't really with me. "Water starved," said Mother, "an unfit, godforsaken wasteland. Pompous, chauvinistic oafs, the service; selfish, shitty man, your father."

And then it's just the two of us inside our house, no curtains up, no beds made, just heaps of clothes and towels and plates and stuff and Mother sitting on the gold linoleum, wondering if she should wait until the General landed home before she started mixing the martinis. Who could see Mike coming? Who saw tree forts and pill bugs? Who could ever see the pits?

Lucky us, Mike and me, we two nearly never happened. Years later, through the later phases of the folks' split, Mother would rerun the day I first met Mike and shoot it at the General like very heavy flak. How the only woman on the block to greet her was a colored. Only colored in the county, mind you. And that shiftless, dopey-eyed, grabber son of hers. They could have been a front for a sophisticated burgling ring, she said, nice scam all right—trot the mother and the son out as the Welcome Wagon, case the joint, and whammo, they have the goods on you, all your valuables laid out as plain as day for picking. Druggies, Mother said, junkies and potheads, where's the daddy? And where was her man, Mother wondered, where's the General when you needed him? Didn't he care about his wife? Didn't he love his son? Shouldn't he have been there anyway to see them settled? No, no, no, he's gone off to the clouds. *Freedom fighting.* Big deal. *Guardian of the skies.* Protecting us from what out here, the wind, the stars, the sunshine? Scared as she was, it was all Mother could do to drag me from that window. Best thing she would tell the General she remembers hoping is that Mike and Mrs. R were just another door-to-door performance in the pitfalls of the welfare state, Mama Rags and Pickaninny, getting fat off hawking tax-free M&M's and key chains.

Mrs. R, as I recall her, held the bucket. Mike held the mop. My mother folded up her arms across herself and asked if she could help them. What my mother did not tell the General was that twenty minutes later she and Mrs. R have pitched in with that bucket and that mop and Mike and I are left to play in a haze of Endust and Pine-Sol, our two mothers set about to make our house a home in a blaze of rubber gloves and elbow grease and small-world swaps of happy chatter.

"Do I know Oklahoma?" says Mrs. R. "Why Talooma, Oklahoma's where we're from."

"I'm sorry," Mother says, "I don't suppose that after all it's all so different from home."

Together, they moved off from missing brisket, and on to missing prairie thunderstorms and south-midwestern twang.

"And lightning bugs," says Mrs. R. "Don't you *even* think you'll find a lightning bug. No, ma'am, not if you are sitting out come midnight, and it's the dead-on hot of August."

"No lightning bugs?"

"No, ma'am. *Skeeters*. And don't you ask me where they comin' from, 'cause there ain't a drop a water in that brush to breed 'em."

The two missed church. Proper, south-midwestern church. They had a church out here, all right, but Mrs. R told mother to forget about a lunch-box social. They missed a gospel station. They missed a tornado cellar, Lee and Esther, Eunice, Thelma, Patty. They scrubbed grout, scoured the sink, papered the shelves, and asked themselves what they were doing. What were they doing in this town, what sort of place was this for anybody to be living?

Don't ask Mrs. R. Mrs. R said most folks living here would tell you they weren't living here at all, but only passing through, sweeping dust, and praying for rain until the next less bleak assignment. Rare to see a proper garden here. Not much lawn. Likelier to see a concrete lean-to than a shade tree. Where you'd maybe like to see a picket fence, you'll be seeing chain link.

"It's the base," said Mrs. R. "Folks go where they get stationed, and they don't put much mind to how they spend the meantime."

It's how Mrs. R and hers had come here, Mr. R a sergeant working ground crew, before he left the service for a life in melons.

"Melons?" says my mother.

"Don't you start," says Mrs. R. "I'm talkin' *cant*aloupes. You'll scoop the seeds and fill that hollow with a dollop of vanilla ice cream, and you'll think you've died and gone to heaven, guarantee it. Hearts-o-gold, we call 'em, and we grow 'em right here in this patch of desert."

Not first rank, said Mrs. R, not the final way and place they wanted to be living, but still it was a happy day when Mr. R quit playing Mr. Goodwrench to the blue-eyed flyboys.

"He spent a good long little while there in that service," Mrs. R was saying, "that man all his life was wanting just to fly. Said if he couldn't fly, then he may as well get on the job of working on those planes he wished he was flying. Seemed most like a sex offender teaching at the girls' school, but I don't ask. I just see him winding up like Stagga Lee till one day he comes home and says a flyboy called him monkey. *Grease* monkey, but a monkey all the same. Uh-unh. Not that. He says he's going to make an offer on that melon patch. Only day he's hearing any monkey is the day they let him be a flyer."

"That's me, too," says Mike. "I'm going to be a flyer, same as Daddy."

And sure the way he says it—says that *I'm*—that's how I know for sure this Mike is kindred.

The ladies were into their drinks, martini for Mother, iced tea for Mrs.

R, and Mother was saying her so-sorries to Mrs. R, pitching in her own two bits about the selfish, chauvinistic, sons of bitches flyboys.

"Don't you worry," said my mother. "I have seen it. They're full of strut and cock-a-doodle-doo right now, but the time comes hard on them when one day they are looking twenty-five, next day looking sixty. The word for it is *decommissioned.* Shot down. Wings clipped. Make way for the next wave up of younger roosters."

But Mrs. R allowed as how she didn't have a bone to pick with pilots. For her part, she would rather keep her meanness to that man—that Murphy—any man who had it in his heart to call another man a monkey. But I could see Mother was mixing, spearing olives. I do not think she heard a word of Mrs. R's desire to see Mike fly. She didn't hear that keeping near the planes for Mike is what was keeping them in melons. No ma'am, Mrs. R, save your breath, Mother has gone off to the airlines, her dream of a civilian life, playing golf and shopping in the outlets in the suburbs of a major U.S. hub.

As for me, I'm with Mike. I'm not listening to Mother. I have heard her. But Mike, I thought, my size, my style, my long-lost, stillborn *brother*—there's a boy who knows his ailerons and trim tabs. Turns out he knew Stukas and Spitfires, knew the fuel it took to fly the Burma Hump, he even knew Elmer "Zipper" Bickerstaff, ace extraordinaire. Easy then for us to stick, say goodbye that day, hello the next; easy for that summer to go off without a hitch, a lazy loop of ice cream cones and long days at the public pool, anyplace our mothers could come up with to distract us from our bombing raids on Frankfurt, our chopper rescues in Saigon, the long formation flights we practiced through the down times of our country's restless peace. Easy then, I mean to say, to understand how all of this with moving and weeping, resettling and befriending could have seemed so short a time ago, before Mike is at my door, and we are leaping sagebrush down the gully for the tree fort.

• • •

So see us, Mike and me, nine years old, tight already, already fast and furious flyers, WWI, as I recall us, guys in scarves and leather hats and goggles, rat-a-tat-tat-ka-boom! Here we come, watch out, you lizard Krauts, you sparrow-legged sons of Bismarck. It's bombs away and gun the trenches, down the gully we flew, leaping and weaving, pioneers of mechanized death by sky. We banked hard, slipped down low and climbed back out of hostile fire at heroic angles of attack. We stalled. Recovered. We set ourselves into flaming spins, pulled the nose up inches from our Dates with Destiny, a certain cockpit coffin in the Danube. Sorry, death. Take that, you, and this one's for my honey in Saint Louis!

In 3-D, real-life life, we tore our knuckles on the wild peach. Barked our shins, gouged our palms, and cracked our kneecaps. We launched off from the upside of a brush never knowing what was on the downside. Broken bottle? Rattlesnake? Cliff? I got so scared I nearly peed my pants, got so happy when I hit the bottom there with Mike I could have kissed him. Sure we stood there panting at each other, amazed, I think, to have flown so daringly and not be broken, heroes, two boys dressed in dungarees and decent sneakers.

"I fear no man," says Mike, just before the first rock whizzes down on us from someone flying higher up than we were.

And so we met Chester and Lester, twins, the current rulers of the tree fort, what they were calling *castle*. Seemed Mike and I had flown into the Dark Ages. These boys here were knights. Apparently, Mike and I had landed in their moat. What were we to do with biplanes? How were these two sirs to mind our goggles and our scarves? Apparently, we risked being chomped on by crocodiles. In this moat were leeches and a rusty can, some pretty pukey, poopy sewage. We had better fall back and declare ourselves, they said, should we wish to spare ourselves the old hot oil in the face, a round of poison arrows.

"Huh?" says Mike.

"You heard us," says Sir Chester. "Ahrrr!"

"Ahrrr?" says Mike.

"Clear out, pussies!" says Sir Lester. "Else we'll douche you!"

The two shake rocks and sticks at us and start to stomping on the floor-boards of the tree fort.

"Douche?" says Mike.

"Douche!" Sir Chester says, and the two commence to hollering and hurling, "Ahrr, ahhrr, ahhrr!"

Mike and I fall back undouched and thinking to each other that these twins up there were maybe made to share a single brain between them.

"We'll wait them out," says Mike. "They'll get bored. Or hungry. You watch. Pretty soon, they'll forget why they were throwing."

Oh, now, turn around boys, I was thinking, you don't *really* need to come on down and punch our lights out, do you, must be something better for you two to do than *clean our clocks.*

"They look pretty big," I said to Mike.

"It's because they're up so high," said Mike. "They get down here and I'll bet they'll be the same as us."

But those two boys were different. They looked big because they were big. Probably we should have run. Chester and Lester, after they had missed us with a few more rounds of rocks, they stood there looking at each other openmouthed, as if the brain they shared had maybe tricked them, and they were circling in some sort of silent holding pattern, poking through some painful-seeming moments of bipersonal interrogation. *What does Chester do when they don't run? What does Lester? We're big, Chester, right? Right, Lester, big. Bigger? Bigger. Both? Both. You? Me. Me? You. Bigger? Much. Much? Much. Ohhh,* says Lester to himself. *Hmmm,* says brother Chester. *So how come they don't run? Little men,* they seem to ask themselves, *how come you're not running?*

Mike picked up a rock and said, "One more step, and one of you is getting smacked between the eyes."

Turns out it was Lester. Nothing melony about it. This here was a smack—like, *crack*, all right—and then the bleeding starts between the eyes an inch or two above the eyebrows. We all stood there for a time, looking through that silence we reserve to measure our response to coming trouble. Adam, Mike, Sir Chester, and Sir Lester, too, Lester looking up and inward at that line of blood so he is looking cross-eyed. When the blood parts on the bridge of his nose and seeps into his eyeballs, Lester says, "Ahhrrr," and Mike and I are lucky to be light and fleet, built for longer, faster running than the twins, who gave up on the chase before we made it halfway up the gully.

"What now?" I say.

"Stealth," says Mike.

So next thing we have junked our biplanes for a spy plane, and we are cruising Mach speed, off the radar, flying for the hideout, which is a crawly kind of thicket-tunnel-cave deal, which is where I get the stick in the eye, which is really finally how we came to hunting pill bugs in a weed lot. I sat back from my pile of bugs and listened to the wind. Every day, it seems, about the time you are finished with your sandwich, got your chip bag crumpled in your pocket, and your soda's down around the last decarbonated drop, then that's the time the wind kicks up and seems to say, wherever you have come to rest, you really shouldn't rest there. I was listening. Wind said: *Move along, son, move along.* I leaned my head back and shut my one good eye and then the bad, trying out the vision on another cloudless sky. Hard, I kept on thinking, to get too much perspective here. One eye or two, most of what I saw seemed farther from me than it ought to.

"Did you get a look at them?" said Mike.

"Naw," I said, "too dark. Felt like I was hardly even started in that tunnel."

"Well, you were in," said Mike. "When I heard them holler, I went in after you. Up to my shoulders before I could get a good grip on your feet to drag you out."

I said, "Yeah, they hollered, didn't they?"

"Names and stuff," said Mike.

"How many, you think?"

"Two. Two for sure. Unless one wasn't hollering."

"I wish they wouldn't holler. Gets me, why they always think they have to holler."

I rolled a bug between my thumb and middle finger, held him in my palm until he must have thought it was safe to open up.

"Which do you like better," said Mike, "Orville or Wilbur?"

"Orville, I guess. Maybe Wilbur. I don't know. I guess I like them both about as equal."

"Right. You need your ground crew if you're going to fly, and there's no sense in a ground crew if you haven't got a flyer."

"Plus which just the sound."

"Of what?"

"Of Orville, you know, and of Wilbur. You don't say Orville *or* Wilbur. You say Orville *and* Wilbur. Orville and Wilbur, as in the Wright brothers."

"Right," said Mike, "sure. So here I'll tell you what. You take that pill bug there and get him rolled up good and tight. Then we'll count to ten, and if he's opened up, then you'll be Orville, and if he isn't opened up, then I'll be."

So call me Wilbur. See me as the one who opens from his shell around eighteen. See me second, anyway, the kid who rides a wheel-length back from Orville, whose idea it was to fetch the bikes and pedal with the wind until we came on something likelier than hideouts and tree forts for flying. We rode stingrays. Sissy bars and spring seats, back brakes for laying down the badass scratches. Mike's was the Orange Crate; mine was the Lemon Peeler. We rode fast, weavingly, hands, no hands, hands, jumping curbs and gutters, popping longish wheelies clear out where the asphalt turned to gravel. *Move along, sons, move along.* But not too far along. Not so far along as we were thinking. *The boondocks*, we were thinking, *the boonies, wow, boy, look at us,* unknowingly coasting over this year's scraped frontier, the leveled ground for next year's subdivided plots, adventures in warehousing, office parks, and franchise food.

Well, what could we know? We thought this was it, the end of town for all of time, a construction site, the future's Last Chance Saloon, a place with a hose, at least, and a well tapped deep enough for finding good sweet water. We took off our shirts and sprayed each other down, drank until our bellies rounded wet and slick and shiny. Nobody hollered. Nobody poked us in the eye or tried to clobber us with rocks. We drank, and then we sat our bikes, and until we saw that fellow come down off the roof-deck, I do not think we would have said that anything we'd seen was putting us in mind of flight. Wind took him. Bad luck for him, good luck for those of us who happened to have looked in his direction. Hell of a ride. Loop and a spin, something of a gear-up, two-hop landing. In the end, he lay there twisted through the spine, his arms outstretched, his hands still holding to the edges of a four-by-eight-foot sheet of plywood, his cheek mashed flat as if he meant to bore a face-sized plug out from the half-inch laminate, and he had not yet given in to failing. *Plywood,* he was saying, *fucking, stinking, motherfucker, fuckass, shitbird plywood.* Flew him like a sail. Some said thirty feet or better from the spot where he was lifted. Mike and I rushed in with all the rest to see how he was doing. *Shitbird,* he was saying, *cuntcheese, asspiss, suckbutt.*

At first you wondered why he didn't move, but then you figured out he didn't move because he had about a foot's worth of that plywood driven in a sliver so it hooked him through the forehead and the eyebrow. Plus which it was pretty sure he'd broken his leg. Plus which, what about his neck? Someone asked him could he wiggle his foot any. Someone else freed up his hands and asked him how about his fingers? When he'd wiggled enough to suit the ones who asked him for the wiggling, there commenced a round of flatteries and astoundments, the likes of which I do not think these men were prone too easily to issue. Seemed they were near to lifting Staley, board and all, to shoulder him away as one among a fighting legion, valor stricken, healing on his shield and in the knowledge of his nation's victory in war. *Oh, man, Staley—shoulda seen yourself! You was up above the peak! Did you mean to land her board-side down? Jesus, Stales, you flipped plumb over! You really did it!*

"I did," said Staley. "Didn't I? I guess this board here sort of broke my fall."

I think we all were relieved to witness his good spirits, though we all seized in a pretty drastic flinch and cringe when Staley tried to lift his head up off the plywood. Stretched his skin, gapped it out so you could see the light shine red right through the membrane. I would swear it was that fellow with the biggest biceps who said, *Ewww!* Certainly, it was the fellow with the biggest mustache who told Mike and me we'd better get along now.

Move along, now, sons, you've drunk your fill, now move along. We knew that song. Takes a first-rate wreck sometimes to see how much a boy will secret in his brain for knowing. Wings, right? Thrust? What we needed was some altitude, a kinder place than Staley's for our landings. We rode on. No talk. No more jumps and wheelies. That was Fortune back there, giving us the elbow: *Hey, you guys,* She said, *keep your heads down, keep your eyes peeled, you've paid your dues today, it's your turn now for glory.*

Glory, I was thinking, what a great idea. Wilbur Oney, Adam Wright. For a time I saw myself as Mike, no problem. Unshelled, purposive, and flexing. If he stood up from his saddle, I stood up from my saddle. He leaned hard right, I leaned hard right. In a climb I think I swung my bike from side to side exactly just how Mike did. We were really living through things here, people here were really getting hurt. Maybe I was riding just then, calling Mother Mama, seeing her as Mrs. R. *Yes, sir,* I could have thought, *Daddy's in the field, riding tractor, moving water, reaping cash from melons.* I know at least for sure I was wishing pretty hard I could have folks look at me the way they looked at Mike. Nothing hep or jive or funkadelic homey boy about it. That's just us. Same hip. Same voice. That's us, there, we two Wrights, destined for the pits, our shirts flown out behind us from our waistbands like a flag.

We arrived. We got there, the end of the road, and it felt to me like an arrival. There we stood, straddled our bikes at the lip of the pit, looking each of us at the other, our two faces lit up with the seeing of a brand-new first, a topper to outrank the hideout and the tree fort. We're there, all right. Runway, altitude, landing—check, check, check. We stood a time and watched the wind pick up the dust and chaffy stuff and blow it out to where it looked like there must be an updraft, hot air enough to float you out and drop you down the fifteen feet or so you fell before you hit the chalky slope and rolled out on the soft dirt slag below. Give us wings, I thought, and what more than these pits could junior birdmen ask for? Gumption? Well, we had it. A guarantee? We didn't want it. A word, possibly, something hearkening to banzai or Geronimo? No, better not to think it.

Best to jump, as we jumped, side by side, without a word, leaping from a running start we signaled by a count, a rundown of our instruments, one last eye to eye before we gave ourselves the clear. *Whaaaa,* or *yaahhh,* or *wheeeahh*—I disremember. There goes the earth, after all, you're open, you're that pill bug treading air, except you haven't got a shell, and it's far down there, and of course there isn't really any lift, and really there is plenty of plummet, that one sharp rock you hadn't seen before you jumped could really, really hurt you. But it didn't hurt. We struck shin-deep in the chalk

dust, tumbled face-first and were finished in a grinning, backside slide. Bare
bodies covered in the fine, white dust, later to be caked. We rested just as
we had jumped, side by side, sitting on the other end of flight, the happy
landing. The high five was fine. We stood up, fine, knocked each other
down, terrific, wrestled in the dust and helped each other laughing up the
cliffside.

Close one eye, close the other, the sky at the lip of the cliff would always
seem too far. Fantastically far. Boyishly far. To climb after so much sky, such
a brightness, so much uninterrupted sun, was to feel ourselves as creatures both impossibly reduced, and impossibly expanding. Not the cliff we
climbed for, but the sky. Dug our fingers into the bank, kicked a foothold,
stepped and dug and kicked and stepped. *Almost there*, we said, pulling ourselves up over the top, same as we were saying *almost there* down at the bottom. We sat with our legs hung over the pit, resting back onto our elbows,
our eyes turned up contentedly, I like to think, as if the sky weren't up at all,
as if we were up there in it, or it was down in us, and our climbing was an
exercise in wanting what we both already had. That I should inhabit a space
in that sky for a period longer than it took me to fall through it seemed possible. It seemed possible, when I looked at Mike, and at myself, and how we
were in white, that we were not creatures born to bones and blood or skins
of shifting pigments, but were really rather simple specimens of happiness,
possibilities for human life on loan, flown down from another planet.

Mike sat up and picked the chalk dust out from underneath his
fingernails.

He said, "Douche."

I said, "Douche."

He said, "How come you think they were so mean?"

"Who mean?"

"You know who."

"I don't know," I said. "Maybe it's not meanness. Could be just a game. Maybe make-believe. A game, the same as we play."

"No," said Mike, "it isn't. It may be a game, but it ain't make-believe, no way."

Naturally, they would return. Sniffed us out, as if Mike and I were game, and those boys, all four of them, were dogs, sent out on our trails by seasoned hunters. They came abreast, on bikes, same as Mike and I had. But before they came we had a time, Mike and I. Loaves and loaves worth. Day-old bread we shredded, spreading peanut butter sandwiches we rode off to the pits to lunch on. Lots of lemonade, two of each of everything, numbering the dozens, a calendar of chip bags and candy wrappers we kept safe beneath a rock for when the wind blew. Feels unreal to think, a happy, sleepy, weeks-long dream, but proof is in the Polaroids. That's us, the tops of our chalky heads, a self-portrait I took of us at arm's length, Mike and I in the patch of shade we built of scrap wood from that job site. We are posed, and not, focused on the photo you see Mike is holding, very excited, the two of us, to see ourselves develop. The arm comes clean against the sky, yes, it's clear, those straight legs, the body bent just at the waist, this one is the Messerschmitt, this one here the C-5, skycow, and here this cube of empty blue must be from when I held the camera and we jumped together, an unsuccessful portrait of ourselves as Orville and Wilbur, before we are discovered.

Vivid mugs, thuggish fellows on those bikes, no question. Seemed to me they'd worked their slouches down their spines and through their seats and frames, clear onto the spokes and pedals. Until they ditched their bikes. Then it's all backram and chest, a stiffened eye, a boy's desire to flex and swell himself where he has yet to grow that one intimidating muscle. As for Mike and me, we had wings by then, these tapered cardboard cutouts, a modified design on Staley's sail. Felt silly. Here they came on in their tough-guy pack, looking for some rough stuff, and then there's Mike and me with string looped through our belts to keep our wings against our backs, our skinny wrists stuck through these cardboard straps we'd stapled on as handholds. You could see that rock Mike had thrown had fetched poor Lester stitches. The way he looked at Mike, you had a hard time saying whether he was meaning to have another go at Mike, or if all this time he was thinking Mike's one throw was luck, and he meant for Mike to have another go at him. Lucky us they stopped. They stopped, I guess, to size us up, to see what we were made of from a distance any boy could make by spitting.

If you name them off by order of their height it goes: Lester, Chester, Hector, and Arturo. By position, as it would come to be announced with every high school home game, it went: Lester Oolag, starting center; Chester Oolag, starting forward; Hector Block, starting forward; Arturo Sanchez, starting guard. Start Mike at the other guard, and you are left with me, Adam Oney, sixth man on the early roster of a team they say was one around here for the ages.

ASK THE BURNED GUY, AND HE WILL TELL YOU HIS ACUTE IS WORSE THAN his Emergent. More nerves, fewer drugs. He knows where he is. He knows a little where he's going, and he can't get over wanting to go back to where he'd been. The going is slow. Better is measured in skin buds, how well that donor site on the forehead accepts the skin from that cadaver; better feels to him like counting grains of sand in building back the beach, like hoping he will be the monster built by Frankenstein who doesn't show his stitches.

The Acute will walk. If he can, he must. He leans on walkers and the four-pronged cane. Leans on nothing, and walks down to the lounge in splints rigged so his arms are stuck out nineties from his body. All dressed up in pressure garments and heavy wraps. Guy looks like a mummy. Stops his walk to rest a bit, lets his head fall to one side and you are thinking some-one nailed a mummy to a cross. His name is Tom. His is the name that sticks to me, in any case. High school dropout. Mechanic. Year or two my senior. Fellow whose mother feeds him Lucky Strikes he sucks between his teeth while we make talk and tune in to the soaps. Guys. Soaps. Five or six of us in the lounge at once, though there are more of us in the unit, and two girls, too, though the wisdom in the unit is to rarely mix us. They mean to keep our hopes up. I talk a lot of team. Mine is talk they like to hear. Five guys, six guys, we could make a squad. The Pain Brigade. Pain makes us. Both kinds.

The wounding kind, and the healing. All kinds. Sharps, dulls, aches, sting-
ing, burning, itching, mental.

The soap is on, and guys are getting hurt. Car wrecks, collapsing bridges,
blows to the head sustained while rescuing a loved one from a fatal peril.
Much, much amnesia. Mrs. Tom, a soap fan from way back, catches us up.

She says, "He deserved that, see. He cheated on his brother. They make
you think he ain't going to make it, but he will. It's good dough, working
in the soaps. Real steady. If he's smart, he'll let them pull him out a better
man."

We learn. We shift in our seats, trying to find a way to watch that doesn't
hurt. We see the mama and the papa and the sweetheart make their visits to
the comatose hero, hear the long withheld confessions and contrition, but,
"Man," we say, "I was that guy's ugly cousin before they slapped this ass skin
on my cheek."

"Really, no, I know, just once you'd like to see those guys get the hurt put
on them so they sweat."

"Right. And so they're ugly."

"Yeah. And hurting, like, so they have to scream."

"Do you scream?"

"Shit, yeah, I scream."

"Me, too, man. I'm bawling like a baby in that tank."

"I don't know, hasn't hurt too much for me."

"That's 'cause you're new."

"Wait till you start sprouting the buds."

"Buds mean you're getting better."

"Getting better means you hurt worse."

"Comfort is deformity."

"And deformity sure ain't comfort."

"Well, at least we're all alive. That guy on the show there, he might never wake up. Look at that. No offense, lady, but he might not be coming back."

"Right, sure. He could be going over to *The Guiding Light.*"

"Right, really, *All My Children.*"

"That's no joke. You know what I mean. I mean what is real and true. I had maybe thirty seconds there where I was thinking I'm a dead man. Shit my pants. That's true. Didn't know I could feel that much of anything and live."

"Well, but look at us here boys, we can."

"Amen to that."

"Amen, brother."

"No victims, right? Survivors?"

"Survivors. Right."

"Hey, what did you say your name was?"

"Tom."

"No, not you. The other guy. Big man there. What's your name?"

"Adam."

"Adam what?"

"Oney. Adam Oney."

"That's what I thought. Didn't we read about you? The optimist?"

"I played ball."

"Okay. Well, let me tell you something. I've been here a little longer than you, and I've lived more, too, and what I want to say is we are not in this together."

"No?" I said. "Well, it sure looks like there's a lot between us that's the same."

"I don't think so, Oney. Let's just start with nurses."

So we started with nurses, and by the end of *Days of Our Lives* the consensus in the lounge was that anything you said was the same could be different, and anything you said was different could be the same. Show is up, and it's time for us to ambulate, and that's the same for all of us, except for Tom, who had some bad burns on his feet and had to lean hard on his mama. Same, except for some of us who didn't have our mamas there to lean on. No mama, no papa, no family at all for some of us to visit with, which was another way for some of us to be the same, except the reasons why our families did not visit us were different. In time, we learned one family was dead. Another family was far away and poor. A father was ashamed. A mother was afraid. There was one old man who had only a daughter in the world to visit him, except she didn't more than just the once because, he guessed, to see him made her heart break.

I told Sue, I said, "It's just the way the General said it was for prisoners of war. Solitary is solitary, right? Well, wrong. And right. You know, you didn't want to have your two legs broken when the other guy got just the one. On the other hand, this was the Hanoi Hilton, you didn't want to seem too hale and happy, either. You start showing signs of superior oral hygiene, word will spread you're a talker."

I told Sue that after how those troops performed in the Korean War, a lot of drill went into making out the model POW for Vietnam. According to the General, it was a question of morale, especially for pilots. There was a time, he said, when it was statistically impossible to fly your tour without being shot down. Statistics showed you were either dead or taken prisoner.

"We dropped a lot of ordnance on them," the General said. "We turned the Plain of Jars into the Plain of Craters. Whole villages, moms, pops, and kiddies. Didn't take them long to learn they weren't safe in their pagodas. A photo we had tacked up on a corkboard in ops showed a cow's head hung up in a pine tree. We had a man eject once, said when he was coming down in that parachute—villagers mobbed around and screaming up at him, got their hoes and picks and whatnot they found to break his bones with—he said it helped to know that pretty soon he'd likely wind up in a cell of friendlies on the same page pretty much as he was. You got shot down," the General said, "you were glad the guys on your side would be living with you in the Code of Honor."

I said, "What do you think, Sue?"

"Well, I think you've been zapped. You've got a whole lot of new skin coming up. Hurts, makes you tired. I believe you're talking and you're silly."

"That's not me," I said, "that's the General talking."

"Then, okay," said Sue. "I think the General is silly. War is war. It's a crime. I'm a nurse. It's silly."

"Did you ever know anyone who went to war?"

"Yes," said Sue. "I knew plenty."

"Did they all come back?"

"They did. Every one of them."

"And so how about it? I mean when they look back, even if they weren't flyers, but were on the ground with the nasty jungle bugs, the bullets, and those land mines, wasn't there some part of them that when they thought about it, liked it?"

"Always," Sue said. "Every one of them. Never failed."

"And still that's what you think? The same?"

"I think that's healing talk. That's how it sounds when they're getting better. Because it hurts. Because they've got a nerve that's open right there on the surface, and it makes them silly. Or sad. They cry sometimes. They drink. They get to needing drugs as much as you do."

"You know what Hector told me once?"

"Who is Hector?"

"The guy in the tunnel, in the hideout, the one who poked me in the eye with that stick. He told me, I remember, he said, 'Only reason any of us hangs around is ball.' I think that was mostly true. It's almost all we ever did. That's a lot of sweat on us. Slippery, leaning on each other in the post. Made the ball slick if it hit you in the chest. We shined with it. Stung your eyes. You could hold your arm out from your side and watch the sweat run off down your fingers. Really, it's an armpit sport. Other sports—uniform sports—you don't get to see the body. You don't see that sweat. Made your hair stiff, when you cooled off some beneath that cottonwood for a drink of water. I'm the one discovered Saltines were the fix for when you dizzied. Look at me. Can you believe I played?"

"I do," said Sue. "I know you did. I read about you, too, you know. I'm an avid reader of the sports page."

Some days, I told Sue, we would go to the court in the cool of the morning and play straight through the hot and on into the cool again before we quit, lay down there in the grass and listen to the mothers call the littler kids to dinner. On the court, we got on all right. We argued some, which is better, the chain net or the rope—chain because it sort of grabs the ball before the ball can drop, rope because the net can back up through the rim on swishes. Lots of stoppage in the action over disagreement on the score. Who walked. Who fouled. Was someone too long in the paint. Hector kept on calling Chester midbrain, made Lester mad enough to knock down Hector with a flagrant on a break. Had we been somebody else, we could have hurt each other's feelings. But we survived, a snap, we loved the game, we're all together thinking ha-ha-ha about Arturo having thrown the ball at Mike and missed, the ball making pudding out of Arturo's bean-burrito sack lunch.

But off the court, you understand that Hector's name is Block, and Arturo is a Sanchez, and no way is the son of the man who owns a solid wall of downtown storefronts going to pass his playtime digging worms with the son of the man who labors by the season in alfalfa and potatoes. Needs the ball. Roll a ball out on the court and something in both of them will make them chase it. Yessir, roll the ball out and here come the twins, farmer's boys, here come Mike and Adam, an Air Force transient and a black kid, boys I learned the local boys were not supposed to play with.

"Hey, Sue," I said. "You know what it is?"

"What what is?"

"An optimist. I wouldn't say that, I was thinking. Not about me. What I think really is I have a talent for happiness. I can be pretty happy."

And lucky. Happy for being lucky to have at least a nurse like Sue to say she was sorry when she hurt you. Not all of them do. It's not in the contract, being sorry. Pain Contract, they call it, the arrangement they make out for how and when you want your medications, when and where to yell or not, how loud, what words, what your nurse will do, and what you can stand to do yourself. I had a good contract. I had a good nurse. That was my difference.

I said, "You're in the wrong line, Sue."

I said, "Why soaps? Why so many doctors on the soaps? And why so phony, and still we watch them?"

"I've thought about that," said Sue.

"And what did you think?"

"I don't know. It's what's on. That's as far as I keep getting."

"Most people in here are pretty poor, right?"

"They aren't too well off, that's true."

"So why is that? How come poor people get burned?"

"Same as why you watch the soap, I'd say. It's what's on, how dangerous it is to make your living."

"Do you think I'm poor?"

"I think you're tired."

"Will I be poor?"

"I think you'll rest."

"Sue? May I see your hair?"

"Not yet," said Sue.

"Let's see those teeth."

"Are you making fun?"

"I am not."

Nurse Sue pulled her mask down. I said with a mouth like hers, her line ought to be in movies; when you had a wide, live face like that, it was better than a ward of raw-skinned men who must desire to kiss you.

"You're sweet," said Sue. "Now sleep."

"You know with Mike," I said, "why he doesn't come, it's money. Not to mention transportation. They've only got the one car," I said. "And you maybe didn't know it, but this year really wasn't much for melons."

Ms. Santoro is the grade they have you write out your thinking on love. Compare and contrast, definition, confession, analysis. Choice is ours, she says. So long as it is written. So long as it is love. This assignment from September of that year, due by two weeks from tomorrow. April in the school world, a classroom lurching on pubescent hormones, hungrily emergent from the hibernating months of June, July, and August. Plenty of chair scraping, giggling from the girls whose breasts have budded out, hoo-haws from the boys who lately lie in bed at night and stroke their purpled bones. Questions, too: *Does this have to be typed? May we write about a dog? My horse? About how many words? Just because it isn't spelled right, does that mean that it's wrong?*

Ms. Santoro walks the rows of desks in go-go boots and sandalwood perfume. She swings a string of puka shells around her index finger, winding it tight the one way, then tight again the other. The team's all there for her. Mike and I, the Oolag boys, Arturo Sanchez, Hector Block.

Love.

Did she say love?

"Some say God is love," said Ms. Santoro. "Once, not so long ago, there was a summer of love. Some said the Summer of Love wasn't about love at all. Others said it was the same as 'love thy neighbor' in the Bible. Of course, some of you are thinking now that sex is love. You might ask yourself: How much do I really know about sex? You might ask: If sex is love, is sex still sex without the loving?"

Ms. Santoro touched us gently on our heads and shoulders as she passed us by. Mostly, she would touch us with her fingertips, though every now and then she laid a whole hand on a person, such as Hector, and appeared to rub his shoulder just a bit; I know she had Mike's wooly head flush in her palm and gave him one fine squeeze. I thought Ms. Santoro showed good judgment not to touch an Oolag.

"Any length," says Ms. Santoro. "Typed, preferably. Due by two weeks from tomorrow."

Any other day, the bell rang and so long as the weather was fine and the ground was clear, the five of us would follow on Arturo's dribble to the court. No more pits then. No more PBJ's and lemonade and leaps into the chalk dust. No, a boy will grow his inches, bother with his hair, search the mirror for the image he believes will be most pleasing to his crowd. Flight comes to be beneath him. That ball Arturo Sanchez carried on the day the four of them rode out and found us at the pits was real. It did what it meant to do. Bounced. Scored. Won. Made the crowd go wild. Made the chicas want you. That ball made Arturo walk in a crouch. Made him change the pitch of his voice, the length of his pants, made him change his name.

"No more Sanchez," says Arturo. "From now on, I am Doctor S."

Point guard. Dish man. We follow in a star-shaped, roughly strung-out cluster. Hands ready, eye on that basketball. He will not turn, Arturo. He is Doctor S. He sees. If we do not see him, we are apt to have the wind knocked cleanly from our bodies by a hot pass in the brisket.

But not this day with Ms. Santoro. We followed Arturo from class, all right, but you could tell he wasn't seeing us. He had picked up his dribble. He'd gone stiff in the legs. I know my nose was there for flattening; Hector's hands were in his pockets; the Oolag boys appeared to be sub-Oolag. As for Mike, he seemed Mike. He shot the lights out. Arturo and I are shooting ducks and air balls, Hector and the Oolag boys are shooting bricks, and there Mike set himself at fifteen feet or so and worked himself around the outside, baseline to baseline, Drs. Swish and Click. Was he made of steel, this guy? Could this guy be unboned? The rest of us, we nixed the three-on-three. No way were we up to running. How about a game of 21? How 'bout MISSISSIPPI? HORSE? We shot, and missed, shot and missed enough so by-and-by we worked it down and found we couldn't shoot our way through PIG.

Blamed it on love.

Women.

"Love. The love bug. We've got it bad," said Hector, who easily had it worst.

We sat down on the grass beside the ball court, lay on our backs and heard how Hector couldn't keep himself from seeing titties in the thunderheads, whereas the rest of us were tamely naming knights and planes and mule deer.

"Tell me you can't see a tit in that," says Hector. "That shit's even got a stiff-ass nipple."

"I don't see it," Chester says.

"Me either," says Lester.

"Shit you don't," says Hector. "That's Santoro there. You'll be seeing it again tomorrow."

"What do you mean?" Arturo says.

"I mean you boys are going to have a hard time keeping the sap down in the wood this year. You'll be glad you've got a desk across your lap when Ms. Santoro stops and asks how you are doing with those fractions."

"Wood?" says Lester.

"Wood. That's right," says Hector. "As in woody, dummy. As in boner, hard-on, stiffy?"

"Chester doesn't get them," Lester says. "Me either."

"Bullshit," Hector says. "Listen, dummies. Here's a question for you all. Snatch: up or in?"

"Snatch," Arturo says.

"Jesus," Hector says. "Pussy, then, all right? Va-gi-na? The little holey-hole the girl has there instead of dickey? Question is, does the hole go up, or in? When you get the woody, which way do you stick it?"

"It's a trick," Arturo says. "Don't anybody answer."

"I'm not," Lester says. "Me and Chester, we don't even get them."

"You do," says Hector. "And here's more, dum-dums. Ms. S, she doesn't wear a bra. You'll be sitting thinking what it feels like on her nipples when they rub against that silk. Feels good. Don't doubt it. She'll lean right close to you, and she'll say, 'Chester, do you need some help?' You'll have the big bone then, boy, and all I'm asking is, which way do you stick it?"

Mike gets up and dribbles to the foul line, hits a free throw, clean, no rim, all net.

"Hole goes up," he says. "Answer's in your pants. Bone goes up, same as the hole, just how God intended."

He was goofing, dribbled high behind his back, moved in fast and straight down through the lane, rolled the ball across the front rim of the basket.

"Okay," Hector said to Mike, "we all give up. What is it? You telling us you don't want to cork her?"

Mike moved out and shot from the top of the key.

He said, "I only want what I can have. If I was you all, I'd start looking for my love outside of sex."

What should I write?

"Why not basketball?" my mother said.

"How 'bout flying?" said the General.

Both, I thought, and more, and more specifically, I got to thinking: *Food.* Because I really loved my food by then, and not just as the stuff I ate, but food as an idea. Illumined Food. Ethereal Food. No way was a deviled egg about the base perpetuation of my human body. I sat down with a fork and poked around that creamy yellow yolk. Observe the brick-red flecks of paprika. Please appreciate the mounding yolk, verging on the slick, rimmed white. It glistens, that white. It complements. It cups. A true beauty, a perfection. A love. I know I wanted it inside me. Lots of them, whole, in nibbled bits, with extra salt, or little drizzlings of vinegar, ends and ends and ends in themselves, all of them inside me. I pushed my tongue straight through the yolk and drew it from the slick white cup by means of a gentle suction. I hummed. *Yolk, paprika, albumen, mayo.* I think there must have been a better word for my affectionate displays than *cram.*

As in my mother saying, "You don't have to cram them down your throat, you know. It's not like you're competing with a sister."

"I'm practicing," I said. "Seeing what I could say about your deviled eggs for Ms. Santoro."

"Oh, well, in that case," said my mother, which is also what she said about her meat loafs and pot roasts, the plates and plates she watched me put away of buttered noodles. Ma's kitchen. Home-style cooking. *Praise the creamed corn, and what's your secret, Mom, to such sublime chipped beef?*

"I suppose it isn't all so easy as I seem to make it," she said, "now, is it?"

Though when it came to Swanson's TV dinners, tater tots, frozen fish sticks, frozen pizza, Doritos, Cheetos, Fritos, Ho Ho's, Zingers, Ding Dongs—then what?

"What?" I said. "What're you looking at?"

"You're crazy," said my mother, "that's what. Did you hear him?" she was asking the General. "That's a Funyun he's talking about. It's not natural.

It's porn, almost. Try looking at his face next time he's eating deep-fried cheese."

"I don't know," the General said. "Looks to me he's on a growth spurt." The General chucked me guy-like on the shoulder.

He said, "When I was a boy, they had me playing forward."

He polished off his eggs and bacon, meaning, I suppose, to show me how a forward grew up from a guard. He stood up tall, drank his coffee down, made as if to dribble in and dunk behind his head, a showy two-hand slam that had him hanging from the basket. He kissed my mother on the cheek and told her not to worry. He turned to face us from the doorway. He looked good there, fresh-faced in his flight suit and his flyer's cap, the morning light cut out around him for his one last word, an order from Lieutenant Colonel Oney.

"You go on ahead and grow," he said. "But not too tall. I expect you'll be wanting clearance for that cockpit."

Such a violent quiet Mother made in the General's cheery wake. *Shut up, sunshine,* she seemed to say, *can't you see that I'm unhappy?*

I poured myself another bowl of Froot Loops, stirred them through the milk until they had achieved the right degree of sog. Maybe if she brushed her hair, I thought, or what if one day she stepped into something other than those sweats? How would it feel, I wondered, to see the General leave the house each day as fresh-faced as he left it, no more mustache, no more goatee, the General seeming to unage as he moved up the years in rank, while here I sat as Mother with the bed crease in my cheek till noon, a grump, perpetually hungover, a woman who could not return a kiss or see her way past ranking all her life as wife, as plain old disillusioned, isolated Mother. My scalp itched, being Mother. My eyes burned. I watched myself through her cigarette smoke, heard the milk soak through the pores of my Froot Loops, I could hear dissolving sugar.

"That sound you make with your nose? Uhnn, mmm, uhnn? It's disgusting," said my mother. "I'm going out to pull some weeds."

I followed her out to where she sat on the low brick wall of one of her garden beds. She flicked her cigarette into the bed, stabbed around in the sandy soil, deadheaded a baby mum. Not a single weed in there. Nor much evidence of flowers. No leaves either, when I thought to look, Mother having cut down the shade tree the General planted on the Mother's Day the first year we arrived here. Made a mess, my mother said, damn tree, same as the flowers. Between my mother's stinginess with plant life, and the General's passion for projects in concrete, there wasn't much around our place for a gardener to be busied by. Still, it was September. In September you put your garden to bed. And so there's Mother, stabbing and flicking, putting hers to bed in a mulch of the summer's butts.

"What?" she said. "What is it?"

"Well," I said, "I guess I was wondering about the General."

"Honestly," my mother said, "your old man tells some whoppers. He never played a minute of basketball in his life."

"Well, I don't mean basketball. I mean you. I was thinking, about this paper, with you and the General, if that was love. Not now. More when you first married, if *that* was love, something you thought was worth me writing about."

Mother shook out another cigarette, flipped the lid on one of the General's Air Force-issue Zippos. She kept flipping the lid even after the cigarette was lighted, seeming to have dropped herself into a trance.

I said, "Could be something else. Your gardens, maybe? Anything, so long as it's love. It's due in a week now. I'm having a hard time keeping focused."

My mother tossed me the lighter.

"What plane is that?" she said.

"Here? On this lighter? It's a B-52."

"Good," she said. "You've known that for a long time now, I guess, very good."

My mother took the lighter back, snapped it a time or two and put it in her pocket.

"What do you think of your mother?" she was saying. "I mean, when you think of me, what do you think?"

"I'm not sure," I said. "I can't remember. Seems like probably I'd be thinking about dinner."

"That's honest, isn't it? And how about your father?"

"The General?"

"Yes, all right, *the General.* Do you think he thinks of me?"

"Sure I do," I said.

"Do you think, if we asked him, he would remember what he thought?"

"About what?"

"About me."

"He might."

Mother smoked. She looked me up and down and told me I was just as big as she was, maybe bigger now, imagine that. She started off across the yard and led us into the garage. She opened the door, she said, to let a little light in.

She said, "It's musty in here, don't you think? You wouldn't think must was possible. Not here, would you?"

She walked us over to some cupboard shelves, asked me would I reach her down a box. She carried the box over to where the shade met up with the sun and sat us just inside the shade side. She stubbed her cigarette out on the concrete. She studied the burned-out, stubbed-in end for a time, then flipped it out into the driveway. She hugged her knees up close against her chest, closed her eyes, and said, "How do you feel when I tell you that the day before yesterday was my birthday?"

"Your birthday?" I said. "You never said you had a birthday."

Mother raked the prong of her gardening fork through the taped-up seam of the box flaps.

"I've got something here to show you. Something for us both to see."

My mother blew the dust off a photo album, opened up the pages from their wedding, those classy, glossy black and whites.

"I remember these," I said. "From Texas. You used to keep them on that table."

Mother turned the pages slowly, touching them a lot like Ms. Santoro touched our shoulders.

She said, "Maybe this is something more what you thought you should be writing."

I thought so. I remembered it so, certain pages I used to turn to: Mother in her white gloves, satin to the elbow. White lace, white veil, white train spread out wide across what you could guess right through the black and white must be a crimson carpet. The General, too, austere, all angles, high collar and brass, the Air Force dressed up at its best, a young man solemnized, a young man with his kiddish grin, the General cleaving gleefully to my mother. My mother turned a page, another. First Dance, Throwing the Garter, Catching the Bouquet. Then came my favorite, the one I call The Hall of Swords, two rows of men in uniform who face each other, ten men in each row, swords in hand, extended straight off from the shoulder, crossed, unshakable and gleaming. A spell, I thought, must have been cast by these sober, stony men: *To all who pass this way, enchanted love, eternal love, regal love and holy.* They feel the spell, I believe, the General and my mother, they stoop beneath the gleaming swords, or do not stoop but crouch, or do not crouch but seem to be in rapid motion, as if my mother and the General are about to take flight as a pair of birds emerging from a sheltered, cliffside perch.

"It does, doesn't it?" my mother said. "Seem that way? And it felt just how it seems, like I was taking off. First time I met your father was a double date. Fellow I was with is rich now. Arnold Sievers. Sells cars. Owns five dealerships in the greater Lubbock area. That man, when he kissed me, it tasted like a very comfortable retirement. But I was all eyes for your father. A novelty, you know. A person humored him, any of the ones who came from off the base. He said he was from Louisiana, which got me thinking, *New Orleans.* I wasn't a dummy, either. I knew enough so when I thought of New Orleans I saw the live oaks and the Spanish moss. I could see this boy who grew up where the ladies hung like flowers from the iron balconies and knew which catcalls were the ones a lady ought to blush for. I kept myself good and turned around in Arnold's car. I even reached back every now and then and touched your father on his knee. I thanked God Patty Jenks had got that lipstick on her tooth, and hoped your father wouldn't be distracted from that tooth by Patty's cleavage. She was really making a show of it, I'll tell you. Kept on wiggling around and pressing her arms against herself so she's about to pop her boobs clear out from her brassiere. Shameful, I thought. And smart. My worry was she would go ahead and scoot up next to him and push those things against his ribs until he figured out how much she wanted him to kiss her. I didn't want to see that. I didn't want to carry any picture of your father with another woman around with me forever, which is how long I told myself I wanted to be with him. Seems he never saw her. Or me. Back then, didn't matter where he was, or who he was with, all your father saw was what he might have seen out through his cockpit. He moved his hands a lot, doing what he'd do in planes. You could almost have thought he was simple, like maybe he would start in making jet sounds with his mouth. I liked it. Made him seem more lifted up. Most boys we knew, their lifted days were over with their sport. Arnold Sievers wasn't twenty-three years old, and he was up there next to me and talking like he'd done his homework on his chairs and sofas. Prices and upholsteries, you know? Not your father. He grew up in New Orleans. That's what I thought. I thought if I could get his head a little off the airplanes, then I might learn what happens after the jazz, like underneath a big magnolia, air full up with honeysuckle and wisteria, soft green light of a new day dawning, birds to whistle good morning to sleepy lovers on the garden bench. You couldn't say where he was heading, except that it was up. This was still the 1950s. Look at us," my mother said. "You don't need the color film to see the color. That man's eyes are *blue*. Up," my mother said. "Up and up. So young. I must have thought he would always take me with him."

My mother hitched her bra strap up from where it fell down off her shoulder. She lit another cigarette. She closed her eyes and let the sun shine on her face and smiled.

I said, "You're pretty, Mama. You have a pretty smile."

Mother said, "It was not my birthday, you know."

"What," I said, "just now?"

"Day before yesterday," my mother said. "September seventeenth. It was my anniversary. Ours, I mean."

My mother opened her eyes, squinted my way through the sunshine. She fished around in her sweats for the Zippo, handed it to me, and told me I could keep it.

She said, "Here's what you say for Ms. Santoro—love is most especially imperfect. Love is what's forgotten. Love is life, and love is only once and then it's elsewhere."

Hard to say where this much put me. I thought maybe she was over-minding the wisdoms written in her soaps. Did she not love me? What was love, if not that lady screaming for her Adam from the bleachers? Ever since

I'd started playing ball for leagues with drafts and uniforms and coaches, Mother came to watch me with a clipboard and a pencil, a drawing of the court where she would mark my shots, makes and misses, her own notations signifying jump shots from drives, fast-break shots from half-court shots, shots defended by a zone, defended man-to-man, shots I put up uncontested. Embarrassing, sure, to hear her whack that clipboard on the bleachers every time you score. Worst, though, to listen to her poor-mouth your opponent over pizza when you lost, especially when you have asked your opponent out to eat with you, especially when the opponent you are eating with is Mike. Still, that was love, I thought, and I liked it. I think Mrs. R and Mike did, too. *Mother love. Mama's boy. Hear that mama love her baby.*

"You know what?" I said. "Seems a little corny."

"Suit yourself," she said, and she left me sitting with her Zippo and her pictures.

I sat there with that Zippo till the sun had found me from the shade and wondered what could be the truth in Mother's corn I felt carousing in my rib cage. No kidding, why should Mother's bra strap be so unappealing? When did I stop wanting her to kiss me? *Elsewhere*, says my mother, *all your life is elsewhere*, says the General, *All your life is now.* I wonder, Ms. Santoro, what happens when a person locates love in life's places, rather than its minutes? And is a minute a place? And can there be a place without a minute? Ms. Santoro, I confess I am confused, is this the way you want us thinking?

I fetched myself a piece of paper and a pencil from the house, put the wedding albums back inside the box, folded up the box, and used it as a desk, deciding I would sit out there and write a thing I could not doubt without much thinking. Wasn't hard. Because I was a kid, maybe, what felt truest from my mother's talk of love was lift. And when I thought of lift, I thought of the General. And when I thought of the General, I thought of flight, and when I thought of flight, I thought of the General's Pitts. Not the pits, as in the pits, but the Pitts, the General's airplane. Biplane, stunt plane, the General's brand-new, serious investment in civilian aviation. September seventeenth was not my mother's anniversary; September seventeenth was the day the General took us out to see him fly the Pitts. Love. For the General, sure that airplane was a love.

And for Mother?

Jealousy, the peevish reach of love, why not?

Not the sort of love a mother wants for, not a good day by her lights at all, but think of us. Me, Wilbur; Mike, Orville. September seventeenth, no big deal, except we were eating Oreos and watching Navy fighter action, World War II, Pacific Theater, lights off, curtains drawn, sound turned up so we could feel the jitters when we lay our hands out flat across the coffee table. We talked radio talk. *Roger, two-six-niner, toro-toro-tango, that's a kismet!* We squirmed and twisted to see the Tigers hit the flight deck, thinking body English is what makes the cable catch, sees our heroes to their bunks at night where they can write another letter to the folks back home. We took dictation from a memory of books we'd read, war reels, a heated mash of pre-teen punk. *Dear Ma, Today we really gave those dirty Nips whatfor. Should have seen Joe Reilly send that Zero down to Davey Jones. Whatever they are telling you at home, it's true. The guys are swell. Tell Pa I am good. Tell Sister if a guy's not over here with us, then he's no kind of guy. There's heroes coming, tell her. She and you and all the girls can make a big parade. Ma, I love you. Love From Your Boys, Mike and Adam.*

Mike and I were lying on our backs on the floor, our feet propped on the coffee table, and for love I think I could have stopped right there. That's a lot of lift, all right, but add the General to the mix and we are moving from the prop age to the supersonic. He did not walk, the General, he surged. He banged in through the door, drew the curtains wide, and told us get a move on, there's still a lot of sky left. Who could say what that meant? Who cared? Mike and I, we understood the General's odor just the way Hector likely understood perfume. Breathe deep, don't ask, just follow. Smell the Winstons in that flight suit from the hours smoking with the flyboys, talking recon; smell the scalded coffee and the breath mints; smell the jet fuel in the General's boots and know enough to follow. But shouldn't he be at the Sanga, five deep in martinis, pulling rank on captains? That's what Mother wanted to know.

"No, ma'am," said the General. "Twelve hours, bottle to throttle. We're going to do some flying."

"Haven't you flown enough already?" said my mother.

"Not hardly," said the General. "Come on and get your jacket, pretty. Mix us up a thermos. I want to show you all what being Lieutenant Colonel buys you."

But Mother wasn't being bought. The thermos of martinis she was mixing could have been half hers. She could have kissed him on the mouth.

He said, "C'mon, c'mon, c'mon."

Heavy gin, light vermouth, ice she shattered on the kitchen counter with a weighted cracker.

He said, "That's a mean martini, Mrs. Oney."

He held her from behind. He had a little hunch on, rested his chin on Mother's shoulder. You could not see what he was doing with his hands but you could see that it was something. He kissed her on the neck. He leaned around her for her mouth and I thought of the smell in the General's whiskered face of oxygen, a day in the rubber G-mask. My mother turned away and faced us. I could not say if she was saying *caught you* or *I told you so.* She could have come. But she told the General go away; he needed a bath, she said, when sure she could have told him yes, of course, I'm coming. I thought maybe that's what freezing milk too long could do to you, freezing day-old bread, that habit. I thought driving eighty miles around the town, redeeming coupons from eleven different markets maybe got you saying no to all things fine, once you saw how much they cost you.

The General watched her shake the thermos.

He said, "Sure?"

Whereas Mike and I ran straight out to the General's good-time ride, a '67 Comet convertible, top down, just waiting on us and the one-handed vault, never mind the doors, which is okay by the General, so long as we clear ourselves and spare the paint. We knew the drill. We knew that once we rolled, the Comet wasn't the Comet but a Phantom. Soon we would be Mach speed, hunting pinko Commies. Folks on the ground back home depended on us. Good folks. Freedom-loving folks. Folks like you and me. The General drove us through a neighborhood where kids played tag and men pulled home from work and said I'm home to old-style housewife women and we knew, should we falter, these happy folks were in for bread-line miseries and thin green soup, annual allotments of shoes that never really fit them. We waved to them, saluted. We rode in back, our heads hung out to catch our speed, the feel of the warm air and the cool and warm again as we left town and quickened through the irrigated acres.

The General was talking back at us, shouting something we could only hear about the half of, stuff about Mother, how she could have lain out on the hood of the car and watched the sun set, seen the moon rise, the stars fall, then something else about some help with those martinis. Mike and I said *what?* a lot and thumped each other on the chest *just kidding*—who wanted to hear more about a sulky mother?—till the General gave up shouting and we made the turn off the highway for the airport. Airstrip, more like. Pretty primitive operation out there in the desert. You had the north-south runway, and the east-west, paved, but rough; you had an abandoned coffee shop and several rows of well-kept hangars. An uncontrolled strip.

No tower. This meant no controller. Pilot cleared himself for takeoffs and landings, sited himself and called in his position by the radio for traffic. If he had a radio. Which the General did not.

He pulled us up in front of his hangar—*our* hangar, he called it—said for us to close our eyes. We heard the hangar door roll back in sections on the steel tracks. "Okay," the General said, "come on ahead and have your look."

He rolled her out into the sun. Cherry red. Maraschino cherry red. A miniature biplane. She shined, a showy bird on the cusp of song. This little sweetheart here, the General explained, not only turns the inside loop, but she'll also turn an outside. She spins, rolls, hops and jigs and saunters. She'll do pretty nearly everything, the General said, but jerk you off and serve you dinner. Only thing he didn't like was the glassed-in cockpit.

"Couldn't figure how to lose it," he said. "Got rid of the radio. Transponder. It's all junk, really, gadgets, pretty much crapola. If I thought it'd work," he said, "I'd be like you boys and jump off that cliff and beat my wings like hell till I was flying. They build them better every day, but we'll never beat a bird. How do you like her?"

Like her? We two boys were speechless, had our hands jammed in our pockets and our feet stuck to our spot so we didn't run and maul her. We shrugged. When the General asked us, we said sure, yessir, you bet we'd like to have him walk us through a preflight. We watched him drain the water off the fuel tank. We saw him check the oil and tires, the leading edge, the trailing edge; we saw the way he used his fingertips to test the aileron and rudder. He seemed gentler, an expert with his hands, a doctor maybe, firm, sympathetic even, more a woman than a doctor, a woman with an only child, a single, doting mother. What must it be, I wondered, to be the loving pilot's airship? What would it be to feel his touch from within a skin of lightweight steel? Made sense for them to call their airplanes her and she.

Right off when he opened up the door you saw the General kept that hangar floor much cleaner than our mother kept our sheets. He would polish her struts, brush her grille, flush her fluids, monitor her airflow. He talked to her. He dressed for her, strapped himself inside the cockpit, produced that crazy leather helmet and the scarf, the real things, the ones Mike and I pretended.

He said, "Okay, baby, let's go fly."

He waved us back a distance, hollered clear, then contact, and then the engine turned, the prop engaged, and Mike and I exchanged the thumbs-up with the General, who taxied for the windward end of runway 34, readying for takeoff.

No junk there, I thought, no sir. When the pieces were all soldered, cut, and riveted together, that Pitts was awfully pretty. She hopped right off the ground, just as the General said she would, looking not so much like a bird, but more like an idea, a new thing in the world, the birth of an old desire. The General snapped her in a roll, flew her once around the pattern, came in low, and turned her over so he flew the runway right in front of Mike and me inverted. Felt then like my stomach was inverted, too, flopped up in the hole left high inside me by my sinking heart. This was the General, our leader and my pop, same guy who had told us many, many times about the fellow and his wife who flew this stunt and ended both their lives as two heads rolling off the tarmac through the sagebrush, the rest of them cremated in a fireball of gadget and crapola.

Naturally, the General righted himself. He flew the runway with his tail a foot or two off the asphalt, climbed, waggled his wings at us, the southern boy's, *How do?* the magician's flourished handkerchief, *How 'bout that?*

Funny we weren't cheering. It got quiet while the General climbed, you saw a quieting toward the sun, a speck of him and silence where he disappeared as if into another, farther sky, a taller dome to vault the western ranges. Weird. And quiet. Quietly, Mike and I had moved off from each other, too far to hear each other breathe or think or feel. Far enough. Then back. Both of us starting off as if what we thought and felt was something of the same, required the same time and the same space in the feeling and the thinking. I liked believing so. I liked believing we continued not to speak because we neither of us wanted to know that what we felt was not the same, that Mike had felt desire, say, where I was feeling fear, that Mike had thought *keep going*, where I had thought, *come back.*

We kept our chins up, eyes on the darkening sky. Empty sky, fair to say, emptier than cloudless. Nothing, I was thinking, for the sky to hold, no trees, no barns, no rivers, lakes, or oceans, no nearer object than the far horizon for the sky to body up and be defined by. The horizon seemed to pull the sky, stretch, and drain it from its center. The sky seemed a bowl, then, a basin Mike and I were watching flare and dim through shades of pink and purple. Yet there was nothing of our General to see, nothing we could hear beyond ourselves save hearts and breath, a biological quiet deepened by an unfulfilling expectation. We listened for his engine, the wind on a wing in flight. Hurt my head. My neck. Felt my skull and chest cave. I felt hungry, sleepy. By-and-by I squatted on my haunches, doodled with a stick in the sand.

"He's there," said Mike. "That's him."

I stood up and tried to see what Mike was seeing to make him look the way he looked. I saw the sky had gone a little purpler. I saw a star. I saw a flicker, something lit beneath the sky, higher than the ranges, above the shadow line, a shine and flicker of the General in the privileged minutes of the aviator's lengthened day, high above us in the sun and falling. He fell through the sun. He did not fly. You could not hear him. He fell out of the sun and into the shadow of the range and still he did not fly and still you could not hear him. We should have heard him. He should have flown. He fell. He was red. He was falling as a leaf falls, maybe, weirdly, by an indecipherable law of lilt and sway and plummet. I saw it that way, only heavier, there was time to see the General as a leaf, and then maybe more like something of a flattened stone, a winged slab, time to see him as my father falling in a little red biplane, called a Pitts. Where would he land? If he were a leaf, how hard would it be to chase about and catch him?

I sat. I wanted to stand up for him. I wanted anyway at least to see. But I didn't have the knees, didn't have the heart. I felt my stomach coming up in me again with this time nothing there to stop it. A splatter on the canvas tennis shoes of Oreos and milk, that's me. I never heard his engine catch. I did not see him fly out from his fall or show us another waggle when he turned his final leg and landed. It's a loud sound in your ear, that getting sick. I wanted to run out to the runway, greet the General while he taxied, but I had those shoes to scuff off through the sagebrush, a shirt to rub down with the sand. I told Mike thanks, I didn't need his help, he should go ahead without me. I took my time, rubbing and scuffing; I didn't want the General to know I gave in to my stomach; I wanted him to think my heart was where it ought to be, right up high and his for having.

Was that love? Was that what I should write about—the General and his Pitts? And if so, how to say it? I felt a little stuck for sure, laid my pencil on the box, went inside and made myself a peanut butter sandwich. I ate it at the kitchen window. I made another. I poked around in the refrigerator, found a Coke, some cream cheese and some celery sticks, a jar of bread-and-butter pickles. I made up a little plate to take out to my box and when I saw the paper and the pencil on the box I was surprised to see the paper still unwritten on; all this time and thought and not a single word of writing. I told myself don't panic. Keep it simple. Ask yourself what happens next, and next, until it's finished. I dragged a celery stalk through the cream cheese.

Calmly, now, recall the General walking you and Mike back from the hangar to the Comet. September seventeenth. A boy on either side of him, an arm around each boy. Even me, especially me, the General's true-blue puker.

"Don't sweat it," said the General, "I've seen guys lose it in their G-masks."

We had questions, asked the General where a pilot sited when he flew inverted, and how tempting would it be to pull the stick back when you ought to push it forward, and how high did the General need to climb to do that last trick where he cut the power? Mike's questions, mostly, sober, narrowly defined, factually answered, whereas mine were steering nearer to the stories we were used to hearing of the General's glory days at war. We sat in the Comet with the top down while the General smoked his Winstons, sipped at his martinis, delivering us increasingly expansive answers as he worked his way down to the bottom of his thermos. A more vivid answer to Mike's plainest questions, anecdotes to supplement the facts; new details to the stories I was asking him to tell us over, contradictions Mike and I would later reassemble in the fabrication of a truer truth. The General rested his wrists up on the windshield of the Comet. The smoke curled off his Winston hand, rising silver in the starlight. He pointed out the figures in the stars and told us what they meant as myths to steer by.

"You start out as a navigator," said the General. "Used to be. I flew second seat."

Cassiopeia was out there, the Pleiades, the General said, but I was watching out for the oily streaks the General set in motion through the gin and ice when he would shake his silvery martini. I sat down low to make him seem a little taller, a little silverier. I liked the look from there of the tips of his slim cap against the black and brightening sky. He looked large, I thought, responsible for and prior to the constellations he was naming. It was cold. The air felt thin and cold and hard, though until the General turned the heater on for Mike and me, he seemed not to feel the air as anything except a free-form volume best described by flying.

He said, "You boys all right? Okay for me to leave the top down?"

The General offered us a sip from his martini.

"Takes the chill off," said the General.

He flipped open his Zippo, mate to my mother's. He struck a flame and snapped the Zippo shut, put the Zippo back into his pocket.

The General said, "Where I come from, kids were having babies by your age. You don't want to do that. Unless you want to be a Kirby Boudreaux all your life. You want to be him, have the baby. You want to fly, then don't. I logged nine lives in a T-38 before I even met your mama, nine lives more before you were a plum pit in your mama's belly."

The General leaned across me, asked Mike did he hear him.

"Yes, sir," Mike said. "I hear you loud and clear."

"Good," the General said. "I like you, Mike. Shame, what happened with your daddy. I heard he was a hell of a mechanic."

"All I hear about," said Mike, "is how he wanted just to fly."

"He'll see *you* fly," the General said. "If you want him to, he'll see you. You've got the fly bug in your blood, son."

The General finished his martini, lit another Winston. "Adam's mother," said the General, "your mother, Adam, she's over forty. Women fade. Around thirty, really. They can look damn good, but I think Adam's mother thinks she's faded. I invited her, didn't I? Well. Maybe it's the onslaught. How she says, *the onslaught of womanhood.* She says she isn't fresh. I think she thinks her country disappointed her. Could be. Lots of women maybe never had much chance. But still, I think a person makes his chance. What do you think, Adam? How about it, Mike? That's what I did. I'm not being any Kirby Boudreaux. Hell. Shit. You know what I think? I think we ought to go and get an ice cream, bring one to your mother."

Sounded fine, I thought, a great idea, though as I sat there with my pencil at my box I saw that I had maybe finally thought things too much through. Because as soon as I have pushed the nexts and nexts to ice cream, then I can't help seeing that the ice cream was a bad idea. For Mother it was. Because instead of eating ice cream, Mother had the lights out. Inside lights, outside lights, a statement. She hadn't come. She could have come, but didn't. She had her birthday, she said, her anniversary. She mixed her own martini, celebrated by herself.

"Go see," said the General. "Then we'll run Mike home."

I opened the front door and stood with Mother's ice cream at the threshold. I did not go in. I did not call to her. The house was dark, and quiet, and through the quiet I could hear my mother in her bed, her wakefulness in bed, her impatient wait to make her statement heard in all its bravely suffering detail.

I ate Mother's ice cream. Mike didn't want it, the General didn't want it, so I ate it. It was just a cone. I had it polished off before we even left our block. Plain vanilla, peewee. She didn't miss much. I didn't gain much. Not too good, that is, as a next, and then the next next even worse with Mike, whose mama made her statement where she waited for him in the doorway, their house lit up around her like a double exclamation point, concluding in a question mark, *Where'd he been!!?*

I put my pencil down. My paper kept on being empty. Pretty unuplifting. Life, I thought, was a poor self-punctuator. Really, a person must become an editor in life, if he would find his periods in love's most elevated moment. Myself, I felt down, a seabird, useless feathers glued together by that oil slick oozing from the tanker on the reef. I supposed I ought to cut back prior to the cone. But where, I wondered? Navy fighters? Top down in the Comet? I asked myself how anyone should rescue his few unadulterated moments from the feel of what is yet to happen in the past.

After Mother, after Mike, the General looked tired. His eyes were red-dish yellow in the white. His Winstons looked to hurt him when he smoked. He sat up with me while I ate a bowl of Froot Loops, watching me as if I were an organism smeared by science on a strip of glass, the microscopic parasite the General has recently been told we all are made to host, all our lives, within the pores and follicles of our degenerating epidermis. Certainly I saw he had a nasty scab from another knock on the crown. Lots of little nicks. Scars and sunspots. The scalp of a tall, bald man, I was surprised to think, the hide of an aging mammal. Just that morning he had looked so good, fresh up from his sleep and boyish for the day. I had seen this look to him before, it occurred to me, and I wondered then what made a man the General's age so vulnerable to the passage of his waking hours.

I took my plate back in the house and thought I might go cheer up Mother. I found her in her chair, in the TV room, curtains drawn, darkish light, fishing cashews from a tin of nuts, staring at *One Life to Live*, seeming to be thoroughly uncheerable. I stood a couple of arm lengths behind her, asked her could I bring her something from the kitchen. She did not turn or answer, but waved the backside of her hand at me and kept on fishing for the cashews.

"You could have come with us," I said. "The Pitts. You could have come."

Mother found the nut she wanted, made a show, I think, of tossing the thing up and catching it in her mouth.

"I think you're jealous," I said.

She leaned her head out to have a look at me. She probed around her teeth with her tongue and said, "Of course I am," then turned back to her program.

I went out to have another look at my paper, check again to see if maybe

I had written something after all, I don't know, a boy will wish, if he is up against a deadline and his paper is a wordless blank between the darkened margins. I tore my paper from the binder. I carried it out to my mother's garden beds, held it up in front of my face and lit it with my mother's Zippo. I dropped the paper when the fire burned up to my hand and thought the way it fell down to the bed was something like the way my father fell out of the sky, that hapless, unflown movement.

I decided to ride. I packed myself a lunchmeat sandwich and a bag of chips. I tore off several sheets of paper, folded them and put them with my pencil in my pocket, swung a leg up on the Lemon Peeler and rode. I felt sort of flash on the old Lemon Peeler, cool. You rode a bike like that for long and you were even feeling groovy. Lazy, dippy little S turns down the sleepy little lanes—*whoop, whoop, whoop, whee-hee!* My knees bumped up a little high when I would sit down low in that banana seat, but if I stood up on the pedals I was king. Used to take a maximum degree of me to run this bike, but now I was a size to own her easy. I popped a wheelie from the gutter curb and rode it half a block.

I said, "I dig you, sissy bars. I am king of my banana!"

I rode. Out of lane and block life. Out of town. I steered west, eyeing the sage and piñon ranges where the sun set. I am Amelia Earhart, Charles Lindbergh, if I fly these lonesome miles back home it's ticker tape for me, I told myself, it's wine and poetry, a little airtime on the AM band in pretty decent pop songs. Until I reached the site where Staley rode his plywood off the roof-deck, I do not think the pits were in my thoughts at all, though when I passed the gas pumps and the glassy front of the convenience store I felt the pits rush to my head as if from every cell that rushed to build my growing body. I leaned my Lemon Peeler on the kickstand, went inside and bought myself a cherry pop. I counted out my change for an unhappy-looking woman who had rung up the amount I owed on her machine.

I wondered if the polka-dotted smock she wore conspired to make her any more or less unhappy seeming, and what it was in women such as this one and my mother that discouraged them from brushing out their hair.

I said, "Did you ever know that guy, the one who got hurt here, long time ago, named Staley?"

"No," the woman said, "why should I?"

"I just thought, since you worked here, maybe you would."

"I haven't been here long myself. How long ago are you talking?"

"Like when they built this place."

"Jesus," said the woman. "No. Hell, no. I been here just two months, and if I'm still here in two more months, then that'll be too long, believe me. Anyway, what happened?"

"With Staley?"

"Yeah, the hurt guy. Something fall on him, or what?"

"He flew," I said. "He got blown right off the roof, sort of flew there for a minute on a big old piece of plywood."

"That's it?"

"Well, he went pretty far, I'd say. He even did a flip."

"No," the woman said. "I don't mean the flying. Wasn't for the old man being branched in the flying arm of the service, we'd never have been based here. I'm sick to death of flying. I mean, what got hurt?"

As it happened, I could not entirely remember. I had to say I had not followed up. The woman looked at me as if I were a kid incorrigibly determined to become the man who risked his life by saving baseball cards and diaries from the house of burning orphans. She said I owed her two more cents. The name on the tag pinned to her smock was Jen.

I said, "You have air, Jen?"

"Have what?"

"Air," I said. "My tires are soft."

The woman looked out at my Lemon Peeler, said, "I don't know, kid. You sure you're not just way too big for that bike?"

I rode on, a little less rushed in the cells, pedaled up the gravel road until I saw our scrap wood lean-to. From here I took the ride in stages, a stop for every hundred yards or so to savor. Not bad, I was thinking, for a job done up from rusted nails and scrap. Still gave shade. Still could keep you dry if you were small enough and caught out in a thunderstorm. I ducked to fit down under. I wondered at the new kids who must come here, waves of them who made the place their own by painting their names over ours. How many kids? Had they made themselves a team? Did they jump? Did they have the hankering for flight Mike and I did? Ned, they were called, Jasper, Gordy, Nick.

I stood up and stretched my cricks and cramps out. I went and sat out on the lip of the pit, unwrapped my lunchmeat sandwich. You got big, eating, no question. Moved you up from guard to forward, according to the General. Or it made you fat, said Mother. Made me hungrier. Once I got going eating, felt almost like I was emptying instead of filling; like whatever want I meant to feed by eating one chip only opened up a bigger wanting for another. Felt light to me. Felt up. Give me a lunchmeat sandwich, a bag of Ruffles, and a cherry pop and I am flying. I studied the drop for a proper landing, paced myself away from the lip of the pit for what I thought would be a realistic length of runway for a takeoff. I sort of looked around, like maybe someone closer to myself than God might see my flight, and there I saw this kid come pressing up the trail, hollering and waving.

He was the size I guess I knew he'd be.

He said, "Hey."

I said, "Hey."

He said, "What're you doing here?"

"Nothing," I said. "I just ate a sandwich."

"You going to jump?"

"Maybe."

The kid leaned over his handlebars to get a look over the lip. He spit down there.

"Well," he said. "You going?"

"Not just yet."

"What're you waiting for?"

"Do you know who we are?" I said.

"No," said the kid, "What do you mean, we?"

"Me and Mike," I said. "We built this place."

"That so? Well, it's mine and Ned's now," said the kid. "So just don't wreck it."

"I'm not," I said. "That's what I said. We built it."

"There's weirder things than that been done," said the kid.

The kid stood up on his pedals, working his handlebars, balancing in place.

"You going to jump?" he said.

"Not yet," I said.

"Didn't think so," said the kid.

He shoved off for the trail, never having lost his balance.

"Wait," I said.

"What's it?"

"I'm going to jump."

"No," said the kid. "No, you ain't."

"Wait," I said.

"Naw," said the kid. "I got to eat."

Kid was right. He had to eat. I didn't jump. I was big. Maybe too big, after all. I sat back down on the lip of the pit and saw it was a long time ago with

Mike for sure, a long time since the team came out to jump with us, almost twice our lives ago, too bad. Because look at that, in those days the General even made it out to watch us jump. He brought his camera out to take our picture, better than those Polaroids by me and Mike, no contest. Best of the bunch he took was when he stood down at the bottom of the pit to catch us on our takeoff. Holding hands, going six across.

"Moral fiber," said the General. "What we have inside this box is six boys flying under serious duress."

I think he liked being there at least as much as we did. He liked the array we made him as a band of allied satellites who held him at the center of a constant, smiling orbit. He obliged us with earful after earful of the war. He took us out to see him fly formation. He told us where to be and when if we would like to hear a sonic boom. Once he picked us up from school and drove us in his Comet to our house to watch an eighteen-minute reel of air-to-air refueling. He used a pointer. He drank scalded coffee from a Styrofoam cup. We all sat at his feet, watched the tanker and the Phantom couple through a haze of Winston smoke rolling in the cone-shaped flicker. We heard the General simulate cockpit communications, synchronizing compass bearing, altitude, and airspeed. He flexed his knees, bit his lip, anticipating, lurched and thumped the screen for emphasis when there was any variation in the motion of these planes that he could differentiate as either turbulence or pilot error. The sky was so cloudless, so uniformly blue, the motion of the planes so regular that if it weren't for the sound of the projector and the General's expert eye, you could think what you were watching was an eighteen-minute still. When the reel ran out, and the General asked me please to turn the lights on, I think it was an Oolag who asked why they called it air-to-air. Was Arturo who got up without a word and went outside to dribble in the driveway. By-and-by, Hector said he really liked to shoot, and unless the General could promise food, the Oolag boys admitted they would rather rebound than drive the hour north of town to see the Phantoms fly the canyons.

Maybe I thought these defections might take some of the lift from the General's wings, but no sir, not at all, the General seemed as glad as Mike and I to be back down to purists.

"Well, it takes all kinds boys, right?" the General said. "We ought to thank the gods not everyone was born a flyer."

Sorry enough to picture what the sky might look like, driven like an interstate by citizen pilots; sad to think of a sky erupting every rush hour with the sounds of props and turbines; but it was downright scary, said the General, if you could really see these folks competing for a runway when the fuel gauge shows them coming up on empty.

"Might be plenty of room once you're up there," said the General, "but all that room gets squeezed down in a hurry when you've got to land your bird on planet earth."

No, sir, better to be Orville and Wilbur, originals, true bloods under the General's wing, nothing of the weekend dilettante about us. Take your lawyers and your doctors, says the General, folks with too much cash to burn, too many courses to golf, too little respect for the heights their airship flies them to—it's them you'll read about, plowing themselves into mountains, spiraling nose down in the desert. This is the General's speech, the mission he lays out for us. I sat and let myself believe I could hear the General down there from the bottom of the pits. Saw him dressed out in his flight suit, got his Winston and his drink.

"Stick with me," he says, "and you'll be flying the elite. It's all right to play ball. I appreciate the sweat. You've got a gym, fans, cheerleaders, I know. Maybe you will be the guy to hit the winner at the buzzer. In my day, you played for Lucy DuPree. You know what she had? *Knockers*. Knockers in a sweater. Lucy DuPree at her peak. Rumor was you hit the winner and you got her. But in the end I'll tell you what, you leave those Lucy DuPrees to the Kirby Boudreauxs. There's a million, ten million Kirby Boudreauxs out there, and for every Kirby Boudreaux there's a Lucy DuPree. He's the guy who works the pump at the filling station. He's got eight kids back at home, and it isn't any one of them he's seeing in your dipstick, no way, no how, it's an ice-cold beer he's seeing. He's got his eye on a barstool with his Kirby Boudreaux buddies down at Chet's. Something nice. Go to work, shoot some pool, get a little liquored up, and go home to the wife and kiddos. Easy. You're a star, you've got Lucy DuPree, sweater meat. You've got your friends who saw you hit that winner at the buzzer. It's fun to joke about your Lucy's sweater meat, you know, the knockers you have got to calling paps and dugs. How's that for a word? Dug? Dugs? They're all stretched out now, sacks. You can see them flopped out on her belly when she sits on the side of your bed, just before she swings her legs up. Poor girl. Tired things. They've done a job you can't imagine hiring on to. Of course, you don't say that to your buddies down at Chet's. She's a cow, your Lucy—that's what you say, that's the spirit—nothing like the sweetheart in the pink Camaro you filled up today, nice high cleavage in a lacy satin bra, not Lucy, shit, your Lucy, she's all haunch and cotton, she's got fucking udders! Don't laugh, though. Commonest life a person volunteers for. Hard to turn your back on the crowd. They're mad for you in that gymnasium. And that's where you'll want to be, this year's champ. What's yours? Lucy DuPree, she'll tell you you can do it all, you're that kind of hero. Your buddies tell you skip that ground school stuff, the action's on the floor, the real score's at the party after. Lots of Kirbys, boys," the General says, "not too many Mikes and Adams. You stick with me, I'll take you two flying."

He was saving us, he said; for us, the General had big wants. When he said God, he meant God.

"You're alone up there," he said. "It's a very clean feeling. Just you and your machine, doing just exactly what He put you here for."

"If you're going to be a bear," he said, "be a grizzly."

He said, "Mike, my boy, I see it, you were born to fly the fighters."

He showed us to the darkroom, introduced us to a sergeant who developed film the General shot on recon. He led us out onto the tarmac, let us climb the ladder to the Phantom where we sat inside the cockpit while the General ran us through the avionics.

"Go ahead," he said. "She won't bite. Go ahead and touch."

He took Mike's hand and placed it on the stick. He guided Mike's hand, front and back, side to side, to feel the range of motion.

"Feel that?" said the General. "Imagine what that means when this bird's in the air. Wait until you grow the leg to work the rudder."

We grew. The General helped us grow. He moved us through the kid stuff in a hurry. It was an accident, but certainly it was the General's hand in helping us to grow that year, which finally finished us from jumping at the pits. Halloween, and Mike and I are ten, eleven years old, and we are thinking aliens and devils, trying to talk the General into buying us something store-bought. Why that? he asked us. We could be Orville and Wilbur, couldn't we? Or if we had already been them, then we could be a fighter pilot, an astronaut, or better yet, the bird itself. A raptor. An owl was a very scary critter. Think of a falcon, hawk, an eagle. A five-foot wingspan, big hooked beak, some wicked-looking claws for piercing and for tearing.

The General stood on one foot and spread his wings out wide, showed his fiercest eye, and did his best rendition of the eagle's scream, the General saying there were reasons why the greatest nation in the history of the world should see the eagle as its airborne icon. He had us sold. Even helped us with our beaks and claws, found us each a pair of angel wings we fixed with jet-black spray paint. Now let Mother sew us up a rayon eagle suit, put a white cap on our heads, and what you've got is a couple of trick-or-treating baldies, ferocious flyers swooping through the blocks for sweets and popcorn balls, terrorizing little skeletons and Spider-Men who must have wished they'd had the wherewithal to be us. Until the rains came. Until the paint ran off our wings and showed our pink. Until some bigger kids whose costumes weren't anything except a penciled set of whiskers came and asked us what we thought we were, Mike and I, did we think we were fairies? We knew to let them take our loot, these boys; we stood still for them to snap our beaks back in our face from the elastic. *Dirty fairies*, said the one, and then the others, and then the gang of kids who gathered there to see if we would fight pitched in so it could be a chant—*Dirty fairies, dirty fairies, dirty fairies.*

That did it pretty much for playtime. First thing Mike said we should do is ditch the wings. Meet him at the pits, he said. Bring your wings, your toys and models, too, anything that wasn't real and we would throw it all over. Say good-bye, make it official, he was saying, move on to the stuff that really gets us flying. Sure, sure, sure, I said, move on, that's right, I thought, but *really?* Already, I was thinking, now, now, *already? Throw it over? All of it?*

"All of it," said Mike.

We traded off, one item at a time, saving the wings for last, said Mike, in honor of the principle which finally moved us out of kid stuff. We made a game of saying good-bye to the games. We threw for distance, for height and stunts and targets. Could you explode that 747 on that rock? Think you can fly this Piper Cub to where the chalk meets up with sagebrush? Gone, there they went, touched together in the manner of a pair of glasses in a toast, and then over. The one that got me though, the thing I saw that Mike had same as me and I was keeping safe at home inside my drawer was *First Flight.* He made a real show of that book, tore out every page of it, folded every page in planes and flew them. Sure I knew he knew I had one, and I believe you see Mike at his Mikest when you hear he never asked me why I did not bring it. I wished he would have kept his, too. By the time we got down to the wings, I wished again he hadn't been so ready to be done with kid stuff. Of the wings he said we ought to throw them at the same time, stand at the lip of the pit and do a countdown just as we had done when we first stood up there and jumped. Pretty uneventful, as my mother might have said it. We gave them all we had, but those poor wings turned out to be the worst flyers in all our stuff combined. Maybe it was funny. I know we laughed. We gave the count, heaved-ho, and there they went, smudged pink and broken, a flat flop stuck against the chalk wall, not ten feet down the cliffside. I itched for us to go on home so I could come back out and fetch them.

I sat there on the lip of the pit with my paper and my pencil, counting back the years, and wondering what Mike might say if he could know I had saved our wings back in my closet. I thought some way he might like to see how they would always fit us. These pits, too, I thought, would always fit us. From where I sat you saw the steep scar carved from the chalk, our gentle landing, and the line of sage which showed you how far out the slag ran. You saw the low hills farther off in grades of purple-gray, and farther off from these you saw the ranges big enough to catch the rain and snow and grow the shortened forests there of juniper and piñon, surprising little creekside groves of quaking aspen I recalled the General took us up to view one autumn from a rented Cessna. One day Mike and I decided we were counting seven different weathers in a single sky. How many weathers were there? How many views of sky? I sat and asked myself if I had ever really liked what I was seeing from an airplane any better than what I was seeing right here at the pits. Then I wondered how long would it be before the town decided to expand again in this direction, fill the pits back in, build on them, plant this slope in clover or in winter rye, and mow it. We'll miss it then, I'll tell you that much, Orville. We'll miss it just as true and freshly hard as all these Neds and Gordys who have come here after us to jump and sit inside our shade the same as we did. They wrote over our names, Orville; they picked up our toys. But we were first, Orville and Wilbur, Wilbur and Orville, Kitty Hawkers, dune jumpers, the original brothers Wright.

And I guessed the question was, so what? From here, this time of day, this time of year, you felt the wind come up as always, you heard the wind delivering the bypass traffic from the interstate. You felt the lights come up in town and knew the mothers soon would stand out on their porches to call the littler kids to supper. He had to eat, that kid. He was right. I didn't jump. I was bigger now. I heard the same sounds from a different head. I sat this time and listened to the wind and heard the wind keep telling me to move along now, son, same as always, except I did not move but sat. I had that pencil in my pocket, too many empty sheets of folded paper. *Love*, I thought, I had entirely forgotten. I waited on the wind to die. I saw the star come up I thought the General said was Venus, then I lit the afterburners on the Lemon Peeler for Mike's house.

I rode hard, leaning out across the sissy bars, squeaking in my seat springs. I throttled back some when the country turned a little greener. I thought when I slowed I could hear the water. Not the running sort like in a creek, but more the water running out across the ground that really needs it, more the way the water sounds when it is feeding fields of stems and leaves through months of desert heat. Pumped water. Channeled water. Water drunk down and exhaled in rounds I thought I heard of, *Thank you, thank you, thank you.* This is where Mike lived. I had never heard it. Water in pipes, water in ditches. Somewhere where I couldn't see it, I could hear a tractor drone along before it shut down for the evening. Lights were coming on in kitchens. I heard the blackbirds quiet down, and the crickets come to voice, and then I heard what I was sure was Mrs. R, calling in her boys to supper.

I stopped off pretty far away from her and watched her cup her hands around her mouth to holler. She stood beneath the porch light, looking like a person looking for another person. *Something good here, boys, come on in, where are you?* I straddled my Lemon Peeler and listened with Mike's mother and I think I saw myself in her again when Mr. R and Mike came chugging up behind the barn, waving from a tractor. The kind of dark it was, and the kind of dark they were, all I saw of them was T-shirts and teeth. I heard their voices only well enough to know which voice was which. Mrs. R let out a whoop and Mr. R and Mike were laughing. I'd never thought of Mr. R as laughing. I hadn't really ever thought of all of them together. I wondered that we hardly ever played at Mike's house but we almost always played at mine. When they went inside, Mrs. R stood at the door and touched the backs of Mike and Mr. R as they went past and then she followed.

You can feel so good. So emptied out and good to see. A lady touches her husband and her son, just a nothing little touch like that one on the back, and then the soft sound of her closing door can really knock you off your bike seat. Somebody should tell a boy at times like these it's okay to cry. I'm telling you, the wind let up, the stars spread wide, the melons sighed, and things felt big, able to include me. I walked on down the lane to watch this family at their beef and carrots. Did you think I would get caught? Give myself away? Should I report on anything too awfully different, the black house from the white? Cleaner. That's a different thing. More talk. Otherwise they ate from plates, same as us, in the kitchen, same as us, same forks and cups and manners. Only cleaner, and brighter, maybe, and maybe Mr. R and Mrs. R talked more than my mother and the General. This was a house that left its curtains open through the night, a house that went to church, the house of Mrs. R, the lady I remember had to put her bucket down to offer up her hand by way of introduction.

So what if they had only just said *fairies?* It occurred to me to wonder what if they had dropped the dirty? *Dirty fairies.* I thought maybe if they'd only called us fairies then we could have kept our wings. I got to thinking maybe Mike would not have flown his *First Flight* into the pits, you know, maybe we two could have stuck around to welcome in the next flock up of future flyers. Could be when a person grows up in a house as clean as Mike's that *dirty* strikes him harder than it does the likes of me. Either word. *Fairy, dirty*, any word at all, I thought, rolls off my skin like water. But what if I was black? What if I was black and made to walk around the house in sock feet so I didn't track the dirt in? What if I didn't have a mom, but had a mama, and my mama kept the glass on all our picture frames so shiny I couldn't see the picture through the image of myself in a reflection? I had not thought. Mike once said his daddy cleaned the engine on his tractor every month by steam. He kept his shop the way the General kept his hangar. What if that? *Dirty. Monkey. Dirty nigger monkey fairy.* What if?

I stood there through their dinner proper, watching, then turned away when Mrs. R brought on dessert. I walked back up their lane, hungry, tired, and thinking. I felt cold, then, and I remembered Mike explaining how a melon held the heat, so I lay down in the melon patch to warm myself before I pedaled home. It's true, what Mike says, a fact of science. It must be the best warmth of the day inside those wrinkled rinds, as good a thing to know about as Mrs. R's good greeting. If it hadn't been for those mosquitoes, I might have fallen off to sleep and dreamed right there of vines and seeds and Hearts of Gold served up on paper plates with sides of homemade ice cream. But I didn't sleep. I stood. I stepped up on my Lemon Peeler and plotted a course for home.

• • •

The upshot is I got a C. Ms. Santoro said a C meant average, but I knew average meant the worst. I sat beside her, in her office, where each of us was given five private minutes to confer about our papers. My paper wanted focus, she was saying. Take the Oolag boys, Hector and Arturo, those boys stuck to basketball, wrote mostly on their own positions. B, B+ work. Whereas what I wrote? Long, she agreed, lots of pages; Ms. Santoro did not doubt me when I told her how many yellow pencils I chewed through to fill them. But love? What wasn't love? Was that my point? Everything was love? She passed us through the highlights of my pages: sex, basketball, my parents' wedding, the pits, the Pitts, the melon patch, the light my mother left for me, the scolding she put on the night I got back from the melon patch, which I had tried to say was Mother's statement meaning love.

"Love is a many-splendored thing," said Ms. Santoro. "But this isn't really how you write a paper, Adam. What you have here is a funny sort of mixed-up list."

Plus which, too many fragments. My participles dangled. I misspelled. I ran on. I counted too much on the future tense.

When we had all concluded with conferring, Ms. Santoro walked the room and told the ones of us with Cs to see our marks as opportunities. She repeated that a C did not, repeat, did *not* by any means mean failure. Still, you got the feeling she was not too pleased. Certainly she wasn't touching near so many shoulders. She sat up on her desk and fiddled with the zipper on the backside of her boot. To do it, she had to turn her knee out, which Hector said she did so we could see the softer, inside part of her leg, the place where Ms. Santoro's skirt split and you saw up underneath as far as it got dark. Ms. Santoro fingered through our papers on her desk until she found the one she was looking for. The Cs of us were slumping lower in our desks, whereas the As looked like they might jump up and snatch the paper out of Ms. Santoro's hand to read it.

"If Michael will oblige us," Ms. Santoro said, "I'd like for him to read his paper. Although it's overlong," she said, "and I don't happen personally to agree with much of what he has to say, I think Michael's paper is a model for us all of shape and focus."

She stepped away from Mike, held her hands toward him, palms up, and made a gesture a magician makes to levitate a wooden prop—rise, rise, rise, you know—and Mike is on his feet, a steady hand and even timbre, reading:

WHY I LOVE THE PHANTOM F-4 FIGHTER
by Mike

In society, many people feel that the greatest good is love. They say love is what makes the soul, and the soul is what makes us human. Yet in order to be able to love, one must first be safe and free. If a human is not safe and free, then their love is trapped and they will spend their life in suffering instead of loving. When the Jewish people suffered in those camps in World War II, I do not think that it was radically because they all got starved and killed and beaten. At root, I think that why they suffered was because of being separated from the ones they loved and that they could not love again because the ones they might have loved were killed before they had a chance to love them.

In society, when a person's love is trapped too long I think it feels like being Jewish. History explains that this is true if one will also remember the Indians, and also if they think of slaves who were not safe or free to love from Africa. This is what it means when people say that they were "treated like an animal." In Moses's time, the people called on God to fight for their freedom. In the Civil War, the people used the industries to manufacture weapons for the North. By World War II, we saw freedom being fought for by the Spitfires and the Flying Tigers. Why I love the Phantom F-4 Fighter is because this great machine is one of the latest signs for us right here at home of why our country is so safe and free and therefore is the best place in the world for love and being human.

For hundreds, and maybe even thousands of years now, societies have understood that winning the war and keeping your freedom was much easier if you were fighting from a higher place than your enemy. This is why they built their forts on hills and why they built castles with big towers. In the beginning, they fought hand to hand, with swords and clubs, or even just bare fists. Then they built crossbows, catapults, and cannons—all because they knew they needed to take their fighting to a higher and higher level. Probably from the first time a man sat in a tree and ran his neighbor off with rocks, society has dreamed of dropping bombs from airplanes. Indeed, after the British flew reconnaissance and dropped the first bomb from the BE 2 in World War I the race was on to see who would achieve superiority of the air.

Some early problems were with weapons. As an example, how could the gunner shoot a machine gun from the front without hitting his own propeller? That problem was solved in 1915 by Anthony Fokker, a Dutchman, who invented an interrupter gear that prevented a machine gun from firing when a propeller blade passed in front of the barrel. But there were other things to improve if a certain society wanted to win as well. Airspeed was one. Another one was maneuverability. Greater altitude was also necessary to escape an enemy's radar or his ground fire. After nearly a century, these remain the general areas for improvement in military aircraft. To see what some of these improvements look like, we may investigate some of the specifications of the Phantom F-4 Fighter.

The Phantom F-4 Fighter was designed during the Korean War in response to some of the difficulties encountered by foot soldiers and tanks fighting in a mountain jungle-type setting. The Phantom F-4 Fighter is equipped with terrain-following radar which allows the pilot to fly so close to the ground that he avoids enemy radar. It has a laser ranger and marked-target seeker for close-range attack, and for long-range attack the Phantom F-4 Fighter has guided missiles and infrared sensors which allow pilots to engage in combat with enemies who are outside visual range. For high-speed flight and greater speed control there are the fully variable afterburner nozzles, thrust reversers, and air brake jacks. For increased maneuverability, there are port and starboard tailerons and a variable-incidence gust alleviator. There is a flat, bird-proof windshield. With a cruising speed of seven hundred knots, and the ability to fly Mach 2, and with the capacity to fly in undetected over enemy terrain and deliver over sixty megatons of bombs, the Phantom F-4 Fighter is a highly feared and respected warrior in the sky. Of course, the past has shown us time and time again that it must give way to the future, and higher, faster, stronger, more maneuverable will always be the rule and place society should pin its hope.

In conclusion, every time I hear a Phantom passing overhead I think of freedom. And when I think of freedom, I also think of all my loved ones like my mother and my father and the comfort that I feel with them when I am at my prayers before I go to bed. I love the Phantom. If I hear one, I give it a salute. Without the Phantom, I know we all could be a slave again or Jewish. One day, I like to think the wars we fight for freedom will be fought by military aircraft we can't hear or see at all. The pilots will be flying so high up above the planet that we won't know if they are there until we read about the wars they fight or hear them on the news. Maybe we will shoot a bomb that won't explode. We could keep our freedom without blowing up the churches and museums. There could be no blood. Nobody would be a POW or tortured. Maybe certain segments of society would get a card in the mail that said they had been killed. Society could build a building that looked nice to us outside and had a better way of killing on the inside. You would just go there, and not know ever what was taking you except it was the war.

In the meantime, you could live in happiness and freedom so that you could love and be more human. You could look up at the sky and not believe you couldn't see the war, or else you might forget that it was there. Society could maybe live the *way it did before there ever was a war, and it was just the people in the world who when they used to look up at the sky could not believe they weren't seeing God. God is up there, and we are under God, one nation, undivided, how the pledge of allegiance tells us. For me, the Phantom F-4 Fighter is like God except that I can see it. It fights to give us "liberty and justice for all." We are free to love, and that is why I love the Phantom.*

Mike sat. Did we have any questions?

MAYBE WE THOUGHT THE MORE WE TALKED THE LESS IT WOULD HURT. TALK, the great anesthetizer. Jesus loves you. Walk with Him, talk with Him. Chaplain talk. Poster slogans. Lombardi-isms from the sports world. I played ball. It hurt. Winning hurt, and losing. It hurt another fellow, being Baptist. Another fellow hurt to be a decent father. We all agreed it hurt to be a son. Talk about it. Hear it. Film today, fifty-seven minute running time of Ernie Gallo, a real-life survivor who burned himself by lighting gas-soaked rags he tied around his frozen pipes one ordinary January morning in his crawl space.

"It was as dumb as it sounds," says Ernie. "And it didn't even work."

What he said *did* work was therapy.

"I have loved ones," Ernie says, "I didn't want to see me suffer."

"Did you hear that, guys?" said Nurse Nadeen. "Did you, Tom? Mrs. Tom? You keep loosening Tom's splints, it's just more surgery to loosen those contractures."

We all sat nodding all right, already, we know: *Position of comfort is the position of deformity.* But after Ernie wound his fifty-seven minutes up, we had ourselves a little talk about *comfort*, the word, given our condition.

"Like," said Tom, "I do these exercises, and it hurts like hell the whole entire time. Or I can hurt like worser hell if I let the doctor cut me, or what, do nothing? And just get deformed? Which part of that to you is choosing comfort?"

"It's relative, of course," said Nurse Nadeen. "You heard Ernie. You saw his face. He'll never be handsome. But he'll be handsome compared to what he would have been, and maybe that's a comfort."

Mrs. Tom took a fat drag off her Lucky Strike, then held it for her son. She said, "Bingo. Now you're talking turkey."

We talked pain. How Napoleon wept. Knute Rockne. That guy, the TV one, who called the Hindenburg, he wept. Burning bodies leaping from the fiery balloon. *The humanity, the humanity*—let's talk.

We limped, hobbled, shuffled, crutched, eased our way out of the lounge and back down to our rooms, where most of us looked forward to our post-tank, post-lounge, pre-nap medications. Sue tapped out my dose, asked me how I liked the Xanax next to Demerol. I started working off my johnny.

"You know what Doctor Noggin says," I said.

"Some of it," said Sue.

"About the drugs, at least, why one seems to work more than the other, he says it's *affirmation*. He says that when you ask, and a doctor gives you a different pill, it tells you your pain is real."

"Is that right?"

"It's what he says. Says it's a trick. Your body tells you it's hurt, but it can't start feeling better till the hurt is okayed by the head. Pills are pretty much the same, he says, one to the next. I'd say the pill I like the best is whatever pill is newest."

"Of course," said Sue, "it could be your body acts a little different with a different pill. Or it could be also your body is simply getting better."

"But you said getting better here is hurting worse."

"Sooner or later," Sue said, "getting better is feeling better."

Sue stood by me while I tried to lift my feet into bed and helped me when I couldn't. She handed me my pills and water and she said, "Sweet dreams. Here's to feeling better."

"Did you know what," I said, "except for my mother, you're the only female who has ever seen me naked. And my mother hasn't seen me since when I was maybe five. Time my neighbor fetched me from a pile of fire ants in Texas. I was bumps and bites all over. My mother didn't touch me. Had the neighbor lay me on a dirty sheet she spread across the couch. After that, she was always giving me my privacy. *Tell me when you're finished*, that sort of thing, *come out when you're dressed*."

Sue pulled up my sheet, the way I like it, without my even asking.

"I'm tired," I said.

I closed my eyes and heard Sue move through her routine.

I said, "She's all right, you know."

"Who's all right?"

"My mother. You look at the body of your five-year-old, something near to perfection, and you'd be afraid, I think, how easy things go wrong. We didn't talk much. I'm just saying. She liked to shop for clothes. She liked to dress for it. Dress up, you know? She liked clerks and trying on. She used to take too much into the changing room to make the clerks pay special care. She's a big woman, but she put on this small girl's voice and told the clerk she just loved them all. *Oh, I have the hardest time deciding*, she would say, *don't you?* She would introduce me to the girl, make us both her audience. In and out, talking to us all the time, *I'm not sure what this does for my hips, you tell me, be honest, now is not the time to flatter*. When we were finished, she drove us straight on past the burger soft-serve place, went to the regular sit-down place, and ordered us a salad. She patted her bags and crinkled up her nose to show me we were really pulling something off. But this one time, the one I'm thinking of, I didn't go with her at all. She went by herself. All the way to San Francisco. She left a note to say what she was doing. The shopping part.

San Francisco. But then the funny thing, when she came home, I asked her, What did you get? Let's see your stuff. But she didn't get a thing. Instead, she showed me to her closet. All of it was there. None worn. Stuff we'd bought together, stuff I'd seen her try on, still in bags and packages. I didn't know what to say. What she said was that she was a very sensual woman. Or sexual. I can't remember. *I'm a very sexual woman, Adam.* Or sensual. *San Francisco is fabulous,* she said. She said she spent most of one entire day just driving back and forth across the bridges, blowing kisses at the city. She told me Pacific meant peaceful, but don't believe it. When I asked her why she didn't buy anything, she said everything was too expensive. How about that? Sue? Are your parents still alive?"

"Yes," she said, "they are."

"Do they talk?"

"Not much," said Sue. "I don't know, they're Lutheran."

"Surprising," I said, "how worn out you get."

"That's all right," said Sue. "Sleep," she said, and I slept.

They say our skin grew while we slept. If we slept, they said, the healing might not hurt as much. If we slept, we couldn't talk, and it wouldn't hurt, said Doctor Noggin, to sometimes give the talk a rest.

WE CLEANED A LOT OF CLOCKS. CREDIT THE OOLAG BOYS WITH RECALLING the expression. Or with never giving it up. *We'll clean your clocks,* they said to Mike and me when we were kids, remember? Sir Chester and Sir Lester, got their rocks and hollers, saying if we didn't run right now, then they were going to have our asses, punch our lights out, clean our clocks? Well, you see us graduating Ms. Santoro, moving through Ms. Brogan and Ms. Yee, and Chester and Lester have dropped the *lights* and *asses*, the *havings* and the *punchings* from their threats so they are left with clocks, clocks and cleanings, an orderly mode of destruction more in step with their emerging, science-minded selves. The familiar scene is Chester in the circle, center court, squared off with a kid who crowns out somewhere near to Chester's pectoralis majors. Tip-off. Referee has got his whistle in his mouth, the ball in his hand between these boys, and Chester's looking down on both of them. There is hardly anybody's dad in town he can't at least look eye to eye to. He leers, generally, fair to say he's leering at the kid, not mild, but polite, polite, not to worry, the next four quarters will be supercool and ruly.

"I'm going to clean your clock," says Chester.

For three seasons, every game begins with the ball out to Arturo, where it's two, maybe three bounces on the dribble, then a lob to Hector or to Lester, breaking on the basket. Clockwork. Money in the bank. Downright Swiss. Our first year all together as a Husky we were kept down on the JV squad where folks were saying maybe now we boys would meet our matches. Ha! *Traditionally, the Colts are pretty strong.* Ha, ha! *The Raiders have a hell of a shooting guard, new kid up from California.* Ha, ha, ha! *Likely it'll be that new coach for the Tarantulas who finally* . . . ha, ha, ha, ha, ha! New coach, okay, new name, different colors—but still those boys were boys we played with through the church leagues. They knew better. They saw the tip go to Arturo, to Mike, to the hoop, and they were down. They saw Lester with his hands up on the inbound man and they were downer. They spelled each other, Lester and Chester, took turns on the baseline, harassing their inbound man, giving him an eyeful of arms and legs, baggy pants and jersey. Poor kid couldn't hardly see, and when he did see, what he saw was just another one of us. First pass and he throws it out of bounds. Second pass he throws it right to Mike. Third pass knocks it off of Lester's knee. Fourth pass they bring in another inbound man who gets the ball past Chester and Arturo but the kid he hits has got a bad case of the stony hands and drops the thing to Hector.

Home game for us, and we JVs have got a loud house going there. We maybe never played so hard. Those boys start off looking scared, then you think they might cry, and then they shrug it off and some of them are laughing. New coach is yanking the laughers out of the game. He's shouting down the refs, calling for fouls. He's kicking chairs. He's called his last time out at the start of the second quarter, takes a seat, and throws a towel across his head so he is looking less a coach and more a shepherd. Got his elbows on his knees, chin in his hands, and then he's laughing, too, stands and waves his towel to our coach across the scorer's table, I surrender. Halftime, and it's fifty-six to zero. New coach holds his palms up at the rafters, beseeching God, could be; he turns and blows a grateful kiss off for the referee whose whistle signals the expiring clock.

Thing is, people liked us. We were pretty to watch. We passed. Boxed out. Set picks. We hustled. We had the fundamentals pretty much nailed down, were playing down the road to showing folks how we could be creative. Looked to people like we all were having fun. *Looks like they've been playing together nearly all their lives,* people said, and they were right. Plus which, people said we were nice. Smart, too. Chester took a shine to chemistry, they'd heard, wasn't that nice? Sure it's nice, people said, you don't see the young ones anymore too interested in science. Yes, sir, chemistry for Chester, and for Lester it's biology, can you believe it? They say he's shown a good hand with his fetal pigs and frogs. Branching from his twin. But not too far a branch, mind you, he hasn't taken up piano. Sanchez boy, of course, he's volunteering in the grade school, tutoring the Mexicans. And that Hector Block, well, he's a good, bad boy, if you know what I'm saying, chasing skirts as soon as he has helped his mama with the yard work. All of them, I'd say, tomorrow's model citizens. Why, Mike and Adam there, they stand close to Colonel Oney, they're a shoo-in for the Air Force, maybe the Academy. Boys today, they're mostly out to serve themselves. Nice to think some are left who want to serve their country.

Farmers, flyers, local wives and wives of military passers-through, they packed the bleachers in their overalls and flight suits, their cotton dresses and their diapers to watch us. After the Tarantulas, we packed them in for our away games same as if away were home. They brought out the band for us, the majorettes, announcers, they opened up concession stands for halftime. Varsity stuff. The varsity. I mean the teams, the older players also came to watch and likely were relieved they didn't need to play us. Drums, trumpets, and pom-poms. A hot gym on a snowy night. We could hear them from the locker room, stomping on the bleachers. Here it comes now, game time, and we are jogging through an alleyway of girls in little skirts and lettered sweaters, sending up the cheer for *Huskies, Huskies, Huskies!*

Mike's idea was we should thank each quadrant of the bleachers with a crisp salute. Homage and respect, he said, something rare and dignified and right. They loved it. Desert rats who didn't really know the rules. Migrant folks whose kids were tutored by Arturo. Unhappy idlers made happy by the spectacle of something they could hope would last.

Certain teams we played against, you got the sense they would rather be up in the bleachers with the rest. These boys knew a fifty-six-to-nothing halftime was a message. *Save yourself for second.* This was the message. *Take it easy, keep on growing, practice, play together for a while, and then we'll think about a real game maybe when you're seniors.* Meantime, we young Huskies will be treated to the prospect of historical unprecedence. We could be local legends. A nation's myth. An international nostalgia. Six boys living out the manufactured dream of cinema by Disney. In other, bigger towns outside our ranking, we turned up every now and then as a curiosity, a challenge. You could not invent us, not enough to be believed. Already, we had the big-town coaches lining up to knock us down, a move to bend the rules and work us in their schedule. Get it, right? Goliath going after hometown David? Human Interest wrote up our early strife. Sticks in the eye, rocks from the tree fort, stitches in the forehead.

"You could tell Mike was a good shot," Lester told the paper, "because he hit me right exactly where he said he would."

Someway Lester's scar looked worse and better when you saw it pictured in the *Crier* as "a symbol of the troubled past and hopeful future in the politics of race."

Each one of us, our own day, our picture, and a feature article and interview devoted just to us.

"We eat a lot of beans," Arturo told the paper. "Frijoles negros, frijoles rojos. I tell Mama she could open up a restaurant—I would help—like start out with a taco stand and move up to seats and tables? First is State, though. A taco stand can wait. It's only once you get to work to be the champion. After that, your work is work."

Easy slant. Our trajectory was the flight of any decongested heart. Unfettered, innocent, totally American. This was written. How we healed our differences by jumping in the pits. How we came together as a team. How our team became a family, our family a community. Our community became the country; our country would become the world. Sure Human Interest was disappointed some to not discover collard greens and chitterlings in Mike's mama's kitchen, but he gave the paper melons, didn't he? Wasn't Mr. R a monkey, the victim of a racial slur? And me, wasn't I Mike's bosom buddy? White? Pure white? Oney, O'Mahoney, couldn't be much whiter? Get this, too, wasn't I the son of a barefoot, orphaned, self-made man? Only way to make us any sexier for TV was to cast us with religion. Any Jew to Block? You a Muslim, Sanchez? Oney, Adam, please tell us you're the son of the Gypsy, bayou Sikh!

We were a small pot here in the desert, not too tough to set us boiling. There were folks there in the bleachers scheming how to take us all to market. Wondering how old a kid would have to be before you used his face to sell a shoe. Hoping we would not break out in pimples. Thinking maybe he could sell the dolls of us, why not, there's worse crap he's seen coming as a free gift from his children's sacks of burgers. Make us out of rubber. Bones of bendable wire. Collect all six of us. Come up with a line of tough opponents. Imagine all the good, clean fun your child might have with us, hours in the sunny vigors of the sporting spirit. Do a quick scan of the bleachers, every two of ten of them is looking at you from a face that says, *Eureka!*

Well, we were going to clean their clocks, no matter.

Chester Oolag, starting center, half-court, faced off in the circle: "That's right, friend. We're gonna clean your clock."

Though I think Mother's was the shrillest voice to cheer us through the JV season, when it was over she decided not to join the rest in praising our performance, but said we were a freak show. An undefeated, nice-guy, old-school freak show. We were eating pizza, celebrating down at Cecarelli's. Whole team was there, parents, coaches. Picnic-style tables, six tables, two larges per table, pepperoni and cheese, pitchers of Coke and root beer, infinitely refillable. People made toasts.

"Proud to have you," said Mr. Cecarelli. "You've been a big boost to my business."

"I think they've been a boost to several businesses in town," said Mr. Block.

"I don't know about any of that," said Coach. "I'd just like to say these boys have really showed a lot of heart."

"Heart, hell," said Mr. Oolag. "These boys here just flat out cleaned a lot of clocks!"

They were taking turns, standing up from the tables, and rapping the pitchers with their knives to quiet us so we could hear them. All the stuff about our guts and hearts and teamwork, how we really could take State, the possibility of all of us receiving full-ride scholarships to college. We were fourteen, fifteen, just. We rolled our eyes a lot, said please, please, please just let us eat. We needed to shout. It's a chugalug we wanted. *Drink, drink, drink!* we shouted, *eat, eat, eat!* and there I went, big news, huge upset in the making, Adam Oney on the verge of burying his second Oolag. Seventh Dr Pepper, thirteenth slice of pepperoni . . .

And then Mother standing up to tell us we were freaks.

"I just want to say," she said, "you all best be careful. You've made yourselves a story. You've got three more years of ball here. Better watch your six o'clock."

Mother sat back down. Except for Mr. Sanchez, who likely missed the gist of Mother's speech, people tried to keep their eyes on anything except another person. Lucky us we had the General. Sure a man who flew his Phantom through the jungle wasn't there to be shot down by anybody's mother. His arms were folded on his chest. He did not rap a pitcher with his knife but only waited till we all looked up at him before he started speaking.

"Mrs. Oney," he said, "she has got a point. But if it's our clocks we've got to watch, we ought to think of Chester. It's catchy, that saying about clocks. I'm thinking, if you all are something of a story, then why not find a way to have a hand in how the story's written. Infiltrate, you might say. Make them think they're taking part instead of mostly watching. I'm thinking, we could make a mess of clocks from cardboard, pass them out before the game."

PR work. Best defense is a good offense. Any publicist could tell you. Think *fast break*; think, *blitzkrieg*. Tell the people what to think before they start in thinking. These clocks, how big should each clock be? What went on the faces? Movable hands? Photos of the team? Should we pass out little towels to wave that signified a cleaning? See it as a start, at least, these clocks. Then pace ourselves. Be humble. Respect our opponents. Clean their clocks, okay, then take our hats off to them, tell the paper they were worthy.

"A war plan, if you will," the General said. "Enlist the aid of the civilian populations. You don't want the people to perceive you as a conqueror. You're a liberator. You want them to think they are just as free as you are."

So right off, then, we had the help of Mr. Cecarelli, who said he would sponsor a buy-one-get-one-free extravaganza every game night. Later, Lou Gramza, of Gramza's Furniture World, volunteered a La-Z-Boy recliner for a raffle. We had Hal "Tiny" Luger, owner of Sweet Dreams soda shop, confect a sundae in our name, proceeds going to the Husky Fund, a charitable institution that could send a troubled kid to camp. And how about a ladies' halftime free throw competition, winner to receive her choice of pedicure or tanning at the Hair Loft? How about a good old-fashioned car wash, and instead of girls in swimsuits doing all the dirty work, we boys dressed up in bikinis, manning the hoses and showing the folks we were not above scrubbing their dusty hubcaps? Sure we had folks offering their cookies and their apple pies, their horseback rides and turkey shoots and Valentine's certificates for Hallmark. We even had Ms. Santoro, who had given up her go-go boots for sandals, saying she would do *whatever*.

All we had to do was play. All we had to do was win.

A reminder from Mike, cool as the General, "These boys we're coming up against are two or three years older. They're big. I'd say it's time we work up something in our game that doesn't lean so heavy on the Oolag."

The General helped us there, went out on recon, fetched home tapes for us to study of the Celtics and the Lakers. Who would be our Bird? Who was our McHale? Who would be our Worthy? Great names. Earl "the Pearl" Monroe. Wilt "the Stilt" Chamberlain. Pistol Pete Maravich. For me, for hoops, this off-season was the last time I could change my shot by changing my name; for sure it was the last time I remember all of us at ease in the belief that if we wanted hard enough, then ours would one day be the names a kid pretended to, ours would be the game he wished he could be playing. We watched the snow give way to rain, rain give way to the dry heat of another summer. All along we played. We never quit. Doctor S was Doctor S no more. By the time the summer leagues began he had picked up what he could of Magic, Clyde, and Tiny, a little of the Harlem Trotter showmanship of Curley Neal. When we took the court against those older boys, we were a team of hybrid champions and Hall of Famer men. Hector Block, aka Bill Bradley. Lester Oolag, Dave Debusher. Chester Oolag, Chief. We all had another name except for me and Mike.

"You got to find a name," said Hector.

"A new look, new sound type of thing," Arturo said.

"Part of the war plan," Lester said.

In the end I said okay, they could call me Wilbur.

"Wilbur, man, who's Wilbur?"

"Wilbur Wright. The Wright brothers? He was a flyer?"

"Good enough," said Hector, "and how about you, Mike? You Orville then, or what?"

"I'm Mike," said Mike. "Rule is, if I can't have it, I don't want it. You remember? Shots I'm working up are coming straight from me."

"Easy for you to say," said Hector. "You've got the whole entire package. You can flat-out leap. And you've got chest on you. Little Doctor Whatsit tries to score inside the paint, he's getting up off his Mexican ass too sore to shoot the free throws. Whereas you're the guy who puts the hurt on."

"Magic," said Arturo.

"Clyde," said Chester.

"A specimen," said Lester. "A landmark in the evolution toward the ideal hoopster."

"The whole entire package," Hector said. "That's you, then—*Package.* Tell me you can't hear the fillies at your barn door. Package! *Oooo, Package. What's that mean, Hector? How come he's called 'Package?'*"

Hector minced around the court and wagged his backside, cupped his hands to hold what would have been a double-D-sized bust. He batted his lashes, raised his voice, and asked if *package* meant what they said it meant, was it true about those black boys, that, well, you know.

"Go on," said Mike. "Talk that way. And then go ask the General about that Kirby Boudreaux."

I was lying on my back, taking in the shade beneath the courtside cottonwood, and I could feel the eyes on me as the General's stand-in.

"Kirby Boudreaux," I said, "is the guy who's boinking Lucy DuPree. He's the one that pumps your gas."

"Okay," said Hector. "Now I get it. Give us the ball here, Oney. We're shooting free throws. Game is you say what you're going to be, and if you make your free throw, then you'll be what you say you'll be, and if you don't, then you're a Boudreaux. Me, I'm going to be the guy who fucks his way through the entire pep squad. I'll be the guy with the biggest, fastest ski boat on the reservoir, and I'll always be remembered as a Husky."

Nobody missed. Which meant our team fielded a future playboy millionaire, an owner of a national taco franchise, a marine biologist, an astrophysicist, and a couple of Air Force fighter pilots. Trouble is, you can believe that sort of game. You pretend not to, you goof at the line, stand on one foot, start off like to shoot with one hand or else granny style, but in the end the shots we took were square and true. You did not want to be a Boudreaux. You knew what a person wanted to be wasn't easy in becoming. You didn't want the jinx. You wanted the luck, the blessing of the game.

When I got home I saw the General in his blue jeans and a T-shirt, mixing concrete. He could sweat, that man. And swear. Seemed sometimes to me that anything outside aviation in his life was cussed. *The goddamn warping form boards; cheap-ass flimsy Japanese steel; and for shit's sake, look at that, old man smashed his thumb with that brand-new, waffle-faced hammer.*

"Look," he said. "Those teeth took a chunk out. What're you holding there," he said, "a melon?"

"From Mrs. R," I said. "She said we should share."

The General sucked his thumb and spit.

"How's Mike?" he said. "You know that boy is going to make a hell of a pilot."

"I know," I said, "you keep saying so."

The General worked his hoe in the wheelbarrow, turning the lime through the water. He wheeled the mix over to the forms, poured his load, got down on his hands and knees, and floated. What he had going here was a concrete mowing strip to line the concrete walk which linked the concrete patio to the concrete boat pad. I thought I could judge the sizes of the jobs he'd done by measuring the yellow rings he'd gathered at the armpits of his T-shirt.

I said, "There's getting not to be a lot of yard left."

"Listen," said the General, "if I wanted green, I'd have kept us down there in that stinking bayou."

"Yes, sir," I said, "If you'll excuse me, I think I'll put this melon in the fridge."

I stood in front of the refrigerator, shook the melon close up to my ear, smelled it, squeezed it, ate it. Not just my fair share, the way Mrs. R had wanted, but the whole thing. I watched the General out the window while I ate, saw him bent and straining over his mud, his yellow stains and ass crack, and I thought how when you took away his cockpit and his wings, a man was never very far from being Boudreaux. I went outside and toed around the butts in Mother's pansies. I listened to the General run his trowel across the concrete, watched him stand back from his work, light himself a Winston, regard the curing pad from several distances and angles. He asked me what I thought.

I said, "Am I as big as you when you were my age?"

He got back down to flatten out a couple peaks I think only he could see.

He said, "Bigger. Same height, but bigger. I told you, when I played they had me playing forward."

"What I heard was you never played at all."

"Your mother say that?"

"Yes, sir."

"Well, she doesn't know everything I played. Not then, not now," the General said. "With women, you'll not want to let them in on every little thing you do. Remember that. Now why don't you take this hose and trowel and go ahead and clean my barrow. Think I'll go see if your mother knows me well enough to know it's time for my martini."

I hosed and poked around the General's barrow and was glad not to depend on metal wings for lift; I thanked the genius and compassion of the minds that brought me fast foods and convenience stores, four-course microwaveable confections I could fly in under twenty minutes—freezer, oven, plate. I felt weak enough and strong enough to tell myself for the first time then that I would maybe never fly the Pitts. And so what? I told myself. I flew plates. I flew my head. Ample altitudes to navigate inside myself, I thought; after food, my aerobatic spirit did not want much past the loops and spins I felt inside myself whenever I would see the butts in Mother's pansies, say, or whenever I would watch the rain dry on the General's concrete, wishing it were grass. Mine were crib-sized flights, jumps from cliffs on cardboard wings, quiet rides on thermal drafts of a seasoned whisper. *You can do it, Adam, you can do it.* I finished up the General's barrow, asked myself, *Okay, freak, so do what?*

As it happened, I did ground school. I was Wilbur, and even though he'd quit at being Orville, I stuck by Mike as if he hadn't. I still rode the Lemon Peeler, but I could hardly ever get Mike out to ride the Orange Crate.

"Can't keep riding these silly-ass bikes," he said. "We threw all that kid shit over."

Remember this year we were playing with the big boys, he was saying, the General was sitting down with us to real-life, grown-up texts, giving us a jump to ace the written. Ask us anything you please about our compass navigation. Have us calculate our fuel consumption based on knots and winds aloft and distance. By late September, the General sat and spread our sheets across the kitchen table, unable to devise a flight plan to confuse us. We all were moving on. Our bodies gained and smartened. We played those bigger, older boys from our varsity squad that summer, unofficial scrimmages, embarrassments, scores that fell in widening margins in our favor. We would be the new timekeepers, the clock cleaners. We had endeared ourselves so every game should seem like home; thanks to Arturo, we even seemed to have the official blessing of our state.

Started local, with our senator, who said he would help Arturo draft a letter, apply for a grant to form a night class in English for Hispanic immigrants. The letter reached the governor, a cinch. Governor okayed the grant himself, another cinch. Only hard part was the governor meant to deliver the check himself, by hand, in person, for the cameras. Question was, where to take the picture? Mrs. Sanchez said the living room, whereas Mr. Sanchez absolutely said the driveway, get Arturo and the governor shaking hands in front of the paternal El Camino. In the end, the senator and governor, agreeable amigos, were happy to pose for both, though what finally made the paper was the living room, the altar at the Casa Sanchez. Section C, page eight is where you saw the color photo of the smiling servants of the people handing over fifty thousand dollars to the brown-skinned lad, our very own Arturo, the smiling "spirit of hope and faith" at the foot of the velveteen Jesus.

Bless us, we were looking good, well-rounded, even, we had in Chester a boy who passed his summer testing up to the next class in biology; we had in Lester a boy who switched from chemistry and wasn't long in figuring the worth for basketball in mathematics.

"Brand-new game," he said, "when you divide the court into geometrical units. Court's a rectangle, right? Cut the court in half and you have got a square. Cut that square in half diagonally and you have got a triangle. Defense keeps the opponent in that triangle, you give them very heavy traffic to try to score through. We pass the ball around the perimeter, we open up the square. More room to pass, more for them to cover. By the time the ball gets over to Mike, those guys are tired. Now consider Mike's jump shot as a trigonometric function. It's calculable. You can figure it—why Mike wins or loses for us at the buzzer."

We would win. We were good. Maybe too good for our own good, Hector said, made him sick to his human heart to witness such angelic virtue. He himself was working, busing tables, washing dishes, learning the value of a dollar as his father had instructed, which for Hector meant a straight lay at the Villa Joy, paid for with a mayo jar of nickels. Kid of the richest dad in town, and there he paid in change. Ten percent of the waitress's take, maybe more, said Hector, if your waitress is a hottie. Hector picked out April at the Villa Joy, girl who held his hand and walked him back into her room where Hector said she called him *child*, Hector dressed in nothing but his stiffy on her shag rug, counting out his silver.

Yes, sir, we were ready. We said good-bye to summer, attended classes, passed the first round of exams. We did not dress up for trick or treat. We ate the turkey and the pumpkin pie, passed another round of exams and asked for new shoes, please, new socks, presents we would need to open prior to the Christmas date for tryouts. Yes, sir, time to make the jump up to the bigger boys official. Coaches and whistles. Running ladders. Running crunches. Running presses. Running breaks. We broke off into positions. We shot, then ran. We rebounded, then ran. We passed, then ran. We dribbled, then ran. We ran, then ran. I don't remember ever being near so yelled at.

Coach blew his whistle.

He said, "Take a lap."

He told us, "Take another."

He held our bunch of six together after practice, said he knew all about us. He lined us up sitting on the first tier of the bleachers, walked back and forth in front of us, tapped his whistle in his palm, and used it every now and then as a pointer. Gave us the coachly stuff about desire and belief. He talked about leaving it all out on the floor. He talked about fourth quarter. He reminded us of Husky pride.

"With me," he said, "it's either put up, or shut up, gentlemen. My way, or the highway."

But we all knew who was in charge here. First mistake Coach made was trying to run the legs out from under us; second mistake was playing us against the older players one-on-one; third mistake was trying to play the six of us apart. What he fetched on all three counts was more embarrassment, the official version of the lessons we all learned without a coach that summer. Those boys were dropping down in cramps. They were heaving in their sneakers. Mike drew out his man by hitting threes, then gave his man a simple juke off a cross dribble that blew the fellow's knee out trying to defend it. I think enough for Coach was when his last year's starting center took the third ball from Arturo off his forehead.

Well, we six were in charge, but as players on a court without us, those older boys were really not too bad. Coach made his cuts, and you could see with the six left over that they meant to see their names behind the glass there in the trophy hall the same as we did. They pushed hard. Rough, Coach said, we might be surprised how heavy boys could get in just two years, how mean and sneaky. Chester picked up some solid elbows to the ribs; he showed us where a pretty purple bruise was blooming in his sternum. If he didn't know it before, then Arturo learned for certain there were no free passes for the little man who drove into the center lane. Coach ran them six against our five. You had two and three guys coming after Mike so Mike could see how hard it was to shoot when he was made to run at the top of his lungs before he even touched the ball to get his shot off.

Lucky for us that good luck liked us. Where there might have been the ill will and the loaded quiet on the court and in the locker room, you saw us slapping backs and giving hands up from the floor. You heard Arturo in the showers, leading us through the second verse of "Feliz Navidad." You saw the steam go thick and heard a loud and echoey bunch, whoops and hollers, mock arguments over who had slid the farthest on his ass across the soapy tiles. Guy stuff, well, and so we were guys. Our shoulders had broadened. Our voices had changed. Another song we sang went: *Men, men, men, men, men, men, men, men.* Sure we were a scene from the pagan bath. A stunt was to grab a guy by the shoulders at the urinal, shake him up so he was pissing on his shoes. Another stunt was to piss on the leg of the guy who closed his eyes when he got his head wet. And meanwhile who had the longest cock? Who had the biggest balls? Whose bent left and whose bent right when he got a woody? What did it mean for being fag or not if one hung way down lower than the other? Yes, sir, we were into something old and classical, an ode to the Grecian homo.

Fourteen, fifteen years old we were, the kings of our season, smooth gods in the bright halls. Girls, mainly, they were saying, *See you later, pig-skinners, hello to you now, Mr. Hoop!* I never knew how many girls wore braces on their teeth until I saw them smiling my way; I don't remember one who stood so close to me I could smell perfume. I went a little blind by them, I think, pretty dumb to have their company. Nights, I ran their names and body parts together, practiced my seductions on a girl I could only dream of, the kind of built-up one Hector said could help you pound your pudding. *Cathy Hull, Nancy Hawn, Paris Rich.*

"They've got our schedule taped up in their lockers," Hector said.

Our schedule was printed in the paper, was plastered on the windows of supermarkets and drugstores; Mr. Cecarelli had our schedule printed up on paper place mats. Come, hear the band, sing the song, worship with the senator and mayor, our reverend and our rabbi. We invite you. Join our congregation in the Husky gym this Friday night at eight p.m., this January fifth.

• • •

Game day, Mother wakes up just to fix me breakfast. Eggs Benedict, real Canadian bacon and hollandaise sauce, eggs poached so the broken yolks were slow but not too slow to spread across the English muffin. Now throw in a side of French toast and a bowl of frozen berries, the picture of my mother standing at the juicer, juicing oranges, and you have us.

She said, "Don't think this is every day."

"I won't," I said.

"It's not."

"I know," I said. "It's the only day. A first. One first once, I know. You keeping stats?"

"I am."

"Got your clipboard?"

"I do."

"Predictions?"

"Yes," she said. "But I'll let you know after the game."

She helped me tie my tie, my first, told me I was at the mercy of the school for lunch, said for dinner we were having New York strip. She took me off to school and what do we see there on the parking lot marquee but a message telling us to clean some clock. Big block letters just like how you see them at the movies: C'MON HUSKIES, LET'S GO CLEAN SOME CLOCK!

Believe it, all day game day is the achy wait. I've got the tie on and the jacket. I've got the voices going in my head. I feel seen. I'm supposed to stand a little straighter. I am a representative, a diplomat, a holy vessel brimming with the word. This one asks how 'bout it, big win tonight? How do I feel? Do I feel good? Oney, man, you must have put on three feet over Christmas. How much do you weigh? You keep growing, you'll take over there for

Chester. All day game day is the drift of fifty-minute daydreams, bell to bell, where the bells are buzzers and in my head is not the sound of Mr. Mabry or of Mrs. Muth but me. I'm the player, crowd, and the announcer. Sixty seconds, down by three, no time-outs, Mike gone out on fouls, Arturo hurt but playing, Hector cold, it's me who is our shooter. Listen: *Sanchez passes in to Oolag, Oolag out to Oolag, Oolag swings it out to Oney on the baseline—score! Huskies will be wanting a miss here, or they'll have to foul or—oh, my, Oney on the steal! Husky ball! Ten seconds, folks, five seconds, four, it's Oney off the dribble, Oney pumps, fades, it's off the glass, he scores again, Huskies win, Huskies win, Oney wins it for the Huskies at the buzzer!*

Was this art? Was it mathematics? No, a day of school was not a day in church, though here on game day it felt as long, and something, someway worse and greater than the fear of God for feeling holy. Such as missing that shot. Such as losing the girl. Such as being born the guy without the luck of legs and heart to play the game with. The clock was ticking, slow, slow, then sure it seemed that game time jumped right up and caught me thinking there was nowhere near the time for being ready. Weird rapture. Scared? Sure. Hungry? You bet. Dressing out, dressing up. Tape the ankles. Turn the sock down. Stretch the old Achilles. Hey, Coach. Hey. Hey, Lester. Hey. Mike. Adam. Boys.

"You nervous?"

"Yeah."

"You?"

"Some."

"Hear them out there."

"Sure."

"What all do you think they're doing?"

"Beats me. Waving clocks?"

A shame for sure that no one else could ever be us; good news for those who found out something of us in themselves. Faith. And doubt. The nervous little spark between the two that charges the heart of the true believer.

"I don't know," Arturo says. "We're gonna have to keep our heads on straight. I saw one dude coming off the bus and he had whiskers. Seemed like all night long I couldn't sleep."

"Me either," Lester said. "I kept having dreams they changed the court from rectilinear to oblong. And then, when I figured out the math for a pretty decent half-court set, they changed the court from an oblong to a circle."

"I got the shits," Arturo said. "That squirty stuff that burns your asshole?"

"That's enzymes," Chester said. "And synapses. Those dreams are just your brain burning out from running through the same old circuits. Those enzymes are acids. They're like a battery in your belly. Next thing you'll be feeling is adrenaline. Adrenaline will be our friend if we make our first few shots. Or it can be our enemy if we miss them."

"Right," said Hector, "adrenaline. That's Oney's stutter if he's standing anywhere closer than fifteen yards to some major babe. Tell you something? You won't find any enzymes up my asshole. You want a tip, Sanchez? Lay off the chili. Get down to the Villa Joy. Only dreaming I did was of Lucy DuPree, and what I'm planning is to shoot the lights out so as Lucy DuPree will come real to me, same as always."

Only this time would be different. Tonight would be a round of firsts. First time playing the late game. First time there might be a college scout to see us from the bleachers. And sure it was the first time I would play in front of Hector Block. We all leaned in close where Coach had gathered us around him in the locker room, but I don't think we heard much of what he said until he read the lineup off his clipboard. All's well, the customary word about pulling together and doing what we know how to do, going out and having fun and such until we hear him reading Oney in for Block. That's right, for the books, it's Adam Oney, original varsity starter.

Also for the books, we won. You had a spell there in the locker room where we were sitting on the benches underneath a comic bubble saying, *What the* . . . You saw by the way Arturo squeezed the ball he was thinking, *Now what the hell about my enzymes?* With the Oolag boys you watched them studying Hector, Coach, and me as if we were the variables of a very tricky algebraic formula, a chemical combination Chester seemed to puzzle over whether there could be a mix that wouldn't blow up in our faces. But the thing is that we won. *Handily*, the paper said, with *style* and *poise beyond our years*. The headline: HUSKIES START THE CLOCK. Made Hector pretty mad, and I'm not sure I was ever thinking how a starter ought to. I thought of Adam Oney. As in, *Wow, Adam Oney got the start?* You know, another fellow stood out there at center court for tip-off. His name was Adam Oney, okay, but he wasn't me. Felt like all game long it would be my job to keep an eye on him. He did all right, I think. Ran the plays the way Arturo called them, boxed out, passed, kept a hand on his man. But what was he thinking? What really did I think?

Stuff I never thought before for sure. Such as was my hair all right? And should I keep my hands on my knees, or keep them spread out wide there at the tip-off? Also, once we started running, I thought it was strange, with all the band noise and the cheering, not to hear my shoes squeak. For certain I was glad I didn't have to guard the guy with the bad back acne. I was happy not to worry over enzymes, and that the General's paycheck fed us steak instead of chili. Sometimes, when I went down low with my man or worked the post, I had the feeling maybe nobody could see me. I felt hidden away, like in a stand of big, thick trees, felt as if I'd like to live out all my life there in that sweating, groaning forest. The first time I sat down for Hector, I looked up in the stands and hoped that somewhere from those tiers of bobbing cardboard clocks at least one face of them was mine. Celebrity, I figure. Adam Oney's inkling of the psyche in the limelight. I liked it a lot. Weird rapture, all right, the unquiet serene. If they scream loud enough, the crowd will push its hero way out where the hero is a hero to himself, where he pleasures in the sound of himself, describing his own name.

I sat and watched us run the floor awhile and then I leaned up close to Coach.

"How'd I do?" I said.

Coach jerked up and straightened in his seat.

"Amazing," he was saying, but he wasn't meaning me but Mike, who had just gone straight into the lane and dunked, another Husky first.

I missed it. I missed plenty, but I didn't miss what Coach had told us all about Mike and Mike's being the guy who took us to another level. Before he dunked, our lead was six. After he dunked, we ran off fifteen points unanswered, went in at the half with nineteen points to give away, more than enough to play the seniors. Thing is, except for moms and pops, not too many folks had come to see the seniors. The clocks came down when they went out. You saw the extra-saucy leave the hipswing of our Huskiettes. Gymnasium went a little ho-hum, back to high school, the squeaky sneaker sound of mortal competition. Hector thought to rally the folks by having us play the game there on the bench where on the count of three we all crossed our legs the one way, and on another count of three, we crossed them on the other. Folks liked this all right, but not as much as ball, and after Hector had us move them through the wave, Mike said knock it off.

"It's clown stuff," Mike said, "it's disrespectful. If Coach ever turned around enough to see this stuff, he'd bench us."

Maybe some coach would, but not this coach. We all knew he'd already seen us and pretended not to. He had gone as far as he would go in showing us who's boss by switching me and Hector, six and five. His name was Jerry.

Jerry looked to be saying, *Oh, Jerry, geez, Jerry, those kids are making a fool of you, aren't they, Jerry? No, Jerry, they're not. They're having fun, they're kids.*

Jerry sucks on a towel the way he's seen the Jerry from Las Vegas suck it. He brushes dander from his suit shoulders. When he sees folks are leaving, he looks back down the bench at us. He won't play us, though. He cinches up his tie, reading himself in the morning paper. Right there, front page Sports, Jerry describes the worthiness of his opponent, says they gave us a run there, really showed a lot of guts. He confesses to some early jitters. He likes the quote: "We've got a ways to go before we really jell." But best he likes those few lines that make him out to be a man of great compassion. *Jerry, you stuck to your guns, played your seniors. It's a game, Jerry, you remind us of that, and for your reminder we are grateful.*

Truth is, he was pretty sad to see. Way too much in Jerry's action of a predefeated hope. Game's over—*you won, you won, you won*—and there I wished Jerry's face could have some share of our face in the feel of winning. Smile, Jerry. Hear us in the locker room, shouts in the shower steam, *That's one o'clock, buddy, sixteen games to go, 1600 and we'll see 'em down at State!* He was there, he heard, he saw, he stood outside the locker room, waiting in the darkened halls with the folks he called our "core fans," greeting us as we came out, a scene he seemed to warm to even more than coaching.

"Great game, son."

"You were terrific, sweetheart."

"Hey, I waited for you. Lindsey and them are going out for pizza. Cecarelli's? I was thinking maybe we could meet them?"

I think it's fair to say Coach murmured. He stood in the doorway of the locker room, shaking hands and taking hold of shoulders. He murmured. I thought how many of his players and their folks had not invited him to pizza. I thought how if you didn't know him, you could think he was winding up for a good, hard cry. From a photo of the man, I think anybody would have said he had played a good, fair game and lost it. I walked with Mike and thought we could invite him. Coach, we could say, *C'mon now, Jerry, first win, we're on our way, let's take you down to Cecarelli's!*

But we weren't going to Cecarelli's. The way the General stood there with his foot up on the bumper of his Comet, smoking, making small talk with our mothers, I could see that Mike and I were in for news, a risky, classified style of celebration. We came up close to where I saw that Mother hadn't hung her game face up, and Mrs. R was looking most to be exactly what she was, a good old open-bosomed soul attempting to be civil with a spoilsport. And more. More meaning the Sanga, more meaning Mr. R, the man who left the service owing to a night out at the Sanga when that stinking, son-of-a-bitching flyboy rode up on his big white bird and got a little mean and slurry. You could see Mrs. R was wishing hard she had never heard the General's invite. She gave Mike a hug like to not let go, squeezed him into her so he might disappear inside that open bosom. Mrs. R was saying, *Mmm, mm, mm,* and on and on about how proud she was of all of us and how we ought to take some pride in how we did our ownselves. Mother said we had our moments. The General said it was a goddamned rout. Mike and I said thanks and right and we all stood about and held ourselves more closely in against the cold while nobody said *monkey.*

Sanga. How did that sound to Mike, I wondered, that name, the Sanga? More like Joe, or more like Jen? More like a tree fort, or the pits, or more like a cinder block basement, earwigs and millipedes, black widows and Murphys?

"A victory," the General was saying, "and good news from the ranks. Let's come out of the cold here. We've got plenty we can celebrate. Quick martini for the past and present—I propose a Roy Rogers to the health of future pilots."

Mother would not look at him. He hadn't said anything to her about the Sanga. She wasn't dressed. She had her back to him, faced off to the stragglers in the parking lot.

The General said, "How about it? What say, Mrs. R? You want me to reconnoiter with the mister?"

"No, sir," said Mrs. R, and we all looked over to Mr. R, who sat across the lot from us, idling in the family Buick. Mrs. R said, "That man isn't moving."

"All right," said the General. "I respect that. Tell you what, then, what do you say we take Mike here with us, have a time, then bring him home at a decent hour? There are people there I'd like to introduce him to. Can't hurt to get yourself connected."

Not too sure, yes and no, Mrs. R appeared to say, too polite and maybe too afraid to say that being hurt or not depends on how a person is connected. I thought the way she looked at Mike and then across the parking lot to Mr. R was not too different from Coach when he was looking to the floor and then to us all on the bench when Coach could see his crowd leave. What was safe? What was the principle? How should she be written up for fairness and compassion?

"Well," said Mrs. R, "I don't suppose we stayed here so the boy could raise melons."

"That's the spirit," the General said. "So let's load up, men. You, too, sweetheart, unless you want to hitch a ride with Mrs. R here? Come on, Mike, we'll have you home a captain."

Off, then. Don't ask questions. Be happy the General keeps his Comet up. Heater works. Mother's toes are warm, the defrost keeps the windshield clear, she can't complain now, can she? She was a sweet old ride, the General's Comet; the only surface with a slicker shine, I thought, must be the skin of the General's Pitts. Mother said the car was an embarrassment, but looking at her warming up there with the General I could see she must have had her moments with the top down, chilly nights beneath the starshine when she helped the General to the bottom of his thermos. Mike had his cap pulled down across his brows and he was sitting pretty far down in his collar, his nose and mouth tucked down below the zipper so the only part I saw of him was eyes. I never saw how little I could say of Mike by looking at his eyes. I thought how looking at his eyes was like the time I parked my Lemon Peeler in the melon patch and watched Mike and his folks at supper. Like how few times I had been over. Like if I was such a friend to him, shouldn't he invite me in?

Monkey, Sanga, monkey, I was thinking, Sanga, monkey, Sanga.

Whereas look at us, we Oneys all were up, privileged ignorants, even Mother. The General seemed to me to be his self of twenty, thirty pounds ago. Captain Oney, the new dad with the mustache. And Mother seemed to maybe be his date, slowly, grudgingly excited, I was thinking, by the sudden rearrival to her night of prospect. That's lipstick she's putting on, Adam. That's some curl she's putting in that eyelash. She sat turned partly toward the General. Her arm was resting on the seat back. She had her thumb between her teeth in a way that let you see her teeth, touched the General with that thumb against his face and held it there so he could move his face around where it was wanting touching.

I nudged Mike to tell him, *look at that there, have you ever known my mother to be such a flirty vixen?* That's the Sanga, Mike. Sanga magic. Cheer up, partner, I wanted to say, it's the base bar, where the pilots hang. They've got these Christmas lights strung up December to December. They'll let us play whatever on the jukebox. Give us quarters from the register for pool. If we're lucky, there will be a gang of younger flyers there with girls who aren't mothers, some who aren't yet even wives. They get bored. What do they care about pulling Gs? They've already heard the one about their heroes greasing landings in a nasty crosswind. They'll think we're cute. We might get a look or two at some pretty decent cleavage, playing teams at shuffleboard; I've played with ladies in their halters who were showing off some primo side-tit.

But that's not what I said.

Me, I said, "You watch, they'll have all the peanuts you can eat there. Sometimes, they've got these spicy, coated bar snacks, a whole big mix of stuff. Free refills on the Coke."

Mike said he could go for a Coke. He didn't move, but spoke right through his collar.

"Coke'd be fine," he said.

"Oh, it's great," I said. "Those bar snacks make you thirsty."

I thought he maybe nodded.

I said, "It's a bar, you know, it's to make you drink more."

After I was pretty sure he heard me, I could see he didn't want to talk, and after I could see he didn't want to talk, I wondered what I thought I could be saying. I thought maybe I did not know what to say or how to live; I wondered could there really be a race of boys who lived more for a salted nut than for a flyer's girl and flying. I pulled my cap down low like Mike's and settled deeper in my collar. Would I ever dunk? Would I fly? Was I queer?

Monkey, Sanga, monkey; come in there, monkey Sanga monkey; monkey Sanga, do you read me?

Poise, right? Poise, think *poise* while the General lands his Comet in the parking lot; be that guy with the tiger's eyes, the killer champion, that's Mike. Get out, stand straight, look up high, the stars are with you. Now hold on tight, Adam, hear that music, feel it thump up from the sidewalk through your boots, messing with your heartbeat. The General holds the door. It's a splintered plank, that door, cheaply built and badly cared for, a wooden record of last night's kicks and vomit, bleached by desert sunshine.

There goes Mother, ladies first, then guests, then you. Poise, I told myself, poise, but once we left that car I came a little all undone. Was the storm in there, the bad soup up from the delta, a heavy flak aimed straight at us of shouted wit and question—

Who, me? What, me? Sure, I am, I'm the General's boy, the one and only Adam Oney. Lemme shake that hand. You're a sturdy one, now, aren't you? Pants? My pants? Ha, ha, yessir, that's a good one, really good, waiting on a flood. Him? He's Mike. Mike, I said, a friend. Here's a quarter, kid, now go and pick your own, so long as yours is B-19, A-2, and C-7, in that order. Hear that? That's an order. You hear the news? About your daddy? News? What news? How long's it been since we've all seen your mama? Buy yourself a drink, kid, step right up, he don't bite, just tell him what's your pleasure. What's that? Pleasure. Him? He's Mike. Mike, I said, we play ball. A flood? Yessir, really good one, very funny, she feeds me beans and taters. Taking care of herself, I see. Hear the news? Big night, tonight. Must be pretty proud. Yes, sir, she can make herself be pretty pretty. Us? Ball. I'm going on six-three, Mike I think is just this side of six. And over there's my mama. Coke. And nuts. Nuts? Those snacks, then, with the spicy stuff, got some? May we have a bowl to take with us? Two? Ho, ho. Good one, really good, a flood . . .

We pushed, surged, ebbed, panicked to the back room, Mike and I, stood with our bowls of bar snacks and our pockets full of quarters for the shuffleboard and pool. From where we stood I saw the Christmas lights were every one of them a red. Blinky reds, steady reds, reds the size of standard, plain white, household light bulbs. The people all were red. And smoky. And crooked. Packed and shouting. The whole thing looked to me to be the real life from the movie we were shown in school that meant to teach us why we ought not act the way we saw these folks were acting. Except these were our folks. Or not exactly our folks, but the folks we were supposed to age awhile and come to be.

"It's not how I remember," I was saying.

We watched a fellow put a lighter to a shot glass. A blue flame burned around the surface of the glass and a chant went up along the bar before the fellow tossed it down the hatch.

Mike said, "Looks to me it's been this way forever."

I wondered could that be too true.

Mike said, "Rack 'em up."

He won the toss to see who broke. He stood at the head of the table, chalked his cue, and looked somehow again to be the guy who was the Huskies' leading scorer.

He said, "It's Valhalla, man. They start breaking barstools on each other, we'll know we've died and gone to heaven."

We shot around some, feeling our way back, I thought, toward our older, younger selves. We said an uninspired word or two about the game, and by the second break I thought of us more as Orville and of Wilbur, less of Magic and of Worthy. Through Mike, it's the General's life for me all over. I licked the peppered salt stuff off my fingers, set up to take my shot, sighted down the far end of the table where I saw a fellow pick a lady up and drop her hard against the dance floor. The fellow got down on his hands and knees to maybe ask if he could help her. She smacked him. A regular slap. The woman sat cross-legged on the dance floor, smoothing her skirt across her knees. Looked to me like she was thinking something funny. She slapped that guy. *I slapped him*, she was thinking. The woman looked up through the lane of legs between herself and us and caught us standing flat-footed with our sticks, a couple of lean-bodied gawkers. She hauled herself off the floor and headed our way.

"I'm Cindy," she said, "Whose are you?"

"I'm with him," said Mike. "Him and his folks. They brought us here. I'm the guest."

"So whose are you?" she said.

"Oney's," I said. "Colonel Oney? I'm Adam."

"Then that must make you Mike," said Cindy. "I've heard about you two. I understand you boys have got a lot to celebrate. How about I give you some quarters for the jukebox, you each pick out a couple of songs, and whoever's song comes up first, that's who gets first dance."

"With you?" said Mike.

"There's no one else."

"There's always someone else."

"Okay, Mr. Mike. But I'll bet your pleasure no one else is me."

"What's my pleasure?"

"You don't know? Smart guy like you? Well, maybe you just need a teacher."

Classic corn, we knew that much. Too much, we said on our way to the jukebox, can you believe it, *maybe you just need a teacher?* We dropped her quarters, and I punched up the Marvin Gaye, a little "Sexual Healing." Mike went with the Haggard, "Misery and Gin." The third play we talked over, said if "Muskrat Love" was first to spin, she was dancing with us both.

She'd got into her kit while we were gone. Livened up the perfume. Fetched her mirror out and powdered in some color to her cheeks and eyelids. She was working on the lipstick when we manned our cues and asked her who was up. She didn't answer us but kept on studying her mirror. I believe the way she worked her mouth against that tube was less to get the red on, more for us to count how many ways she might remind us of our pleasures by a kiss.

"What did you choose?" she said.

"Surprise," says Mike.

"I doubt it," Cindy said. "See if I don't guess."

I said, "Hey, Cindy, did you ever think you would slap a guy?"

"I've slapped lots," she said.

"For real?"

"Sure, I have. It happens."

"Only in the movies."

"Oh, boys," she said. "Let me tell you. We *are* the movies. Live awhile and you'll find out we're as real as they are."

That's when Marvin Gaye pipes up, and sure we tried to tell her it was me, my song, but those fingers she was peeling off the cue were Mike's, that elbow she was hooked into was Mike's, those eyes I saw were looking back at me and wanting help were Mike's, no way could we tell her "Sexual Healing" wasn't also Mike's—"Misery and Gin," she said, was me. Too late. She had Mike out there trying to do the no-touch two-step to the slow groove, Mike looking more to be a stiff-legged descendant of the folks who brought us polka, than a proper brother from the blood of soul.

Credit Cindy, though, she kept him moving. She must have known when the right song spun our man would summon up the funk we white folks in the audience assigned to him as the nearly scientifically established privilege of his people's pigment. Pick up the tempo, give him the big boom bass, the jungle chorus, stuff to scare us into ghetto scenes of spears and .45s and lip plates. Boys grown up to nine feet tall, three-hundred-and-fifty pounds of Mandingo muscle, shamelessly unemployed, sucking on a pacifier fastened by a clothespin to his hooded parka. Give him the R-E-S-P-E-C-T. Have him take us to the waters. Oh, man. Oh, God. Oh, merciful, brotherful Jesus. That's cheetah love. The long cock on the Serengeti. Keep the record spinning, and soon enough we see hyenas on the entrails of the newborn antelope; the bullet in the brain of the jump rope princess, drive-by number six-o-one, brother's sister, mother's daughter, gorillas picking nits from the scalps of sleepy toddlers.

Monkey, Sanga, monkey—do you copy?

"Look at him dance."

"I wouldn't let him dance like that with mine."

"You know she could move like that?"

"What's that called?"

"That's not dance. Is that dance?"

"It's dance."

"It's sex."

"It's what?"

"It's dance."

"It's boogie."

"It's mojo."

"Disco."

"Could you do it?"

"He's a kid."

"Not at heart."

"Well, with all your all's permission," says the fellow Cindy slapped, "I think it's time I bust these dance champs up."

There he went, Cindy's man, a big-backed tool called Weisolmirski. He had a grounded walk, a weight to him that told a fellow Mike and my size we were boys; once we stepped out from the toy room we were mixing with the men and women. Volume's maxed out on the jukebox, folks are loading in the quarters, pumping in the jungle. All I saw was back. A bald spot on the crown. A big green wall of Sergeant Weisolmirski. He gathered Mike and Cindy up into a real reluctant-looking huddle. Folks were booing. They had paid out quarters, picked the songs they had a right to see Mike dance to.

I kept an eye on Mike, another eye out for the General. Sure I thought the General might have stepped right in and pulled a little rank. But the General, when I saw him, was seated at the bar, hunkered over his martini, feeding olives to a lady who it looked to me like could have passed as Cindy's sister. I know he could see the goings-on with Mike by looking in the mirror because I saw the General duck his head and jump when Cindy broke out from the huddle and raised her hand to have another slap at Weisolmirski. Lucky for us Sergeant Ski was slapped once already that night and wasn't looking for a second slap but caught her hand and kissed her. Double lucky for us all Cindy kissed him back.

Well, all right, I thought, okay, so folks were trying really to be pretty good here; must be folks are happier to cheer the kisses than the slaps. They let Mike go, cheered him when he walked off under a salute.

"What'd he say to you?" I said.

"Not much," said Mike. "Nothing. He's just asking me how to do it. You know, could I show him some moves."

"That's it?"

"That's it."

"Must have been more. I mean, she slapped him."

"She didn't slap him."

"Well, she would have."

"But she didn't. If she wanted to, she would have. Anyway, we got to go," said Mike. "Gets too late, I'm going to catch it."

I said we could check with the General, which is how we found out the lady he was feeding olives to could pass as Cindy's sister because it happened she was Cindy's sister. Two stools down I could not say if she was closer to the twenty side of thirty or the forty, though when I leaned across the General to shake her hand, I saw that she was working hard to show her thirty side of forty rather than her fifty. Bad tobacco tooth, voice on her as if she'd spent the last two decades shouting in a bar like this, hashing over what she'd done and someday meant to do, eating olives off the General's toothpick and smoking up his Winstons.

"You're this guy's kid?" she said.

The General put his hand on my shoulder and he kept on saying, *This guy*. He pushed me on the chest and pulled me. He lit a Winston off the Winston he was smoking and he handed it to Cindy's sister. He shook me by the elbow saying, *This guy*, like he didn't know what else to say or how to really touch me.

"Where's Mom?" I said. "We're thinking we should leave here pretty soon for Mike."

The General drank from his martini. He made a gesture with the backside of his Winston hand to show that Mother could be anywhere except where he was sitting.

Cindy's sister said, "Your friend here have the hots for Cindy?"

"He's just fifteen," I said. "Sixteen pretty soon, but still we're both just a kid."

"I know fifteen," said Cindy's sister. "There's nothing fifteen in that dancing. That kind of dancing is as old as Eve."

Mike just stood there, looking like a fellow who was looking for a clock.

"They played ball," the General said. "All worn out. Big game. Boys are big winners."

"Well, congratulations are in order," Cindy's sister said. "It's not every night a person has so much to celebrate. What'll it be? Sarsaparilla for the boys? Roy Rogers? And how about another extra-dry martini here? To the players, and to the U.S. of A.'s most recent General!"

The General lifted up his glass, and Mike and I said cheers, though I am pretty sure we both were thinking we were drinking to ourselves. We had called the General *General* for so long we no longer knew the difference between what he was and what we called him. But he'd made it. He hadn't told us, but he'd made it finally for real, a general, the General really was a general.

"Most guys go their whole careers throughout the service," Cindy's sister said, "and they don't come nowhere near that star. Show him the star," she said. "Have they seen it?"

He fetched the stars from a zippered pocket on his chest. He wasn't old. But he wasn't lean now, either. If I didn't know him, I would have said that slouch was shaped around his belly, not his cockpit. I saw the ash hang longer off his cigarette, and I recalled he said a captain recently had called him Pops. He showed us the stars. A victory, a promotion. But how come Mike and I should hear it as the late report, a special bulletin from Cindy's sister? The big green bug sat squat onto my heart. Sure I should have pitched right in with Mike and said hooray, congrats, but I was feeling awfully boo and hiss right then and wanting more to look for Mother.

"Did you tell Mom?" I said. "How come you didn't tell us?"

The General tossed a star up in his palm. He closed his hand around the star and held it out so he might drop it in my palm and asked me would I like to hold it. I thought about it, and while I thought I saw Mike reach out his hand and say he would like to hold that star, all right, with the General's permission.

The General raised an eyebrow, gave Mike a two-finger salute and said, "Permission granted."

So it was me again, wishing I was Mike again, when Murphy pushed chest first into our business. Hard to believe, but Murphy looked to be as deep into his martinis as the General. Some dangerously high octane breath between these two. Remember him, Murphy wanted to know, and I answered, sort of, yes, I do, but he wasn't asking me but Mike.

"I knew your daddy," said Murphy. "You don't mind, do you Oney, if I talk a little to this boy?"

The General moved his head around from Mike and Murphy and the mirror, narrowed his eyes and widened them as if to make a better focus. He wagged his finger in a circle and said the country was free, last he'd heard, he guessed Murphy could talk to anyone he wanted.

"You weren't here," said Murphy, "but I knew this boy before he knew himself. Mama used to come in with a belly out to here. She had religion. She'd come in and holler at the old man and drag him by the ear for home. You know, she's the boss. She know you're here, kid? Surprised she let you. Old man, for that matter, if she gave him any say-so. He's got religion too, I heard. That right, son? Your daddy got religion?"

"He goes to church," said Mike.

"Hear he's picking melons."

"Got a farm," said Mike. "He owns it."

"Well, that's fine. Found his place, sounds like. Comfy cozy. Nice soft melon patch, dressing up for Sunday school with the ladies, hard to beat it."

"Cantaloupes," said Mike.

"What's that?"

"I said *cantaloupes*. Hearts of Gold. We grow cantaloupes."

"That right? Well, you should have used to've seen your daddy. Time was, he got religion from the engine of a jet. He worked for us out here. Long way from a Heart of Gold. Mechanic. Monkey. Pretty good one, too. Tried to mix it up with us, but then your mama. Damn, though. A monkey in a melon patch. I got to say, it's rich to think it."

"Mechanic," said Mike.

"Mechanic?"

"My father was a mechanic."

"Isn't that what I said?"

We sat, all of us, considering what Murphy said, because it was all of us and not just Mike that Murphy wanted to be heard by. I think Murphy was looking to the General to pick the glove up. He wasn't looking at Murphy, either. Who would want to? Ugly uglies. Beginning with his skull, a balded liver-spotted patch he'd thought to renovate with chest hair. Plugs, hundreds of these festery-looking sprout holes his surgeon threw in as a half-price bonus with the face-lift. He jabbed his chin at you as if to say, *Okay, so they botched the hair, so maybe it is sissyish to have them pull the skin up, so what of it?* You looked at Murphy and the General, ran them back as boys, as teens and young cadets, and I believe the General tells you he flies for flight, and Murphy says he flies for killing.

No surprise. No, sir, surprise for us was Mother. Where'd she come from? What happened to her lipstick? How was it she was only partly zipped? She put her arm around Mike's back and held him by the shoulder. I'd forgot how big she was until I saw how small she made Mike seem compared. I'd forgot how fierce. Eagle eyes, the raptor diving on its prey—that's Mother. Believe it, please, she was even deeper into her martinis than the General was or Murphy. *Light a match between these three,* I thought, *and you will blow the bar down.*

"Monkey," she said. "You said, *monkey,* not mechanic."

"Same thing," Murphy said, "what's the difference?"

Mother held out two hands of fingers in front of Murphy's face and counted them down by letters, spelling one word from the other.

"Monkey," she said, "six. Mechanic, eight. Monkey live in jungle, mechanic live in hangar, see? Different. It's all right," she said, "we know, we understand. All these years, you've been thinking with your hair. Poor dumb flyboy. His hair never was much but sprays and fancy combing, and now it looks like it's all gone, looks like he'll be thinking with the hair the doctor yanked up from his knuckles."

Murphy jabbed his chin at Mother, zeroed in on her, another killer searching out the weak spot.

"Hiding behind the skirts," he said. "Hey, Oney?"

Murphy turned away from Mother to the General to wait and see what next. You had a feeling this was not the time to spend your hope. Though I could see how maybe Mike thought different. He took this time to give the General back his star.

He said, "Here you go, General. Thanks for the look, sir."

The General came up with another two-finger salute, lit the filter end of his cigarette, and flopped his head down on the bartop.

I said, "Say something, General. Get up, sir, tell him."

The General lifted his head and said, "Get up."

"Say something," I said. "Go on and tell him."

"Tell him," said the General, and flopped back down. "Get up."

"You see there," Murphy said. "Can't answer the bell. That's exactly what all I'm talking about. Only guy to earn his star by ducking from the war I ever heard of. There's guys here they've flown on over twenty, thirty missions. Your so-called General here, he hasn't flown a single . . . " Murphy said, and then my mother called him asshole.

"You asshole," she said.

"I . . . " said Murphy, and she hit him openmouthed—gin, vermouth, and crushed ice—movie moment number two, the old drink-in-the-face bit.

She didn't wait around but told us go and get our coats. Mother was trying to get the General up and moving with us, but the General looked around and told us go ahead without him, he had some cleaning up to do. He grabbed ahold of Cindy's sister's wrist and had her have a good long look at Mike.

He said, "Forget about that basketball. That's Boudreaux. This guy here is going to fly the fighters."

Mother and I took Mike home that night, Mother steering an awfully quiet ride to the farmy part of town, swerving the General's Comet into the drive where the light was left for Mike so he might know someone waited there who loved him. Nice. Lucky. Lucky Mike, that's what we told him when we dropped him.

"I'm sorry," said my mother. "Assholes, all of them. You know, to be a flyer, you don't have to be an asshole with them."

We waved to Mike, watched him through his door and I was thinking maybe that's why church; maybe Mrs. R said he would have to go to church to learn how not to be an asshole even when he was a pilot flying fighters. He could shoot up the beaches, bomb the Commies, fly the prime years of his life defending freedom for us first-world Christians, and still not be an asshole. He could be humble pie, clean as Jesus. Maybe Mrs. R believed Mike could be the General. Except the General never flew a mission. And don't just count on Murphy, ask your mother. That's what I did. I asked. The morning after was a sunny winter Sunday when I asked her and she said, yes, the stuff about his mission days was stuff.

"He got out," she said. "He taught, passed on his commission, flew the trainers for a year, then when it came up time for action, your father failed his vision. Temporarily. Never understood how. How do you fail your vision even once," she said, "then get your vision back?"

The way she spoke, I had to quit my chewing so I could hear and understand her. What she said was clear enough, all right, it's just she kept on holding her mug up against her cheeks and to her lips while she was talking, warming up her face, I guess, or maybe making it so I would seem as hot to hear what Mother said as she had been to say it. Anyway she stopped me chewing, she had me leaning out across my bowl to listen. She didn't look good. She looked swelled. Looked as if a dream recurred to her each sleep in which she acted out a seven-hour fistfight.

"For a while there," she was saying, "he was working on a private shrink to tell the board he was crazy. You know, not certifiable, not all the way disabled. He thought if he could come up with something pretty specific to a war that made him psychologically unbalanced, then maybe they would keep him in the service, but they wouldn't send him off to fight. Why would Uncle Sam keep a fighter pilot who didn't fight? That's what I wanted to know. So then he came up with the failed vision. That's what's crazy about your father. He called himself an optimist. What I think is he thought the jungle would be too much like the swamp. It's a thing with him, you hear it, his saying how he's worked too hard to ever in his life go back there."

My mother turned her mug across her cheek, squinted through her swollen eyes at me, and asked me would I like to see where all the General flew his missions. Think, man, what it might mean to have your mother show you where your father flies his missions when she only just now told you he's never flown a mission. Ask yourself what brings a girl to shove a Zippo lighter and a pack of cigarettes into the pocket of her ratty robe and leave the house unwashed of last night's sins on a Sunday morning. Where does she mean to take you, Oney? Why the General's Comet? She drove the old car hard, lovelessly, I thought, purposely through gutter slush and washboard roads to the prefab part of town, where people stapled Visqueen to the windows and the roofs were flat and covered over by a cubic yard or two of small white stones. Oil slicks in driveways. A Confederate flag nailed to a wall. An old dog hunkered up to pass its morning stool. What mission?

Mother pulled up to a curb, fetched out a cigarette, and settled in as if we might be in for an appreciable wait. I looked out to the side of the road where Mother parked us, searching for some sign of what might draw the General here, something that might show me he had been here in the name of freedom.

"Surveillance," Mother said, "get it?"

"No, ma'am," I said.

"I guess not," my mother said. "You're not even looking out the right side, dummy. Surveillance always parks on the opposite side."

She handed me the General's aviator glasses from the dashboard.

"Put these on," she said. "Didn't your father teach you anything?"

My mother watched an ember fall from her cigarette and burn a hole through the vinyl between us.

"What exactly are we waiting for?" I said.

"The enemy," she said.

"How will I know him?"

"Blood," my mother said. "You'll feel something going funny on your insides."

When Cindy stepped out on the porch to fetch the morning paper something funny went, all right, then something funnier when Cindy saw us and pretended she hadn't.

"Cindy?" I said.

"What do you think?" said my mother.

"I think my feet are cold," I said. "I thought you said this was about the General."

"Wait," my mother said. "Observe."

So I observed the flat-roofed house, the white stones, and the melting snow. A period through which the house seemed to shimmer in the sun, then vibrate, I was thinking, from its sense of being watched. Then a curtain parted wide enough to peek through.

"Wave," my mother said. I waved, and then my mother started up the Comet, asked me was I warm enough, turned on the heater for my feet. She lit another cigarette and started counting down from ten. At three the door to Cindy's house was opened up and Mother said, "Our General."

Forgive a boy for thinking all this time the General was at home, sleeping off his celebration. Anybody might have seen him coming. He was squinting. He raised his hand to wave across to us. I waved back. Only Mother had the good sense not to. Her sense was to set the Comet in gear and ease out from the curb. The General kept on walking toward us, showing us his half-tucked shirt and a face that said, *Don't do it.* I thought he looked a little balder. The stars pinned to his collar were as dull as nickels. Until he took his first few running steps, the General looked like maybe he had summoned up the stuff to do the killing here with just his hands that he had never done there on the delta with his Phantom.

But then he ran. Mother put some foot to the gas, and instead of sticking to his ground, the General started running. Not far. Steps. Maybe two or three steps in a burst, and then a sudden jog, as if he'd run into a thicker avenue than air, as if the thought had just occurred to him that he could never catch us. And if he did, well, then what? He ran, I thought, as if he'd seen out to the last page of a failing explanation. He wasn't bad. He was sorry. I turned around to watch us leave him. He waved again, gave me the two-finger salute. I had that sickly feeling in me from the day I watched him fall unpowered in the Pitts and knew I could not save him. That's a hard earth from a high height, Mrs. Oney, did you want your husband to survive it? I saw Cindy's sister come out of the house and then we turned off from the block and left the General, as my Mother said, "to his own devices."

I felt him falling fast in me. When I saw the steeple and the cross I wanted to believe I saw a sign, something abler than myself to save the General from his fall, but when I saw the little crowd of people on the walk, and saw the crowd was gathered there for Mike, I guess I knew right then the General would likely never pull his nose up.

Why? Why duck? That's a handsome boy there, Adam, the center of his flock, your good best friend, a hope. That's Mike in church. White shirt, blue blazer, and a tie. Sure that is a happy congregation. There are Mr. R and Mrs. R, shaking hands with folks, patting backs and laughing. Why hide? I think Mother felt the same way I did. Wanting to hide and not knowing why, liking what she saw and wondering why liking what she saw should make her sadder. I know she put her cigarette out. She turned the mirror on herself and looked into her puffy eyes and tried to smooth her hair down.

She said, "Congratulations, Adam. You played a real fine game." She said, "I don't know about you, but when we get home, I am going to give myself a good hot bath."

You do heal. Unless you die. The fellow with the face died. Another fellow died I never saw. And then a girl we boys had heard about who tried to kill herself by gasoline and matches also died, even though she changed her mind and wanted hard to live. We talked her over in the lounge. How here's a girl who checks in at over eighty-five percent, likely looking at a three-to-four-month stay here on the unit, better than a year or two of grafts, some topflight plastic reconstructives, and still a life of permanent disfigurement, a face of the skinny reptile, and now, now, now she wants to live? Of course, now, naturally, except she didn't live, she died. Granted, we agreed, she was on the morphine, never made it out of her Emergent, still, it made sense one thing she would want to live for was her marble. Cat's-eye marble she kept asking for but nobody of hers could find it. The mother tried to fool her with a newly bought one but that girl said hers was scratched. Word leaked she died right in the tank. Too bad for us, who had to go in after. If we would heal. Which we did.

You could mark our healing by our talk, how far the five or six of us who came in pretty much together had moved away from those more recently arrived. I myself took pleasure showing rookies how to help themselves at camp. Tips on how to space the meds. How to flatter Nurse Nadeen about that gastric bypass. What kind of gossip would engage Nurse Jill. We told them they might reasonably expect to wheedle Mars Bars and Coca-Colas from the nurses, but don't think flattery and gossip will ever fetch you your morphine.

"We know a lot," said Tom, before he left with Mrs. Tom, which was the last way we knew we were getting better.

We thought to have a party. Usually, said Sue, you do, though for Tom and Mrs. Tom, the nurses weren't rallying much muster. Mrs. Tom was puffing like a locomotive on her cigarette, and I thought it showed good taste that Tom was not.

He was saying, "I guess this is it, gentlemen."

He was saying thanks to Nurse Nadeen. Said for us to say a thank you, please, to his surgeon. Thanked a therapist who happened by and said to thank the chaplain, too, though Tom could not make God or Jesus seem to be his saviors. Mrs. Tom stubbed out her smoke, crossed her arms across herself as if to make sure no word of thanks could come from her. I thought at least she could have helped Tom hold those rolls of gauze and salves. She could at least have said good-bye to us. Before I thought how sore we were, I thought we ought to hug him. We looked in need. Weepy, the younger of us.

"I don't guess I'll ever see you guys again," said Tom.

Nobody would disagree. We wished him luck, told him take care, don't play with matches, keep your fingers out of the socket, don't smoke in bed. Burned-guy jokes, another step along the get-well road. *Did you hear the one about the burned guy who . . . How many burned guys does it take to . . . Okay, three burned guys walk into a bar . . .*

I went back to my room and waited there for Sue and asked her when she came in how she thought such jokes would translate.

"My opinion?" said Sue. "Keep your burned-guy jokes to burned guys."

"Still, I want to practice," I said.

"Practice what?" said Sue.

"I want to practice being out. Like you stand there, pretend you're squeezing loaves of bread or something, minding your own business in the supermarket. And I'll walk up and say, excuse me."

"You mean role-play?"

"That's Doc Noggin talk. I want to call it practice."

"Okay," said Sue. "Except, if you don't mind, I'd rather be in the library than the supermarket, let's say, and I'm reading."

So Sue sits down and makes as if to hold a book, wets her finger with her tongue as if she's turning pages. I walked up to her, meaning to approximate the less-disabled version of myself I tried to see off in my future. I touched her on the arm and said, "Excuse me," and she shrieked. A joke, right, a thing I think surprised us both to see how much it scared me. We ran the same scene back with Sue enacting variations of politeness, pity, indifference, disgust. I touched her arm and she said, *Can I help you?* Or, *You startled me.* She said, *My best friend got burned, I don't work here, sorry.*

She was saying, "So what? What do you want?"

"I don't know," I said. "I forgot. I was just . . ."

"What?" Sue said. "You just what? Is this how you get your kicks? Scaring old guys with those paws? You ought to be ashamed," she said. "Why don't you go out and get a job? Be a credit to your kind, why not? Now go on, get out of here. You let me read in peace."

She asked me how was that.

I said, "I think that one needs more practice."

We practiced dates, job interviews, elevator rides; we put two chairs together and practiced sitting down beside a stranger on an airplane. Would I want to hold my hand? Serve me food? Or if I saw me walking down the street, would I cross over to the other side because I was afraid to pass me? Would I worry I might find me in my dreams as someone else's nightmare?

"When he sees you," she said, "then whatever a person is, you can bet he'll be more of it. People have a hard time keeping character a secret in the company of open wounds and sickness."

"And what is a burn?" I said. "Open wound, or sickness?"

"Could be both," said Sue, "if you let it. Always it's an open wound. Sickness comes by your head. How you treat the wound by thinking."

"Head sickness."

"Psychological."

"Doctor Noggin."

"That's right," said Sue. "Have you been talking?"

Yes, I said, and no. I said it seemed to me Doctor Noggin these days was more interested in telling me his story than he was in listening to mine. Apparently he had an allergy to those horses he married into. He said he felt ashamed of his face-lift. He could understand plastic surgery in the case of the man I described in Murphy, whereas in himself he could not.

"He did this funny thing with his hands," I said to Sue. "Held them out in front of himself and made them like to talk. He kept turning his eyes on one hand and the other, listening, you know, nodding same as he would nod for me, really giving those hands his full, professional attention. The one hand said, *Vanity?* The other hand said, *Youth? Youth,* he kept on saying, *vanity? Vanity, youth?*"

He got a good laugh out of that game—*heh, heh, heh*—but I told Sue it didn't look too happy. I said it didn't seem to me the doctor was too crazy about his new wife being pregnant, either.

"Is that character?" I said. "You think when he sees me laid up he can't keep secrets?"

"I think it's pretty unprofessional," said Sue. "It's uncommon. Have you told anybody else?"

"No," I said. "I don't want anyone to know. I like it. Makes me feel good.

Days he really talks, he leaves me saying he believes I'm doing much, much better."

Sue wrote down some scribbles on her charts, thumbed through several pages in my folder.

She said, "Anyway, you're gaining."

I said, "You know the General had his secrets, too, and I don't mean about his serving in the war. I mean Louisiana. Past it not being New Orleans, and that about being Boudreaux and DuPree, you couldn't say too much about Louisiana because the General didn't tell. A kind of secret was his daddy, who the General never knew. The General hinted about crime, something in the line of robbing banks as why he never got to know his daddy, but Mother thought the story there was that the General's daddy plain got scared when he saw the seed swell in the mama's belly. If he had robbed a bank, Mother liked to say, then the General and his mama would be free to visit him in jail. An Oney broke the law and he was thrown straight to the wolves. Bad luck. She said a plague was on the General's name. Could you really call a suicide successful? That was Mother's question. And when you said no, you know, it proved her point—bad luck—because in the case of the General's mother, she succeeded. I told her the General's mother wasn't really Oney, though, Oney wasn't really in her blood, but she said the curse was in the name, you could bring it on yourself by marriage. Me, she liked to say, I was double-cursed, name and blood, if she had known back then what she knew now, she never would have had me. She always had an answer, Mother did, always had a way to doom you.

"Still, I know a bad luck thing the General told me I believed once was a story on his cousins. I don't know which, or how, or were those his real cousins, or if, how Mama says, *cousin* was a name the General gave to anyone who fed him. It was a fair day. The General was six. Big-boy cousins telling him how cotton candy makes the peanut brittle taste like twice-boiled greens.

Plus which, you could shoot at the fair. Win a treasure. But the best for the General was the Aerowhip, these unwinged cockpits on chains. Pretty crude, I guess, but when you're six, and it's fair time in Louisiana, and you're the General, then that Aerowhip must pull at you like something of a private, sugar-coated newness. Except the General didn't get to go because those cousins tied him standing to a dogwood. There was a tethered goat there in the yard with him, named Bijou. According to the cousins, Bijou could eat the General if he wanted to, that goat was an animal a boy should keep away from. The General said he hadn't even seen Bijou till after the cousins pedaled off and left him. But there was Bijou, tethered to a stake not twenty feet from the General's dogwood, chewing at his tether. The General said that goat stared at him the whole time he chewed, too, as if the General would be next. The General closed his eyes, said he tried to feature himself on that Aerowhip, saw himself unchained and riding on the thermals high above the fair site. He was still up in the clouds when Bijou chewed free from his tether. The General heard him snorting closer, evil sneezy thing, come across the yard to eat the General like a suckling piglet roasting on a skewer. He's hot, the General, really dripping, scared, scared, scared, but it wasn't Bijou made the General foul himself, it was time. Bijou only nibbled some, tickled at the General's pant leg. Then he's cropping up some stinkweed, jumping up on the roof of the car, and then that goat is gone.

"That was still the morning. Wasn't till after noon, the first time the General wet himself, five hours, maybe, another five or six on top of that before he wet himself again and shit his pants. The aunt and uncle found him. Beat the hell out of the cousins, which the General said it only made things worse. Was nothing, the General said the first time he told it, same as he said it wasn't anything the second. But you know it was," I said. "It was something, all right. Character is what. That's the story where the General sees how anybody flies without an airplane. That's his secret. That's mine. On the outside, you might say with Mother that the Oney name is cursed, but on the inside, if we've got our heads on right, no matter what all's wrong, we're flying."

"That's fine," said Nurse Sue. "That's good. Only not too high. Right? Not too wild? You always keep an eye out where you're landing?"

"Look at me," I said. "I've got a talent, remember? I'm a word to spread. When I leave here, only reason I'll be coming back is to treat you to a real nice dinner."

"That's fine," said Sue. "You let me know ahead of time so I can bring my appetite."

I lay there in bed, feeling this week's meds roll over me in warm, pink clouds that spoke to me in tickling surges of a lover's whispered French. I lay quiet, listening—*ooh-la-la*—then asked Sue what that pill was and what color. But Sue had gone. I listened for her step in the hall but couldn't make her out, one step from another, couldn't even make the steps out from the cartwheels, or a closing door, or from conversation at the nurses' desk from way down at the front end of the unit. All French to me. All lovers. How did anybody die here? Give us the beautiful pill, people the planet with Sue, lie down in the memory of screams and moanings of the sick and wounded and know the Oney secret: *You and I, friend, we're immortal.*

I lay listening, trying to convince myself I had not gone a little loopy. Wasn't just the drug. Not fatigue. Was a lovely scream, I thought, that poor girl with her marble must have heard; such pain must privilege us with views of less disintegrating truths, something fuller than the Catholic's wafer, a more humanly embodiable transubstantiation. Brother, brother, born into the fire—have you been saved? Who spoke through your fever? You dog, Jesus, was it you? Who is talking? Who's responsible? Phuat Yung saw his pup obliterated by a land mine, saw his sister cut in two by the big guns fired from the Phantom. The girl with thalidomide flippers plays at mama with her Easy-Bake. The meds are strong in here, they're good, but that's TV up there, it's real, don't doubt. I understand that man was convicted. He murdered in the first degree. White guy. Westerner. Bought himself some leather chaps and cowboy tools and bound a college girl in baling wire, branded her, notched her ears, shot her full of steroids, raped her twenty-seven times before he roped and hung her. His plea is innocent, by way of his insanity; he says before he killed her that the college girl assured him he wasn't bad, not a bad person, he just did a bad, bad thing. True, Allah? Beauty of beauties, the mushroom blooming over Nagasaki, Yahweh, is that you? The blue whale feeding from a wide mouth in a radioactive sea, Lord, is that you? Needs a god in us to conjure such excruciating trial. Needs at least a resurrected Elvis, a James Dean in a race car, needs a president to spill his brain in Texas, needs at least the General. Give us all you've got, sir, we will survive it!

That's coming home, Adam. You'll be going home soon. Tom went home. You will be well. Remember, I was well. I played ball. I flew. I crashed. I burned. I was son enough to hear a General's secrets.

I lay and listened. I wanted the French. I wanted back the lover stuff. But it's hard to hear the French, when French is what you're listening for. I listened and I knew no step I heard was Sue's. I heard the cart wheeled to the tank, and was happy that it wasn't me. I hurt. I was healing. Soon, I thought, the hurtful part of healing would be over. I heard another cart go by with empty plates, half empty from an eggs and porridge breakfast, and for lunch was hoping *enchiladas.*

MUCH OF THAT FIRST SEASON ON THE VARSITY I MISSED. THIRD GAME IN I HAD a fall, backpedaling on defense, caught myself a little how Staley caught himself off the roof. Broke two arms, that is, spiral fractures running upward to the elbow from the wrist. After that, life moved through so fast it seemed to me I was looking back on things that hadn't even happened. We lost. That much happened. We lost one in the regular conference season, won the tournament for zone, were routed in the first round by a team down south at State. The clock fad passed. The local news moved on to track a dominating middle-distance runner from the high school on the other side of town. To keep himself in girls, Hector turned to baseball. Chester and Lester turned to their books. Arturo gave the ball a rest to tutor at his night school, and Mike said he was flat-out on the farm, discing fields, and planting seeds for melons. At home, Mother kicked the gin martinis, joined the church, and drank iced tea with Mrs. R.

She said, "I strayed, Adam. I forsook the Lord."

After she agreed to pose for a family photo of the governor presenting General Oney with his stars, Mother told the General to find his own apartment.

She said, "I've been carrying around a lot of anger. I've lived this way too long."

I wished I knew which way that was. Or else I knew which way that was and told myself that way was Mother's way because she chose it. Curtains closed. Footrest up. Sleeping in and taking naps, *One Life to Live* until the news came on and it was time for cocktails. I suppose the General's way was also chosen. He sat on a folding chair in a studio apartment he rented in a complex built beneath the final leg for the north-south runway. Planes took off and landed and the sound waves shook the ice cubes in the General's martini, rattled the picture of the General as a fresh cadet, the blue-eyed flyboy smiling from the ladder mounting the cockpit of his T-Bird. Sure the glass and frame might shake and rattle, but the image of the General there would not. This boy was resolve, permanent gleam, the promise from above that when the ground troops marched into the jungle, they would march back out into a clear blue sky, intact, unscathed, happily embraced in victory's immortal song. Look up there, soldier, and salute him. Give him your hand, your heart, pass with him through the hall of swords, up and up, this boy will take you with him.

"We're just biding time," the General said.

The General made as if to shoot a jump shot with his toothpick, missed the trash can and asked me would I fetch the pitcher from the fridge and pour him, please, another drink. When I brought his drink to him I saw the General staring out the window, fingering the stars on his collar, sort of picking at them, sometimes, sort of petting them and rubbing them, I thought, the way a kid will pick a scab, the way I thought a lady might pet and rub a brand-new pair of bigger breasts. My superior. He set his drink down on a U-Haul box he used as a side table for his folding chair. He said we'd learn what all was in that box when the soggy spot wore through the cardboard. And anyway, what difference? Three, four months now and nothing in that box had been too needed.

He said, "Tell you something? I am happy. That gal was a first-rate toss."

If he had it all to do over again, the General liked to say, then he would do it. But he did not have it. She was gone. *You should see the one I'm working now,* the General liked to say, and now, and now, and now, but she was gone, Cindy's sister, Cindy, Cindy's sister's sister, her cousin, niece, daughter, mother, friend—all gone, all passed through too fast to cause the General to change his sheets or cook or think about a rod to hang some curtains, all passed through before I ever had a chance to even meet them or believe for sure they were for real.

"I don't know," I said. "I'd at least not like to see you drink from off a box."

"Well, maybe when you get your arms out of that plaster I could let you open it. Could be there's a table in here. Or if it's really got you bugged, we could go and buy one. Pick up a table, a burger and a shake, then give you a lift home?"

"You know that won't fly," I said.

"Doesn't want to see me still?"

"Still," I said. "That's the Lord in her, it's Jesus."

"Baloney," said the General. "What burns hottest in your mother isn't any Lord. What's hot in her is what she sits on. Pretty soon here she will get too hot for sitting, then we'll see if it's me she's looking for or Jesus."

I told the General I hoped he was right. Meantime, I would walk.

"Nice day out," I said. "Lots of sky left. Walk would do me good."

And it would have. Lots of walks would have. But the trouble with those walks was people didn't like to let me take them. I'm a celebrity, right? And who wants his celebrity to slub along under the summer sun, a pedestrian in Car Town? Sure it could be because I skipped most walks is why I put the softer weight on. Let myself grow out of the feel and habit of the harder weight. It would come back to me—my *fighting* weight—this was the word, what the General said, what Coach said, too, what everybody from our starting five, to our teachers in the classroom, to fat old Mr. Dobb who picked me up while I was walking said—lean, quick, hard—"Oh, no," he says, "you're a young man, Adam. You put your mind to it, you'll trim right down to where you want to."

Another ride, another reminder, another point of view. It was the off-season, a little letdown after State, I broke my arms, they didn't heal right, had them rebroken and recasted, ouch, what did I expect?

"You're growing," says our bone man. "You come from some pretty big parents, don't forget. Your body's telling you it needs those calories. Calories are energy. You don't use the energy, the calories are stored as fat. Once you start running again, you'll be a calorie vacuum. You might have a hard time holding onto any weight at all."

Funny thing is how much I liked it. I liked the universal clearance I received to eat, and the optimism I inspired in other people for the youth I carried in myself to lose what I had gained and keep on eating. Except I sometimes thought I might not like to lose. I thought I liked this fold I could pinch and roll it on my belly. Felt creamy. Felt easy. Was something I could do. Couldn't play, couldn't practice, couldn't help my mother cook and clean, couldn't even help the General move his boxes. But I could grow. I could take a ride when it was offered. Dobb. Ms. Yapp. Mrs. Scully. Doctor Scully. Sometimes, too, a kid, a boy who wondered what the odds were he could make the team next season. People I knew and people I didn't picked me up and dropped me off and said they were glad to finally meet me.

"Saw you play," they said.

"Saw your fall."

"Recognized the casts."

"Sorry piece of luck," they said. "Those boys could have used you."

Wasn't hard to see that even if they hadn't said a word about the fat they were wanting to. Sneaky peeks, politeness, except from Ellen Swinson, widow, she explained, to Eddie Swinson, who farmed pigs.

"Damn, boy," said Mrs. Swinson, "you got fat."

She took me down to Cecarelli's, her treat, so she could see me feeding.

"There's good things," she explained, "about a husband being dead. A good thing, just for starters, was unloading those damn pigs."

Without those pigs, she said, where would she be? She'd made quite a life in rentals off the sale of those pigs. Bought herself a duplex, which bought her an apartment, which bought her a bungalow, and so on till she was the lady of leisure I was seeing right before me, owner of eleven properties in all, a self-made lady, doing just whatever all she wanted.

"Life is big that way, once you line it up with what you want."

She allowed herself a monthly perm, for instance, played a round of mini-golf on every summer Friday. Her dachshunds slept on beds of laundered sheets. But maybe Mrs. Swinson's greatest joy in life was ball. Husky basketball. A true fan of the red and blue, she knew these were her glory days and she'd made a clock to prove it.

She said, "Would you like another pizza?"

She watched me eat, as pleased, I thought, as if I were the pig she'd sold to send her on her road to riches.

"You decide," she said. "One day it's all hoof and swill, then maybe something happens like your husband dies and Lord, you're up there with the birdies and the angels."

"I see your point," I said. "When these casts come off, I'm going to work on losing. My age and build, they say there's nothing to it."

"Could be," said Mrs. Swinson, "or else pretty soon you could be posting on the Oolags. Could be growth is why you broke those arms. I knew a boy once who grew a foot in a year, and in that year he'd also broken seven bones. So what is it? I'm ready to go. Happy to take you anywhere you want. Or I'm also happy to leave you here, order you that other pizza."

I took the other pizza. I went up to the counter, sat down at a stool, asked Mr. Cecarelli what he thought, was I on pace to grow up on the Oolags? Had he ever heard of growth inspiring bone breaks? Or was that something from another generation and the farm?

"I don't know," said Mr. C. "Myself, I'm a Brooklyn boy. I don't know farm. I heard of different things. The nose. Grow into your nose. Or the wanker. Heard that, too. I usually go with feet. What size shoe you wear?"

"Twelve," I said.

"Well, that's a big foot. You might ask those Oolags what size they're in, give you some idea what you're coming to."

I went home and found my mother gone to Thursday church group. Or else to Tuesday church group. Friday Bible. Saturday pre-church service. Sunday Sunday school and Sunday service proper. Drill with Mother was to read the note, look inside the oven, turn the stove to low, find the frozen tortellini in the freezer. She might be home in time to join me. If not, don't wait up. If so, then it's Mom and Adam at a sit-down dinner, Mom assuring me I was welcome in the Lord, I could come along, wouldn't hurt me, would it? It's Adam saying, It's not me I'm thinking of, ma'am, it's the General, though he, of course, was welcome, too, my mother said, a little God and humbler worship wouldn't hurt him, either. I found a boiled potato and a roast pork in the oven. Cuisine for the tepid Baptist's palate, a plate I seasoned with the memory of Mr. Cecarelli's sausages and kalamata olives. *Another meal there, Adam? Oh, it's fine,* I told myself, *don't want to hurt the mother's feelings.* I watched some tube, picked up the phone to dial Mike, and then remembered better. I was welcome, wasn't I? The General was the reason why Mike wasn't allowed to see me. I wished I could believe. I made myself a nighttime sweet of Cool Whip and chocolate sprinkles. I made another and was someway through the eating of it when my mother came back home and asked me how I liked the pork roast.

She said, "What's that? Straight cream? From a can? You're just eating cream and candy?"

"It's good," I said. "You ought to try some."

"Not hardly," my mother said. "Some of us are trying to keep our weight down."

I followed my mother to her room where she undid herself. I remembered that, how she liked to say from the shopping days, *Will you undo me?*

I said, "Do you want me to undo you?"

She looked at me as if she did not think she knew me, or knew me maybe once, a time she might refer to as a *phase,* days she hoped she had outlived and happily forgotten.

"I see," she said. "No, thank you, Adam, I don't need to be undone. Listen, Adam, if you want to, you don't have to eat the way you do. There are other pursuits you might follow. The door is open. You are welcome anytime. It may well be the only way you'll get your friend back. You might be surprised to learn how deep a person lives in his belief. Your friend Mike believes. That's a good boy, your friend Mike."

"That's a change," I said. "Two months ago you told the General that church stuff was a front. Remember? Time that Mrs. R showed up to help out with the cleaning? Mama Rags and Pickaninny? I heard you say you left off seeing Mrs. R because she wouldn't spring for pizza."

My mother sighed, weight of the ages exhaled from her weary bosom, the miraculous transformation stitched into her brow; Jesus and the seven weeks of Sunday school, I thought, have made a sage of the shewolf, stalker of the year-end bargain basement blowout.

"I confess," she said, "and I repent. The Lord works in mysterious ways, and I am the Lord's. Now," she said, "if you'll excuse me."

I called up Mike and got the runaround again from Mrs. R.

"Mike's gone to bed, honey. Can you call him in the morning?"

Or, "Oh, hello, Adam. I'm sorry, honey, he's out in the field with his daddy."

Or, "Can he call you back? Right now he's in the shower."

But he never called back. After Murphy and the Sanga, I would see him in the halls at school and he was busy, busy. Math, practice, game tonight, he said. Neither one of us could say it, *Sanga*, neither one of was saying, *Murphy, Sanga, monkey.* We would leave off from each other with me understanding, with school out and summer coming on, and me back on the telephone with Mrs. R, saying, *Yes, ma'am, fine, okay, sorry to be calling, I didn't see it was so late.* He was a good kid, you know, responsible, I heard, mature beyond his years, he's off to church, gone to worship with the mothers.

I lay on my back, rested my casts across my belly, wished I could sleep straight through the week and wake up to the weekend. Back to the General. Fried eggs and Tabasco sauce and bacon, English toast with extra butter. Forks on plates, that's the General and me, two appetites for spice and excess, two big guys really digging in. The General and I had fun with Mother, a good laugh at her pork roasts, her unsugared, lumpy oatmeal. Morning time the best time of the day for us, the General's second-cup-of-coffee time, time to stretch and scratch and shake the gin, okay. This was a shaved General I was looking forward to, a showered General, an antiseptic smell about him of the cure, an ethery release.

The General saying, "Just leave those dishes in the sink."

Time he was on leave, off-duty, dressed out in his civvies, time he bounces his keys up from his palm and says, "Where to?"

Off to the rodeo, why not, the county fair, events, and nonevents, something like a simple weekend drive out to the reservoir to cast for perch and crappies. Burgers, onion rings, and cones the way we like them, large, please, extra salt and ketchup, a double cherry twist. Lots of Country Western on the General's radio. Listen to the old man sing a lyric. Did I think he had it in him? Pop-style country, the dumb stuff with the corny rhymes, song lines written out so you could sing the chorus halfway through a first-time hearing, catchy tunes you knew you'd be ashamed to say you liked them. If you're me, you've got an extra-biggie-bacon-cheese, hot, foil turned down to the meaty grin, that moist smile saying, *Eat me.* You've got the Comet doing sixty, sixty-five, top down for the summer and the General singing, *I've got friends.* Sure, I liked it. Felt like Mike and I and being winged at the pits. Felt like shouting clear, like shouting contact, like blubbering your lips to make the prop sound; felt like leap, like lift; felt again like this must be the man my mother married. There we went down Aviator Way, home of the General's Pitts, home, I was to learn, of a guy named Hal, a name I liked. The General's Mike, he was a kindred spirit, "great guy," the General said, another man whose holy moments came by working over vintage aircraft in a vaulted hangar, flying loops and rolls through radio-free zeniths of uncontrolled airspace. There were lots of them. Franks, excellent Jacks and Hanks and Bills, Mike-like guys the General said it was "high time" I should meet.

"This is my boy," the General said.

I stuck my cast out, offered up my greasy fingers.

"He plays ball," the General said. "You maybe read about him in the paper. Broke those arms diving on the floor. Fella fell on him must have gone two, two-fifty."

Yes, sir, these were men who looked at life in terms of where the wings fit. Ball, they seemed to say, you play it on a court? Basketball, a ground game? We stood together in threesomes of greeting, and by-and-by you saw a fellow's face saying he wasn't seeing you or any kind of ball at all but depths and heights of sky. What machine will fly it? What shapes of flight might be inscribed there? I followed. I listened. I was a guest, a possible initiate to a secret league of men on furlough from the wife and kiddies for the weekend. Except for Hal, who never had a wife or kid. Hal lived there. In his hangar.

"Super guy," the General said. "You'll like him."

One look into Hal's place and you saw his difference. Two, three, four looks and you saw his difference deepen. Hal's was done up right, righter even than the General's. Fuller, anyway, less stripped. He really lived there, Hal did, you walked around his hangar the way you would a house, reading personality through plants and chairs and bookshelves. His house was a museum of all the things he said had led him into flight. His first rod and reel, model no. 801, by Zebco. A bat rack for the twenty-eight-ounce Louisville Slugger, a homebuilt, lacquered stand to hold home run ball number one. Hal's Harley. Hal's old-guy Golden Wing. Pictures, too. Hal, the Eagle Scout. Hal, the winner of the pinewood derby. A toothless Hal, gaping with a toothless Felix, Hal's best friend, said Hal, a boy who never flew at all, but fought by foot, stepped on a mine, and came home in a body bag at twenty.

"Make yourself at home," Hal said. "Go ahead and touch."

You saw that not much here was not touched, and retouched, buffed up to a Sunday shine. The General walked me over to a '57 Thunderbird, had me sit down in the driver's side and tell him what I thought. Very cherry. Healthy-looking woodwork, scent of Murphy Oil Soap, softer-than-Italian leather, gleam of chrome, simple lines, and sense of last-stand, post-war pride. The General shut the door and the heavy swing and the tumbler clicks and sucking rubber hush all made a sound that said, *We won*. When you passed from all those other hangars into Hal's, you passed from a display of someone's earliest and one desire in life, to someone's life as all desires.

Hal's desire in wings showed up in a barn-red tail dragger, a crop duster, "A hoot," said Hal, "don't fly her all too much, except for laying down the fog on spuds and melons."

What I liked? I liked it that the General, not Hal, told me Hal flew choppers in the war. I liked that the General could tell about his missions and not have Hal remind the General he never flew them. Best I liked the loft Hal built where you could climb a ladder to a walled-in space that had a bedroom and a living room and a kitchen.

"Help yourself," says Hal, and there was a man who noticed enough of what you ate to double up for you on what you'd eaten for the next time.

All in all, there were next-times enough for me to change my taste in Hal's supplies from tinned Vienna sausages, to spreadable cheddar, to frozen egg rolls and the microwaveable burritos. I could thaw, heat, and eat in under seven minutes, unmolested by the Lord, or my mother's escalating need to tell me, on the Lord's behalf, that I was welcome. Okay for the General and Hal that I should disappear from them, lie down on the couch upstairs and rest a bowl of chili on my belly, snooze, watch a little tube, practice tracking planes and raptors with the telescope that faced the runway from a man-sized picture window.

After food, the telescope at Hal's was my favorite feature of his place. Took skill. Especially with casts. You focus once, leave the focus be, screw the whole shebang down tight there on the tripod, and still I guess a wind blows up, a teeny, tiny tremor sends up from the spinning earth, and the part of the world you thought you'd focused in on is a blur.

"That lens is true," said Hal, "and what it says is that the world is never sitting still. You want to see out past your eyes, you have to learn to work that scope, you've got to jump where the world jumps."

Where, he said, and how. How the world jumped, it didn't show its seams. Trick to jumping with the world was learning how to keep yourself in seamless focus. I learned. While the General and Hal were talking engines, I was focusing on stop signs; while they whistled over women, I was tracking beetles. I got to where I could follow a plane around the traffic pattern, no problem. The General and Hal took off for fly-in brunches, club stuff where the talk was total wings and mostly vintage, and there I sat back at Hal's hangar, watched them through the telescope, saw each man taxi out and lift off from the runway in his single-seater passion. Poor Adam, daydreaming of plate-sized cinnamon buns, scratching with a butter knife at the gaps in his casts, catching flakes of skin he folds up in a paper picnic napkin while he waits to hear about what all he hasn't eaten. Except I never heard. I watched the General and Hal approach at 0100, spot-on with their flight plan, held them through their finals, sat and waited in the loft for news of food—something Spam and eggs, country biscuits floating in a boat of sausage gravy—but only heard of airplanes.

Flight and flight. Formation flight. Communication, cockpit to cockpit, without the aid of radio transmissions. World War II club. World War I. Club whose membership required the fabric wings and handstart prop, a machine that conjured scenes of smiling pilots with their thumbs held up, goggles down to holler clear and contact. Was that for the General and Hal? Would they really like to own that house-and-hangar combo on a private PGA designer golf course? Myself, I stuck to the scope. I practiced seamlessness. I could move with the soaring birds, sometimes even hold the flitty little sagebrush birds for decent viewing. By the time the casts came off, I could work the scope and listen to their conversation both. Soon also I could listen, talk, and eat. I set myself up behind the scope and held the General in his Pitts, ate my grilled cheese while I called his stunts for an imaginary grandstand. Times he stayed behind, I co-called with Hal. We held our hot dogs upright like a microphone and spoke into the mustard and the relish.

I said, "We want to thank you folks for coming out today. Not a bad seat under the sun, we think you'll agree. Winds aloft are blowing fifteen knots, we've got eleven miles of viz, refreshments off the east end of the runway, General Homer Oney flying his amazing, death-defying Pitts. Now, Hal, tell us what we can expect today from the General's program."

"Well, Adam, as you know, the General is a fearless flyer. There's no gainsaying the courage of the man behind that stick. General Oney wears that aircraft like a second skin. I think with him you've got a pilot more bird than man. I don't know the details of this program, but I don't foresee a lot of slack between the aerobatics. With Oney out there, you have got a flyer who is all-out stunt."

"Thank you, Hal, and with your permission, I think I'm going to sign off now and eat this dog."

Happened pretty often the General flew and left us at the scope like that. Often enough, at least, so a person might believe I ought to know as much about the General's Hal as I know about Mike. Which it turns out wasn't knowing much beyond a feel. I felt I liked him. *I like you, Hal. I like you, too, Adam, you're all right, pal, let's play ball.* I asked the question once about Hal's wartime flying and the answer wasn't any news. He didn't want to go. No idea what he was doing there except somebody called his number. Whole damn thing was dumb. After Felix, Hal figured he would rather be shot down from the sky than blown up by a land mine.

"Agonies of Mimosas," he said. "That's a poem. Ever see a mimosa in bloom? Ask your old man, they've got them thick where he's from. Poem says why the war, you know, like it's enough to die in agonies of mimosas. Always figured I would rather go down by a beauty."

I knew that much, and not much more because I saw how Hal was not too ready with the telling. I knew that home run ball was Hal's mimosa. Hal's Ducati mimosa, his mimosa T-Bird. I knew Felix's last name was Fattaruso. PFC Felix Fattaruso.

"It's a name," said Hal, "he was living up to."

And how about Homer Oney? Air guy, a serviceman, spokesman for a war he never flew for. For Hal, I wondered, and what Hal liked, what part of the man in Homer Oney was the General living up to?

When we leave Hal's, the General talks his war talk more than ever. It's the cocktail hour, a long time since the sunrise in the General's kitchen. The General says he's felt the seconds ticking in his head as if a tiny mallet has been tapping on an open nerve, a bundle of nerves he feels as tracking backward from behind his eyes to focus on the place his skull fits to his spine there at the nape. Says sometimes he can't see straight. He might be sitting in his chair, plugged into the news, or maybe if we've fished then he is standing at the sink, forearm deep in gutmuck, asking me the time. It's 4:15, 1628, 4:40, Adam, what the hell, why don't you just mix up those martinis, it's 1657.

The fog rolls in then thick and fast and you can see the war come up inside his head and understand it really hurts him. You want to help. He needs to see. You want to feed him gin till he is clean. I wanted him to say just once okay he had never been. He never went. I learned to mix for him—gin, vermouth, cracked ice, and a splash of water—the double-cast martini. I served him, listened to the same old stories from the General's private war zone, only plus some, only minus. He was flying up the Mekong, right, laying down the napalm, blazing trail for the ground troops and the gunboats, banging on about what heavy fire dropped at Mach speed does to people living in a house of sticks and grass. I'm listening by duty, it's no fun, no game, it's a guy who tells his story who's really done the killing, seen the mothers running with their babies from his cockpit, a guy whose stories you don't want to have repeated. Smoke, he said, that's who those people were, scattered hot spots, less than dust. He said those few short years on tour were the livest of his life. Outside the cockpit, out of action, his life seemed more a dream to him than life, mild scenes of mashed potatoes and boiled meat from which he held his wakeful self remote.

The General watched the ice cubes shimmy in his glass, quieted himself in reverence to a passing Phantom. I think the less I liked his stories, the more I liked that he was ever faithful to his airship. I liked that he was also someway faithful to my mother. He sat at his box, his drink glass softening the cardboard.

"She's tough," the General told me.

Or, "She's weak."

He said, "Your mother never was too sure what all she ever wanted."

"Goddamn," says the General. "Am I right?"

I do a little KP, freshen the General's drink, settle in for the duration. The louder the General, the quieter the Adam. His voice comes on a thicker tongue; the light goes gray and grainy.

He says, "Any thinking on how long she'll keep me out here? Hell, no. She'd've thought, I never would've been here in the first place."

There he is, though. Me, too. Weekend warriors, off-season vets, men without women, ripening through another sultry Sunday evening in a marinade of alcohol and saturated fat.

"I feel good," the General said. "I'm doing what I want."

He said, "I'm the General. They don't really want me in the cockpit. We went off to war right now, I'd be grounded in command. They would keep me stateside."

He said, "Your mother ever tell you once she could have married into money? Guy sold cars. She always wanted me to go commercial. I could never go commercial. I thought to fly would be to be like birds. Bird's not a carrier, he's a flyer. He's up there doing recon, hunting. When you're a kid, bird looks like he's up there just for having kicks. We get a lot of flak from hippie activists, you know, the peace, love, and dope crowd. Say how threatening we are. Harass the cows and wildlife. But goddamn if an everyday commercial airport isn't what Americans should throw their peace and love at. Take any day you please at LAX or JFK, it's D-Day. How many thousands? Every hour? You don't know who those thousands are, what they're carrying into our country. What, they've got an uncle? A green card? It's a free country? Answer me this, who's keeping it free, baby? I've got a theory. If you want to travel, it's better anyway to drive or take a boat. Give yourself a chance to see the change in how you got there. It's weird," the General said. "Step into the tube and folks are saying bye-bye and I love you, step out of the tube and then it's gaga laga. There're mountains down there. Corn's growing. Maybe if we had to cross the ocean so we saw what's in it, we'd be better to the fishes. I'd gone commercial, I'd go crazy, wondering all those years what I had missed that came between me."

He said, "Your mother had the softest hair."

He said, "She still going to that church?"

"I used to have a mustache," said the General. "Maybe you remember that. Your mother said she didn't like it. Got into my soup and ribs. But back when we were kissing, she sure liked the way it tickled."

The General said he had to use the head. He touched his way down the hallway walls, came back out and freshened his glass and settled heavy-lidded in his chair, his drink perspiring in his hand for me to make my private bet on whether this would be the one to go unfinished. The General's face was a putty someone seemed to pull from somewhere in his head to make his mind up. Seemed this time of night to be two someones in there, each one pulling in the opposite direction. I watched the General's eyes fall shut, then open when his hand jerked so he almost spilled his drink. After that is time for him to rest his hands up on his belly. His hands slow with his breathing. Sleep soon, deep down in the fog, done in for the night.

From somewhere down and worn-out in himself he says, "You think she's ready to forgive me?"

Well, I say to myself, forgiveness is a negative, sir. The person most afflicted by betrayals of sex is the person sex could not be sold to in the first place. That's your wife, sir. She keeps me fed all right, in case you're interested. My socks are clean. Monday morning comes, and I go home to Mrs. Oney's house to find a tidied room and freshly laundered sheets. She dusts these days. In addition to going off martinis, she's gone off Winstons, cold. She herself looks ironed. She hums and sings. Hard to tell if maybe she has lost a little weight.

I tap the General on the shoulder.

I say, "Up, sir."

If he is awake and able, the General will make his way to bed. If not, his bed will be his chair. I take his shoes off. I fetch a sheet and pull it to his chin. In the morning, I find a bag of cookies he waked up enough to eat, crumbs of pecan sandies trailing down the hallway to his bedroom. I lay out a breakfast, leave a note explaining what I know about the healing possibilities in complex carbohydrates. I sign off saying the walk will do me good, and I will see him in a week.

I never left a word for the General of my mother. Partly, I suppose, because she never asked for any word of him. Seemed undignified to me. Beneath his rank, that kind of unrequited need for news. Mother did not want to know. If I tried to tell her anything about the Pitts, or the telescope at Hal's, then Mother held her hand up with her palm faced out the way the General did so he could quiet me to hear his Phantoms. Mother's Phantom was the

Lord. I never knew if that meant God, or Jesus, or both of them together, or neither but a third. I knew at least she didn't want to hear me. No surprise I didn't want to hear her, either. We understood each other. By the time the casts came off and Mr. Sun was working up some color to that mealy forearm pigment, understanding meant for me and Mother that we didn't need to talk, didn't need to see each other save to stay out of each other's way. We were see-no-evil and speak-no-evil, two monkeys with an ear out for the mysteries we felt most moved us. I spent a lot of time in my room. I came to have a regular candy shelf in there, a good selection of the salty snacks I hung up in my closet from a clothespin on a hanger. Mystery for me was how light I kept on feeling, big as I was, fat as I could see myself when I stood up on my bed to get a fuller look there in the dresser mirror. The Big Buddha. Honey Pot. Tub O' Guts. I sucked it up and let it out. Anymore, I didn't need to hunch my back to roll it. I stood up on my toes and bounced myself to make it jiggle. I counted three folds of back fat. *Adam Oney, fatty; Adam Oney, flyer.*

Mine was the mystery of the bumblebee, the fat mass hoisted on the gauzy wing, Nature breaking laws that She herself had written. I knew versions of those laws, something of the laws as I could see them through the telescope at Hal's, and then something of the laws as I was rediscovering them through the toyland relics in my bedroom. In my desk I found an unbuilt model Stuka. I pried the cap off a tube of glue and it smelled to me like Mike; I dug around and found a slip of decals and those little model paint pots, a couple of gummed-up skinny brushes. I found a Big Chief tablet and a coffee tin of broken crayons. Lots of thick-lined drawings Mike and I had made there of planes of different eras, different attitudes in battle. Tracings, then on to freehand sketches of the aircraft we had studied from a deck of spotter cards. We knew landscapes, too, desert lands and jungles and cathedrals we picked up from watching movies set about the world's great theaters of war.

Wasn't much. A drawing of a dogfight over the Rhine, a drawing Mike made of a Phantom I remember we pretended was the General. I found *First Flight.* Very often *First Flight* came to bed with me. I thumbed through Orville and Wilbur at the drafting table, scratching their caps over drawings of the Wright Flyer. I saw the cap I had given Orville from Ohio to Kitty Hawk was green. I saw blue dunes and a yellow sky. Crayon-colored clouds of yellow, green, and purple. I remembered anybody I was with when I was drawing. I could turn to Orville chasing after Wilbur and know I was in the kitchen with the metal chairs, the days from the table with the red Formica; I could know I was drawing mustaches on Wilbur while the General ran me through his personal narration of events as they transpired at Kitty Hawk.

Very often then I would lay my colorbook across my chest and wonder what the General might be doing. Down the hallway, I could hear my mother fussing with her sink stuff. Splashes, soaks, and rinses. Sounds of metal lids screwed off and on again to ceramic jars of healing salves and ointments. Mother slathering her neck, dabbing at the corners of her eyes; Mother saving her face from a wrinklier tomorrow. I thought the General by now must be a good way off to sleep. I hoped he was in his bed. I said what I would call a prayer for him to not be in his chair. I made a roll call of the things arranged there on my dresser, the model planes and colorbooks and whatnot.

I said, "All here, sir. All present and accounted for."

I slept. I woke. I built my Stuka. Adam Oney's convalescence, Adam Oney on the lam from the Lord, peeling glue from his fingertips, doodling in the Big Chief, filling in more realistic versions of *First Flight,* seasoning his pork roasts with the memory of burgers, shakes, and pizza. I took my clothes off, pulled a bag of Funyuns from my snack rack. I stood while I ate, rocked my head from side to side, sort of swung my hips around in slow-mo circles, figuring to burn the calories as I consumed them. One night I hauled the old pink wings out from the back of my closet, stepped up on the bed and held the wings up to my back, and made a go of simulated flight while I was finishing a Snickers. Pretty decent, I was thinking, pink wings, fine pink skin, round and pink and smooth except where I had lately gotten hairy in the privates. I stopped the flight so I could have a clearer look. I listened to myself. I asked myself, *Well, goddamn, Adam, look at you, what all are you saying?*

If I hadn't felt so high right then, I could have been real low. Anybody watching through my bedroom window would have said what that boy requires is a good stiff dose of concrete living. Somebody give him a barbell, something smutty he can keep in his sock drawer, someone take him out with Hector to the Villa Joy and get him laid. Seems the General must have watched through something like that window. By the last few weekends of the summer he was telling me at least that he was worried.

"Not worried so I'm scared," he said. "I've just been thinking it's high time you broaden your horizons."

He made a joke or two about what broaden did not mean in terms of weight, and then the Saturday before we started back in school, he showed me something of what broaden did mean. We drove out to the hangars, a top-down, end-of-summer, cooling day, climbed the steps to see Hal where he was washing dishes in his loft for what I thought would be another round of our traditionally unbroadening conversation. Their conversation, my listening, or not, but working on my focus. But then the General said for me to sit and join them. He pushed a magazine across the coffee table, had me looking at a glossy advertisement of an airplane he had circled there in Magic Marker. He pushed a couple of Polaroids of the same plane across the table and asked me what I thought.

He and Hal sat back and held their hands behind their heads, stuck their chins and chests out like to say they'd built the world's first fence that told a fellow which side he was standing on. I could see them over there, through that fence, the question in their chins and chests, you know, *What say ye, Wilbur? For, or agin? Have ye not been born a flyer?*

The General said, "You know what this means?"

"We're going to buy a plane?" I said.

"Bought one," said Hal.

"Partners," said the General. "She's a Cessna. She's a get about, a starter."

"A starter?" I said.

"To learn on," said the General.

"Or just toodle," said Hal. "Take us all together out to breakfast."

"Idea," said the General, "is that we could rent it out for folks who wanted lessons. Plenty of instructors out there would be happy to lease."

"Me," said Hal.

"How about it?" said the General. "This time next year, you could be a licensed pilot."

I held the Polaroids at different angles to myself and shook my head and blew my breath out in a toothy whistle meant to demonstrate my grateful unbelief. But what I really thought was that this Cessna rig looked pretty shabby. Bigger than the General's Pitts, longer and wider, but also lighter looking, like maybe it was built of thinner metal, fewer rivets. Felt scary looking. Felt like Adam Oney's dreams come true too soon. Plus which, it was yellow. Canary yellow, butterfly yellow. Except not living yellow, no sir, yellow more like how the feather the cat picked over from the meat looks, more like how the powder from the wing looks on your finger.

That's the broadening I am shown on Saturday. Sunday morning comes and I expect the General to pick up where he left off with the Cessna, the eighth or ninth martini place, where the Cessna has become a fighter you

can fly by where you point your eyes, a mating of a man's machine and his
volition. But the General's fog lifts over simple coffee, eggs, and bacon, and
I see the mission for the day is nothing doing with a Cessna. The General's
broadening of Adam Oney on this day is sex. Real sex. Live girl sex.

The General said, "Today we're going to get you a proper bed."

By proper he meant bigger. Queen.

"Takes some room to romp," the General said. "You need to romp. Big
as you are, you might find that with a frisky girl you'll need a king."

I told the General he might be premature with me; his apartment wasn't
big enough to fit a king, and no way would a bed at Mother's house be any
place for romping. We weren't really talking, though. That I should let the
General buy a bed for me was an explicit order.

"Soon enough," he said, "you'll be swinging up in my league."

We drove. Ought to have been a lark, I thought, all that talk about romping and swinging, but the way the General worked his Winston seemed to
me to be at odds with the ease of our mission; something going on behind
those aviator lenses was decidedly unlarklike.

I said, "What's the hurry?"

"What hurry?" said the General.

"A mattress. Why today?"

"Well, it's time," the General said. "We're here together, right? You must
be what, sixteen now? I figured you were due. Might be something of a back-
to-school sale going on."

"Fifteen," I said.

"What's that?"

"Fifteen. I'm fifteen. I'll be sixteen in a couple months."

"Of course you will," the General said. "That's why I think we should
take advantage of that sale."

Except there wasn't any sale. There was an empty parking lot, a sign on the door that said the place would not be open for another twenty minutes. At twenty-one minutes the General tried the door to the place, tried it again at twenty-two and twenty-three or so, and then at maybe twenty-five I thought it was lucky for the girl who showed up late for work she was a girl and not a boy, luckier she was a girl I saw the General thought was pretty. The girl let us in, said she would be right with us. The General had me lie down on the Velvet Dreamer while the girl went off to turn on lights and open up her register.

"Pretty little clerk," he said. "Perky little titties."

I stared up at the ceiling, wishing the General were not so loud. You get loud flying jets, I learned, because the other thing you get is deaf. The General had me on the Beautyrest and he was saying he would be away some nights, and if he knew me, if he knew anything about a healthy, strapping boy the kind like I was, well, let's just say he was springing for the pillow top because he wanted me to keep mine out of *his* bed.

"Deal?" he said.

The General gave me a hand up off the mattress, put his arm around my back and held my shoulder, leaned his head to mine so I was thinking next he might go on and punch me in the ribs to show what pals we were. We came upon the girl where she was squatting out of sight behind the counter. The General leaned across and shouted down at her.

"I am General Oney," said the General. "And this here is my son, Adam."

Famous as the General told the girl I was, she did not know me. She did not know the General. She said cash or charge and would we take the mattress now or did we want to make a date to have it be delivered. Delivered? No, no, the General was saying, we would move that mattress and the box springs by ourselves, despite my withered arms, the obvious inadequacies of the General's Comet. The General asked for rope, twine, string, dental floss, hell, he said, if you knew the knots and where to tie them, you could hang a hippo from a hank of thread. How manly, was the big idea, how heroic. But that's not the girl's thinking, because the girl isn't even watching.

With the top down, and the Country Western playing all the General's favorites, I could pretty well forget how silly we must look, packing that big Velvet Dreamer on our backs, making lefts and rights with no apparent sense of destination. But by-and-by I saw the General had plenty of sense. He had a time, too, judging by how often he would roll his wrist up on the wheel to check his watch. I watched for other signs of mission, saw him light up, fix the cap on his head, look out searchingly through every quadrant of his clock.

"Okay," I said, "what's up? Where we headed?"

"You don't know?" the General said. "We're almost there. Run your numbers back from ten."

I counted back to five and guessed our target by the steeple. I counted four, three, two as we came full around the corner for the church. Mother's church, and Mike's, where their entire congregation gathered on the lawn to hear the General's gentle toot, to look up from their handshakes and their hushed words and wave to us in passing. Mike waved, Mrs. R, Mother and the Reverend, all the principals I had my eye on, and me, too, I waved, after they waved; seemed to me as if the General's toot had rallied us beyond our private grievances to almost neurological observances of His more neighborly commandments. *Peace be with you. And also with you.* And then we're past, and then it's over. A gutsy stunt, I thought, though nowhere near so gutsy as what followed. Meaning Mother's house. The General's former house, and mine. Meaning that he meant to move that Velvet Dreamer into my room, break the truce of total separation.

"Let's move," the General said.

We got the old bed out and the new bed in, in under fifteen minutes. Another blitzkrieg, I was thinking, an allied liberation. The thing was huge, dominant, regal, my queen.

I said, "I like it."

But the General was gone. I found him in my mother's room, in her closet, holding up a pair of hangered dresses.

He said, "What are these?"

"Dresses," I said.

"I know what they are. What I want to know is, where'd they come from?"

"Stores," I said. "I can't remember which."

"You were with her?"

"Long time ago," I said. "Years, even."

"Have you ever seen her wear them?"

"No, sir. Last I'd seen, they were all still in the boxes."

The General hung the dresses up and moved to Mother's dresser drawers and went through Mother's underthings with something of the same surprise as he had gone through Mother's closet. He said *damn* a lot, and *goddamn*, and *for shit's sake, will you look at this?* He worked quickly, clearly looking for something other than what he was finding, though when he must have figured he was up on time, I saw the General stuff a pair of Mother's underpants in his pocket.

We went back to my room, had a satisfying look, and then the General plucked a bag of Bugles from my snack rack. He opened them, sampled a few, gave the bag to me.

"On the house," he said, and left.

I took the Bugles out, sat and ate them on the porch, watched the General wheel away, and wondered why he didn't take me with him. Sunday was our day. Had it not been for the bed and for the Cessna, I might have felt the General was a traitor. I polished off the Bugles, fetched a bag of Cheetos to the porch to help me ponder the General's motives. I didn't get too far with motives though, because here came Mother home from church a little early with the Reverend.

They came rolling down our lane, the Reverend at the wheel, and my first fear was conversion. They had seen me with that mattress, the entire congregation on their gentle lawn, they were witness, that was Satan Adam Oney was possessed by; they had finally sent the big gun in to save me. Or not. Because my second, more sustaining fear was something must be wrong with Mother. Why else would she let the Reverend drive? How come Mother couldn't stand up all alone but needed the Reverend to support her? And more, and different, how come I didn't notice Mother's dress? The General and I, we must have seen that dress when we drove by the church, yet neither one of us remarked it. Neither its newness, nor how sexily she filled it. Strongly, too. She was out now, a power in the world. The way she walked, the way that dress was cut, I had to confess the Lord could really work a wonder in a woman's bosom. Drawn up, I would say, lifted; that's not straps and underwires working there, I thought, that is light, love, inspiration, hallelujah!

They came up close and I could see in fact it wasn't Mother leaning on the Reverend at all, but the Reverend leaning on my mother. Mother had a whole half-head on him for height, was wider through the shoulders, had a wholesomer appearance to her cheek. I couldn't blame the Reverend, his petting my mother on the arm there where she held onto his elbow. We said our hellos and then my mother bumped the Reverend in the ribs and said, "Well, tell him."

I got ready to receive the high word from the Reverend then about the General and my new big Velvet Dreamer, a sermonic pitch to draw me to His flock, I thought, but when the Reverend opened his mouth it seemed to be from need of air and not for speaking. Open and closed, like a fish on a bank, sunstruck and clammy, God's less lucky creature in the world, looked like, too far from his native waters to appreciate how near he was to drying up and dying. Mother stopped his hand from petting her.

"Listen," Mother said. "This is important, Adam. I am leaving. Your father is giving me a divorce. Uncontested. I'm going back to Texas, Adam. We think custody should be entirely up to you. I'll be leaving in a month. I want you to know you are more than welcome to join me. Of course, if you decide to stay with your father, I'm leaving him the house, you see. I'm leaving. You're welcome, I'm saying. It's a good school there in Texas. Christian school. More football, more baseball than basketball. You could star there. Of course, I'll understand if you don't. If you want to stay, I mean. Of course, I won't have that red convertible to drive. I can't guarantee you'll fly."

I sucked the gritty cheese stuff from my fingers. The Reverend squeezed my mother's arm so she would look at him, I guess, to see him nodding God's approval. I was old enough not to have been surprised. Still, I was surprised.

I said, "Okay. I get it. But what's he doing here?"

The Reverend straightened up and held his chin out so he was looking down his nose the way I thought he must if he was at his pulpit.

"Him?" my mother said. "Reverend Marsh? Reverend Marsh is taking me to Texas."

BEST TO DONATE STRAIGHT OFF FROM YOURSELF. BETTER TAKE, LOWER RISK of sepsis, the inevitable rejection. Makes sense, they tell you, doesn't it? Harder to reject what is yours than what is mine? My skin is pinkish. Mine is more a yellow. Mine is olive, grayish, brownish, heavy cream. Of course, maybe you have not got healthy hide enough to make yourself your own donation. Well, good luck, you can grow some in a dish! If you've got a month to wait, you can grow the skin from one square inch to cover two entire football fields. And if you haven't got the month, well, good luck again, they can patch you with a pig's skin. Skin of a fetus, skin of the deceased. They keep banks of skin. Sheets of skin, HIV- and hepatitis-free, maybe not your color, not your texture, but it's clean, certified, temporary—stuff will shed, slough off, good news, right?—just a way to keep you closed up till you've healed enough to take your own skin, simple. Called an allograft, coming from the bank and from the pig; coming from yourself it's called an auto.

"We've got to close you up, Adam. There're bad bugs in the air, you don't want them in your bloodstream. With you, we've got some options. The insides of your thighs are viable. We could take from your scalp. I should caution you, though, that even with the autograft, the patient sometimes will encounter complications due to an infection. You're lucky, son. You're strong. We think you'll do fine."

They wheeled me to the bright room. A lady nurse said breathe into this mask. Deep breaths, deep and easy, she was saying, she would count, and before she counted to ten, I could expect to be asleep. While I slept they peeled me. Partial-dermis swatches roughly one-inch square. They notched the swatches in a mesh so they could stretch them, give the body fluids, and the blood a place to drain. They went at the wound, excised down to fat, excised down to fascia, beneath the fat, right down to the tough stuff covering the muscle, cleaning up. Now take those swatches, stretch and stitch and staple them across where they have cleaned, and when Adam Oney wakes up in recovery, he has got himself a graft.

"Congratulations," Sue was saying. "They think two more of these and you'll be patched."

I blinked up at Sue through IV lines and grog and screaming needle pain behind the eyeballs. Big thirst, a brand-new version of the please-God feeling that where I was waking up was not the place I dreamed I would wake in. I felt the pull between my legs, recalling that where I had given up the skin would feel a whole lot like the place where it was given up to. I sucked shaved ice, watched the vital goops drip into me and dribble out.

"Funny thing," I said, "I was dreaming of one summer back when Mike and I, we made big plans for sneaking out. Mike said there would be these coyotes in his melon patch. He always wanted to, but his mama wouldn't let him out to see, no way. I don't know, but I just had the clearest picture of me, climbing out the screen and pedaling the Lemon Peeler. It was bright, and quiet, all the stars when you rode any way at all from town. Thing was, he didn't show. Coyotes did, but not Mike. I sat there on the Lemon Peeler and the things set up a racket way too close beside me. Close enough so anyway I thought I should see them, though I wasn't sorry not to. I wasn't supposed to be there. I listened to them yipping farther off and pretty soon they quit. Got real quiet again, and brighter, seemed like, from the quiet.

In that much quiet, you believed you could hear those melons being sweet. I twisted one from the vine and I can tell you I felt awful when I found out it was green. I ate it anyway; I didn't waste. Tell you something else, it wasn't bad. I almost saw my way to thinking if you took a proper pleasure, and you said a prayer of thanks, then instead of killing what you ate, you saved it. I remember that was also the year we tried our hand at retail. Set up a roadside stand. Didn't sell a single melon. I was thinking price, but Mike was thinking more location."

"I think he was right," said Sue.

"Sure, me too," I said. "Location, like the Mississippi Delta. But you know the reason he never showed that night was he got caught. Mrs. R. I spent a lot of time, still must, figuring which way to feel, thinking how much easier a life would be if you could ever not feel both, you know, lucky on the one hand you made it out that night to hear the coyotes, and lousy on the other hand you didn't have the sort of mother who would catch you."

"That's true," said Sue. "You want a Popsicle?"

"What flavor?"

"Say it and I'll tell you."

"Cherry," I said. "Red. Or if not red, then grape."

When Sue came back I said, "How come we need skin?"

"You know why," said Sue. "Skin is an organ. Biggest one in the body. You can't live without your organs."

"They're making skin, you know. Artificial."

"Naturally," said Sue. "Why not? They've also got an artificial heart."

"Would you want to live with one?"

"I would. I could live with the artificial heart. But honestly, I can't say for sure about an artificial skin."

"Because it's not exactly in the body, you think?"

"Could be."

"Because if it's an organ, your biggest one, and it's hanging out like that, then you don't want for folks to see that what your life depends on is a fake."

"I don't know," said Sue. "I think you're going either very deep or very shallow now. I think if you can keep that cherry down, then you deserve a grape."

"All right," I said, "But listen, Sue, those voices? You know I know that's only me. Myself. Myself overhearing myself. Mission I'll assign myself from here on out is how to listen."

SNOCKERED, THERE'S A WORD. MAYBE IF YOU'VE GOT YOUR ABSENT WIFE IN mind all day, viewing pictures of her kneeling at the pews to grace the Reverend's woody with a fervent hummer, then you would want to end your days a little *ripped.* Trashed, we said in school. Hammered, stupid, blotto. Twelve hours, said the General, bottle to throttle. So long as he was nodding off by eight, he'd say, then the old man would be clear the next day to be airborne. Trouble was, he wasn't getting up much anymore; it was those younger pilots now who did the General's flying.

Shitfaced. Ugly. Wasted. Not nearly so resilient.

Nights I covered him where he passed out in his chair, days I left for school before he waked up in the mornings, I would think it wasn't where he'd been that wore him out so much as where he wasn't going. Didn't go out to the Sanga anymore. Didn't golf. Didn't want to go and shop for clothes and food and lightbulbs, who could blame him?

The General gave me twenty bucks, fifty bucks, a credit card. He was maybe fifty. He could live another twenty-five years, I thought, no problem, more than all my life. I took the money laughingly, as if the General's talk of aging were a joke, and pretty soon became a regular at Buy and Bye, a market not so far from us I couldn't walk to get there. First time in, the checker said she'd heard about my mother, said she was sorry, asked me did I miss her, all of it a repetition of the drill I'd run through with the man in produce, my English teacher, even Coach Jerry. I told the checker what I told them all, which was the truth, which also was the fastest way to move us off from Mother.

"I'm fine," I said. "I like to shop. It's thanks to my mother that I get to. I know she'll be happier to be back home in Texas. Had you seen her lately, how much better she was dressing for that Reverend?"

The checker scanned my Froot Loops and my sandwich bread, held up a package of sliced American cheese.

She said, "You know, we've got Kraft brand going two-for-one today. If you want to save, at least."

I made myself a quick study. I never came to coupons, but I kept my eye out for those two-for-ones; I paid attention to the goods that weren't too shabby as generics. I liked to shop the quiet hours. I liked the old and old-ish women, the old man every now and then in tow, his hands jammed way down in his pockets, a foot dragger, sent off by the wife to aisle three to fetch a pack of Brillo pads, a plunger, and a mousetrap. These old wives, they tutored me, appeared to like the feel of talking down a little bit to someone they would need to tip their heads way back in looking up to. They held my forearms where I held my cart. Sometimes I was beckoned down to hear a whisper.

They said, "Read your labels, son."

"Trick to ripening your avocados is a paper bag."

"Might say it's less per sheet, but in the long run you'll be better off with two-ply."

Happy then to say good-bye to frozen milk, so long, day-old Wonder. Only thing I think could make me feel much better than those days I walked home with a brand-new recipe and all the fixings, was if the General would ever be as satisfied as I was when I served our dinner. Or maybe if he stopped at one or two martinis, I could have felt a little better. And if we hadn't lost our status with the sports hacks at the papers. Or if everywhere I went I didn't see the absence in my life of Mike. There they were though, loss and absence, diverging appetites, invitations life will give you to do better till you finally feel your best. Not an easy invitation to accept. One day I waked up and practiced dribbling in the driveway. One day I waked up and ironed the General's shirts. One day I waked up and just said, *fuck it.* Fuck it, fatty, who're you kidding, *flight?* Bad day, that day, thoroughly unOney. To try to make it better, I pumped up the back tire of the Lemon Peeler and I pedaled off to Mike's. I made it out as far as the near fence of his neighbor's farm before I turned around for home, coasting under noisy bursts of red-winged blackbirds, saying, *Fuck it, it's a start.*

I sat down to breakfast, poured myself a bowl of cereal and milk, unfolded to the sports page, same as always. I checked the box scores, same as always, league leaders, which records stood, which had fallen; I saw we had come into the season it made sense to write about the Yankees' magic number. But no mention there of us. Last reports of us were a follow-up on my recovery, and an editorial debating strategies for greater boating safety in the wake of water enthusiasts who almost tore off Hector's arm at the shoulder in an accident involving alcohol and teens. *Significant,* the doctors said, *though not irreversible nerve damage.* Doctors said a youth of Hector's physical description and desire could be back by spring, summer league by latest. Still, the sports hacks took no chances. In addition to Hector, there was the problem of my getting fat. And fatter. I had personal problems. Word was Mike was finished playing. There were Chester still, and Lester, and Arturo made a solid, handsome three, though no word in the news for us like cleaning any clocks.

What word could there be? As far as I knew, no two of us had come together on a court all summer. Science might have claimed the Oolags from our starting five; Arturo might have finally moved down south to flee the gringo winters. None of us had heard of Hector's wreck until we read it in the paper. We surprised ourselves, I think, had never felt how fast an interruption from our single-minded play could make the time pass. Season is over, school is out, you get a job, sit a tractor, pack your mother up for Texas, help your old man out of your house and back, and when you see your team again you're saying, *Man, I can't believe we let it go so long, or maybe I was thinking you would call me . . .*

I paged through the sports and business to the classifieds, thinking *simplify,* until I saw the ad for help at Cecarelli's. I tried not to pick the phone right up. I left a bowl and spoon out for the General, started him a pot of coffee, loaded up my backpack with the algebra and Shakespeare. I made off for school. I saw a bus drive past, another bus, a bunch of other kids whose parents dropped them off in wagons. A lot of those kids knew me, or thought they did, and maybe asked themselves was that guy who I think it is, can't be, can it, that fatso, Adam Oney? I heard the bell ring saying I was tardy. So mark me tardy. Better yet, go ahead and mark me gone.

Myself, I had some real thinking to do. I walked on to the Buy and Bye to fix myself with some provisions. Box of powdered donuts, pull tab can of tuna, and a loaf of seedless rye. I sat down on a sunny bench in the towny part of town and ate a donut. According to the bank clock, a qualified buyer could find himself in a thirty-year, fixed-rate mortgage at 7 and 3/4 percent. That's a lot of interest, I was thinking, compounded. More than most had in this place. From the base to the pits, from the gully to the melon patch, if it's for sale, there are not too many takers. Passers-through, right, leasers and renters, shallow-rooted folks, blown scattered on the winter winds, gone off in their U-Hauls with the tumbling, tumbling weed. I got up and walked through empty lots of primo real estate, speculated on pedestrians. This guy with the tie and belly, I thought he might be going to a coast out west to ride his surfboard for a fawning blonde; this older one I featured packing up the clubs to play the courses down in Tucson. Road maps on the faces of the folks I passed, geographies and travelogues, heads of graying globes.

Clear enough to me I wasn't going anywhere. Or, I wanted to go back. Back to the brothers Wright. Simplify, that's what I wanted to do, but life seemed not to want it. A life must need to be historical. Historically complicated. The longer you lived, the more you understood how much you owed to complications dating back before you started living. Says Mrs. R, *It's complicated, Adam. Mike's daddy, how he feels about the service, he's a complicated man.* Throw in Mother running off with the Reverend, and there you have a whole new book of sin and complication for Mike's folks to read him saying why he could not see me. *Move on, that's life, Oney, it's in the wind there if you listen, move on, lighten up now, get a job.*

I made myself two tuna sandwiches and started hoofing it for Mr. C's. I was the man. When I walked in, I saw this scrawny kid with unburst whiteheads on his chin applying for the job, and the way Mr. Cecarelli looked from him to me I knew the job was mine. Made me feel bad for the kid, who likely had some hours at a kitchen sink, maybe even picked those whiteheads up from slinging meat and pulling spuds from greasy cooktops and fryolators. I said hey to the kid when he came up my way and the kid said hey and asked me was I Adam Oney.

"Sure am," I said.

"Well, good luck," said the kid, "you'll need it."

I watched the kid go out the door and light a cigarette, look up the road and down it, a boy who all his life might look up and down a road before he set off for a place he had no call to get to. I was moving to the door to wish my good luck back at him, when Mr. Cecarelli took me by the shoulder.

"Hey, Adam," he was saying, "how come you're not in school?"

I saw him wipe his hands off on his apron, palms first, then finger by finger, a thoroughly efficient gesture, I was thinking, the reflex of a man who made his way in life through food.

"I don't know," I said. "I was going there, and then I ended up not going."

"That's not my question," said Mr. C. "My question is how come."

I said, "What?"

He said, "Why? I said, Why not school? Why here?"

I followed him back to the kitchen where he started rolling out a ball of dough on a wooden board. He tossed it, spun it up and caught it and retossed it into a doughy disc, sized small. I watched him brush the sauce, layer the pepperoni, sprinkle on the whole-milk mozzarella. He could do that, I was thinking, without looking.

He said, "Mind if I ask you a personal question? When's the last time you played ball?"

"While ago," I said. "Sort of shot around the other day."

"But ran, I mean, full court. I'd say you look pretty out of shape. Like if I was me, I'd run on you."

Mr. Cecarelli opened up the oven door so I could see inside to the revolving racks. He shoveled up the pizza, slipped it on a rack, and closed the oven door without ever stopping watching me or talking.

I said, "How come that rack revolves? Supposed to be brick, right? Brick-oven pizza?"

Mr. Cecarelli snapped the cellophane across a tin of peppers.

"Supposed to be in school," he said, "right? A student? Look, kid, I felt terrible about your mother. Seems to me there's a very smart lady who made a very dumb decision. She's not alone, though. Lots of kids have lots of moms and dads who are making very dumb decisions. You're not helping yourself, dropping out. Are you dropping out?"

"No, sir," I said. "I'm not dropping out."

"Because you're not helping me, either, you know, dropping out. Because you do, am I right, that's why you came in, you want to work here?"

"Yes, sir," I said. "I do."

"So listen, then. You drop out—"

"I'm not dropping out."

"I heard that. Listen, I'm just saying, this job is after school and weekends. Understand? I'm saying, if you drop out, then you're not playing ball. You're not playing ball, your team doesn't win. Your team doesn't win, the fans don't come in here for pizza. It's a climate deal. Like economics. A lot depends on the mood of the nation. Around here, pizza is the nation's *up* food. Get it? It's a victory food. What you've got when you lose is a depression. A recession, anyway. I've always got the birthdays, but when you all are winning, then I've got a bleacherful of birthdays, twice a week."

Mr. Cecarelli opened up the oven door, shoveled out the pizza onto the countertop between us.

I said, "Are you saying I've got the job?"

"I am."

"What about flying? I'm due to take lessons. That makes flying I'll be doing, plus school, plus also basketball, and work. Some kids can't keep up with just their studies."

"I don't think you're some kids."

"Still, sounds like an awful lot of work."

"No worse creature in the world than a human being out of work," said Mr. Cecarelli. "Let's just try it out, see how well it fits you."

"One thing," I said. "Is this pizza here for me?"

Mr. Cecarelli rocked the big blade back and forth and cut the pie up into slices. He handed me a slice and picked a slice up for himself.

He said, "For us."

I made off for home, cruising at an altitude of thirty-thousand feet. Five,

six miles high, in and out of Mach speeds, banking hard to a two-twenty heading, south-southwest—that's final, our driveway—where I saw the General in
the front yard on his knees again, filling in and troweling mud across my
mother's planters. I came stomping in, breathing hard and wheezy, hands
on the knees, a show by which I meant to let the General know I was way too
taxed to help him. But he didn't ask for help, only asked why I was home.

"It's not time," he said. "What have you been doing?"

"Well, sir, I skipped. Truth is, I got to thinking, and I went and got a
job."

"You got what?" the General said.

"A job," I said. "Making pies at Mr. C's."

"No," the General said. "I heard the job part. It's the first part I don't
think I heard. You say you got to *thinking*?"

"That's right, sir, I thought—"

"That's enough," said the General. "I don't want to know what you
thought. I want to know what you're thinking with. Your belly? Your peter?
You're what, sixteen?"

"Almost, sir."

"Well, that's Boudreaux thinking, a job. You're not wanting. I was wanting. Pizza? That's not Oney. Oney is Oney. Oney is a flyer. Do you read
me?"

"Yes, sir."

"So I'll drive you right back down and you can tell that Mr. Cecarelli
thanks for the offer, but you have got to focus on the flying."

"With all due respect, sir, I can't."

"Can't?"

"I think I can do both. Fly and work. Mr. Cecarelli thinks so also. He said
I might surprise myself. Our deal was to give it a try, at least, and if it's too
much, I quit."

The General bent to smoothing the ripples. Then he stuck his hand into the mud just like a kid to leave a print. He asked me did I want to, too.

"We could get a stick and write our names in," he said.

I got up and pressed my hand into the mud beside the General's hand and was surprised to see mine was bigger by a knuckle. I think that print surprised him, too. He stood up, as if to see what hand size had to do with us by height. He was taller yet, and looked to be relieved, though I think he wished he could smooth us out there in the mud; I know he didn't look around too hard to find that stick to write our names in.

He said, "Listen, now, it's early. You hose this barrow out while I clean up. I've got something I believe it's time I show you."

The way he put his foot down on the highway, I thought the General was afraid he was maybe late in showing me whatever he had to show; the way the fabric in the Comet flapped and strained and swelled at the clasps, I thought if the General drove much faster he would float us. I felt floated, anyway, dizzied by the prospect of responsibility.

"You're taking on a load, mister. You feel those first few shudders, that means you're headed for a stall."

We slowed up off the highway, made it onto Aviator Way, off Aviator to the General's hangar. The General rolled the door back, kept an eye on me as if to gauge what I was feeling when I saw the yellow Cessna.

"Go ahead," the General said. "Don't be shy. She's all yours."

Mine, he meant, and his and Hal's to share. We were official now, he said, partners. Cessna Yankee Hotel Foxtrot. She made her way to us from the catalogue, across the wide Sierras, and had waited in the hangar while we moved my mother out, moved the General in, the General thinking there would come a better time for her to meet me.

"You can touch," he said. "Go on."

I stood at the door. I was thinking 0600 reveille, breakfast for the General, finish up the homework, hurry off to school, to class, to basketball, to shop, to cook, to job.

"No?" the General said. "Well, come on then. Let's go meet your teacher."

Took six weeks for me with Hal to fly twelve hours, twelve hours for him to see I was ready to go solo. Through that time I also got back to the courts, ran some with the boys. Lester, anyway, and Chester and Arturo. Played, anyway, if not exactly ran. We worked half-court, mostly, hoping to discover something other than my height and weight to keep us winning. We made it down to the old blacktop courts from the Ms. Santoro days, where Arturo practiced passing into the key to me from unfamiliar zones at widely ranging angles. I moved from side to side in the box, kept my hand up for the ball the way Arturo told me.

He said, "You keep moving, keep your hand up, and I'll find you open."

He threw me the lob. He fed me the bounce pass with the top-right English, zipped the chest-high bullet through the lane. Chester had me play behind him so he could show me how to use my lower body in the post. Hector showed up with his shoulder in a sling and said I had grown to be a natural.

He said, "You just stick it in there with your big fat ass. Keep that thing between your man and the ball, there's no way he's going to block you."

One idea was to teach me. Another was to see me sweat. Harder for me to lose than we had thought. Needed a regimen. With the Oolags pitching in their knowledge of nutrition, and Arturo drawing up my workouts, we needed only Hector to direct. Hector the Director. His first idea for me was to make up names for fat I wouldn't want somebody else to call me.

"It's lousy being fat," he said. "Get it? You are fat. You're not Adam anymore, no more Wilbur or whatever, either. You see yourself in the mirror, or even just think of yourself, think, Fat. Hey, Fat. Or, hey, Fatty. If you need help with names, you just call me, hear?"

I came up with Fattypants. Porkpie, Butterball, Lardass, Blubberbutt. Pudge, Lump, Slab. Doughboy, Blimp, Blob, Spud. In the end the best, or least I liked was plain old Fat. Most anything other seemed to me to work some kind of charm. Fat, I told myself. I am Fat. Fat. Would it be nice to meet me? No, I told myself, it wouldn't. That body in the glass there wasn't mine, I said. I would work it off me. I would starve it. I dressed out in heavy sweats and ran Arturo's after-practice laps. I took the General's twenties, walked the supermarket aisles and crossed off fiber-diet foodstuffs from shopping lists concocted by the Oolags. Bran flakes, bran muffins, bran mash, All-Bran. Branorama. Branorific. Brantastic. I made some new old friends by listening through their testimonials relating weight loss to prune juice and dried fruit.

"The grapefruit has fewer calories than the body burns up to digest it," Chester said. "The key to loss is process. Basically, you want to avoid foods that stick."

Hector brought the magazines with articles that told me how. Those slicks of skinny girls in sexy underwear, January swimsuit spreads, photos documenting sad Befores and happy Afters, first-person tributes to diet plans and exercise and to the power of prayer and to the loved ones who were there for them through fear and doubt and guilt and through the shaky days of their initial triumphs. At first I thought I was supposed to sympathize, identify with the sad Befores, but Hector pointed out the real idea was to get myself in shape to fuck the happy Afters.

"Face it, Fat," said Hector, "you're pretty much unfuckable."

I made Hector a grilled cheese sandwich, fixed myself a dry, open-faced sandwich of cucumbers and sprouts. Hector wetted his thumb, turned the perfumed pages, cutting out the pictures of the girls he called Most Cosmo.

These he taped over the photos of NBA greats appearing in the calendar Arturo gave me to keep a record of my calories and weight.

Hector said, "Just think. By March you could be prime to cork the likes of this babe."

We watched my calendar, and by the calendar we saw some heavy losses in the early days from Fat, all right; I saw my grades come up from early morning studies, just the way I planned it; I kept the pantry full, the General fed, flew my hours with Hal and held my job down—all good—but the Cosmo babes looked less likely to cork for me the less we saw me losing as we moved up to our season.

"That's because you're converting fat to muscle," Chester said. "Muscle weighs more, it's natural."

"Also," Lester said, "the more you lose, the less you have for losing."

But I don't think we were really looking at my weight as our salvation anyway. I think when we looked each week to see how much I lost that we were saying Fat and really meaning Mike; I came to hear us urging me to be the guy to coax Mike back in honor of our team and friendship.

Hector said, "What do you think, Oney? You guys were deep into that Orville-Wilbur shit, right? How come he won't play?"

"I told you," I said. "Grades. They're gunning for a scholarship at the Academy. They say it's too much this year, him working in the fields and all."

"You work," Hector said.

"That's different."

"Different how?"

"I don't know," I said. "You want me to, I'll ask again. But if I were you all, I wouldn't bet on any different answer."

Week one, week two, Hamlet, Hester Prynne, the periodic table, a five-day leveling off of weight loss at two-forty, a jump to forty-five, and sure enough the answer I report from Mike is still the same: *No ball.* I never said much more because of course I never really asked. I didn't see him. Didn't call. I didn't and I didn't want to tell them why I didn't.

"Got to go," I said. "Off to the land of fresh-baked crust and mozzarella. Any comers?"

None came. Off the court, I think they could not keep up. I know Hector wondered how I didn't lose the pounds just from the way I moved from one thing to the other.

He said, "No kidding, Oney. I see you in the halls, see you on the courts, and then I've got my mother telling me she sees you shopping? And then you go to work? Wears me out just thinking. I did what you did, would run me down to bones."

How did I do it? Got myself up from a low B to a low A student. I could hold my altitude and execute a very pretty S turn, stall, recover, plot my way through a three-point flight plan. Cake. Fluff. I was rising to the occasion, simple, we have more in us than we think, boys, get yourself a Mr. Cecarelli and a General and you'll learn. You walk in washing dishes, and then presto change-o, you can toss and spin. Myself, I could swap out canisters of soda for the fountain, tune the ratio of syrup stuff to carbonation. I ran the register all shift and rang out even to the penny. I made up an item for the menu I thought best depicted me, as I saw myself on the court, an all-meat, pesto pizza I was calling The Enforcer. Super heavy on the flavor. Salt, garlic, and nitrates, available in large only, a mozzarella-Gorgonzola finish I thought might be advertised along the lines of thirty-two-ounce rib eyes, an appeal to the competitive spirit of eating.

Mr. Cecarelli ate it up. I mean I told him my idea, built the pizza, and we ate it.

He said, "That's fine, Adam. That's more than fine."

I stood up from our table to shut the place down, tidy the salad bar, tally the stock for orders. I was picking out the bacon bits and croutons from the Thousand Island, humming a hit from the AM band when Mr. C came up with his clipboard and his keys behind me.

"Hold on," he said.

I watched him tap his clipboard with those keys, then swing his keys around his index finger. He was thinking about me, I saw, weird, like he was just about to give me the kind of speech that starts off, *Son.*

Instead, Mr. Cecarelli asked me how it felt to be back playing ball. He asked me did I need a lift. He said he had a present for me, and on the front seat of his car I saw he had a book called *Fundamentals: The Lowdown on How to Heighten Your Game.*

"It's old," he said. "But there's some basics in the game that never change, in my opinion. I took the liberty to highlight some of the stuff on playing center."

He turned the dome light on while we were driving, told me go ahead and feast my eyes. These were pages dated by the uniforms for sure, tight shorts and the knee-high socks, the low-cut shoe a person used to call a sneaker. Guys looking too posed, too short, guys in funny looking crew cuts, guys too white to look like they could jump or be quick to put a move on.

"See there?" Mr. Cecarelli said. "Those elbows? Tell me they don't tell you to keep the elbows out like that these days. Two hands on the ball. Nobody's stripping that, boy. You can't tell me the game's evolved beyond the elbows, can you?"

"No," I said, "it's still elbows. But I think now it's more conditioning and footwork."

"Better shape, eh?"

"I think so."

"Faster?"

"Right."

"Better jumpers?"

"Yep."

Mr. Cecarelli pulled up in front of my house, the old ranch looking lower down and stripped and meaner to me when I looked at it with somebody I didn't think had ever seen it. Darkened windows, darkened porch, all vegetative life cut down to narrow strips of grass surviving through expanding pads of concrete. I kept looking at the book, letting Mr. Cecarelli talk about the game from his day.

"You want to know the truth?" he said. "There's just something un-American about basketball. Take baseball, football, those are sports invented over here the same as basketball, but they're just more American. Why should basketball not be American? Same organ, same peanuts and hot dogs, same cold beers that cost you way more than they ought to. So, why? Too perfect is why. I mean the athletes. What it doesn't do, it doesn't capture our imagination. Ever see a guy as fat as you out there? Ever see a guy can't really run? Baseball's got its fatties, and football. It's got the god-awfullest, pockmarked, broken faces. Those boys on the line, they leave their helmets on because they don't want you to see them. Notice those games, baseball and football, they're equipment games. Guy can't play the game without his pads and gloves and masks and bats. Guy can't even play baseball till he's done some time as an apprentice. Hell, he's been married into the minors so long he can't afford to ditch the homely girl he married coming out of high school. That's human. That's American. I see number 64 trying to tie his shoe over his belly, he's got me. My number, you know, *that's me*, I'm saying to myself, *I am number 64.* Who is basketball? Those guys with their lean teeth and their muscled stomachs. They play half-naked. And with what? A ball! That's it! Perfection is perfection. It doesn't need your imagination to make it any better. And I don't want to hear a word about the ghetto, either. How those boys climbed their way out of gangland and food stamps. Ghetto isn't American. Ghetto isn't anything Americans are hoping to imagine. It's Sunday afternoon, you know, it's a Saturday doubleheader; you're either cozied up in your den or outside working in your yard; you don't want any junkie's needle in your head, nobody's daddy in the slammer. Americans, they want corn, they're dreaming of that milky Swede, the beef-fed tackle they remember blocking in the Orange Bowl for the Huskers."

Mr. Cecarelli said, "And now they're palming the ball."

He said, "But that's just me."

He said, "I realize."

He looked up to the house to see the lights not on and seemed to want to say something but didn't. He turned on the radio.

The radio said, *Enter now. See sweepstakes entry forms for restrictions.*

"Must be something, though," said Mr. Cecarelli, "going solo."

"Oh, it is," I said. "Just like I told you, by yourself, up there in the clouds like that, it's the best."

I got out of the car, leaned in to say a thanks, not wanting to rehash the tale of Adam Oney's premiere solo in the little yellow Cessna. I let myself into the house, switched a porch light on so Mr. Cecarelli could appreciate my thumbs-up sign, thanks again, good night.

Not sure why, but of the life I tracked across my radar through that time, the solo flight and the retelling of its moments after was the only troubling blip. The solo flight, at least, and also nights I came back home from work and found the lights out. Mission was to see the blips, figure how to fly above or underneath them. Get those lights on, find the General in his chair, turn the TV off and clear his drink and see what our commander has found himself to eat. Nothing, turned out. Sometimes, nights like these, I had the funny sense that having eaten nothing, the General was becoming nothing, something of a ghost. I opened a can of ranch beans, put them in a pot to heat for when the General waked up later in the night and hungry to rejoin the living. I set a bowl out on the table, a bag of pecan sandies and a glass of milk. I covered him in his chair. The way he twitched, the way his head bent down into his shoulder, seemed he put a kink into his windpipe, seemed a fight for him to breathe. He gurgled. He ground his molars. He moved his mouth around enough so sometimes I could see his eyeteeth and the canines. This man got me up, I thought, he is able to be happy yet. I saw him happy the day I soloed, folks, and we have got the video to prove it.

I looked around and found the tape and plugged it in, sat down at the General's feet to watch it. Maybe thirty-seven minutes total, shot from pre-flight to tie-down. Begin with me and Hal there on the TV screen, neither one of us an actor. There we are, pop-up from the blank, Hal and I standing side by side, answering the General's questions for the record.

"Tell us your name, lieutenant," the General is saying.

"Adam," I say.

"How's that?" says the General.

"Adam Oney, sir."

"And who's this guy beside you?"

"Hal."

"How's that?"

"My instructor."

We see Hal wagging the A-OK sign.

We hear him say, "That's me."

The camera jerks away and up from us, wobbles through the sky to complement the General's commentary on the weather.

"Temperature is fifty-eight degrees," the General is saying. "Winds aloft are nil, visibility at seven miles, no ceiling."

The camera jerks back down to us where Hal has made his exit and we see me crouching underneath the wing to reach the cockpit.

"Hold on," the General says. "Any words? You're going up a student, coming down a pilot, any thoughts?"

I look down to fiddle with my jacket zipper, look up to the camera with a dumb, here-goes-nothing, good-luck-to-me-type smile, and shrug.

"Flight plan?" says the General.

"Oh, yes, sir," I say. "Two go-arounds. First go is a touch-and-go, second is a full-stop landing."

"And how about a waggle on the downwind?" says the General.

"Yes, sir," I say. "One waggle on the downwind. First go, or the second?"

"Why not both?"

"Yes, sir, then. Both it is."

I crouch. I blink. I seem a little cramped.

"Well?" the General says.

"Both," I say. "Both downwinds."

"Right," the General says. "So?"

"So what, sir?"

"So what are you waiting for, lieutenant? Show us your stuff!"

I salute and step aboard. I'm a real hulk, a visible strain on the little Cessna, hard to think this machine will lift me. There I go though, same as I had seen me go off every other time I watched this video, not entirely believing. I looked back to the General where he worked his teeth and fought for breath there in his chair, surprised some that the sound of airplane engines and his own voice rising in narration did not rouse him. Because the man was on. Since Mother left, it seemed to me the General was more and more either one of the two: On, or off. On the tape he's on. I come around to my second final and the General hasn't left much on this shoot for natural effects. It's voice. Deaf-eared, fighter-pilot voice. *Now he's flying straight and level, there's the waggle, good, hello, he's about five-hundred feet, that's traffic pattern altitude, holding, straight and level, soon he'll turn that base, good, he's turning base . . .*

I looked back again to where he slept before I muted him with the remote. I kept watching and then there I came on the second final, too high again; I flared too high, too far down the runway. I stalled, throttled up, lost more runway. We see me coming close to running out of tarmac, rolling Cessna Yankee Hotel Foxtrot through the sagebrush. I unmuted the General and heard him saying . . . *down, boy, throttle, whoa, boy, whoa, boy, whoa!* I got the cold sweat and the clammy palms to see that one played back. I watched the camera turn on Hal and *damn*, I heard the General say, *who taught him that?*

Hal makes up his finger and his thumb into a pistol he points straight back at the camera.

"That's you," Hal says. "That's the blood of the guy who flies the Pitts."

The General pans around to find me from the desert on the taxiway. You can hear it from the way he says his *I don't know* that he is smiling, hoping Hal is right. When I roll close enough to see my face, I see I am smiling, too. It's the hoo-boy smile of the survivor, the postpartum face of happiness and unsuspected grief.

"Look like you're about to cry," the General says.

"Well, I bet he damn near peed his pants," says Hal.

The tape runs on with Hal shaking my hand, offering some words we cannot really hear of his congratulations. Instead of Hal, we hear the General cussing out the flagging battery; we see a little jostling of the landscape in the picture frame, which means the General has propped the camera on the Comet so he can come around with Hal and me to have himself be pictured in the moment. I closed my eyes and let the picture in my head of us dissolve: the General, Hal, and I standing quietly beside each other, three stiffs waiting on a battery to count them out on tape. Off tape, though, is the part of that flight you'd want to see. For exuberance, I guess you'd say, the scene of so much joyful meat crammed into the cockpit, packed behind the yoke, quivering inside the yellow can for takeoff.

I turned the TV off, took off the General's boots, turned the lights out, and stood in the room with him until my eyes were better suited to the dark so I could see him.

"Good night," I said. "Thanks for the ride, sir, you really got me up there."

I went down to my room, undressed, lay down on the queen beneath my satin sheets, and asked myself, *What blip?* Today was a good day, I was thinking, I was learning the post, I invented The Enforcer, what blip? I flew. Solo. I was Big Boss in the cockpit. I spoke aloud in there, what you don't see on the tape, the same talk and the same voice I would aim into my palm in airships I commanded from the days of pure pretend. I was saying, *Flaps, check. Magnetos, check. Oil, check.* Right tank, left tank, check and check and now dial up the weather. Do a little duck and crane, a high-side windshield visual clearing of the skies, announce myself by letter and by number, Cessna Two Nine Seven Yankee Hotel Foxtrot! Give her the full throttle, maximum r.p.m., easing back the yoke for my rotation, just how Hal had taught me. Only, there's no Hal. No rubber on the pavement, no groundling sounds and drag.

What a cinch. What a snap.

I stuck to standard patterned traffic, remembered my waggle for the General, but it's nothing up there for the camera to see of Adam's hollered invitation to the foot-bound crowd to join him. Nonflyers, I was meaning, the unprivileged herd I thought must feel flight was just as near and far from them as I had. All the short length of the downwind I was shouting.

"Fuck!" I shouted. "Fuck, fahk, fahhhhk!"

Happy fucks for sure. Good luck fucks. Fucks for blue skies and zero turbulence, a long view to the pale peaks ranging better than a hundred miles away in the direction of the broad Pacific. Rain there. Snow. A gentler western slope where cattle fattened on the green March grasses and the citrus groves bore heavy fruits and it was not impossible to feature naked ladies stomping grapes in oaken hot tubs. That's what I did. I featured a fellow cracking walnuts underneath a walnut tree, three guitared señors, strumming something like flamenco for the ladies. And lookee yonder are the mythic redwoods. Hear them from the shaded forest floor, swapping yarns about the good old days when they were saplings in the time of Christ. Sunset on the wavestruck cliffs. A bottle and a wicker basket. A toast. Clam bake on the rocky beach tonight—the thirty-second proclamation from the guy on high, the flyer, Adam Oney—*yes, yes, fahk yes, yes!*

I got myself on the radio.

"Hey, you all," I squawked, "I'm flying, did you notice?"

Which is when I saw the hawk. Up there, with me, another solo flyer. He seemed surprised, I thought. Happened fast, but I thought I saw him be surprised and then a little mad to have me up there with him. And then fine. Fine like I might like to play with him. Spar. That fast, and that much I was thinking I was seeing. He banked hard, dropped hard, and was gone from me. Shut me right on down. Got real quiet in that cockpit. I was turning final, feeling way down in a brand-new, holy kind of happy, so what blip? Well, blip comes on the second go-around. Second go-around I felt the yoke weigh. I heard the engine surge and saw the bits of leg and wing and yellow smear of bugs crushed on the windshield. Second go-around felt less like flight, I guess, more like being lifted up and flown around as airborne haulage. Truth? I felt like something of a soft nut in a Coke can. When I called the crosswind turn I heard my voice shake like I had the old-guy's nervous palsy. A sick, soft nut. I was at best a pilot, not a flyer. Still a privilege, I was thinking, what is wrong here, come on now, Oney, this is coming close to God, remember?

"Most folks," said the General, "closest they will come to God is on their knees."

I remembered this, the General's saying, repeated my good fortune to myself and made my second waggle. Except I didn't see the broad Pacific on that second go-around; I flew my pattern and I knew when I turned my base I would not see that hawk. I saw a dry ground needing trees, mounting in diminished ranges back to Texas. I saw Mother, and was doubtful she was finding any God by kneeling with her bottom propped up on a Lone Star pew, her head bowed to the Reverend Marsh, infallibly intoning from the Baptist Bible. A congregation of them, kneeling in the prairie. I looked down and saw the sage, looked farther down and out and saw the irrigated acres, straw-colored stubble fields this time of year, lots of work to look at it by foot, a tiny livelihood by air where you compared it to the skin of planet Earth and saw those fields as follicles, and the cultivation of a hundred-acre melon patch as the maintenance of a single strand of hair.

A person could want better. Field dust, tractor fumes, and gopher holes. A person waked up with the sun, baked his brains beneath the sun, cocked his hat against the setting sun, and rode his tractor through till dark before he thought about his supper. Walking checks in rubber boots, moving water. Hot wind, if you're lucky. If not, a hungry swarm of Mrs. R's improbable mosquitoes. For snack: A warm cheese sandwich. For lunch: A warm cheese sandwich with a chunk of last night's meat, deviled ham, or a thick-sliced round of fried bologna. Of course, I knew some folks passed their tractors down to sons and daughters who were just as thirsty for the farm as dirt is thirsty for a drink of summer water. These were kids who ate their cheese-bologna sandwiches with milk, smiled at you through sunburned, milk-fat cheeks, told you the truck they learned to drive on was their daddy's truck, their granddad's truck before him. In a town of passers-through, the blond-haired, blue-eyed farm child was a blessed soul who might look forward to a line of blond-haired, blue-eyed sons and daughters of his own, a grandchild running at him through the stubble, the harvest's gold and purple twilight.

But he wasn't Mike. Not my Mike. My Mike didn't have a blond gene in him. Mike was passing through. He was flying. Except it wasn't Mike who was flying, it was me: *Adam Oney turning base. Cessna Two Nine Seven Yankee Hotel Foxtrot, turning final.*

Truth? I sort of blanked myself. Fuzzed my vision out of focus, rode the rudder and the yoke as lightly as I could, thinking I could maybe have that feel of flying if I gave up being a pilot. When I made my flare and saw how little runway I had left myself for rolling out, I also saw how such confusion in the air could kill you. My stomach understood, my palms understood, and my heart, and then my knees, which felt like maybe somebody from Mr. Cecarelli's stomping grounds in Jersey, some Joey or some Jimmy, some-body who knew the kneecap and the ball-peen hammer, had been working me for hours, helping me along to a confession—*I want to live, don't kill me, please, just let me keep on living.*

You look like you've been crying.

Well, you get over it. You learn to say okay already to the comforts in your life, okay I've got it good, no reason you should cry except sometimes when I'm logging solo hours in the clear blue sky I want to. I looked fine. I was fine. Go to sleep, I told myself. Have a dream. The touch is coming on that jump shot. Sleep. Sleep and dream of how to fix those blips mañana.

Next day I waked up and I was thinking, Mike. Simple. Offer him to fly. Ask the General, *How about it, sir, how 'bout let's get Mike up, too?* I got busy, brewed the joe, punched the toast, cleaned up the bean pot from the night before, buttered up a pan, and said good morning, sir, when he walked into the kitchen scratching at his armpits. I poured his coffee. He made way for me to serve his plate behind his paper. He dug in as if in need, a man who likely had forgotten he had eaten beans and cookies as an early a.m. nightcap.

He said, "You mind telling me what you're doing?"

"Nothing," I said. "Just standing here."

"That's what I mean. How come you're standing there?"

"I don't know," I said. "I guess I'm thinking pretty soon we're into winter, you know, and it's going to be hard to log the hours. Truth is, I'm wondering if maybe we can't help Mike get his license."

The General mopped his yoke up with his toast. He pushed his plate across the table, stood up, and looked to me to lighten up.

"Mike," he said. "Your friend?"

"Yes, sir, that one."

"Haven't seen him in awhile, have I?"

"No, sir, you have not."

"I've been missing him. What's he up to?"

"Work. He's working on the farm a lot, I think. And then his folks, I think they ride him pretty hard about school."

"He playing ball?"

"I believe he won't."

"Sissy stuff," the General said. "Basketball. I don't like the uniforms. Seem light, a little faggy."

"Yes, sir."

The General lit himself a Winston.

He said, "I don't see why not."

"Sir?" I said.

"I said I don't see why we couldn't help him."

"You mean it?"

"Was your idea," said the General. "You know some reason why I shouldn't?"

"No, sir," I said. "I don't believe I do."

"This is serious," the General said. "It's dangerous. Nobody needs to shoot at you to have an airplane kill you. It's a good life you boys can have. You play this right, Kirby Boudreaux isn't anyone you'll have to think about again forever."

Of course, if it weren't for the General, I wouldn't think of Kirby Boudreaux much at all. I was thinking *minutes* at the time, how long till I dialed up Mike, heard him say, *For real?* Funny thing though is I didn't call. Didn't ring Mike's doorbell, didn't hunt him down in school or in his church. Those minutes passed and pretty soon they came to being hours, days, weeks, months. Plenty of time to feature Mike and me as long, fast friends again, scenes I floated through where Mike and I flew tight formation for our fans who thought all we knew was ball. I saw us as I'd seen the General and Hal, except Mike and I were partial to a radio, we talked, we were young enough to flight that we could lose ourselves to the thrill of the speed our shadows passed en route to a pretty mediocre breakfast. On the other hand, I often saw us finished for forever. Mr. R slamming the door in my face, or worse, Mrs. R, and worst, the three of them together, standing in their doorway, telling me to clear off from their melon patch, they didn't want my charity, who did I think I was, who were they, how dare I?

In the end, I kept not daring. I walked the canned meats aisle, squeezed bread, tossed crust, studied Hester Prynne, and stepped up on the scales, afraid to think how little I might live with what I wanted, because I was afraid to ask if I might have it.

"What's going on with Mike?" the General said. "He on, or not?"

"Haven't called," I said.

"What are you waiting for?" the General said. "You want me to call him?

Talk to his old man? Now's the time, you said it yourself. You wait till winter, it'll be too late."

Yes, sir, I said, I knew what he meant. I watched the calendar come up to where you set the clock back, passed the candy out to trick-or-treaters, thinking *too late* meant *forever*; I stuffed the turkey, mashed the yams, baked a grated apple pie with lemon zest, and by the time I rendered sandwiches and soups and hashes from the carcass, I was giving thanks that *too late* was not quite yet, there was time, a couple of weeks in any case before we started in officially with tryouts. Because by then I had it in my head that Mike, if he could fly, would come back to playing ball. I thought maybe if he played, I would lose that weight, and if I lost, we would win. And if we won? Then the sports hacks would feature us as comeback kids; then every game day is a birthday in the pizza world; then we have grown up after all, Mike and I, a big dream of the brothers Wright come true, maybe buzzing low and waggling for the new kids at the pits, a thrill for one of them to chase and vow to make a large part of his lifetime.

But then the snow fell, and I myself had left off flying till the springtime, and still I hadn't called. Coach Jerry called. We came up on under a week till tryouts, and Coach's version, what he told us and the paper was the line on grades. Mike had his sights set on the Academy. He was a smart boy, they didn't have much, farming melons; the surest way for him to earn his way was making honors. But the other word, the one you could be pretty sure was coming down from Mr. R was *black*. Mike would not play ball because it was too black. No boy of his would dance a soft-shoe for a teenage desert minstrel show. Folks here wanted to see a son of his jump, wasn't going to be from any hardwood, they would have to wait and see him jump from this town straight into another. Word from Mr. R, I thought, was something of the General's word, if you wrote in *black* for *Boudreaux*, if you thought all the General and Mr. R were saying was that there were truer places for a person than the safer grounds of a familiar affection, where the crowd will clap and cheer to keep him.

Said Coach, "Boys, this leaves us with a tough road."

We agreed. Tryouts were up, and the clock, I thought, was running supersonic. Big lapse between what I would see and hear and when I understood it. Coach has got us seated in the bleachers, got his clipboard and his whistle, and I see him move his mouth and pace, but it wasn't till I walked out on the floor that I could see the speech he launched on us was aimed at Mike. The guts and whatnot we would need to win without him. How deep we would have to dig, how much we would have to suck up and the like if we wanted any shot at State. Sure we wanted to win. We expected the victory. Us, alone, though, minus Mike and Hector, we didn't run like victory. We got out on the floor and learned last year's juniors were seniors, shouldery boys who came at us to take our place as starters. They could smell us not being us. Good chemistry gone bad. We stunk. Seemed Coach Jerry might sprain his cheeks from working out that whistle. Accustomed as we were to winning, it took a beat or two before we understood that whistle was for us.

"Sanchez," Coach was shouting, "what're you doing, picking up that dribble?"

"Oolag! Oolag! You catch it that low in the post, you've got to take it to the rim!"

"Oney! Jesus, Oney, you got to at least make it from the one end before the rest are running for the other!"

By the time we finished tryouts and our squad was picked, I don't think Coach had too much left for making speeches. He read some names off his clipboard, thanked the boys who "ran real hard, showed a lot of heart" but didn't make it, told the ones of us who made it he would see us after Christmas. No ass skids in the steamy shower room, not this year, no "Feliz Navidad." When we walked past Coach's office, we could see him in there in the dark, his back to the window and his desk swiveled to the wall, puffing on his whistle so it made a squeaky sound too soft to make the little pea inside shake.

"That's trouble," said Arturo.

More trouble was me, my falling off my schooling. Fell off the diet, too. Shopped the canned fruits aisle, mixed the General's martinis, wondered how I ever found the time for flying. I blamed the dry air and the cold wind for my blurry vision, but I think really what was in my eyes was time. I could not keep up with it; I needed just another minute, please, to finish up this reading, thirty seconds more to do these dishes, just five more minutes, please, of sleep. Lot of work, speeding myself around, imagine, big as I was, I got tired. I sat at my desk to write out my exams before the break and saw my pencil tracking through a soup of sweaty socks and grated cheese; I lay down in bed at night and tried to slow the rush of bouncing balls and Cosmo babes, anything I told myself was why I couldn't find the time to think too much on Mike.

Christmas break, and without the school, without the flying, without the ball, it ought to have been a down time. But there's the General, home too much, with too little to do. Man just didn't want to see you sit; he had earned that star by giving orders. Bring him drinks, drinks, and just plain drinks, no need for the olive, though of course if we have got a can of beans somewhere around the place, he'd eat some if I opened them, and bread, white bread, if we've got it, buttered, and while I'm at it, go ahead and fry us up a steak. Mornings, for a working man, I saw he was getting maybe too good at the crosswords; evenings, come the third pass through the local news, I thought he sounded too much like the old boys at the barber shop, cussing taxes, Jews, and blacks.

He said, "I'll tell you exactly what the problem is with the economy, is wetbacks."

"Look at that," he said, "now that's a program. That's just plain folks using common sense. Nothing government about it. You see? They got those little girls to tote around a five-pound sack of flour, see how much they really want that baby."

"Let me ask you," said the General, "how they going to get off the state's tit, if they're not even speaking English?"

I sat with him sometimes and sometimes didn't, and he carried on about the same the one way as the other.

He said, "This is not the place I risked my life for."

He said, "Where the hell's that Mike?"

We put our Christmas tree up, rang the New Year in, pulled the tree back down, and took the court for our first game, and what is happening with Mike is suddenly a question with folks who never even knew him. The clock wavers, shopkeepers, the farmers, farmers' wives, and gray hairs seated in the bleachers feel they have a right to know. They named sodas after us, gave out special game-day discounts, they carried our schedules in their wallets, here they were, they'd bought their tickets, so where's Mike?

I got the start that game but didn't last. I ran fine, easy in my head, had the lope and lungs I ran on last year. Except of course this year I'm packing thirty pounds of flab, and these boys here we played against were lean, small-bodied runners, coached to press and break, get our larger-bodied version of the Huskies running in a track meet. I took myself out and sat down on the bench and hung my head, afraid for real that I might throw my lungs up. Coach called time-out with us down by eight. Had us take a look around the bleachers. Kid with a flag on a stick, woman I remembered holding last year's clock. What had they been promised? What did they remember? Lots of folks, the only stake they had in being here was us. They hadn't gone to school here. Some would move before the finish of our season. They meant to witness something rare. Us, Coach said, we were rare. Solid, deep, a team. People wanted something they could fight and scream for. Not me. Not the Oolags really or Arturo, either. There's Hector, dressed out in his street clothes, but it's not him they are looking through us to, it's Mike.

When we came out for the second half, I think the spirit in the bleachers had evolved from a confused hurt to a righteous anger. Uppity stuff. Goddamn uppity stuff. Goddamn uppity nigger stuff. These were good people, I thought, people I thought I knew. Weird to me to see how hard-about a crowd can turn when they have come to see you as a face to sell their shoes, a rubber doll with wire bones to give away with burgers. We won, though if you asked the folks there in the bleachers, I think they would have said some wins only show you how far down the road you've played to losing.

We lost one game, two games, three games in a row, and I never did call Mike.

"No panic," Coach would tell us. "Remember these teams we've been playing are out of our league. We scheduled them when we thought we had a different lineup. Not time to panic yet. Let's just hang together here and focus on conference."

But two games into conference we were lucky to have come out with a split. Won the first game on a prayer Arturo threw up at the buzzer. Second game we lost by twelve, outrun on the break at home, Coach up shouting from his seat for us to move, pick it up, for Chrissake, were we men out there or trees? From our huddles in the time-outs I could see folks weren't looking anymore for Mike. They looked at us, looked out to the doors, and they were leaving. Last two minutes of the game you might have thought were scrimmage. Quiet so you heard the shoes squeak, more volume from the ball off the dribble, less the feeling in the gym of two teams bent on winning, more the feeling of the one team having given up. Even quieter in the locker room after. I pulled my shoes off and headed to the shower and I had the definite impression I was why we weren't talking. I was the one nobody wanted to shower next to, who nobody would look at. These boys changed out fast. The last of them was gone while I stood drying off at my locker. Seemed a race we all were in except nobody told me. When I passed by Coach's office, he called me in, told me have a seat. Tough news, Coach Jerry said, didn't know how to break it, but here it was, Oney, there had been a vote, and the vote was Coach should bench me.

"They came to me last week," Coach Jerry said. "You've got a lot on your plate. I thought maybe you would be all right. But unless you make some serious changes, I can't hardly play you."

Coach read off my stats, numbers I was glad my mother wasn't there to keep: 1.6 points and 3.7 rebounds wouldn't cut it. Coach meant for me to be the guy you called a *goon*. My job was to come in and commit the hard fouls, put on the kind of hurt that *sent a message*.

"We've got to get a whole lot more aggressive," Coach said. "And you have got to lose some weight. These boys are giving up on you, Oney. Might not feel this way to you, but your best friends right now are me and Hector."

Could be true, I told myself, because except for Coach and Hector, I was being shown a lot of back. These boys don't want you at their table, I was thinking, your blue-haired lady friends are shaking their heads at your selections for the snack rack. They are pulling your schedule down around town, too, no more soda-fountain specials, the sports hacks are already writing forward to that middle-distance runner, and look at that, Arturo lost his grant, rumor is the governor this year will have his picture taken in a teepee with a Paiute. Even Mr. C had something, something hard along the lines of Coach's telling me I would be benched. Mr. C was wanting to talk hours.

"Look at this place," Mr. Cecarelli said. "It's dead. And look at you, you're talking to the cauliflower. It's not healthy. You don't look too healthy. Give yourself a break, kid, focus on the hoops. It'd do the business good. I'll pay you the same, give you back the hours at the end of the season. What I'm saying is, I'd like to cut you back by half."

I kept at my work, changed out the anchovies, wiped the hood down on the salad bar.

Mr. C said, "Really, Adam, you don't need to be here."

"But I do," I said. "I do."

But I didn't. Excepting the early family or two, a birthday in the afternoon, and the auto player on the jukebox, it had been dead for weeks. Quiet. Post-loss, locker-room quiet. Quiet so if you are Mr. Cecarelli, I supposed you could hear the food spoil, you watched your cheese and olives like your last sad dimes and nickels.

"They'll be back," I said. "If there's one thing people need, it's food. And if there's one thing people want, it's pizza. I am the Enforcer, Mr. C. Trust me."

"You're a good kid, Oney," said Mr. C. "So let's say this. Let's say you guys win tomorrow night, then you'll keep your hours. If you lose, you cut back."

So we made a deal to shake on, I went home, picked the phone up, dialed Mike. Then hung up. Then dialed again, let it ring until I heard an answer, or a question, more rightly, the plain hello of folks brought up to be hospitably polite.

"Hello?" says Mrs. R. "Hello? Who is this?"

But I hung up.

She was saying, "Hello? Yes? Who is this, please?"

And I hung up.

I held my hand down on the phone and thanked her; her voice, turned out, was all I needed, never mind what Mike might need from me. I set the General's food out. Later was the time for Mike, I told myself. I could go it on my own awhile and come back to him strong. Thank you, Mrs. R, I felt strong. Strong enough so maybe I could play the goon. Taking the legs out. Elbow to the ribs. Elbow to the ear. Goon.

I went to sleep and didn't seem to really wake up till the next night, midway through the second quarter. Decent crowd, considering, cheerleaders are swinging, we're alive, still in it, and there's Coach Jerry, looking my way.

Coach is saying, "Okay, Oney, number 26 there, watch him. Kid is killing us. You go in, and next time he comes off that pick, I want you to clothesline him. Get it? You just make like you're going for the ball, then take his head off."

I went and sat down on the floor in front of the scorer's table, waiting to go in. I knew that kid, this 26. Kid who turned his face away from the ball because he got his lips mashed once against his braces. Coach looked over my way and I thought I saw him move away from wanting me to take the kid out how he told me to. He was Jerry, remember? Sat us on the bench last year to play his seniors? What would they say in the paper now? Terrible to see a big dread on a softy's face. I thought he said, *No dirty stuff, Oney, hear? You go out and play the way you are supposed to.*

So I played it square. I ran through the transitions best I could, made myself a presence in the middle, kept a hand on my man, called and watched out for the picks, though I know a lot of what I did when I was in was wonder what that number 26's name was; I asked myself if somebody was readying to put the hurt on me, then would I know it? First time the kid scored without me flattening him I heard Coach holler something, something Oney, something else and Oney; and then the second score I'm yanked, sent down to the far end of the bench, far away from the game, where I remembered the name of the kid was Will. *Willy,* said his folks. *Go, Willy! Good job, Willy! Run,*

Willy, run! Good kid not to hurt, but boy did he hurt us. Killed us, just how Coach was saying.

After, in the locker room, I was being worse than just not talked to. Seemed to me the answer to my question whether you could feel if someone meant to put the hurt on you was *yes.* I watched out for my six o'clock. I kept the soap clear from my eyes so I wouldn't need to close them. I dressed with my back to my locker. I walked out through an empty locker room, to a nearly empty parking lot, thinking I had maybe gone a little off. Did I really think I could hurt someone? Did I think someone from our own team would be hurting me? Turns out Hector would. I was working the key in the Comet, and here I hear these footsteps running up behind me. Big, hard stride belonging to a power forward. I turned around and caught a forearm in the forehead. Knocked me down and silly. I didn't try to stand right off but sat there blinking up at Hector.

He held out his hand and said, "Get up, dope."

I let him help me up and sort of crouched in case he thought to knock me down again.

"You shit," said Hector. "I like you, Oney. You're a fat fuck, and a dope, but I like you. But I don't get you. Look at that, all you had to do was knock him down and help him up."

"But I knew that kid," I said.

"Of course you did," said Hector. "We all know them all."

"His name is Will," I said. "Church league. Back then, he couldn't dribble with his left. He had these sweats we all made fun of because we thought his mother ironed them."

"That's what I mean," said Hector.

"What do you mean, that's what you mean?"

"Jesus, Oney. I mean, the kid dribbles with his left now. I'm saying, wake up, Fat. It's not that kid back then that's killing you. I don't even think it's fat. You're soft. Softer even than fat. I don't know what to call it. Better go on home and ask yourself," he said. "Then ask yourself if whatever the hell you call it helps you."

Most nights, postgame, I would have had some quiet time to think on Hector's question. Cover up the General, lay him out some food, spread myself a blanket banquet, and consider what soft thing was killing me beyond the fat. But here's a night the General has survived to see his nine o'clock. Before I even stepped up to the door, I heard him shouting outrage at the liberal network. He stood there in his T-shirt and his jockey shorts, leaning over his belly, pointing at the TV. He stood far enough from his chair so if he fell I saw it would not catch him. He was going after the bleeding hearts again, the goddamn richy-rich-bitch Democrats behind the ruin of our country's upright, working middle class.

"People like us," the General said, rounding me in with his drink hand, as if the two of us had been involved here with the TV since the front end of the p.m. news. "Killing us," the General said. "Raising our taxes and gutting the military. And for what? For who? Hardly pays to work. They penalize you for working. Give it all to the guy who won't work. And there they're closing bases. All for *programs.* It's a disgrace. It's a joke, is what it is. We're weak."

"Soft," I said.

"Goddamn right," the General said. "Soft. That's a goddamn right way to put it. Some crackpot someday, he'll see it, too. Some Commie, raghead. He's over there right now, and you know he's not taxing folks who work to pay some welfare mama to feed her habit while her sixteen children are in counseling or rehab. We're all supposed to think it's our fault? Me pay the bill? Look, hey, it's tough, I won't say it isn't. I wasn't born myself. I worked for what I am. And I'm not perfect, either. I've got my addictions. Nicotine addicts you. I drink. But doesn't mean I have to go out raping and killing.

I never thought I was owed. If he's smart, you know what that raghead's doing? Sonofabitch is sterilizing. Tying tubes and cutting off the nuts. He's putting those people to work, got them in the factories, building planes and ships, wear them down before they can make more of themselves. You've got to understand, Adam, in those countries, these are people who shit in their living rooms. He sure as hell isn't paying them to be who they are. It's, ah, it's—what did you say it is?"

"Soft?"

"Soft. Goddamn right. Soft. Would you look at that? What they're selling now?"

The General and I stood together, watched a lady in a smock degrease a seabird while she talked about the fish and whatnot out there choking on pelagic tar balls.

"See that?" said the General. "You see? Now they're going to shell out millions cleaning up, just to save some guppies. What they ought to do, they ought to take that money, turn it right back into exploration. Make up for the oil they lost, that's what."

I asked the General did he need another drink. He lowered his drink hand, looked into his glass, tipped the glass way up so he was spilling ice around his mouth, and I was thinking I would have to catch him falling backward. He handed me the glass and said why not. I mixed him a drink, took a sip, asked myself why not, and made myself a drink to join him. The General raised his glass to mine and told me welcome to the ranks. I choked a little on a healthy swallow I thought might impress him, shook my head, and wiped my mouth off with my shirtsleeve.

"That's jet fuel," said the General. "Martini's a high-octane cocktail. Two or three of those'll have you flying off the radar."

I think I was up there after number one. I know I was glad to break from the bleeding eco hearts before I told the General, with all due respect, sir,

I was right there bleeding with them. I sipped, watched the ad where the truck spins donuts on the tundra, the ad which said my teeth could be as white as hers were if I brushed with Pepsodent, the ad that ended with the whispered side effects I might expect if I should take a drug whose name I can't remember for esophageal reflux. Please, I prayed, don't show us Africa's distended belly next. Don't tell us how much wheat we owe the world. Don't ask us to adopt a Guatemalan. We know, we know, we know, but, please, God, for tonight, please keep them off the air; I don't want to see the General when he's told it ought to be his mission here in life to save them.

The General scratched his hairy leg up near the crotch, and the good news here was yes, God had heard me, loud and clear, the Supreme Commander had seen fit to favor us with part two of the five-part series documenting man's career in flight. The bad news was the General had seen part two, at least six times; he'd seen them all, he said, telling me to watch, that plane there is a DeHaviland, pretty quick here she'll be dropping ordnance on the railroad. I was losing him. He murmured, same as I'd heard Coach Jerry do. He rolled his head my way and smiled a sleepy smile as if he'd heard himself and was relievingly embarrassed.

I said, "We lost."

"Of course you did," he said.

"Of course? What do you know? You never come to our games anymore."

"Why'd I want to see a bunch of losers?"

"But you didn't know we'd lose."

"I did."

"How?"

"You lost your winner."

The General set his drink on his table.

He said, "That there is the Douglas SBD. Called the Dauntless. You imagine coming down like that? Guys who opted for that duty, if they hadn't lost their nut already, then after one or two missions in that bird, they had. Same way for us there, flying F-4s in gookland."

The General closed his eyes, breathed a little deeper toward sleep. I stood up, finished my drink, asked did he mean Mike.

"Mike?" I said. "That winner?"

The General got the smile back on and looked at me through one eye only partway open.

"He's a beautiful flyer," said the General. "Could be a real killer. Lead a squadron one day, bet you."

"But he's never flown," I said. "You've never seen him."

The General closed his eyes again, rested deeper down and easy.

"I have seen," he said. "If you're lucky, you'll see, too. One day you'll wake up and see your season is over. Mike'll be that sound you're trying to spot there in the sky, way up high above you. That boy, that boy, that boy is tomorrow's general."

I went and fixed myself another drink. I fixed the General's nighttime plate, covered him up, brought my drink back to my room, and laid into the snack rack.

I never would have known how much I ate that night if it hadn't been for all those wrappers I waked up with in the morning. I waked up also with a bad case of the spinning dizzies. The heavy cavalry was trampling riderless inside my skull. My mouth was packed with sand and shiny pennies. I held up the various food sacks, unremembering, feeling cheated of their flavors. I made it to the kitchen, recalled the General's cure of cigarettes and red beer. I poured out the tomato juice. I twisted the top off the beer and came to being pretty nearly sick to smell it. I wanted the couch, several hours downtime with an ice pack, a *TV Guide,* and the remote. I covered myself with the General's blanket, punched around the channels through the morning news shows, gave up any thought of making it to school. When the game shows ran into the talk shows, I got to wondering where the General was. I watched the talk among the wives whose husbands turned out to be gay, the talk among the mothers of the babies having babies, then got up to check.

He slept. Midmorning, and he slept. I watched and listened to his breathing and I thought, *With your permission, sir, I think your men must need you.* Still, I wasn't the lieutenant to step up and wake him. I thought my duty here would better be to let him keep on sleeping. I went back to the TV, saw the talk had turned to fat. Before fat, after fat, the guilt, the doubt, the usual. The four-hundred-pound vegetarian, there she blows, my hero, swearing to God above she has fantastic sex, says she doesn't want an *after,* says she's fatter now than last time she was on this show, just look at the pictures. She points out to the ninety-eight-pound stud in aisle three who keeps her happy. She is the only one of seven on the show who did not lose. She shouts. The audience shouts. The man of the seven who has lost the most says he, for one, does not believe her sex, her happiness, nope, no way does he believe her.

He says, "My bleeping gut was hung so low I couldn't find my bleep to bleep the broad side of a bleeping barn."

"That's fine," the woman says, "that's you, that's *your* imagination."

Some that's-rights and some hear-hears go around and then a less fat gal who I don't think lost too much says, "Honey, that's your *body* you are bleeping with, not your imagination."

The fat gal holds her mud. Hollers for her sweetheart to come on up and join her. Big fat bleeping chance. You see his scalp bead up with sweat and shine a taillight red through webs of sticky hair he combs from the heart side of his head and over to the heartless. She blows him a kiss. She hefts herself around in her seat to face the hostess of the show. She says she realizes none of this is super dignified. She says we won't believe it, but she was once a gymnast. And then from love, and memory, and not without some grunting effort, she takes her foot and lifts her leg up so her heel is hooked behind her head. She smiles, red-faced, huffing, grins, really, so her eyes are squinched and buried in her happy, fatty cheek. She leaves her foot up there and holds her hands out wide and beckons with her fingers for applause. She gets it. From me, too, she gets it. I am clapping, one of the folks back home, thinking, *That babe is for me.*

When the hostess broke for a commercial and returned with several feuding couples and their shrinks, I made my rounds and gathered up the junk food that survived the night from all my stashes. Mars Bar, a Butterfinger, a bag of Cool Ranch Doritos. Brave foods, unafraid of health and smeary-lipped nutritionists, fads in anti-caloric dining. Foods whose expiration dates would indicate they were practically immortal. I wanted not to die. I waked up thinking maybe I could die, but here now life was good. Flavors, absolutely. Sights and sounds. I liked life as it landed my way by the senses. I liked the sound of wrappers. I liked calories. Memories, too, I liked, the anticipation of the senses in the abstract. Some part of me must always pine for brisket.

Could I eat? Or had I ruined myself for a whole entire day? And if a person carried on the way the General did, how many days in him were left to ruin? I decided maybe I should slow down some, ease my stomach into the Doritos, maybe test myself on toast. I went out to the kitchen, where it smelled like toast and coffee, and the General sat behind his paper blowing smoke. He looked at me over the top of the paper, seeming no worse off on this morning than he did on any other. I suppose I thought he ought to be as bent and stirred inside as I was. But he was straight, from the outside anyway, and still. He was good; he was the General.

He said, "You guys lose again last night?"

"Yes, sir," I said. "I told you that."

"That's right," said the General. "You did. No Mike."

I leaned back up against the counter.

The General said, "He get back to you yet? About those lessons?"

"Well, sir, truth is I haven't actually asked him."

"Still?" the General said.

"No, sir, not yet."

"What's the matter with you, you sick?"

"No, sir. I think it's more a thing of time. I keep not finding the right time to ask, I guess."

"No," the General said, "I mean now, you sick right now? You're looking pretty puny."

"Well, that, right. Jet fuel, I think. I don't think I'm really ready yet to join the ranks."

"Takes practice," said the General. "Try a red beer? Red beer, fried egg, and some grits should cure you. Listen, you want me to call him?"

"Call?"

"Mike. I could call him right now. Fine day for flying."

"No, no. No, sir, I mean. I'm pretty sure he must have school."

"None for you though, huh? Well, so how about you and me go up? Red beer, grits, and an hour or so at altitude?"

"I don't think so. Nothing sounds too good right now. Red beer nearly made me sick."

"Let's fly then," said the General.

"Not me," I said.

"What do you mean, not me? You're a pilot, aren't you?"

"I don't know," I said. "Lately I'm not sure if airplanes are for me. I have a question, sir, did you ever do a fat girl?"

"How's that?" said the General.

"A big girl," I said. "Really big. Did you ever take her—"

"No," said the General. "Never. What are you talking about? Airplanes aren't for you? Haven't been thinking again, have you? What you need is to get back up again, remember what it is. Look, let's go. Right now," the General said. "That's an order."

I was to get dressed, warm the car up while the General shaved. I could hear him running water, splashing water at his face, and whistling. Tuneless, toneless notes, private ditties he let out when he was on an upswing. Going flying. *Don't forget your logbook, Adam, bring your shades, the sun up there is fierce.* Maybe he was right. I pulled the Comet out into the driveway. I stood outside the car, thinking maybe the colder air might help me, and thinking also of how long the General had kept this car, how good and loyal he was to her, how easily he might have sent her down the road, swapped her for a newer version. This is the car the General, Mike, and I had watched the stars from. Same car my mother drove away from him the day she made him chase us there at Cindy's. He stuck by her. She looked good. I wanted him to drive me. I thought then, *All right, I've had a good time in that Cessna, let's give the girl another chance.*

The General came out smelling clean and looking smooth, straight, and springlike in the eye, his steady, unpitched exhalations signaling desire's triumph over black lung. So many years, that many Winstons, how'd he do it? Not a drop of booziness in that man's brain. His blood was running pure, distilled, high-octane aviator savvy. Fifty, sixty miles per hour, the General hunched across the steering wheel, as if just by looking he might make out bumps and ripples, maybe choose out regions of the sky that made for smoother flying. He whistled Dum-dee-dum-dum. *Take me with you, sir. I will hang on your wing, General, I'll maintain your altitude and airspeed, I'll grow a mustache soon, you'll see. I'm coming into my own now, soon enough and I'll be weller.* Except I was slipping into something sicker. By the time we pulled it into Aviator Way and Hal's place, my guts were in a tailspin; I went watery in the mouth; I told the General I thought I'd better not go too far from the nearest toilet. We climbed the steps to Hal's loft and I eased myself onto a couch and how I looked was rough enough to have the General keep me grounded. I think he got a charge out of seeing me, calling me puny, lily-white, and whatnot.

"You lie down," he said. "I'll go see about some aspirin and water."

I heard him go off hollering for Hal, poking through Hal's drawers and cupboards, running water from the tap, and cracking me some ice. I opened my eyes and saw him go to the door and step out on the landing to look down on the hangar. He came back with my water, said, "The dog, that Hal, he's gone off flying. You take these," he said. "I'm going to see if I can't track him down."

I sat up and drank. I went and looked down at the hangar how the General had, saw the space where Hal's old tail dragger would be, and I wondered what it meant about the way we got along with Hal that what we hadn't seen was missing from his hangar was his airplane. I moved over to the window, got a fix on the General through Hal's telescope and thought I could see the General whistling while he rolled the Pitts out. When he lifted off the tarmac, I told him *Bon voyage, sir,* and then I lay down in a patch of sunshine on the carpet, feeling well enough to doze.

There was a cure for me. I felt it coming. Heal me, sun. Draw me up there with you. I am on my way, born again, notify the General. Come in, General. General Oney, do you read me? This is Yankee Hotel Foxtrot, do you copy? There's a thirty-two-ounce rib eye and a bowl of ranch beans waiting at the O Club, sir. Our own Kansas beef, flown in daily to Saigon. Got a good Kentucky bourbon and an English gin. We'll toast the funny little yellow man, hunkered in his tunnels. Cheers, Charlie! Here's to stir-fried rat and centipede. You're a worthy adversary. Only let our leaders fight you with our other arm, then see what. The rout is on. We've got the full-court press on you, running the fast break, shooting threes, lobbing in the tall-boy dunks, stepping to the charity line before they know they're in a ball game.

But that's not me at all. Me, I am just a sick dog on an olive rug, drooling in the sunshine, panting after the minor ecstasy of lapsing consciousness, the expectation that when I wake my stomach will be well enough to eat that bone. Sleep, sleep, I thought, and slept. Not long, though. Not nearly long enough before the General bombed Hal's hangar, dived on it, roared and shook the windows, put up a volume and a tickle in the floor more urgent than I thought a shoeskate stunt plane had a right to. Shining his ass. After I uncovered my head, untucked myself, and hobbled groggy-kneed to the telescope, I caught the General at the far end of the runway, fifteen feet off the ground, tops, rolling upright, climbing, wagging to the folks there in the grandstands. I looked for him to make another pass, an eight-point roll, maybe climb straight through to an inside loop, but saw the General had finished with the stunts. After a quick jump up to altitude, the General entered standard pattern traffic. I saw him reach and work the throttle, saw him well enough to have the feeling we could talk.

I said, "Come on, sir, give us another run. Thrill us, General. We've got the glass on you. Folks," I said, "that's General Homer Oney up there, best to keep your nose out of those hot dogs. Be alert. This man's seen some hours in that Pitts, he's got something up his sleeve, I'll bet, our commander loves to throw a treat into the old routine to wow you."

But he never did. I focused on him so I saw the shine of sky across his aviator shades, so I thought I could make out the scent of limes from his shaved face. He was talking up there, too, I saw, talking to himself, or to his bird, I thought, coaxing her, thanking her, his baby, confidante, his sweetheart. I watched him search the skies to see who else he shared the pattern with. Must have looked to him like no one. Through the scope, it looked to me like no one also. I followed him to base leg, and got to thinking of sardines. I stood back from the scope, wondering why sardines, and whether Hal might have a tin around and also crackers, and as I bent back to the scope I saw Hal in the bigger, unscoped sky, flying low into a lengthened final. The General, too, had turned to final, so it looked like they were flying something of a staggered, stacked formation. But nothing of formation to it. The General came in high and from behind, so if you hadn't seen his face, but only saw the plane, you could have thought he meant to dive on Hal. A slow dive, all right, a sneaky deal, the biplane's best approximation of a tiptoe. Only look there through the scope at General Oney's face, find Hal's face in the cockpit, and you knew these boys were only pilots flying final, eyeing gauges, keeping busy with the trim and throttle.

Sardines, I thought, were certainly good on soda crackers. They're good, very good, in either mustard sauce or wine sauce, or even better smoked. I watched. I wondered why sardines. I thought maybe I had a fever. I liked to think right then what I saw out there was just a thing I saw and wasn't so. I watched out and figured these boys must be three-, four-hundred feet above the sage. I figured by their airspeed, and their distance from the runway, maybe they should meet at two, two-fifty. *Sardines*, I thought, *sardines*. I thought, *That flyer is my father.* I zeroed in and steadied, had him focused all alone. He had a good shave. This close to the runway, he looked to be all business. He didn't give you much behind those shades. One tic, I felt, two tics now. A view back to myself, could be, a simple mirrored Adam in those aviator lenses, a tiny, giant, fat guy at the telescope, tensing for the bang, praying for the miracle so he might tell the folks back home how General Oney had withstood it.

One tic, two tics, three tics, then, and good-bye, sir, the General is blasted out of sight. He's there, and then he's bounced up out of focus, and then he's dropping straight and wilder anyway than I can track him. I lost him. I looked up from the scope, and even then I had a hard time finding him, and never did find Hal, though I looked, both without the scope and with it, thinking how could I not find him, a whole plane, a whole man in the desert? I turned the scope back on the General's Pitts, which wasn't any Pitts but was a fireball, a blazing heap in the blackened smoke, not what even General Homer Oney could be bet on to survive. But there I saw him, through the scope, very clearly, crawling burning from the burning wreck, slapping at himself, rolling in the sand and sagebrush.

I sat. I thought, *We need help.* Something needed doing. A man might live. Two men. Something needed to be done. I picked the phone up. All my life, I think, whether I will be much in the daily way of dialing them or not, I will be able to recite the sequence of those seven numbers I first learned to dial by heart. I sat, listened through the first ring to the lucky third, and when I heard him on the other end, I knew the time was finally right for calling Mike.

Along about the tail end of my stay there on the unit, Nurse Sue took me on a field trip. Raptor museum. Hawks, eagles, falcons, owls. Fighter pilots of the aviary. Dead ones, all right, and stuffed, taxidermic miseries for some folks, undignified, sacrosanct, but still I thought, *Okay, pretty good, so how'd you find this place, Nurse Sue?*

"Gold's Pawn?" I said. "Were you buying, or selling?"

"Neither," said Sue. "I just heard about Mr. Gold's birds. All these birds, he finds them. He harvests the power lines."

Skinny, old, short guy with a beakish nose comes at us with his claw stuck out, our Mr. Gold, a raptor-man with the eagle eye to spot unluck, frailties, degrees of desperation.

"You'd be surprised," he said, "what gets zapped."

He looked me up and down and said, "What's yours?"

"What's mine what?" I said.

"What zapped you?"

"Fire," I said.

"Too bad, kid, looks tough. Better than a scald, though, lots better than electric. You're in good hands here with Suzie. I'd almost roast myself if I knew Suzie would take care of me. You come in to do some business, or admire?"

"Adam flies," said Sue. "He's an Air Force brat."

"Aha," said Mr. Gold, "you're saying F-4s? You're telling me the Phantoms?"

"Yes, sir," I said.

"*Sir*, he says, the boy says sir! That's fine, that's good, but you're not telling me you intend to fit the cockpit?"

"No, sir, that's my father, General Oney. Mine's a Cessna."

"General, is it? Well. I should be honored. The General's son. Okay, Mr. General's son, what may I do to help you?"

"Nothing," I said. "This is practice, my first time out. I'm with Sue."

"We came to see your birds," said Sue.

"It's a tragedy," said Mr. Gold. "You think? A tragedy. I tell them, I say, you should do something, some insulation, what, you could insulate those lines, but do they listen? They don't listen. It's a tragedy. Am I right? I am right. Let me tell you also—fences. Look at this guy here. You see? Redtailed hawk. Weighs maybe, what, three pounds? Soaking wet? He's shot dead off a fence. You know what I think? I think people think this guy will kill their sheep. Sheep! Look at this. This one here is my favorite. Golden eagle. You see that wingspan? You like that eye? Well, he was a sorry fellow when I found him. He needed work. For him I paid a pretty penny. For him I broke my knees to pick up feathers. You know what I think people think? I think they think if it's strong, and fierce, and beautiful, people want it dead. Makes me sick, is what it does. They kill and say they're killing for the aphrodisiac, for the *schwanz—verstehst?*—ancient culture, or what, you tell me, they think this eagle here will carry off their babies? Makes me sick. People come in with their kids to gawk. You know what I tell those kids? Thanks for coming in, I say. Have a look. Now write your congressman, I say, and tell him insulate. So write," said Mr. Gold. "I'll tell you, too. I'm telling you, write. Insulate. You will excuse me?"

We moved from owl to eagle, Sue and I, quietly, as if our quiet were a sign of our respect, though mostly I was keeping quiet so I could hear old Gold harass a sap who came in needing cash for his guitar, his camera, and a heap of gyppo turquoise. I couldn't hear much from the sap, who kept on looking one way and the other, talking soft and saying, *Geez, okay, okay,* while Mr. Gold was plenty loud, and pretty rough, as if he wanted both the sap's bad luck and Mr. Gold's responsibility for such bad luck to be on record for the public.

"Is that my fault?" Mr. Gold kept saying. "Is this my problem? Am I to blame?"

The louder Mr. Gold was, the softer was the sap. They kept at it till I guess I showed a face that told Sue more than I was telling to myself. I mean I felt bad about the sap. I felt weak and didn't have the sense to tell myself that it was time to leave. Food break. Imagine, Adam Oney needing to be told it's time to eat.

"I know a place," said Sue. "Aren't you the guy who said he likes the chili-cheese?"

We walked a block and a half down the street and sat down at a greasy spoon called Landrums.

"Well," I said to Sue, "So what do you think?"

"I think I'll have the chili-cheese, of course."

"No," I said, "I mean, how long do you guess till I'm released?"

"I don't know," said Sue. "Soon, though, very soon I'd say. If it were up to me, I would say today, right now. What do you think?"

"I'm surprised, I guess. I thought I'd get more stares. You go through those treatments, you almost want the stares. Like you deserve them. Earned them. Something. I don't think this waitress even noticed. I guess when you get out you see how little of us really shows."

"That's true," said Sue. "And also I think you'll see how much people aren't really looking. Anyway you're lucky. You got to keep your pretty face. What are you having?"

"Chili-cheese, of course."

"Sure you can handle it?" said Sue.

"Sure I'm sure. I'm strong," I said. "I'm beautiful. I'm fierce. I'll eat the chili, only just don't kill me."

"Very funny," Sue said. "He's an odd duck, don't you think? Always trying to get me to buy. I think he likes me because I don't. Only thing I did buy was this crucifix, you like it?"

"Not much," I said. "Sorry. I never knew you wore one."

"Why should you?" said Sue. "I keep it underneath my shirt."

"Right, well, I think I have a hard time with the old cross, owing to my mother, you know, her deal there with the reverend Holy Joe."

"Does she ever call you?"

"No, ma'am, she does not."

"Do you want her to?"

"I do. Sure I do. I've been sick. Wounded lamb and all. Sure I want my mother."

"Why don't you call her?"

"Tried that," I said.

"And?"

"And she said she had washed her hands of me. Me and the General both. We were unclean. She's come around to be a hard, hard woman. Said the only way back to her heart is if I come to her through Jesus."

"Doesn't sound like any Jesus talking to me."

"No, right? Me either. Funny thing, that Reverend Marsh, he called me up to say he was sorry. He said it wasn't right of her or natural, how she was with me. Except in church, he said it seemed to him there was a dam built up in her, and when it broke, those most rightly dear to her would know a flood of love—a grievous love, I think he said—and healing."

"That's awful," Sue said. "She sounds scared sick. Did you tell any of this to Doctor Feigenbaum?"

"Noggin?" I said. "Not yet. I'm thinking how. I don't want him figuring I've got more on my plate than I can swallow."

Sue said, "So you'll tell him?"

I said, "Do you think I should?"

"Tell him?" Sue said. "Yes, I do."

Our waitress brought our plates to us, and after Sue sent back her dirty silverware for clean, we dug into the tastiest chili-cheese I never had the luck to fly out on a Sunday brunch for.

For Doctor Noggin, the story of my mother and the Reverend Marsh provoked him to unweigh himself of his own family history. Stuff I had heard from Nurse Nadeen and since forgotten from the early days of my Acute. Son he hadn't spoken to in thirteen years. Unnatural relations between the son and mother, Doctor Noggin's first wife, remember? Another head doctor. Woman brought her son home from the hospital and after three nights found another woman in another house in which the boy would pass his nights so Mrs. Doctor Noggin wouldn't be deprived of sleep.

"This was in the days of assertiveness training," said Doctor Noggin. "The boy was eighteen, twenty hours in the care of a woman two blocks down the way. He was five before he lived with us, and even then Francine refused to yield her time for putting on her face to stir the boy a bowl of oatmeal. I don't blame him, blaming me. My response in all things was to patch. What must that seem to a child? The man charged with his son's protection and his loving, rushing to fix an amputation with a box of Band-Aids? I am old school. I thought we should stick together. At least until the boy had grown up and gone away to college. Best for all of us, however, would have been divorce. Nowadays, we call me an enabler."

He sat gazing at his hands in his lap, having given up completely on the clipboard. His eyes were red and scratchy-seeming so I thought to tell him he'd be better with his glasses. But I didn't. I thought there might be something more he wanted to tell me. But he didn't.

"But you did," I said, "didn't you? Get the divorce? I heard you remarried, moved out there with horses."

"Ah, yes. That," he said. "That's true."

"Well, let me ask you something. That's pretty rural, right? Place where you raise a horse? Pickups with gun racks? I mean, do you ever hear of neighbors shooting raptors off of fence rails?"

The doctor looked up from his hands at me and said, "My God, no. Is that true? Where did you hear that? Raptors?"

"At Gold's," I said. "Mr. Gold, he collects them."

"Collects them? Collects them how?"

"He walks power lines, sometimes fence lines. They get zapped and shot. Mr. Gold, he stuffs them. You should walk the fences one day, see if you can see one."

Doctor Noggin blinked at me so my eyes were burning, watering the same as his were.

He said, "Should I?"

He looked back at his hands, and I wondered if the reason he kept looking at his hands was so he would remember not to rub his eyes with them. We sat too long again like that, not talking when I thought our job was talk.

And then old Doctor Noggin said, "You know, I'm really not too happy. I think I chose the wrong career. If I weren't so afraid of nothing else to do, I believe I would quit."

OUR SENIOR YEARS PASS FAST. THEY TELL YOU SO. YOU LAUGH AT THEM, OF course, we are young, they are old, impossible that you and I could leave so many years behind ourselves to be them. Only think, so soon, and here already comes the year you vote each other in your yearbook. Most likely to succeed. Handsomest, prettiest, funniest, cruelest, poorest, fattest. Doesn't need to be a sanctioned, paper vote. The vote is in the face. Senior portrait. The camera shows you knowing how you're seen and what you will likely come to. Trapped in there. Unintended. Just say cheese. Say pickles. Just say Boudreaux. After the General went down, I walked the halls and saw how far our senior years were made out from our junior. I looked harder, after the General, or a harder look at life was shown to me when I stopped seeing through the softer. Most of what I did that year I quit. I was helped to. Ball, I quit myself. I would have a spot next year, said Coach, no problem. Same scenerio with Mr. Cecarelli.

"Anything you want," he said, "you keep the keys. Job's yours when you're ready."

As for flight, with wings, sheet metal, rivets and gizmos, I gave it up for keeps. For one thing, I had lost my teacher, Hal, who died, and also I was getting something of a scary eyeful from the General, who did not die, but burned so you would have a hard time telling him from any picture of himself, junior year or senior. Hardly human, how he looked. Creep show Hol-

225

lywood. A bona fide special effect. Melted. Head blown up two, three times what it was before the burning. He's blind. Could be blind. Won't know until his eyes can open from the swelling. They gave me a mask and rubber gloves, a smock and paper booties.

"Is that you?" the General asked. "It's hell," he said.

"Hal died," he said. "Never saw him. Authentic, huh?"

"I can't see," the General said.

"I know," I said.

"I can't see."

"You're blind," I said.

"But I can't see a thing."

"I know," I said. "That's what they said. They said you couldn't. Might be awhile."

"Hal died. I killed him, you think?"

"You never saw him."

"No."

"He never saw you, either."

"But he died."

"They say he broke his neck. Likely killed him instantly."

"I'm blind," the General said.

"You can't see," I said.

"I saw things. But I never made anything from what I saw. Listen, tell me what you see till I can see again, all right? Make something from it. That's an order, hear?"

I pretended I could understand him, said yes, sir, roger, got it. I drove his Comet. I made the trip from home to town and back two or three times during the week, spent the night in a motel room on the weekends. I told him it didn't look to me as if the Communists were any threat. I said I saw a mitten on the road. Watched Hector make his comeback. Scored thirty-one points, sparked a Husky turnabout, a 3-1 run that let them close the season at .500. I watched the General's vitals and I told him he should have seen it, Hector's thirty-one. New wrinkle in his game. Had a real nice jump hook he could throw up from ten feet or so with his left. He could go behind his back with his left, too, pass or dribble; you couldn't guard him for a weak side.

"And what do you see in that?" the General said.

"I don't know," I said. "Two strengths are better than one?"

"Negative," the General said. "You see in that a boy who knows which side his bread is buttered on. That's a boy who's got his nose up Lucy DuPree's skirts. But that's not your bread. Do you read me? Adam Oney is an Oney. Adam Oney flies."

"Yes, sir," I said. "I fly."

"You're my son."

"Yes, sir."

"Let me tell you something else," the General said.

The General did his best to lift his chin, sort of rocked back from his neck and chest so I could see two slits and maybe even eyeballs shining through the swollen goop.

He said, "Can you see me in here? We've got light, buddy. I think by tomorrow I could maybe see just fine."

He smiled, looked like. Through the Silvadene and gauze, I thought I saw him smiling. He was alive. He would see. For a while, the miracle of sighted life was drug enough so he seemed not to mind how much it hurt to live it. You fall out of the sky, crawl burning from your burning bird, and you don't have much in you for question and complaint, you give thanks. *Very well,* the healers tell him, *that's the spirit, yet I must tell you, sir, it will be weeks, months along of grafts and surgery, you'll have to push yourself through therapy if you expect to ever feed yourself or look up well enough to see what's flying.*

"That's gravy," said the General. "That's cake."

Except it wasn't cake. Not the tank, not debridement, not chewing, sipping, pissing, shitting, none of it, not even seeing, said the General, because guess what, the first thing he had asked for when he started seeing was a mirror. I wasn't there, but they told me he dummied up the whole first day he saw himself, and when I came in the only thing he said to me was I should have told him.

"Well, you look a whole lot better than you did," I said. "If you could have seen yourself before, then you'd be happy."

But the General wasn't happy. But then he would be. Then he wouldn't. Then he would. Sure the General worked a crazy stick and rudder, putting on the spiritual acrobatic show of the Acute. Never mind your rank, your age, religion, or your race, you've been stripped clean down to nerve. No stoics here, boys, this kind of pain will take you.

He lost a lot. Fluid weight, muscle weight, weight. He leaned on me, and each time I would visit I felt him being lighter. No more Winstons. No more gin and dry vermouths. Thought of the olive made him sick.

He said, "I get out of here, I'm going clean."

He said, "I get out of here, first thing you will do is mix me one stiff drink."

I went in one day and saw him weeping, kissing at the backs of his hands while a nurse worked in his catheter. I saw him sweat and ooze and stream while she went at him with the scissors and the blade. I held his hand, walked beside his gurney from recovery, promised him a can of ranch beans and a bag of pecan sandies, don't you worry. He watched the soaps, sat through chaplain talk, survivor talk, talk about what next, what kind of life he might expect among his fellow patients.

He said, "Great guys. Great. You'll like them."

He said, "Boudreauxs. Kills me, knowing I have come off so far from the swamps, and here I am, cheek-by-ass with a bunch of stinking Boudreauxs."

I sat beside him in his bed, watched him twitch and flutter, roll his eyes and lick his lips and come up from his meds.

He said, "Was I sleeping?"

"Some," I said.

"Did they let me skip my breakfast?"

"It's afternoon," I said. "Late. You're looking next at dinner."

The nurse came in, said, "Look alive, General. Time for the p.m. session."

The General started beading up before she touched him. When she did, he whimpered. He asked her please to stop, please, wait.

To me, he said, "You should go now."

I went, turned to say good-bye, I love you, saw him squeeze his eyes shut tight, sucking on his johnny.

Discharge for the General came in June. That's a long stay on the unit, a record of the reach and the degree of burns, the battles won and lost to bugs in the blood, rejected grafts, one surgery to loosen a contracture. The last day of grand rounds, the team gathered around the General's bed, the General sitting upright in his street clothes.

"Congratulations, General, you've won the war. You're going home now."

I wheeled him out in a chair, and anyone we passed who knew him gave him a salute. *Farewell, sir; good-bye, General; love life, Homer Oney, that's the brave campaign, you have earned it.* Dressed out the way he was, long sleeves, long pants, and a hat, you could not see him right off as a man who should have lost his life to fire. Some redness to the one side of the face, a little yellow eschar needing work still on the high part of the neck, the hands wrapped so he couldn't really use them. He had a stiff walk, too, a gingerly manner to his move that said he was a little worried for the world to bump him. But the man was out, that redness would fade, I had learned to dress his wounds, practiced on the unit, soon the General would lose those last few wraps, and the only one to see the ugly stuff would be the General's next new sweetheart. *Next* was our word, *forward* our direction. We'd go fish, we'd maybe learn to shoot, drive out to the mountains, stalk the wily chukar. Fine for him, my quitting ball, that's good, now don't look back. Don't look back for sure, and never, ever mention Mother. *The Lord will provide*, she'd said, the closest thing to sorrow or to offering a hand back when I called her up to tell her. When I pulled up in the Comet to fetch him from his wheelchair, I thought she might be right.

First command from the General was for me to put the top up. Sun would cook him. From here on out, he's flying on the doctor's orders. Wasn't just the skin he'd damaged, but the inner organs, too. He got in the car and said, yes, sir, he was a true believer, what wins the war is one day at a time. Nothing more of the Acute to him. He would be straight and true, coming through the Rehab, his General's days were finished as a drinker and a smoker. Outside of town I opened up the Comet on the interstate and the General told me easy, slow down, what's the hurry?

He said, "It's a nice drive, isn't it? Why don't you show me something you've been seeing?"

"Yes, sir, right," I said. "I've got just the thing."

We climbed up through the first range headed home, descended through the pass onto a spread of basin wetland, water running flat and shimmering, silvery and blue, boundless from this distance, so you could easily believe this water was mirage. But then you saw the exit sign—Stillwater—and then you saw the waterbirds, and when you parked, and got out of the car, you heard them.

"Look at that," the General said. "I've flown this way before, but it's nothing like the same as getting out here with them, is it?"

"I don't know that, sir. This is the only way I've ever known them."

The General walked out toward the water, held his hands behind his back, stopping every now and then until he reached the shore. A bit of a spectacle, I guess, not the sort of winged life you might expect to fly the mountain desert. Sharp, short-legged racer birds, mud peckers, and the longer-legged wading birds, heavy bodies balanced high up on unlikely sticks, curlews, herons, cranes, geese, ducks, gulls, gulls, and pelicans. They paddled, dived, skimmed, hovered above the water, one small kind of them, whistling at the fishes. They cawed. They squawked. They honked and quacked and cooed and chortled. If you looked across and fuzzed your eyes, tuned your hearing like between two stations, it seemed every plane of sky and every wavy length of sound was taken up in song and flight.

The General looked to be a man relieved, I thought, breathing deep, looking up. Up. Up and up. That's the man, a little less the showbird, more a stately sort of flyer, his eyes a little less blue, more a shade of brighter gray, that's my pop, the General. He walked back up to me, leaned beside me against the Comet. He seemed to me to have grown smaller. By the pound, sure, and by the inch, and smaller somehow even by the year, as if the age he'd put on through his months there in the hospital had summoned up a last reserve of youth, the stamina to look at life and see it newly. He pointed a lot, hung his bandaged hand out in the air, saying look, look, and look, asking me how deep I thought the water got, whether the geese were here all year or passing through, asking me the name of a bird that screamed and made as if it had a broken wing it dragged around in crooked circles.

"How come you never told me about this place?" he said.

"I guess I was saving it."

I saw a mood swing through the General's face and remembered to expect it. According to the nurses, he would require naps. He might refuse to eat. I should be prepared to comfort him from nightmares. I asked myself okay so was it something I said, or was he tired, or hungry, but it wasn't me or him but was a pair of Phantoms. He was looking higher than the bird life, tracking faster than the local feathered flight. They came in low, very near to twelve o'clock, and I never found them from the sky until the boom shot straight down through and shook me and I knew to look behind us. I watched them out of sight and when I turned to ask the General what he thought, I saw him off toward shore again, his hands behind his back, toeing at a dead one of those birds he'd asked me what its name was.

"Killdeer," I said. "She's likely got a nest around here somewhere. That broken wing thing is an act."

The General walked along a ways and found another.

He said, "We get complaints about this sort of thing. I never thought it really happened."

He pointed out to several birds you saw were also dead and floating on the water.

"Ducks?" he said.

"Looks like. I don't know, maybe mallards?"

I followed beside the General back up to the Comet.

"They aren't supposed to fly here."

"Who's not?"

"F-4s."

"Well, now you're back, can't you find out who they were? Write them up?"

"I am not their general," said the General.

I eased us off the gravel to the blacktop, asked the General what he meant.

"I mean those boys there were Murphy's. Truth is, I have been officially retired now for going on six months. Politics. Ran me out. Here's a thing I've learned I'll tell you—when you hear about the good old boys, you best find out who they are and bust your ass to join them."

"You never told me that," I said.

"Well, I'm telling you," the General said. "Consider yourself told."

The General tipped his hat down low across his nose and looked like he needed to sleep.

I said, "But what kills them?"

"Birds?"

"Right, the birds."

"Some say shock waves. But I'd say more the fear. You saw that. Big green bird, fast as that, and loud, you can see how something little as a killdeer might be scared to death."

The General slept the next few ranges on to home, waking up when we descended through the drier desert. Before we even made it to the house he had me drive us out to Hal, the canister of ash and flint his brother thought it would be best to have Hal's charry corpse reduced to. We stepped inside the chain-link gate, crossed the grassless grounds, stood at the foot of his plot, and kept a time of quiet.

By-and-by the General said, "Was it religious?"

"They got Father Mac out," I said. "It was small."

"I wondered. Anybody speak?"

"Everybody. You know, the Father, Hal's brother, couple of guys out from the hangars. Mostly what they had was stories."

"You?"

"I said a poem. Poem about how to die not in a war. Or why a war, at least, and not by beauty. 'Agonies of Mimosas.' That's what Hal said, what he liked about this poem, about how it was best to die in agonies of mimosas. He said he'd never seen a real mimosa, but probably you had."

"I have," the General said.

"And would that be a good way to die?"

"I never thought much on it. But I can see it. By a mimosa, yes, I believe it would be."

I waited to hear more from the General, but the General was finished. I looked up to the sky, thinking there should be some sort of flyover salute, but the sky was empty, pale blue in the later phases of the post-noon bleach. Time for the wind to pick up, the whisper from the cooler ranges blown across the flat to tell us *move along, it is time now, move along.*

From that day there with Hal, and for weeks long after, you hardly ever saw the General out. Too hot, too dusty, didn't want to risk his skin. He napped a lot, just as the nurses had predicted. It was hard to feed him. I went down to the Buy and Bye with recipes I copied from the local paper, from cookbooks of Chinese and Italian dishes, cuisines I thought might let us eat more healthfully. Mostly, in the early days, he was an easy man to cook for, attentive to the kitchen's effort, though I noticed more and more the stuff that called for goat cheese, say, or bean curd, anything that smelled to him like ethnic, he would at first politely ask for small portions, and then later, less politely. Some of it he came to say he simply would not eat. Reminded him too much of the mystery meats the VC ate, the General would say, too much of the deck of an unhosed shrimp boat.

"Gumbo?" said the General. "Listen, partner, no offense, I know around here gumbo must be pretty highfalutin, but for me, I'm smelling swamp."

Stick to pork chops, he would tell me, green beans, and ribs. Honest foods. Cuts of meat you could say which part of the cow or pig they came from, vegetables you could say had either hung from vines or grew down in the ground as tubers.

"There's some truth in the saying," he said, "you are what you eat. Could be I just like to think I could tell you what I am."

Take his headaches and his flashes, add them to the a.m. and the p.m. sessions in debridement, the General said sometimes he was surprised he was eating anything, said he sometimes didn't know who he was at all. To help him out, we hung some extra-heavy curtain liners; we ditched the oscillating fans, installed the central air. We pushed some furniture around and bought a rower and an exercycle. To help out with his headaches, we seemed to have evolved some canceled topics in our conversations. Still no Mother, naturally, and also no talk of the General losing his command to Murphy, nothing on his Pitts, very, very little talk about Hal. We canceled our subscription to the paper, skipped the morning news shows and the evening, kept the General tuned in to the History Channel, the Nature Channel, the major movie classics. We did all right. We made our drives back to the unit for his checkups and were given grade A marks. Lots of healing here. Grafts took. Minimal scarring. Could stand some improvement, but a pretty decent range of motion to the neck. We were finished with debridement; we could cut down on our trips back to the unit from twice a month to once. Doctor said the General's face was healed enough he might try breathing steam to help his headaches, said to help his pallor, the General might try sun.

"I don't think I've ever seen someone so pale," the doctor said. "You're so white you're blue. Get out and get some exercise. Wear the screens, cover up, and you'll be fine."

We left the hospital and the General said all right, then, let's live it up, as if he all along were waiting on the doctor's orders to appreciate his healing. First move for the General was to make the trip back home there in the Comet with the top down.

"What we need," the General said, "is a sombrero."

So we found a flat-roofed shack in the shady part of town, *tienda del sombrero fantástico*, bought ourselves a pair of enormous shade makers, poorly dyed and loosely woven, el cheapo. The things were flapping off our heads at thirty, so the General's next idea was to rig a cinch with shoestring borrowed from his street shoes. The General stretched himself across the seat, lay his head down in the corner with his brim flipped up so he was happy teeth and ease, the aviator lenses mirroring a sight of faultless sky. If you didn't call us stupid, we were sharp. We didn't speed, didn't honk our horn or wave or take our shirts off. Was other folks who honked—big girl in an open CJ Jeepster, flashing us her titties. Father and son, General and lieutenant, amigos. *Righteous*, I was thinking, *groovin'*.

The General said, "Only thing could make this any better is an ice-cold beer."

So the General had me pull us off at the first last-chance-for-gas joint out of town, said for me to wait right there, came back to the Comet with a sixer and a ten-pound bag of ice, a Styrofoam cooler, and a sack of salsa-flavored corn nuts. Not to worry, Adam, those beers are for you; the Mountain Dew will quench the General's thirst, sugar, caffeine and, okay, just this once, no big deal, a pack of Winston Lights.

Well, it's true, all of it, what they say about our senior year, and how it seems like only yesterday, and how you are what you eat, and how the one thing leads up to another. Try to stop them, the one thing and another. You know, hadn't he started off with Lights?

"Three a day," he said. "One smoke for the morning, one for noon, one smoke for the night."

But there the three would lead to four, would lead him back up to a pack, and from the Lights to Winstons proper. We drove home in our sombreros, and sure I never felt so fine behind the wheel as I felt driving range and basin through the smiley haze of those cervezas, but when the General sat down to the evening news that night and started in on tax hikes, the pussyfoot U.N., and advocates for same-sex marriage, I could see pretty soon those cigarettes would lead the General right back into gin. I sat and watched him more than listened, and I saw how soon from the time the doctor says a person has his health a person will resolve himself to lose it. Winstons and gin, the easy chair and meanness: That's a slick runway, sir, an unsafe place, I thought, for takeoffs and for landings.

I watched the General's blood beat in his temple while he sat through the reports on welfare fraud, or the plight of the desert tortoise and the kiwi fish, a mayor caught smoking crack with a teenage hooker, contending he had been entrapped.

Of the mayor, the General said, "They got his Zulu ass on tape. You watch how he handles that stuff, he looks like a pro. Nobody entrapping that dumb bunny but himself."

Of the tortoise, and the fish, and the birds and air and water, and the long hairs and the Commie lawyers who throw away their hours to protect them, the General said, "What do you say? How do you reason with people who pitch their tents on bombing ranges?"

The thing I think the General really wanted was a fight. He wanted a drink. A knockdown, blackout drunk, the courage to invite the bright new day without complaint, wax the fender, change the oil, mix the mud, pour and trowel another cubic foot or two of concrete. I think he missed his oxygen-depleted brain. Thumbnail stained with nicotine. The feel of bacon grease congealing on his teeth. I served him up, watched him paging through the paper, unfolding rival after rival.

By August, what made the General happy was the Two-Martini Rule. Two for the weekdays, in any case; for the weekends, three. Then three for the weekdays also, four for the weekends, then on, then on, his happiness concluding in the pitcher.

"Look alive," the General said. "It's 1700, time to mix us!"

Us, he said, and *we*.

We Oneys.

He said, "Who's the General?"

"You, sir."

He said, "Who's your pop?"

"You, sir."

He asked me what my name was, as if maybe I'd forget it, as if he needed to remind himself he was not alone in being Oney.

"What's your name?" the General said.

"Oney."

"How's that?"

"Oney, sir. Adam Oney, sir. My name is Oney."

"Very good," the General said, "at ease," as if the only way a person could sustain himself at ease was by a narrow vigilance, a rote conviction that he couldn't ever be another.

"Onliest Oneys in the phone book," said the General. "Ever notice?"

I said I had not noticed. I said I noticed. I said I had and had not noticed, didn't matter, it's the question General Oney never tires to hear himself repeating, *Ever notice?*

I mixed. I cooked. I cleaned. I mixed. I sat down to the news with him and listened myself numb from five o'clock to eight o'clock, the hour the General quieted, rested his drink, and slept. I covered him. I studied his mustache, the early whiskers marking out the shape of a goatee, coarser hair grown from a thinner skin. How must it feel to wake up being General Oney? When he sipped at his coffee, and lit his cigarette, and the smoke turned through his lungs, and his blood felt sick, and his cells were saying, *Sir, we're wounded*, what sort of love in misery was he feeling not to answer them, care for them, those cells, the skin he'd suffered so much in regrowing? The General claimed to be repeating history with a wiser eye. But he looked to be the same old bald abuser, sweetening in the sickly guilt of squandering a miracle.

One day, to simulate the good old days, we drove out to the hangars. The General smelled of last night's gin, the morning's Bloody Mary, a potent breath surviving bacon, eggs, and toothpaste. And then look at the General's unshaved face, his untucked shirt, the coffee stain he'd slopped onto his khaki trousers. Nothing good old days to this old boy; nothing of the sanctity of flight. But why should there be? The General wasn't flying. Neither was I. We had our first good look at the Pitts there in the hangar, and I don't think the General had the heart right off to push me.

Looked scary. Didn't look like anything that could have ever flown you. Looked like even less of something you could crawl out from alive to say you were the last one to have flown it. Nothing to it but the fuselage, nothing to the fuselage but metal frame. A charry, twisted heap the General said we ought to find a cushion for, maybe hang the thing by chains and turn into a porch swing. I thought the General was shaking. For sure he'd lost whatever color he'd got back; I thought he looked a little the way he did when I would see his nurse come in to cart him to the tank.

"So you say you saw me, huh?" the General said. "On fire?"

"Yes, sir," I said. "I did."

"And then you called up Mike?"

"I did," I said. "Instinct. Just like how I told you."

What I didn't tell the General was I never really talked to Mike at all. Mike handed the phone straight over to Mrs. R, who said for me to hang up right now, dial 9-1-1, tell them I have got a real emergency, all of which I did, which saved him. We stood in the hangar with our hands in our pockets, staring at the Pitts. I thought that might be all with Mike, but then I think the vision of that wreck inspired the General to push for him to start in flying with a vengeance. The General went a little bulldoggy, locked his jaw on me, seemed like wouldn't turn me loose until I'd picked the phone up and finally made our offer. We left the hangar, went to lunch, and the General said he didn't understand. Not at lunch, not on the drive back home from lunch, not at cocktails, not at dinner, not through those three waking hours before the General nodded off at eight.

"You're his friend, aren't you?" he kept saying. "Don't you call yourself a friend?"

Think about the implications, said the General. Hadn't he taught me? Didn't I remember? You could have a life? He worked in Mike and me through varying articulations and opinions of the news that passed before us, worked himself in, too, featuring the three of us as brightening points of hope against the rot he said the world was coming to.

"Flying musketeers!" the General said. "Think of us as that!"

A bulldog, think. Or a gator. Got his jaws locked and he's shaking, rolling you so in a day or two you're snapped and twisted under. Sure it felt some nights like I was drowning, and sure it could have been the General and the TV both that drowned me. The volume the General needed for his hearing. Or the tone and surge of all those paunchy, red-faced quibblers, talking heads for shows called *Double-talk, Cutthroat, Backstab*—professional bickerers, grown-ups—guys who watched the footage of babies slaughtered in Rwanda and were gone without a break to making jokes about the Pope's most recent scandal.

I sat thinking, are they for real? Musketeers? Musketeers? Now what the hell is General Oney saying?

"That's what makes this country great," the General is saying. "You get a chance. I was poor. I could have laid right down with all the rest. But that's not what this country's all about. Not what I'm about. I believed. You're smart, you'll believe, too. Think of this—I had cousins once they tied me to a tree while they went to the fair. There was a goat there called Bijou, could have ate me but he didn't. I fouled myself. Both ways. That's America. Did I tell you? These United States. That's what I'm saying. You can go to the fair next year. Goddamn it, I wanted to fly. And I never knew my daddy. You've got yours right here. You are an American. Here I am. I flew the fighters. We eat steak. It's not easy. You come in low across that plain, see those huts, it's farmland. You see the pagoda, place those people worship. There's a little yellow man out plowing. For me, I never wanted to shoot. But I did. Lay it down fast, that's how. You want to cut that yellow bastard half in two. That's your mission. For your country. For yourself. The flak is coming. They want your ass. That's life. Hear? Hear? What I'm saying, you can save yourself. But you better get on the stick, I'm saying. I like a steak. You like steak? For the little guy, poor folks, this country gives you hope. What's your dream? Your friend Mike, he's clear. He'll fly. He knows what this country is about, I can see it. Christ," the General said. "Christ. Let's go. You know what? Let's go. You got a friend, you help him. He's my friend, too. We go back. I know that boy. Let's go."

The General lowered his footrest, stood up from his chair, and punched around on the remote until he punched "off." I don't think we either one of us expected so much quiet. We seemed to me to be surprised without that volume, embarrassed, as if a pretty girl had just walked in to catch us with our clothes off.

"Go?" I said.

The General teetered from his heels and back onto the balls of his feet. His hands hung straight down at his sides and opened and closed as if the one hand wanted for its cigarette, and the other hand its drink.

"One for the road," the General said. "Mix us, then we'll go and see if we can't talk to your friend Mike."

I drove. I was drowning, driving. The General was on, a wide-open throttle, running his engine full rich. Past eight. Unfamiliar daylight for the General. He sounded very far to me and tentatively happy. I think we both were wishing it would hurry up and darken. On the other hand, it's a pretty, dusky light we're driving through. Very nice to feel the cool air falling from the high, thin sky; nice to breathe up the aroma through the irrigated acres of perspiring vegetation. Alfalfa, potatoes there, potatoes, onions, melons.

"Looks quiet," said the General. "Pull up right here to the front."

"I don't know," I said. "Maybe we should have called."

"Bullshit," said the General. "Just pull up right there. Now give them a little toot."

"Well, what if they're eating dinner?"

"Then I guess they'll put their forks down, come on out, and see who it is. The horn," the General said. "Two taps. Two taps is what's friendly. That's an order."

I said, "I'll just go up and knock."

I walked up to Mike's door, and when I came around to the front of the Comet, the General leaned hard on the horn, twice, scared me out of my skin, very funny. Not funny was Mike's daddy, who stood up and threw his napkin down to come and see what sort might make himself at home to interrupt his dinner.

I said, "I'm sorry, Mr. R. We were just out driving and we thought, I don't know, it had been awhile, I guess, I'm sorry."

Mr. R stood at the door not saying anything but looking like to say that *awhile* was fine by him, and even better was a whole lot longer, like *forever*. I had never seen the look before, but it wasn't hard to see Mr. R was saying, *Move your ass now, white eyes, this is my place, ain't nobody in this house to make you feel invited.*

"Sorry?" said the General. "Hell, no. Tell him!"

The General was coming up, tipping forward from his Comet, looking smaller, I was thinking, more wounded, redder on the one side of his face than how I saw and thought of him at home. He kept saying sorry, no, you're not sorry, he's not sorry, tell him, Adam, say it, we got good news here, why sorry?

Mrs. R came up and made a place beside her Mr. R and said hello to us and that the General was looking fine, thank the Lord, they had prayed for him, we must be very happy.

"Well, that's nice," the General said. "Thank you, Mrs. Mike. All the same, we don't believe too much in prayer. We believe in flight."

"Believe what?" she said.

"Tell them," said the General.

I couldn't tell. That kind of flight, it didn't seem enough of mine to offer.

"Christ," the General said.

"Please," said Mrs. R.

"Well, we have a deal," the General said. "Where's Mike? Deal is, we've been thinking, and we want to start him flying."

"My boy?" said Mrs. R.

"That's right," the General said. "That's why you stuck around here, isn't it? Growing melons? Keep close to the jets, get your boy up flying? That's the deal. We have a plane. We'll get him up, and it'll cost you next to nothing."

"No deal," said Mr. R.

"How's that?" said the General.

"No deal," said Mr. R.

"But we want to thank you," Mrs. R said, "that's a very kindly offer."

"You're saying no?" the General said. "No? I'm talking nearly free here. You people can't afford to say no. Where's Mike?" the General said. "You know what this could mean for him? You know how much a thing like this can cost you?"

Mrs. R moved up in front of Mr. R, saying please and thank you, Mr. R looking more like he would maybe like to bust the General's crown to show him how much Mr. R had learned a thing could cost you.

"I'm sorry," Mrs. R was saying. "Adam, honey, could you help us? I don't think this is the time."

"What time?" the General said. "It's always the time. You people are as bad as Boudreaux. What is it, pride? Too proud?"

"Please," said Mrs. R. "Adam? Will you stop him?"

"Where's Mike?" the General said. "Where is he? That boy can fly, I'm telling you. Christ," the General said. "You people. We came to help. Friendly visit. You keep up the holier-than-thou bit, next place we'll be visiting that boy is jail."

"Lord," said Mrs. R. "Please, son, take him."

I picked the General up, just folded him how you might fold your bride or baby, held him tight to keep him safe from squirming free and falling. I was saying thank you, thank you, and I'm sorry, and as small as the General felt, and weak, I was sure Mr. R could easily have killed him.

That's what I said, too. Driving home, the General's mouth run out, his lamps on dim, I said, "You're lucky, you know, what were you doing? He could have killed you."

The General rolled his head so it rested on the door to catch the wind.

"Don't tell me about killed," he said. "I made it. Believe me, lieutenant, fly the missions I flew, not a scratch to show for it, and you come home knowing killed and lucky."

"That's all stuff," I said, "bullshit. You know you never flew. You and your missions. All stuff. Kid stuff. I'm not a kid. You never flew. You never saw an hour of action in your life."

The General sat up straight, and even in the failing light I saw he had rushed back up behind his eyes, his life called from wherever it would fall to. That's a flare sent up in the old boy with the captain's goateed whiskers, no signal of distress, this was the flare the scout sent up to zero in the heavy bombers. I was afraid, and relieved at once to think I was seen, and likely would tomorrow be forgotten as the General's Pearl Harbor.

The General burned behind his eyes, dispersed, flickered out, and faded.

"That's a lie," he said. "And you had better ask yourself who you'll become if you believe it."

Sure we were pretty well-grounded, the General and I. That's a bad turn the General took those days and nights directly after Mike. Every night, the three-hour feed of gin, news, and beef. Volume is up, smoke is thick, and the General isn't going straight at Mike, but singling out his *people*. That's how he says it—Mike's *people*, your pal's *people*, his *people*, right, the woman on the news you see collecting on nine kids. Monkeys are going to stay right where they are, so long as they have got a government keeps feeding them bananas. The General had his feet up. He was near to shouting. The General dropped down way beneath his eyes, ran himself on autopilot. Some very scary low-level flight going on in him for sure. You saw him, looked to me like skimming the tea-green swamp, touching down with the water moccasins and copperheads, diving right down with the bottom-feeding catfish. That's bad magic working up there from the General's bones; something rank and fevery that told you it would kill you if you caught it.

He was asking me who traded us those slaves back in the first place. White guys had to buy from somebody, didn't they? Some Hootsi-Tootsi chief? Still selling each other to this day, according to the General, just pay attention to the news. Spoils of war. Winners rule. White folks used to do it too. War wasn't over, either. Never be over. War now in our country fought with money. White guy has the money now, but you think if the black guy gets his he won't do like any white guy, well, forget it. Winners rule means losers serve; white or black, you lose and you're the slave.

"First rule of war," the General said, "is you had better win it."

"Mix," the General said.

He said, "This smoke all right with you?"

The General said, "You've got your Boudreauxs, and that's trash, and worse than trash, you've got your niggers. Now you'll pass them both on the road with their thumbs hung out, but you don't pick them up. Trash will think he deserves to have the same as you, make you take him to your house so he can live there. Same with the nigger, only when the nigger moves into your house, and you go to the law, they'll tell you the nigger *does* deserve your house, owing to his history. But when you drive back up that road you find out the nigger hasn't got a history. Not the one the law is pointing at. The nigger you picked up has got a daddy drives a top-down, leather-seat Mercedes. No Cadillac for him. He's gone European. Doesn't want to come within a bluesy note of Motown. Nigger with the history you never see because he can't even make it to the road you drive on. He's back there in the neighborhood, place you wouldn't think to drive at noon, *shufflin' with the brothers*. Nigger daddy, he won't drive there, either. Hell, no! He's fat. He married blonde. He's living smack dab at the dead end of a cul-de-sac of solid whites. He knew which road to drop his boy on. He told him, he said, *You want what I got, you best stick that thumb out.* Then he leaves his boy for you to give your house to him, and that daddy drives home with his top down, shaking his fist at his sorry white neighbors all standing there behind their curtains, not knowing whether they should cheer him or shoot him, you know, because the white folks have been making money on the Angry Black Man act for too long now to tell that money no, thank you, sir, we don't need it."

Sit with him, watch the news and you decide the General was reading in between the anchor's lines, reciting from a book a whole lot older in the world than he was. I took to closing all the windows near to six o'clock because I didn't want the neighbors knowing the General was shouting all the same things they were. That's a long shout now. Hoary old voice of war. You might expect we could have moved along by now, maybe listened to the wind while we were eating our potato chips and peanut butter sandwich, like maybe after so many thousands of years of taking scalps and planting heads on poles and shooting babies in the neck so we could rape their mothers, we could be ready now to sit out on our porches when the wind died, appreciate a little grace, watch the stars, and say a thank you for the dream we finally lived beneath them on our round, blue world of peace.

Well, I saw the news. I know that's not a star there but a satellite. Satellite surveillance. There's a bad guy on the planet, and we need to track him. I see the General is relieved to find a man in office who appreciates our need for warfare technological advances in space. Defense shield. First-strike capabilities. Lasers, unmanned drones, smart bombs able to reduce that eighteen-year-old soldier to a splattering of brain and lung and liver on the pavement without a bruise or an abrasion suffered by those citizens who worshipped next door at the mosque. That is some amazing grace, brought to you by the greatest nation in the history of the world, how'd we do it?

"Don't be a sap," the General said. "Kid that age, younger even, twelve years old, I'd say, must make the coldest-blooded killers going. The ignorance," the General said. "If they would just lay down their arms."

I ran the loop—mixed, closed the windows, covered up the General, and laid him out his snack, waked up to another sunny day of eggs and bacon. Repeat the loop till one day I am worried for my quality of mind, and then the next day or the next I'm sitting at the morning table with the General thinking, yes, all right, thank you gods, I am saved.

"Look at this," the General was saying. "Right here. Right here is the real world."

The General handed me the paper and I think I had expected him to mean the real world was a program for exchanging needles, or else a program teaching safe sex in the high schools, a clown dressed in a sperm suit, juggling IUDs, diaphragms, and contraceptive sponges, paid in dollars from the General's taxes, what an outrage. But this morning, real life for the General was sports. Basketball, of course, news that our Coach Jerry had been axed, replaced by some ex-legend from the Hoosier State of Indiana. Showed a picture of this new coach in the paper, a hatchet-headed man whose lean, gray face made you believe it didn't matter if the film that took the picture was black and white or color. Look at this guy, then couple him with Mike, who this coach has talked back into playing, and suddenly the Huskies are reborn; read the article, know our histories, live here in our little desert town and understand how wild a hope is made by hitching it to the short, wild time a person has in life to hitch himself to something famous. *I was there. Should have seen. That town, the movie they made of that team, I lived there then, I waved a clock, that was me.*

I gave the paper back to the General, thinking, *I am coming back . . .*

"What do you think of that?" the General said. "Looks like your friend Mike has jumped in bed with the devil. Too bad. Shame. One ride in the F-4 could have cinched him."

I let the General go. He went on, had a bunch to say, though none of it much new. I tried to tell him something good might come of this new coach, but the General didn't copy. *General Oney, sir, come in, please, Pop, come in, Pop, do you read me?* I saw he gave up on his goatee, wore a face perpetually encrusted by a four-to-five-day growth of beard. Gray, gray, gray. Unless the General had been out in the sun too much, he looked as if he had been dipped in ash. He looked to disappear, and reappear, thinly, a gray ghost, a floaty presence in the room, infected with an otherworldly stasis. Loud, all right, a white-noise volume, a gray man in a gray smoke, who would see him?

I saw Huskies. I made my rounds through Buy and Bye and Cecarelli's, treated myself to an old-fashioned shake at Baxter's, saw our schedules taped to walls and windows, games we weren't to play till late December, dates clear out to early March, and we weren't completely through with August. Call it hope, healthy wishful thinking, but I was inspired with other folks in town, had my head turned pretty well around by what appeared to be my life's potentially most brightly colored season. Though that schedule wasn't handsome, or festive, nothing red and blue or Huskyish about it, but blockier, upright, a format urging an allegiance to an institution in our lives more precious than our high school. A government from back when Uncle Sam meant Uncle Sam, and if the word came down to pitch in, we pitched in; and if the word came down to cut back, we cut back. These schedules seemed to summon up the spirit from the days when we believed victory was ours if each of us would dedicate a little patch of ground to raise a lettuce and tomato.

And our spokesmen? Our warrior leaders? Well, there they were, new coach and Mike, profiled headshots in the upper left- and right-hand corners of the schedule, the new coach looking inward from the one corner, and Mike there from the other. The more I studied them, the more I thought here was a man and here was a boy who knew about their lives because they each had passed through life already; they were miracles, I thought, resurrections to remind us of the sanctity in passing. Very serious. Gray, as the General was gray, only different, the difference being that the General's was the gray of a guy on his way out, whereas the gray of that new coach and Mike was the gray of two guys on their way back in. Stick with them, you'll come to see some cosmic peacock color; run your laps, you'll last the game; step in time, you'll live your moment. The message from these two: *Don't miss it.*

Mike I hardly recognized, figured him to be a trick of heavy touch-up.

The coach's name was Krieg.

Hector called around, got a meeting up of all of us but Mike at Cecarelli's. Couldn't get ahold of Mike. Krieg, either.

"Krieg!" said Hector. "You believe that shit?"

"Krieg," I said. "As in blitzkrieg, right?"

"As in *war,*" said Hector, "you believe that?"

"Well, it's perfect," I said, "isn't it?"

"Too perfect," Hector said. "That's what I'm saying."

"And from Indiana," Lester said. "Or was it Carolina?"

"Indiana," said Arturo. "But what I want to know is, has anybody seen him?"

"Well, Mike has," Hector said. "Anybody checked those schedules out? The way they set it up, looks to me like those two boys are phase one in a red-hot romance. Have to be a pretty skinny slip to fit between those two."

Mr. Cecarelli brought us our pies, sort of hovered near our table. He held his hand out, pointing, checking did we have our plates, our napkins, our seasonings, our soda? The VIP treatment, very nice, all right, felt good to see that Mr. C believed.

"You guys okay?" he said. "Got everything you need?"

"What do you think?" Hector said. "Seriously, look at us here, Mr. C, and tell us what you think is missing."

Mr. C studied our table, stuck out his lower lip and said he couldn't serve us beer, if that's what we were missing, or if it was girls, he couldn't help us out there, either.

"No, no," said Arturo. "He means Mike. You know, how come he won't call us when we call him? How come he already has his picture taken on that schedule?"

"Hurt your feelings?" Mr. Cecarelli said.

"Feelings?" said Hector.

"Sure," said Mr. C. "You want to be in the picture, too, don't you? That's jealousy. Jealousy's a feeling, last I heard. People kill by it. It's life. Sounds to me like your new coach is schooling you in hardball."

We talked it over some and figured Mr. Cecarelli maybe wasn't too far off his nut. We could see how Mike would be the first on Coach Krieg's list of who to talk to, but take his picture? He didn't even play last year! What kind of Husky was he? He let the team down, he let the town down. We saw what Mr. C thought Krieg was getting at, using Mike as an electric wire touched to the heart department of our brains to prod us, and for sure we jumped, what choice? According to Mr. C, the idea was to keep us in that boat, way out in the ocean, adrift with all the rest until we'd got ourselves in shape enough to swim out for the island paradise where Krieg and Mike were. Idea worked. We worked. Met up at the old asphalt courts and ran. Twice a day. Eight till noon, and then again from two till six. Arturo organized. Mornings we drilled. Ran lines. Ran shuffles. Ran the full court backwards, ran the full court in a sprint. Arturo thought to shoot from spots, seven spots, fifty shots from each spot, baseline in an arc from one side of the basket to the other. Then shoot back.

"That's what," said Hector, "fourteen-hundred shots? Is that possible?"

"Mathematically," said Lester, "yes."

"Physiologically," said Chester, "it depends."

"I don't know," Arturo said. "It's like what I remember from those films Oney's dad used to show us. Hall of Famer types. I figured, well, let's try."

We weren't alone. One morning an old gal reined in her pug and watched us for a while. Next morning she brought her pug and her old-guy husband both to watch, and pretty soon we had a pretty good-sized gang to watch us dribble cones and shoot and run the three-man weave. Afternoons though is the time when most folks seemed to want to catch us. Scrimmage time. Half-court, two-on-two with a fifth man coming in to rotate every tenth basket. That's two-and-a-half hours straight, long enough so we would pair up each of us alongside and against the other. I never wasn't grateful for my turn to sit. Not only for the rest, but also so I could watch. Those Oolags, Hector and Arturo, shirtless, shining, tanned. Sleek boys, naturals, nothing of the weight room to them. When Arturo got down low and made his cuts across the key, when Hector rose up high to shoot his baseline jumper, when Chester made his pivot, held the ball up high and cleared out for his famous hook, then if you watched the body closer than the ball, you saw the highlight reel for muscle groups and how they ought to function. Calves, quads, biceps, triceps, pecs, the implication of some seriously steely glutes. Those were fluid moves. Grace in August. *Looks like dance,* I heard, *tough dance, lot rougher than you'd think, nice butts.* Audience made it fun. Talky. The way they sat on the grass beside the court, in folding chairs, on a bench somebody built of milk crates and a pine plank, it was easy jawing back and forth, *Get him, get him, shoot, you gonna let him do that to you, whooee, better get a hose on him, that boy is on fire!*

So we were jealous. The kind of jealous Mr. Cecarelli said we were, a little bit like girls with crushes, or like boys who had imagined Mike into a girl, a poster sweetheart we all taped up on our ceilings, promised to forgive forever, so long as she would take us where we needed to be going.

"That's good," said Mr. C. "You guys are young, idealistic, take advantage."

"True fact," Hector said. "Boy has got the ring through our noses."

I myself never saw him. Not sure how hard I looked, had reasons not to look at all, but still I thought it seemed a little funny, unlikely I should be the only one to never see him till the word came through Arturo that Coach Krieg was calling for a meeting.

I said, "He called you? Krieg did?"

"Not Krieg," Arturo said. "Mike."

I asked Hector, "So how's that make you feel?"

Hector said, "You mean like does it hurt my feelings? Answer is no. Yes, and no. I'm looking down the line here. This is called foreplay, Oney. I'm thinking the way we've been working, when we throw in Mike, we'll be headed for a hell of an orgasm. We'll come off that court at State like we just shot the mother of all loads. I'm thinking I'll be set for life."

We met the day I picked my senior portrait up. The pictures were from maybe just six weeks ago, a surprisingly fatter, paler day for Adam Oney. Ah, well, I thought, who looked? And how much anyway would a pound or two or color in the skin decide what somebody was really seeing? If a person really looked, I thought, then what he saw was current, the motion in the tides of a life and not the sack of bones that held it. A person looked, and right or wrong, he saw the person he was looking at through the lens of the General's question, *Was this guy here a winner or a loser?* Sure I walked into the room and there you had a bunch of twenty-five or thirty of us looking just like that, like *loser? winner? is this guy going to make it?*

Missing in the room was Mike. And Krieg. I sat down next to the Oolags, who were using their free time wisely, studying their science. Hector and Arturo sat apart and seeming calm enough, unquestionable winners. I didn't know what I must look like, but I know when Mike and Krieg walked in, I felt afraid. I think we all were just a little bit afraid. I think we saw how next to those two, we all were kids, something in their focus said if you stepped onto the court to play them you were coming off a loser. Mike took a seat in the front of the room and Krieg stood up before us, motioning us to sit. He didn't say anything, and kept not saying anything until he'd had a chance to look us over, each one at a time. Seemed to me those two drained the room of color, as if they were the poster of themselves, black and white, gray lives they were someway letting us in on to see how well we liked it. You didn't want to move. Didn't want to breathe. You were grateful in believing you had maybe stood up better than the guy beside you, and when Krieg had finished his review, you weren't surprised, but still you wondered why he hadn't looked at Mike.

He wrote his name on the board.

He said, "There has been no meeting here today," and left.

Then Mike stood up in Krieg's place. He wrote his name beneath Krieg's name, wrote out his address.

He said, "Beginning tomorrow, five o'clock, my place, going to have a one-on-one tournament. Top twelve players get to come back three times a week after that to scrimmage, play ball together till tryouts. Any questions?"

Weird scene here. The original five of us looked sort of stupefied, like we were thinking, *What the fuck?* Guy from last year's squad raised his hand and asked Mike was this legal.

"Entirely," said Mike. "This isn't an official meeting. Do you see any coaches? I'm just inviting, if you want to play, then I'm inviting you to come on out and play at my house."

We sat quiet for a while again until some younger kid raised his hand and asked if Mike's was close enough to ride there on a bike.

Lucky for the kid he made it on his bike. Unlucky for him when it came up his turn going one-on-one he got his ass kicked. Lester couldn't figure the math, and none of us could see the reasons for the matchups, but we all agreed the system was devised by Krieg, and that Mike's job was to call and cross the names off. Took a couple days to find our twelve, and when we did we saw the twelve were likely those a coach would pick in tryouts. Only we had *played* to get our twelve. Hard. Head-to-head, mano a mano. Made for good morale there in the Quonset hut. Even the ones beat out on the first day, even the kid with his bike came back for the second day to watch and holler. Big noise in that slim tin tube, some crazy reverb off the corrugated ribbing. Big whoops, lots of laughs, more jawing, yuk-yuk, a ring of courtside judges, the vanquished, the next in line, up-and-comers, the contenders. Seemed an old and happy way to play the game. Just give us the ball. Walk around your neighborhood, drive across the country, right, see a gang of boys out shooting in the driveway. There's a girl who throws a shot up at a basket standing way out in a pasture. There's a basket nailed onto a tree, a netless basket on a crooked pole sprung from the broken asphalt in the projects, basket out back of the town garage where the mechanics play a game of HORSE on lunch break. The wind comes up. A boy is six, he is seven. He lies down on the grass, tries to prop his head up on the ball the way he sees the big boys do it. He gazes. The net is unlooped, stained the colors of its age. One day, he thinks, I will run with those big boys, one day I will touch that net, I will shoot the big ball. The wind feels good against his skin. He hears his mother on the wind, calling him in to supper, and this is Mrs. R, calling us out of our dim hut for melon.

"I've got melons for you all. You come on out to eat. Look at what a pretty sunset!"

Twenty-eight boys, that's the official count of us in paper plates. That's the picture Mrs. R has taken of us, lined up against the Quonset hut, digging into those half-cuts of Hearts of Gold, looking skyward while the desert purpled up, shaded through a deeper blue, then darkened. Handshakes all around, elaborate grips involving wrists, palms, and fingertips through several staged regrippings. Mrs. R apologizing for the cantaloupe, promising a sweeter melon in a day or two, these melons here were sweet, but you would be surprised how much a thing will profit from a day or two of sunshine. *See you later, good game, see you later, thank you Mrs. R . . .* till I am left with Mrs. R and Mike, the three of us all looking out to Mr. R, who came riding our way on his tractor.

"Adam, honey," said Mrs. R, "you better go now."

I stood on a bit, thinking what to say while Mr. R kept coming closer. In the end, I said again I was sorry.

"I don't know what else to say," I said.

"We know," said Mrs. R. "Let's let it go now, can we?"

"Mike," I said, "You can fly. Really. Offer's still good. General keeps on saying it, how natural a pilot you would be. Fighters, too. It's great," I said. "I soloed. Can't we just—"

Mrs. R said, "Adam."

Mike didn't answer but kept facing toward his father.

"Mike," I said, to this gray guy I hardly seemed to know, I said, "Mike."

The tractor rolled on closer so I saw enough of Mr. R to understand how much he didn't want to see me.

"All right," said Mike. "All right, now, just listen. I'm going to fly. Going to fly because I want to fly, don't care about the fighter killer. Killer shit is bullshit. Didn't you ever see? Your daddy isn't any killer. He never went at all. You heard the man."

"What do you mean?" I said. "You believe that?"

"Believe it? I know it. Best part of your daddy, too, him not going over."

"What?" I said. "What are you saying?"

Mike held up his hand and shaped his fingers in a zero sign and said, "Right there. Zero. That's how much you understand about your daddy."

Mr. R rolled up and sat not twenty feet away from us, shut the tractor down, and did not move from off his seat but kept on sitting through the quiet.

"Adam, honey," said Mrs. R.

"All right," said Mike. "You're sorry. So go on, all right."

. But it didn't sound all right to me. Sounded more like sorry wasn't ever going to be enough, like being sorry was not the kind of thing he wanted me to be. Didn't really need me to be anything. Or any of us, really, to be anything. Except for Krieg, he was entirely apart.

When I saw Hector, I said, "He didn't even play. Nobody asked. How come?"

"He's the man," Hector said. "But I've got some ideas for a little something different. Break up that old scowly faced routine. Our game, when it's good, it's got a real joie de vivre. Know what I'm saying?"

So the next time we are there at Mike's, commencing with our twelve, Hector takes the lead and says he'd like to make a proposition. He let us quiet, just as Krieg had; looked us over, just as Krieg had; and sure I thought he did a pretty fair impression of the scowly faced routine he'd said it wasn't ours to play through.

"Gentlemen," he said. "We have a situation here. In this hut, with these twelve talents, we have the tools for making Husky history. We can make our town proud. You have mothers, and fathers, sisters and brothers, some of you are blessed with a steady sweetheart. I want for you to take a moment here and think of them. Now recall our season last year, and ask yourself if last year's performance was the gift you want to give, or if you are prepared this year to make the sacrifices needed to give them something better. A performance they will never forget, a spectacle to last a lifetime."

Hector continued, clapping his hands, smacking his fist into his palm, spreading his arms and looking upward at the corrugated steel as if beseeching God in heaven. By-and-by he came around to talking on division, and unity, the brotherhood of ancient Greeks. A pact needed to be made, some rite by which we showed ourselves to be initiates in the selfless league of team.

Was he right?

He was right.

Was he right?

He was right.

"All right, then," Hector said. "What I propose, as a sign of solidarity, is that we all have got to fuck the melon."

That's right, he said, we heard him right, and no, not metaphorically, but literally, all of us, take the knife, cut a hole, stick it in and fuck the melon. He shaped his hands to fit a ripe-sized cantaloupe, held them at his crotch and bucked. Some uneasy-seeming chuckles went around, a big ha-ha or two, but once it looked like Mike was with us we let go with Hector, bucking into our empty hands, *oh, yeah, baby, talk to me, I know you like it . . .*

One thing though to find your joie de vivre from fucking the space between your hands, another thing to stand out in the field with all the boys and fuck the actual melon. Questions, please: Who fucks first? Or do we all fuck at once? Fuck till I come? In a cantaloupe? What if I can't get it up? Or worse, maybe, what if I can? We met out in the melons on a new moon night, thankful for the high clouds that darkened up the starshine. We went about without much talk, some stuff about the warmness of the weather, jokes about what made one melon sexier than another. Smoother rind, we wondered, earthier aroma? I saw Arturo lift a melon to his ear, shake the thing and smile. I saw the Oolags and a couple other guys who sort of followed Mike, maybe thinking since Mike lived here he would have a better sense of how to choose them. When everybody had his melon, we stood around in a circle, eyeing each other's picks, embarrassed, covetous, proud, in Hector's case, to see his was biggest.

He looked at Chester's pick and said, "Jesus, Oolag. You call that thing a melon?"

Chester held the melon closer to his face and turned it.

Chester said, "I never fucked a cantaloupe before."

"Me, either," said Lester, and the way they said it made you worry what they *had* fucked. We held the things in front of us, turning them as Chester had, unaroused and likely wondering what next.

"Knives, gentlemen," said Hector. "Carve your fit."

Hard for me to feature us, twelve boys in a field, got their brows pulled down, their tongues stuck out, all business, me too, going at my melon with a steak knife. Ripe melon, I could smell it, warm and ripe, sweeter smelling than the melon Mrs. R passed out a couple days before, just the way she had promised. I looked around enough to see we all were opting not to try it through the fly, but dropped our pants, and then I didn't look around at all much more. Nobody did. You didn't want to see or be seen, it's private time, me, myself, my melon. I used the memory of those pictures Hector cut out from the women's magazines and was amazed at my success. I was up! All the way up! I was in! Felt warmer than it smelled in there, and sweeter, and orangier, felt like all that hurried ripening and sunshine meant to swallow me in there, and my brain went blind to stop it. I mean I pulled out. I panicked. I looked around and saw nobody was even in yet, still had their mouths hung open and their free hands diddling their scrotums and their foreskins.

I said, "Heeh!" a high, sharp, girlish sound between my teeth, and then defiled my melon.

I didn't have to look around but felt all eyes on me, my mess, these stringy, seeded gobs of Hearts of Gold hung from my pole, a sticky mix of Oney's misspent jism.

Good news was I made for a lot of mirth. Saved those boys from going in, the consensus being they all had passed the ritual by bearing witness to a newly minted legend. I would get around. My name was made. These boys were the proud and the few to see me make it. Bad news was the other names I made myself to go with Adam Oney. They all were laughing, throwing their melons out into the field, hauling up their pants and saying no way would they have ever done it, they were only joking, saying, *Voted: Adam Oney, Most Likely to Fuck Fruit.*

Mike, who it turned out never dropped his pants at all, came up to me and laid his hand right on my shoulder, saying, "Oney, man, you are one sad dude."

We all went home, and on my way, the clouds blew by enough for me to look up to the stars to try to find some cosmic sign to tell me I deserved to feel the way I felt, and I supposed I found plenty. Because I wanted to, I guess. Because every single star and every grain of sand will give you back the answer you desire of any question you will ask it. *I am bad, cosmos, punish me, anything you like, I'll take it.* Though when I went inside the house, and did not see the General in his chair, didn't find him in his bed, went around the house and called for him and didn't get an answer, then I said, *Okay, cosmos, uncle, I'm not that bad, just tell us, where's the General?* I went out front and sat down on the porch awhile, looking up and down the block to see if maybe he was staggering the sidewalks. I checked the garage. Well, I thought, how much harm could a foot-bound flyer come to?

I took a shower, quick rinse, little soap to the cantaloupey middle parts, and when I shut the shower off, I could hear the General through the bathroom window, in the backyard, singing what I supposed were Air Force fight songs. I yelled out through the screen to him, though I couldn't see him, and he hollered back to me he wasn't singing, there wasn't any singing in the Air Force. When I made it out to him I couldn't really think what I was seeing. A slab, I saw that much, a six-inch concrete platform I hadn't seen before, and on the slab the General, seated with a thermos of martinis in the cockpit of his Pitts.

"What's that?" I said.

"War bird," said the General. "I am shot up pretty bad."

"How'd you get it here?" I asked.

"Truck," the General said.

"Well, why? Why, I mean, why?"

"Why?" the General said. "That's what I asked, why. I said, General Oney, are you ever going to build yourself that gazebo? When you were little, didn't you always want a gazebo? Think you'll ever have a hot tub? Where're you gonna sit outside?"

I said, "What are you sitting on now?"

"I don't know," the General said. "Cushions. It's all paid for. Cash money. Private property. Can do with it what I damn well please. You want to sit?"

"In there?"

"No room in here," the General said. "Pitts is a one-man cockpit. You forget? You're too big," the General said. "How'd you get so big?"

"I grew," I said. "I eat a lot. But I'm losing."

"You're old," the General said. "You're eighteen."

"Yes, sir."

"You could vote. You could go to a war. Any damn thing you want. Move out."

"Yes, sir," I said. "That's true."

"So what do you want?"

"I want to fly."

"No," the General said, "you don't. You're no pilot. Too big. Never be a pilot. Your friend Mike, now there's a pilot."

"That's what you keep saying. He's a natural, right? He'll fly the fighters?"

"Damn right," the General said.

He banged his thermos on the metal frame.

He shivered, said he was cold.

He said, "You don't want to go to war. It's hell. I got shot down. It's hell. Look at this thing. A waste. A shame. Nobody should have to live through this. You want to fly?"

"Yes, sir," I said. "I do."

"No, you don't."

"But I do," I said.

"Well, hell. Me, too," the General said. "I always did. You know what? You know those cousins, the ones who tied me to the tree? I used to go down to a bridge with them, and what we did, we dropped rocks on gators. One time, Leonard, he went down around the side of the bridge to take a leak. He's the littler, understand. Bigger brother, Walter, he stayed up with me, and we were dropping rocks on the heads of these baby gators. I never even saw the mama. But boy she came out fast, and bellering. Scared me and Walter most to death. But it was Leonard she was after. Bit his arm off at the elbow. If that arm hadn't come off, she would have gone and taken all the rest of Leonard with her. You believe that?"

"Not sure," I said.

"You don't have to be," the General said. "Thing is, flight, before the Wright brothers, nobody was too sure to believe that, either. But they'd flown. Tried to sell their airplane to the government, but the government wouldn't even look. Didn't believe. Fairy tales. So those Wrights put their bird in a barn and kept it secret there for a couple of years. Then they took and showed it to the French. The French! God help us. Boudreaux is a French. Place down there is thick with French. Oney, now, Oney, you're an Irish. Irish! Do you know how tiny you are?"

"Sir?"

"Skip it," said the General. "Strike that. Do you know, do you know—well, shit, I think I'd better cut back on the sauce, do you think? I'm cold," he said. "Aren't you cold?"

"No, sir," I said. "But it's cooling off some. Were you in the sun much?"

"Little bit," he said. "Had to help out with this baby."

I asked the General if he remembered to wear his hat, long sleeves, did he use the sunscreens?

He poured himself another drink from his thermos. He sipped, offered me to go and get a glass to join him.

"No?" he said. "No. Just as well, not as good without the ice. I packed this glass with ice. It really lasted. Low humidity. You would be surprised. Where were you?"

"Just out. Goofing. Down to Cecarelli's. Stuff like that."

"Stuff like that," the General said. "It's quiet here, you know. Sometimes, when you're gone, I need to get outside. It's nice. But it's cold."

"You want to go inside?"

"I want to fly," the General said.

"You do," I said. "You can, you flew."

"You know that Orville was the younger," said the General. "He lived to see an airplane break the speed of sound. You know what he said? He said the best thing from his flying days was the dream of flight, that work, wanting and not knowing whether you would ever really do it, get up in the air like that, land back on the ground and not have the whole thing kill you."

I said, "I understand that, sir."

"I know you do. That's why I'm telling you. And let me tell you something else. Don't goof. Don't go to the wars."

"But there isn't any war, sir."

"Bullshit," said the General. "Listen, listen close, now, hear that? That's incoming. Choppers. There's boys they're running off those things on stretchers that they've had their face shot off. Got a four-inch piece of shrapnel cut right through their spine. Eighteen, same as you, and paralyzed for life. Coming home in body bags. You listening? They are always up there. Country needs you. You can go. You're old enough. Country needs to protect itself, country wants its freedom. Be a great defender. Liberator. Decorate your chest with medals. You see my star? What's it? Hey. Hey, they teach you how many stars yet in the universe?"

"No, sir, they have not."

"Know why?"

"Why?"

"They can't. Me, I only wanted to fly. You're a kid, you know, those planes they painted up to look like tigers? Those were handsome men. They were true and right. They painted sexy ladies, swimsuit gals on bombers. Names of people they loved. Enola Gay. There's a name. Another name I can remember. Otto Lilienthal—The Batman. Look him up. First-rank lunatic for flying. Inspired the Wright brothers. He died gliding. You know what he said at the end? *Sacrifices must be made.* How 'bout that? I loved that. I told myself I would sacrifice anything, give anything if I could fly. I was a kid. I was a baby. You are small a long, important time. You're small, and someone big is talking to you, you're looking up a lot to listen, and what I can remember seeing was a lot of sky. Remember that? That's my memory. Seems no matter who I conjure, whoever all I talked to, I will find them from a patch of sky. Not as much as here, but enough. Enough to set me. Do you know Otto Lilienthal?"

"No, sir, I don't."

"Lilienthal. The Batman."

"Yes, sir."

"That name, I guess, and looking at those pictures, as a kid, I always thought he looked more like a butterfly. Otto Lilienthal. Homer Oney. Know what I mean?"

"I think so, sir."

"That yellow bastard in his paddy, you capture him, run him through interrogations. He's got kids. A boy learning to count. Oh, yeah, of course, you're thinking, amazing, they count, too. He likes the Rolling Stones. He said the F-4s scared the shit out of him. Imagine living in the dirt, underground. Truth was, much as he feared the Phantom, he also loved it. He said despite the fire we were laying down, we were breeding a want to fly in a lot of VC hearts down there. I never saw a reason not to believe him. I didn't want to kill him. I couldn't kill him. Kill him. Kill. You understand?"

"Yes, sir, I think I do."

"I'm cold."

"Should we go in?"

"Sacrifices must be made."

"I could bring you out a coat."

"What if they had called him that instead—the Butterfly?"

"Or a blanket," I said. "If that would be better, I could bring you out a blanket."

"It's just the skin," the General said. "Might have overdone it today. Look at us, this thing. Made a few stops with her along the way home here, asked folks what they thought she was. Nobody knew. Maybe should have said a sacrifice. To what? Strike that. I'll tell you, however many stars there are, there are more here than in Louisiana. Damn. Why am I so cold? Give me a hand here," said the General, "this thing needs some ice."

"Yes, sir," I said, though we never made it to the ice. I steered the General for bed, and he didn't do much to resist me. He had gone muttery. Soft. He didn't want to fight. He wanted to fly. He was cold. He worked hard. He got lucky. Flew a goddamn awesome, beautiful machine. It was his duty. But he couldn't do it. Mimosas, he was saying, mimosas.

He said, "My life is pretty unbelievable. Anybody's life, a life, if you think enough about it, that anybody is alive at all and knows it, it's pretty unbelievable."

GRAND ROUNDS, PRERELEASE PARTY TIME ON THE UNIT FOR PATIENT ADAM
Oney, whole gang there to recall the damages, assess the progress, predict
the ranges of recovery they say I ought to know are realistic. Lots of pens on
clipboards going there at the foot of my bed, eleven sets of eyeballs moving
from the clipboards up to me and back to scribble out the similarities and
differences between who I had been when I flew in here, who I seemed to
be today. I tried to put the happy on, rolled out a burned-guy joke or two,
but these folks weren't here for laughing. Not here to talk. No reintroduc-
tions, either, so all I knew by name were Sue and Doctor Noggin and the
chaplain, Thomas. But these three weren't here for talking, either. Hardly
looked at me, except for Sue, whose face I thought was telling me she was
sorry, ashamed, maybe, she was not in charge here, we were following pro-
cedure, doctors' orders, our leaders were debating exit strategies, there was
nothing she could do.

I sat up straight, my legs stuck out from underneath my johnny. I thought
to pull the sheet up over me, cover my feet at least, but didn't. Thought to
turn the TV on, but didn't. Didn't ask for anything to eat or drink. Didn't
say, excuse me, please, I need to use the bathroom. You might think without
their masks and skullcaps these doctor types would not be quite so likely to
intimidate, less for you to not know by their faces, less for you to be afraid
of not knowing. I sat very still. They looked me over, compared clipboards,

leaned in close, squinting, looking over the tops of glasses, putting on the rubber gloves and touching. Then I went ahead and moved myself around a bit, thought to tell them by how well I bent, *Look guys, see the neck, how I can roll my head here, and how about these knees and ankles, great job, team, no contractures!*

Who knew what they saw? They looked and wrote, poked and talked me over, but what patient ever really understands such conferences between those highly skilled professionals engaged to heal him? Those body parts are yours they are describing, those valves, organs, tissues, these are your vital signs, your flows and rates, how you work in there, what dope you've swallowed, the incisions, and dissolving stitches. Encryptions, I was thinking, what you need here is your Navaho decoder. Sure a question every now and then in layman's English, *Did this hurt, did that? Thirsty much? How's the appetite? Feed yourself? Dress yourself? Sleep well? How often do you urinate? Any pain? In general, how would you describe your stools?* But, what? How to answer? This is a test, you are a schoolboy here, you pass this test, you graduate, this bunch knows the answers, they're watching you, they're waiting, they must see you need their help, but they're not telling.

"I've been out to lunch," I said. "I ate the chili-cheese."

"That's good," the General of them said. "That's fine."

But what really did that mean? I was getting out, right? I would be okay?

I said, "Nurse Sue here, she took me to Gold's. You been, any of you? I was telling Doc Noggin he ought to go. This guy Gold, see, he takes and stuffs these raptors."

Nods around, pens and clipboards, unmasked, semi-smiling faces. I was sweating. My ears hummed. I looked from one to the other of them, and what? The blond-haired, blue-eyed intern, looked like, creamy cheek, Mr. C's corn-fed Swede. And there the blue-cheeked guy beside him, veiny nose, bloodshot eyes, could have been, in age, the daddy of the Swede, what was he thinking? Who do we have here? Got the Japanese, which maybe you could say his creaseless skin was yellow since you wouldn't call it pink or red or tan and not at all the brown, brown, brown of that guy there from India, one with the fancy wire spectacles, a mole grown on his nose, him, them, by their faces, those shining, Asiatic eyes, what were they thinking? And the General of them, his lip hung down, his jowls hung down in folds of white whiskers, saying yes, saying no? When he looked at me and pushed his tongue against that lower lip did that mean I was free to go, in a couple months, give or take, I could expect to be myself? He didn't say.

He said, "Well, all right. Thank you for your time, Adam. Please forgive the intrusion," and he held his clipboard in the air and turned around and left my room for all the rest to follow.

You need Sue to tell you all of this was normal here, you did well, you'll be fine, though when she left your room, and it was quiet, and the only person left for hearing was yourself, you could never be too certain.

FOR THE GENERAL, AND HOW THE GENERAL AND I GOT ON TOGETHER, WE were living through some better days there thanks in part to the General's Pitts, in part to the General's having taken up his own advice and laying off the sauce a little, a little off the evening news. We dolled it up some, the General's Pitts, rigged it with tin we hinged so he could sit out in the day and have some shade, fold the one sheet back so he could watch the stars come nighttime. We sat out once and listened to a thunderstorm, somehow squeezed in tight enough for neither one of us to get too wet. The General turned his head to me so we were face to face and close enough to kiss. He was clean. No booze or Winston to him.

He said, "Hear that? I love that sound. Just listen."

I loved that sound, too. A hard rain on the flat tin. There are sounds like that you have no doubt you will love forever. Until you doubt. Because a sound like rain I loved and came to doubt was the sound of a ball, drib-bled and shot, the sound of shoes and the voices of the boys at play with the ball and happy. Because you saw at Mike's that ball—for us—would not be happy. Not much joie de vivre in the Quonset, no, sir, no more, not in Mike's house. In Mike's house, if you played, you played by Mike's rule. Rule was a rule to be followed, not interpreted. At first we thought it was a joke with Mike, like, *C'mon Mike, just let us play.*

But Mike said, "I'm running here to win. When you come here to my house, and you're not with me, then you're out."

"It's brain chemistry," said Chester. "When the fear part of the brain kicks in, you pay a whole lot more attention. Basically, it's the recreation of the infant state. He's treating us like babies. It's what sergeants in the army do. Create the optimum balance between your fear and your desire, then you create the optimum state for learning and performance."

"Makes sense to me," said Hector. "Guy wants us to feel like we're playing for our lives. He wants a squad of killers."

Dark came on a few minutes earlier every day along toward Christmas break, and the cold set in so we were playing with the door rolled down and under the lights, and it looked and felt to me as if that poster gray had soaked right through our skins, filled our bellies, lungs, and hearts so when Arturo scraped his knee, or Chester broke his nose, gray appeared to be the color we were bleeding. You would never guess we were the same bunch who had stood out in the field together, prepared to do it with a cantaloupe. Yet however gray, however humorless we were, however much we said this kind of play just wasn't us, we learned. We performed. We all caught and swapped the same disease. We were good, getting better faster, but I kept on feeling worse. One bright light in that time for me was the kid who rode his bike, come back again to watch us, and another bright light was the General.

I told Mr. Cecarelli, I said, "I don't know, but I'm not having any fun at all out there. I sometimes think I'd be a whole lot better off at work with you."

"You kidding me?" said Mr. Cecarelli. "You ought to want to kill to be you. You've lived through some things, kid. Do yourself a favor. Do us both a favor—you're looking good, stick this one out. Go home to your pop, if that's what helps. Just keep your eye on the kid with the bike."

Mostly I could see how Mr. C was right. Looked to be some kind of spell on us, deepest spell on Mike, helped me sometimes when I saw myself as being just the guy to break the spell and cure us. The way I saw me, I would fly the low-level missions, dropping leaflets urging cheer, laying down great fogs of color. I could do it. Wasn't any time at all ago we were jawing on the asphalt. Depending on the day, what had happened, and its hour, I could hear and see myself as if completely, sweating, breathing hard with Mike, squinting hard against the sun while we were climbing at the pits. We were there. I had only to recover us.

Mr. Cecarelli let me make a pie to take home to the General. A modified Enforcer, a nod I meant to make to Hector's dietary program, an Enforcer Lite. I pulled up to the house and saw the General sitting in the Comet in the driveway, idling with the heat on. I tapped on the window, showed him my pizza, and he made a motion with his finger for me to join him on the passenger side. He had the Country Western going in there, a rocking, sassy gal singer, needing a Do-Good Man to mend her Cheated Heart. I tried to ask the General what he was doing, but he shushed me.

"Good one," he said. "Listen."

He closed his eyes, tapped his fingers on the steering wheel, hummed along, and lit himself a Winston. I went ahead and started eating.

When the song was over, he said, "Good idea, huh?"

"What's that?" I said.

"The car," the General said. "The old Comet to the rescue. It's been too cold to sit out in the Pitts. I miss sitting outside."

The General lifted his thermos, sloshed it some, said, "Makes these things more enjoyable, listening to Patsy and watching the moon rise, instead of those talking heads."

The General said no thanks to the slice I offered, poured himself another drink, and tipped his ash into his palm.

He said, "All around, I think this is better for my health."

So for the General's health some nights we took to eating in the Comet—pizza, chicken in a bucket, Chinese in a box, stuff you didn't need a plate for and could eat with your fingers. Other nights, if I was late, I would need for his health to carry him inside. Felt good, like something I could do, and though it wasn't all the way to cheer and color, I knew sleeping in a bed must beat the Comet anyway for comfort. Made for a better cup of coffee in the morning, made for a better egg.

Fine for home, but on the court I cured nothing, broke no spell, and by Christmas I was happy for the time we gave our play a rest. Home for the holidays. Holiday baking, holiday cheer. We strung some lights around our windows, strung some on the General's Pitts. We sat listening to the Country Western Christmas tunes, eating egg rolls in the Comet when the General said what we needed was a tree.

"A real one," he said. "Kind we cut down how we used to."

We set off next day for the desert, same place we used to go, piñon stands in the foothills. Warm enough for a picnic, we thought, so we stopped for subs, all the good stuff, "Anything you want," the General said, "use your judgment, I'll just sit right here and wait."

Turned out he also sat and waited while I walked up the hill to do the cutting. He meant to come along, but the way he sounded in his chest, the way he said his head hurt, it didn't take too long to figure he should just turn back. I poked around some till I'd found a nice, fat tree, a heavy-scented piñon I dragged back to where I saw the General seated in the Comet with the top down, wearing his sombrero.

He handed me my sombrero and he said, "Surprise, surprise, found these in the trunk."

Another thing he said he found was a cooler full of ice, a bottle of champagne, and two glasses. The General poured us out.

He said, "Merry Christmas, hombre."

We raised our glasses, said our cheers, and when two Phantoms passed us low down through the basin I thought it meant good news to see the General salute them.

"Murphy," said the General. "He'll be gone with the next new governor. Somebody up there will take him out. Always somebody up there who has got a boy that isn't you. Bigwig with some rank and plenty cheek to pull it."

We said a cheers to bigwigs and muckamucks, another cheer to fuck 'em. Said another cheer to the little guy, to killdeer in the wetlands, said a cheer to the last glass in the bottle and being all cheered out. We drove home singing "Feliz Navidad," and sometime after I had covered up the General in his chair that night, I called my mother. I didn't talk to her but to the Reverend, who said she wasn't there.

"Not there?" I said. "What are you talking about, not there?"

"I mean to say just that," the Reverend said. "She is not here."

I waited for more, and when there wasn't more, I asked the Reverend had they seen my senior portrait.

"Yes," the Reverend said. "Your mother thanks you for it. It is displayed in a position of some prominence."

I waited again for more, and when no more came again, I said, "Huh."

"It's late," the Reverend said. "Have you any idea of the time?"

I said, "We don't talk, do we, Reverend?"

"We are far," the Reverend said. "It's natural. However, it is late. If you would like to talk, we might set up—"

I said, "I want to ask you something, Reverend. Do you ever, when she isn't there, do you ever like to rummage in my mother's drawers, put your face in my mother's underpants? You know, like, your favorites?"

"I beg your pardon?" said the Reverend.

"Oh, c'mon," I said. "You know what I mean. You're allowed, right, you're not a priest. I'm just asking, do you ever sniff my mother's panties?"

"Adam," said the Reverend. "I am offended. You offend your mother. Is your father home? Have you been drinking? It's late," the Reverend said. "I will say good-bye now. I will inform your mother."

After that, the General and I trimmed the tree and exchanged our presents; I went through tryouts and was cut. Sure nobody saw it coming. Tryouts seemed to be a done deal, a formality Coach Krieg didn't even bother to attend but ran through his assistants. But there we ran the drills, made our time, lined up sweaty and expectant on the bench, and assistant number one reads from his clipboard, and the name we never heard was mine. We heard eleven of our twelve, and not surprisingly, okay, some new guy who could shoot, but after the assistants walked off, and the guys who didn't make it, and the guys who did and also Mike, then Hector, Arturo, the Oolags, and myself all stood around and asked ourselves what happened. What was any-body thinking? Had there been some mistake?

Hector said, "Come on, Oney, let's go check it out."

Hector dragged me down to the assistants there in old Coach Jerry's office, telling us that, no, I wasn't a mistake, there would be no more mis-takes, that's the word down from the top.

"Krieg?" said Hector.

"Krieg."

I followed Hector to the showers. We stood there in the steam and Hec-tor said, "You're looking good there, Oney, but you're fucked."

Still, I lived. You can live, fucked. Myself, I could go on home, sit up in my bed at night and eye my empty snack rack, seeing maybe that the thing my work had earned for me was some relief. Flickeringly, I mean, I could see a bag hung up on one of those empty hooks. Straight potato chips, nothing fancy, then bang, a bag of Cheetos, then bang-bang, here come the Cajun corn nuts, watch out now, a sock drawer full of Baby Ruths and Almond Joys. Okay, so maybe you were fucked, but you could eat. Work at Mr. C's. You could even fuck, fucked. Think of the gal on the talk-show TV, fatty with the balding skinny. She fucked. The entire nation watched her haul her foot up clear behind her head—could you top that for living?

Yet I asked myself, compared to her, what did I do? Sure some days passed through there with me swinging mood to mood, blessed and damned in minor modes, aping the involuntary modulations I had witnessed from the General's Acute.

"What's wrong with you?" the General said. "You're acting like a god-damn girl. Shape up. Understand? That's an order."

"Yes, sir," I said. "I mean to."

We sat and watched the weather, cold front coming through, low pressure dragging down the big snows from the north, real winter and the likely end of winter flight.

"Could be you're feeling guilty," said the General. "You could be my pilot. I'm looking into maybe a Bonanza. And a dog. Name the damn thing Bijou, hey? Fly us out to the wine country for brunch? And for tonight," the General said, "just to show you I'm a sport, how 'bout I let you grill that London broil, shish kebab it. We can eat off our sticks in the Comet."

The General made himself a thermos, backed the Comet out into the driveway while I went at the skewers, and by the time I loaded our plates with sticks of meat and red potatoes, the snow was coming down and Hector stood there at the door to tell me the reason I was cut was Mike. I faced him with my plate of meat, not knowing what to say. I invited him in, asked him was he hungry.

"No, thanks," Hector said. "I got to go. Just thought you ought to know. I did some digging around, found out he said he wouldn't play if you did.

That was part of his deal with Krieg. Other part is Krieg has got some kind of a connection with that college where you learn to fly. Talk is if Mike can get us through to State, then he's a shoo-in for a scholarship. Anyway, it's not right, you know, nobody thinks so, and all of us, we're sorry."

Hector turned his collar up, and we both looked out to where the General had his wipers going in the Comet, his headlights shining bright against the falling flakes.

"He just sitting there?" asked Hector.

"He likes it," I said. "Sits out there with a thermos of martinis and the Country Western station. Sometimes we eat out there. He's waiting. Sure you don't want to sit out with us?"

"No, thanks," Hector said. "But no shit, Oney. I'll tell you what, your old man is an animal. Or a machine. You could learn from him. He's a monster man, unkillable."

Thing was, I lived with Hector's news awhile and saw I still liked Mike. I had it worked out in my head so there would be a ratio that said the more Mike pushed away from me, the more it meant he was needing me to save him. I didn't know from what, exactly, didn't know how, figured to get my old job back with Mr. C, keep myself a little closer through the other players, get a little perspective from the fans who didn't even know him. Mainly I would talk to Hector, who said Mike seemed further off and deeper down inside himself, mean, mean, the kind of fight in him where if he had you dead he wouldn't even notice but would keep on trying to kill you. That was Krieg's word for sure, no mercy, no prisoners. He sat up in the bleachers, Krieg did, way up high, said Hector, high against the wall, all by himself, without a whistle or a clipboard. You want to know about Mike, said Hector, then you should hear a little bit of Krieg.

"He wears these big old owly glasses," Hector said. "Light shines off of them and it's like he's looking at you through a pair of lamps. Hardly ever says anything. Usually got us running lines or something so we don't even see him leave. Os and Xs come from his assistants. Stuff we get from Krieg himself is Schopenhauer, Machiavelli. It's like he's got a mic in the ear of those assistants, you know, like you go half-speed on your cut, and a whistle blows and we all stop so it's real quiet, and you're thinking the guy who blew the whistle is going to chew your ass, except he doesn't, he just stands there for too long a time and then you hear Krieg there from the bleachers. Soft voice. Sort of nice and also sort of creepy. Uses your first name. Like, *Concentration, Hector, projection. Concentration and projection. Explode on your man, son. Don't let us down. We know you can do better.* He gets into you," said Hector. "Like everywhere you go, you feel he's watching. Arturo says he's got Krieg in his dreams."

First game they played you saw the Krieg dream send a wake-up call to teams across the state: *This small-town, desert-rat squad can compete.* Proof was an eight-team tournament, big-league Holiday Classic, lots of sound, heavy horns and drumbeat and some real heat to the cheerleaders, a big-league team that lost the game before it took the court by looking past our small-town Huskies as a tune-up. If you never played, and called the game by warm-ups, scored for style, uniform, how many guys could dunk, you couldn't blame them looking past us. They had terrific hair. Headbands. Wristbands. Sateen, azure shorts with golden trim, names stitched into their jerseys. They were loose and easy, good enough to run the showboat with a minimal degree of slop. Whereas our guys looked a little stiff. Square, and stiff, maybe even just a little dingy in the socks department, maybe like these uniforms were being stretched out for another year before our school would spring for new ones. Excepting Hector, we looked like who we were, boys styled by the military and the farm, boys who kept their feet on the ground and their noses to the grindstone.

Still, if you knew our Huskies on the court, what they could do to you in forty minutes, if you looked a little closer and knew that stiffness was resolve, then you might have been more seriously prepared for what was coming. Huskies lost the tip, but they didn't lose much after that. The boys in sateen, when they saw Chester's hook shot wasn't luck, and that Arturo could fit a no-look pass between your legs or through your armpit, when they were finished thinking Mike was not just on a streak and likely would keep hitting threes if they stood back and let him, well, by then it was too late for the boys in sateen, they were finished. Those boys were pretty, they were out there to have fun, but they were crushed by a leaner, colder-blooded bunch, men, looked like, dutiful cogs whose sole design was execution. What you heard from those assistants: "Execute! Execute! Number seven, Sanchez! Seven! Execute!"

Not that they ran anything too special. On the shooting end, you saw the picks coming, you watched them spread the court and swing. Difference was speed, reflex, instinct, drill. On defense, if you watched the ball, you saw hands in the face, quick switches, no easy lane for passing. Away from the ball, you saw heavy contact, hard, quick shots with the elbows, knees, and fists. What happened, if you meant to run your offense on the Huskies, you got mad, red-faced, you appealed to the zebras, you hit back and were caught, called for a technical, sometimes called for two, sometimes were ejected. Coaches were ejected. But never once a Husky coach, never once a Husky. Huskies played up to the limit of the rule book. Tactic was to keep calm while you cut their heads off. Run their lungs out, break their hearts, their will.

Our Huskies took the Holiday Classic, winning their three games against those big-league schools by an average of eleven points.

Concentration and projection. Explode on your man. Execute.

When our Huskies played back in their own league, you could see the other teams were plain afraid. Confused, and afraid; betrayed, and afraid; someone kept on telling them basketball was just a game, a sport, at least, where was the fun in tipping off against a team determined to destroy them. *Intimidation* was a word you heard a lot, *revenge. Revenge is mine, sayeth the Lord.* Every team in our small league had beaten us last year, so here we were, big bad Huskies, regrouped, healthy, new coach from the heartland to inspire us, out to even the score, the young lords out to seek their right revenges. Folks didn't like it. They liked Mike's salute. They liked the General's clocks. The way this team played, a person saw it didn't really matter if there was a crowd to care enough to clap and shriek and throw confetti. Made folks mad, old Coach Jerry's core fans feeling more akin to the knots in the pine they sat on than to the boys they came to root for.

"You ever see them look up here just once?"

"Boys act like they're the be-all-end-all."

"Criminy. It's high school! Who is that coach, no talking to the press? The press is not the press—it's Norm, down at the *County Crier!*"

"And what's that with Hector? He's about as zombie as an Oolag. Remember how he used to run down after he would score, thumping on his chest?"

Said Mr. Cecarelli, "Well, that's what I call basic. Those are elbows. But I'll say what, I'd like to see a smile or two. A smile or two and I bet you we'd be selling pizzas."

Mrs. Swinson, the widowed pig farmer, came up and sat down next to me and said, "Adam, you know me, I'm the Huskiest fan in the bleachers. But this just doesn't feel like winning. Not with that Krieg man lording it over. He's a—what do you call it—*life sucker.* Those cheerleaders, did you ever see a droopier bunch? I'm all for God," said Mrs. Swinson, "but I am not that kind of farmer."

I said I knew what she meant. I was mad, too, hurt, too, I told her, I'd been getting close to getting back in shape. I ought to have been out there. But I sat, huge, and getting huger, Adam Oney, the hugest knothole in the bleachers, standing up and leaving early. Lots left early. You see a paper shredder once, and *wowee*, you are thinking, *that's a miracle, show me, show me*. Doesn't take long though to see the shredder is a simple trick, a pretty crude machine, two or three times through, and you are hoping for the more miraculous of miracles that the paper will go in the one end and come out the other end intact.

I sat out with the General in the Comet, told him I'd been duped. I told him what I thought those schedules had promised, the look of them, the apparent invitation to enlist.

"Like we were supposed to be a part of things," I told the General. "But you never saw a bunch so stingy in their winning."

"That's legitimate," the General said. "A tactic. The mystery campaign. If you want to be a god, you've got to act like God. God doesn't give anything up."

I said, "Well, all right, so how about this—rumor is Krieg got Mike to play because of some connection with a coach at the Academy."

The General nodded, said he knew all about that rumor.

He said, "Your Mrs. Mike came by awhile back and had me write a letter—on the sly from the mister, you know—a recommendation to that same Academy. I know about the deal with Krieg. I know because Mrs. Mike, she doesn't trust it."

"And you wrote it?" I said. "The letter? You wrote it for him?"

"I did," the General said. "I wrote him a hell of a letter. I expect he'll get in. They got a quota for his color. Boy's going to be a damn fine pilot. I like that Mrs. Mike. I don't have much use for the mister. But the missus, you know, I think she's all right."

Myself, I didn't know what to think. Didn't know how to feel. I thought the way I felt was fine. I felt steady to myself. Passed a couple of quizzes, did my prep, tidied, turned the pies out. But then one milder Saturday near Valentine's, the way I thought I felt was soft and needy. Coldcocked by those cards, I guess, the Hallmark industry, what I told myself I needed was a sweetheart, maybe Hector could arrange my getting laid. Meantime, I bought myself a box of chocolates, a Whitman Sampler I drove out to pine with at the pits.

I hiked up the path, blowing hard, surprised by how fast I had lost the lungs I had recovered from the months of running prior to my being cut. I started up with myself with the names Hector had suggested for self-shaming, tried to disgust myself with the vision of my crumb-encrusted queen, the possibility that someday soon I, too, would not be able to find my bleep to bleep the broadside of a bleeping barn with. I told myself to get a grip. *Head up,* I told myself, *nice day out, look there, the shelter's still intact, have a chocolate.* I had an orange cream. A nougat. I studied the names on the lean-to, tried to fit myself in there but couldn't. I walked out to the lip of the pit, considered a jump, set myself up for what turned out to be a scene repeated from the last time I'd been out there, the one where I turn around to see the kid come pumping up the hill behind me on his bike, hollering hey, hey, wait, and then the rest about this place being his and Zack's and Gordy's and I had better not be here to wreck it.

Where do these kids come from? When do you become the size in life when kids on bikes must think your mission is to seek out and destroy their favorite places?

"You gonna jump?" the kid said.

"Thinking about it."

"You're not gonna jump."

"No?"

"No."

"Well, why don't you jump?" I said.

"Never said I would."

"Well, how about I throw you off of here?" I said.

The kid looked up at me, way up, so behind me I thought he could see that spread of sky the way the General had described it.

He said, "You're not gonna throw me off of here."

"No?" I said, and picked the kid up. Snatched him, I could say, because I'm big, and strong, and he was little. Thing was I didn't know what to do with him once I'd snatched him. Just dangled him out there over the edge.

I said, "You're not that other kid at all."

"What kid?" said the kid.

"That Ned."

"No way," said the kid. "Ned's in eighth."

I shook the kid a little bit, I don't know if I was thinking I might scare him, or if I wanted him to know this was our place.

I said, "Listen, I come here for the same reason you do."

"No, you don't," said that kid. "Put me down," he said. "You're not gonna drop me."

Kid was right. They're always right. I put him on the ground and he ran for his bike. Move along, son. That's the word. But I don't listen. Whatever I pick up in life I don't drop but carry. Fat, fat, fat, all right, and heavy. What's an Oney boy to do?

I went to Cecarelli's. Sat down as the customer, asking Mr. C what he thought.

"I think you should eat," said Mr. C. "If that's what makes you feel good, then that's what you should do. You got a raw deal, kid. But I'll tell you what, you've got to ride it out. The good life's on the way. Meantime, what you do, you just try and make the bad life better."

"That's it?" I said.

"What more do you want?" said Mr. C. "Pizza's on the house."

"I don't know," I said. "Just seems so dumb."

"Life's dumb," said Mr. C. "Strip her down to naked, there's not too much to see to life. It either is or isn't. To be or not to be, that is the question. Am I right, professor? All the big ideas in the world are the either-or type. For you, the big idea looks like fight or flee. I'd say you tried the fight. So eat now. Flee. It's all about survival. Dumb survival. Nothing smart about it. Do what makes you feel good, kid."

I wasn't too sure how far sold I was on Mr. Cecarelli's thinking, though I stopped along the way to make some purchases to fortify my snack rack just in case. When I got home, I hurried through the usual setting up the General's midnight forage, a spoon or two of ice cream for myself, and then what, a little music, I decided, something new to welcome in the something new, call my big old queen a dance floor for some fat-boy slide and boogie. I got the soul stuff going, post-Motown sound, *play that funky music, white boy, play that funky music right.* I peeled the shirt off for the mirror, peeled down to the big white Skivvies. I got an eyeful. I worked it up. Let the neck loose, loosened up the hips, rolled the shoulders, let the pelvis fly, boys, I got *down.* Ow, I'm a brick, *house! I'm just a love machine, a huggin', kissin' thing! Voulez-vous coucher avec moi, c'est soir?*

Yes, I said, *surprise, surprise.* I rippled out, swells and tides of me, pulled and come back to the shore of me, Adam Oney! *Work it, Adam, work it! Bow wow,* I was singing, *I'm a sick puppy, love puppy, die-hard Husky, people, I'm the Big Dog!*

First slow song, I jumped down off my bed and dialed up Hector.

"Hector, Hector," I said. "This is Oney, man. I've got it. Here it is, are you ready?"

"Got what?" Hector said.

"It," I said, "*it.*"

"What's it? You know what time it is?"

"It's now," I said. "Time to clean some clocks. Listen up, man, I'm the Big Dog. That's it. I'm the Big Dog. I've got something here will save us."

Save he didn't understand right off. Same with *us.* We talked a time and okay, he agreed, he could see some room on the Husky squad for saving, some areas in need of definite resuscitation, breathe some life back into winning, all right, but no *us,* he said, count him out, at least, no Hector in the Oney scheme, likely doubly true of Hector's Husky teammates.

"Dude," said Hector, "I mean, you want to be a cheerleader?"

Truth? I said *entertainment.* Or, *dancer.* Never said *cheerleader.* All the same though to Hector, who tried to talk me out of anything that made it look like Krieg was right to cut me as a player. Not to mention sissy, he was saying, guys like me, they called me fairy. But I could live with that. Something good was up in me. I felt it on my bed there, heard the voices going loud and clear, *Adam, Adam, try again, son, you can do it!* Sure the details were not given all entirely in hand. Sure I needed the connivance of our Huskiettes. The pregame and the halftimes were their show. Technically, I needed their permission. So I called up Captain Tiff. We agreed it might be best for all if we would meet up on the sly. Thinking here was to *unveil* me. Keep me secret, secret, work hard and be clear, pump some red and blue back in these Husky fans, let's go!

Well, I belonged there. I hit it off.

"We talked you over," Tiff said, "and we think you're just what we've been looking for."

Draw a line from my forehead to my navel, paint the one half of me red, the one half of me blue, make me a pair of Husky-looking ears and a curly Husky tail, spring me next home game at halftime and observe. The music went up, the lights came down, I took the court and kept folks in their seats.

They had never seen me. They were leaving, picking up their coats, starting down the aisles, another Husky rout, another gray, ho-hummer, but when I moved you saw these small-town desert folks pull up, thinking I should not be possible. But there I was, me and the girls, a highly cornball, highly digestible routine. The way it worked, I did my dance, a shirtless beast, I woofed and wagged, chased my tail and romped—I'm a lovable stray, come and pet my belly. Then here they came, our Huskiettes, all dressed out in the opposition's colors, trying to subdue me—this is the routine—one girl with her leash, one girl with her muzzle, got a girl who tries to cage me with a length of plastic picket fence. Some kid from the bleachers hollers, Big Dog! and forget it, girls, the Big Dog is unstoppable, the girls hop on and off of me like fleas and ticks. In the end they shed the opposition's colors, lay down their leashes and their muzzles, show their red and blue and dance. *Watch out, now, watch out folks, get those hands together, stomp those feet, let's rock this gym up through the rafters!*

First time out we ran a little long, our boys coming out for warm-ups just about when I am due to catch the two girls on my shoulders for the photo-op finale. I don't think even Krieg knew what he saw or how he wished the crowd would rather have responded. Because we were bringing it down. We had them shaking in their overalls, waving their canes, no kidding, we'd even got the book-bags-and-braces kids to show some closet boogie. Players swung, too, showed us some teeth till Krieg's assistants must have heard the ESP communication from the man himself and told those boys to put a clamp on, next one caught who taps his foot or pumps his pelvis can expect to sit the bench. That's life. We brought it. That's a skirmish, opening salvos fired in a lively war we were to fight for the remainder of our season.

Another truth? We were not so hot. If you saw us and the way we had with our fans, you would think the lot of us were simple, starved for our share of attention, some camera time, proof of our necessity as active witness to our team's historic moment. After me, for Husky fans, you could be remembered for the ears. If you were a girl, you wore a tail. Whereas if you're a Husky guy, you maybe showed some skin, went shirtless like the beast, painted yourself red and blue, barked and howled like the Big Dog. You saw our colors seep around town again, knickknacks and whatnot speaking more to our routine than to our team. Parking lot marquees at our away games, saying, Welcome Big Dogs. A Big Dog burger. Big Dog shake. Husky T-shirts reading, *Do You Do the Big Dog?* I was woofed at on my walks to school and in the halls; an anonymous admirer drew a set of paw prints on my locker, bubble caption saying, *Grrrrr!* My old lady friends at Buy and Bye said they were thrilled, they had never seen me look so happy.

Sure I said I had a mission, and a mission had its dangers. One day, from the bus, one kid threw his lunch at me. Could have been an offering, but for an offering, I thought he could have said my name at least before he threw that sack, or he could have thrown it not so hard and at the backside of my head. For sure I know the dog shit wasn't any kind of offering. Stinking, steamy pile dumped right on my doorstep. Notes, too, letters I received, all of which you could sum up: *Bowwow, Husky faggot!* That's danger, believe it, unauthorized flight, a mission flown out past the cover from the home base, the General's strict command to play it straight and narrow, fly your tight formation. Three or four games into our routine I told the General what all I was up to and the General said he didn't want to hear it. We sat out in the Comet with our finger food and Country Western and he told me he felt good, asked me did I like that song, was I getting plenty there to eat, so dummy up, son, don't wreck it.

"What did you expect?" said Hector. "I mean, if you're asking only me, I'd say what you do is pretty cool. Didn't think you had it in you. But no man is an island, Oney, so I'd appreciate it if you just sort of steered clear of me for a while here. Word gets back to Krieg I talk to you, I'm shit. Plus which, I don't think you do me any service with the ladies."

"But the girls love it," I said. "And anyway, what about the joie de vivre?"

"I don't know," said Hector. "C'est la vie, the joie de vivre. I'm not stupid. I'm rich, you know? My daddy's rich. The end justifies the means. That's my daddy. That must mean me, too. And it's everything of Krieg. We'll forgive a lot of a winner. Forgive and forget. Ask your old man—I mean, the only reason we make such a big deal out of those civilian gooks in Vietnam is because they kicked our asses. You win, then those monks you slaughtered and that kid you blew his arms and legs off, they are called *collateral damage*. Little oopsies. Read your Machiavelli. We love a lawless hero. Only real crime in this country is to lose."

All true, I thought, too true. Sad, as they say, and true; false, and true; don't fight it. Okay, I told myself, all right, and so I wouldn't lose. I'd win back Hector. I'd beat Krieg. I'd get the girl. I'd win back Mike, make the General proud, just watch me. We won. We won, we won, we won. We heated up, winning. I mean the crowd did. Team kept its Krieg face on, kept its cool, gray pace of play, its killer grip through victories of almost exponentially widening margin. Look back, men, behold the ruin of your conquered conference. Boys, all of them, undisciplined Tarantulas, green Colts, nesting Hawks, all behind you now, a march through regionals, through zone, now on to State, the championship round, it will be for you to bring the crown back to the north!

That's ten weeks through an undefeated season: 21-0. Count one week through the tournament for zone: 3-0. Then say, right, good, eleven weeks, twenty-four games later and we've got our whole town come down with the fever. The Big Dog fever, Husky fever now in equal parts. Score that as a victory for Oney, I will take it. Mr. C sees. The widow Swinson sees. We have worked our way in, insisted on ourselves, made ourselves the banner of the banner season. On the evening news, it's footage of the team, all right, swing pass out to Hector for the fifteen-footer on the baseline, Chester dunking off the pick-and-roll, rerun number hundred-thousand. But look, too, and you have the bleachers in the broadcast, living color, and week by week you see that color creeping out onto the court, it's maybe not inside those boys, nothing they have caught quite through the blood, but it's out there, they are playing through it, it's on their skin, that's eighteen years of colored life old Krieg is leading, you had the sense that one more week, one more game would be his final moment to command them.

That was my sense anyway. I saw the Huskies with the lead in the championship game, seconds on the clock, running a flawless, four-corners keep away, the hometown, northern crowd counting down from five, four, three, two, one—then Mike with the ball, flinging the ball into the stands, the fans mobbed on the court, players swinging their jerseys up above their heads, spasms on the floor of indiscriminate embraces. *I love you guys! I never doubted!* Even Krieg, the shining owl, will dim his lamps a notch so we can see his eyes and know that somewhere in there he is smiling. Pretty B-league. But there it is; we are B-league. Should our moment reach beyond the desert, participate for thirty seconds in our prime-time national news, it will not be owing to the greatness of our game, but to the drama of our people. We overcame. Pulled together. We tapped back into our biblical selves, hometown Davids, Goliath slayers, good old American boys, melting pot phenomenons, cucumbers and radishes and iceberg lettuces, dressed and tossed in the American salad, get it, power to the people, we are the rainbow coalition, sing it, Peter, put us on the airwaves, watch us, here we go now, this one's for my mama, my Lord and Savior Jesus Christ, catch it, the *macrotastic, microcosmic, multiculti hustle!*

Even the General saw it some. He sat with his paper and his cigarette and puffy eyes, folded and refolded to the sports and said it looked like we were having fun.

"Think you have a chance?" he said.

"I do," I said. "I believe we'll win."

"They got a lot of blacks down south," the General said. "You've just got the one."

"That's all right," I said. "We've got a team. Those Oolag boys are six feet six inches, you know. And they can pass. We're smart. We know each other. Knowing counts."

"Well, what do I know," said the General. "Wasn't much basketball where I grew up. The South, real south, town where I come from at least, it's more a football place."

"Like Texas?"

"Like Texas."

The General mopped his yolk up with his toast, pushed his plate aside for me to clear it.

"We're having a party at the pits," I said. "Big bonfire. We've already stacked the pallets."

"That's fine," he said. "That's good. I remember those fires."

"You should come," I said. "I mean, to the game."

"Be something to see, wouldn't it?" the General said.

I said, "I could get you a ticket."

"Game's tonight?"

"Yes, sir," I said. "I could leave a ticket at the door."

"All right," the General said. "I might make that. Could be better than another night out in the Comet, think?"

I said I thought so.

I said, "Tip-off is at eight."

• • •

Here we go then, packed gymnasium, streamers and flags, faces painted red and blue, the ears and the tails of the Big Dog filling up the bleacher seats to riot. But where is the General? Did he get his ticket? Did he have time? Have I missed him? He should see the cameras. He should hear the Big Dog bark. Here I had them going on the Husky side, rhythmic bark, cadenced on a heartbeat, a volume timed and pitched to its crescendo as the Huskies took the floor for warm-ups. Zombie killers, those boys were playing into this game just the same as all the rest, which for those other boys meant murder. Death by execution. One pass, one rebound, one bucket, one mistake-free second leading to another Husky victory, another Husky victim standing dumb and bloodless on the hardwood. Until the buzzer sounded, I don't think our boys looked up to see who they were playing. If they had, they would have seen a lot of cock-and-balls-type stuff, big dunks, chest thumping and strut, muscles cut in lines ungifted by God to rural white boys. Who cared? You don't look at them, they don't exist. They don't have a strength to guard against, they don't exist; no weakness to exploit, they don't exist. Run your offense, run your defense, make them play your game, exploit your weakness, let them find out you don't have one.

Forty minutes, imagine. We all heard the buzzer, raised our voices, needing this particular forty minutes to run much longer. But then a minute is everything but what you need it to be when you are needful of a minute. Too fast. Too familiar. We expect a difference, another kind of game, but the difference we have come to cheer is only difference in degree. We are older. Seniors. We have seen all this before. Those boys up from the south start out the game amused by Chester's yeoman put back, a high-percentage tap from off the glass. They're talking at him, grinning, *Oooo, boy, you got to throw that down!* They come down and score their bucket, some spin-dribble, between-the-legs, around-the-back, double-pump and pretty finger roll, pointing fingers in Arturo's face, in Chester's face, and saying, *That's what I'm talkin' about!* But then the Huskies answer quietly, a good-look fifteen-footer by Mike, an open three-point shot by Mike from the top of the key. And then those boys get loose with their passes against the Husky full-court press, turn it over two times running and they're down by six. They're more confused than amused, you know, losing control, taking the ball down through the paint, dribbling off their feet, picking up the charging fouls, playing one-on-one against a team. We have seen this, boy who hollers at the referee, throws the ball at Hector's knees, earns himself a technical, gets himself benched where he will watch Mike sink his free throws. We have seen these boys begin to holler at each other, lose composure in the moment. The cameras are rolling, the Big Dogs are howling, and these boys here are promising to *fuck you boys up next year, c'mon down to my house, we'll fuck you all up good . . .*

Who hears? Who sees? Not our Huskies! Our team is alone out there, conducting operations, firing away at an invisible opposition. Undoes them every time. *We'll fuck you boys up next year!* Except there isn't any next year. No time to look ahead, no look back; there's no time to be amused, no room to be demoralized; everything is now, here, focused. Concentration and projection. Explode on your man, right? It's war. It's metallic. It's beautiful and awful, a squadron of our nation's Phantoms flying for us, our freedom, a victory we ride up from another victory, freedom to freedom to freedom! We wanted bridges burned. Communications knocked out. Electricity disrupted. We got caught up, screamed for heads on plates, skins on hooks, certainly we didn't find the time for contemplating damage. Those boys from the south would soon walk off the court a beaten bunch, humiliated, forgotten. You could feel it, watch the life lift out of them like water lifted from the desert. Believe it, now, the clock was ticking down, we had the eight-point lead, the ball, just as those most hopeful of us had imagined. Five, four, three, two, one—just as we imagined. Huskies in the four-corner offense, just as we imagined, and just as we imagined there was Mike at the buzzer, throwing the ball up high into the bleachers.

But where was the General? Where is he, I was thinking, the General needs to see this. They were coming down. Fans, the crowd, the B-league mob scene, all right, the liberated masses. Did he not see? The cameras kept on rolling, sure I thought we could be live, maybe he was watching there at home, or listening, we must be on the radio at least, he could be sitting listening in his Comet, freshening his martini for a celebratory toast. He wouldn't need to see. I could tell him. I myself could see just fine. I saw Hector lifting two girls up on his shoulders, just the way I did. Saw the Oolags in the bleachers with their folks. Tall folks, straight, folks born into overalls and gingham. Mrs. Oolag gave her boys a hug; Mr. Oolag shook their hands. Those are good people. Saw Arturo's people, broad-faced and brown, squeezing all together six or seven of them in a knot and weeping. The old widow Swinson, pinching up her *Do You Do the Big Dog?* T-shirt at her nipples, screaming at me, *we did it, Adam, we did it, I knew we could, we did it!* We. There was Krieg, he'd won, I'd beaten him, who cared, the man was true, just as I imagined, something of him down there smiling. Too much, you know, Coach Jerry even, come out for this game to shake Krieg's hand, now there's a sport, and there went Ms. Santoro. My town. My life. I thought I might sit down and cry, what a hokeypokey pageant.

I pressed through the crowd, looking out for Mike. I had a good view. People pushed and pulled and slapped high fives with me but still I kept a wide circumference. I saw Mr. R who looked like he might be pulling Mrs. R out by the elbow. And Mike? Had he dragged Mike with him? No, sir, he had not. That's Mike right there underneath the basket, got the net cut down and looped around his neck, front and center for the camera, seeming most alone of anybody on the winning side, the victor in his interview whose face would tell you nothing of what he was saying. The spell is broken, Mike. I wanted to tell him so, it's over, lighten up, you're on your way, here comes your brother Wilbur. I didn't think. This part I had not imagined. I went to him. I grabbed him up and held him and I wouldn't let him go.

"Put me down," he said, not loud, not so I could even tell how far he meant it.

I held him pretty tight, and tighter when I felt him try to push away from me. I held him high. His feet were off the ground. I could hear the people back behind me, reporter types, saying, *Hey, hey, get this on the cameras, that's the Big Dog!*

"We did it," I was saying. "We stuck it out! We did it!"

I didn't know what to say. I went ahead and kissed him, big, fat, wet one on the cheek.

I could feel him surge against me, trying to flex away. I had him. He couldn't hardly move. I was huge. I didn't know how big I was. He tried to get away, and then he didn't try, but put his head up close to mine, his mouth up to my ear, imagine. What is it, Mike? Orville, I was thinking, speak.

I was saying, "It's over, man. We won. It's over."

"Put me down," he said. "You put me down, and don't you ever touch me, you just stay the hell away."

The way he sounded, he convinced me, right, no problem. He backed away from me, kept his eye on me, backed away until a space had opened up between us big enough to fit another person. Then another, and another. Some wanting a piece of Mike, some of me. I couldn't hear. I think I went a little blind. Too much blood in the head. Temporary major setback. I rushed, right? Too strong, Oney. You're a great big bite to swallow. Did you say love? What would you do, love? Ah, well then, next time. Let things ride awhile. Simmer. Big win here, a real crush of people. You, too, Adam, you're a real crush. Look there, son, you picked him up. His feet were up. He couldn't touch. That's scary. I looked at myself. My hands. My red half and my blue. I thought if I were Mike, then I wouldn't want to know Adam Oney was a whole lot stronger after all than I was, either; I might have seen the wisdom in a cool retreat.

Lucky for me the fans, hard chargers, were ready to party with the Big Dog. Was I going to the pits? Was I going? Big beer bash. Chicks. Pallets stacked to burn a house-sized fire. Would I be there? Sure, I said, sure, you bet! Only I would wait awhile. I savored. Okay, I told myself, all right, still a long night still ahead. Except it sure passed fast. The game did, the crush did, and I supposed the fire at the party would erupt and then die back before it ever even seemed to warm us. I watched the news folks rolling up their gear. Not a player in sight. Older folks cleared out. Couple of young romancers kissing in a corner of the bleachers, couple of pimply faced kids down at the losers' basket, trying to touch the net. Surprise, surprise, how fast the gym will empty out and leave you standing on the hardwood while the lights go down on you and pretty much Coach Jerry. Coach Jerry had his hand out, a look on his face like he and I were soul mates, losers in the winner's circle, the symbiotic parasite, hangers-on who couldn't make the cut. He seemed small. His hand seemed small and soft in mine. I thought, when I shook hands with him, the gym, too, seemed small, and I wondered weirdly if I really was so big, or was it more for me that things were shrinking.

"Great game," Coach Jerry said, and his saying so seemed small, as if the size of what you felt would fit a thimble.

Coach Jerry said, "Looks like they did it all without us, huh?"

"Looks like," I said.

Coach Jerry tried to put his hand on my shoulder, but how high he had to reach must not have felt too fatherly to him, not too coachly, and so he let his hand slide down my back to where it rested at my waist. That was my skin, his soft hand cupping on my fatty blue side.

"Still," he was saying, "was a great game. It's good they won. Good for the town. Those boys deserved it. You all deserved it. You've been together for a long time now."

"Yes, sir," I said.

"Still," he said, "it makes you sad. You stand here and you listen, and there's nothing left to hear. No shoes. I love the shoes. And the band, cheer-leaders—that's a great act you worked up, Adam."

Coach Jerry patted me on the back and I thought maybe would have kept his soft hand to himself but didn't.

I said, "Well, you know, Coach, there's a party. You could go. If you wanted. I think it would be fine, I mean, people liked you."

"You think?" said Jerry. "No, no, that's crazy."

I said, "Well, listen, Coach, I'm going to go. But if you want me to, I can call up Mr. C, have him build you one mean Enforcer. On the house, if you want."

"No," said Coach. "No, thank you, Adam. You're a good kid. You just stay out of trouble. I'll be around. I'm not going anywhere. Maybe I'll see you down the road."

No offense, Coach, but I was thinking not. I was going to that party. My mission was to carry the General in from the Comet, if he had nodded off to sleep, revive myself with a firsthand recount of the ball game if he hadn't. Maybe even mix myself a pre-party martini. I drove up and saw the General's Comet wasn't in the driveway, and the first thought I was having was the good one, which said, *Good, this is good, maybe the old man caught the ball game on the TV.* But when I went inside and saw the TV wasn't on at all, and the place did not smell too much like a recent cigarette, I had the bad thought, which said, *Uh-oh.* I poked around some, and then I had the worst thought, voice that told me, *Oh, no. No, no. What is it? What, sir? What has happened here? What have you done?* He wasn't in the house, wasn't in the Pitts, and I had the knowing in me that he wasn't gone out staggering the neighborhood and I was saying, *Ah, you fuck,* right out loud there in the kitchen while I laid him out his pecan sandies. I said, *Ah, you fuck,* surprised to say so, nothing I imagined, *You stupid Boudreaux cunt.* I could have hurried, but I had that knowing in my fat-fuck, freakish body, a knowing like a woman's knowing, a mother's, probably, a premonition, saying, *Too late, relax, it's over, you're too late, take your time, look here, do a nice job with that milk and cookies.*

Truth? I likely heard the engine. As soon as I walked in the house I must have had some flavor on my palate of the fumes. Probably I heard and tasted and I told myself the General is dead but then I would not listen. Wasn't any note, I told myself, no note, and no way is the General giving up his life to a mistake. True, now, though, my father died. He died. He had an accident. My father, a General, one star, burned guy, *Oh, sir, sir, sir, bad timing.* I opened up the door between the house and the garage, stepped out in the bad blue fog and cut the engine. How would you go? For what cause? By what accidental battle? The General had been tuned to us. I wondered did he live to know we won? The General had his glass gripped in his hand, unspilled, the ice unmelted in his thermos. I asked him did he mind, and took his drink from him and drank it.

I said, "Move over, sir," and shoved him to the middle of the bench seat and sat down as the driver.

I pushed the button to raise the door, backed us out into the driveway, took the top down for the stars. But there were no stars. It was cold.

I said, "Sir, I don't have a shirt on."

I poured myself a drink. I tuned in the Country Western. I poured myself another.

"I'm cold," I said.

I poured another. I stroked the General's head, the scar-slicked patch above his eyebrow.

I said, "You bald fuck. You old survivor."

I tipped my glass up high, finished my drink, threw the glass behind me in the street and said, "I hate these things. Don't know how you drink them. And I have to say I'm sorry, sir, but I don't like this Country."

I kissed him, I thought, sweetly on the forehead. Cold, dead man, I told him I was sorry.

"We won," I said, "I've got to go. Big party."

The rest, by now, I think a person likely has imagined. How Adam Oney flew. How Adam Oney burned. How Adam Oney will go down in yearbook lore as the Huskies' six-foot-seven-inch flambé, voted Most Likely to Fuck Fruit.

I carried the General inside to his recliner, dug up those pink wings from Halloween. My red half and my blue half and my flying pink. I stood hunching on my queen to fit the mirror.

I told myself, "You look all right, Wilbur, you look fine."

I drove out to the pits, walked the trail up to the cliffside, stood there on the lip, and looked down on the party. Crazy scene down there, drunken kids all painted up in fire. I hadn't thought. I hadn't imagined. I thought you were this kid once, right, you were a kid, and you imagined you would fly. And then you flew. And then I thought, *So you have flown, is flight what you imagined?*

I stood waiting to be seen, waited till I heard them hollering for me to jump. Simple thing, clear command, *Jump, Big Dog, jump!* The chant from the liberated masses, *Jump, jump, jump! Jump, Oney, jump!*

Good lieutenant, born flyer, I, Adam Oney, jumped.

THE WORLD I THINK WOULD BE A PEACEFUL PLACE IF WE COULD FEEL AS thankful toward it every day as I myself felt toward those folks who gathered round to celebrate my discharge. That's a bleeding feeling I had there, veins and arteries of thank-yous to my team for sure, and then a heart that beat out gratitude for every Dixie cup and four-pronged cane that blessed me by its quiet spectacle of service. Spectacles of joy, and comfort, wild, wild thrill, a world remade, by me, out the window, I remade it—*Hello there, Mr. Sun, rock on, little cricket!* I was prepared to die of beauty, pass thankfully away in the poet's agonies of pink mimosa.

I said, "You doctors ought to work up a concoction we could shoot up so we felt this way more often. You know, like every time our eyeballs start in beaming out the sour, we just dose ourselves and beam the sweet."

We drank lemonade and fruit punch, ate angel food and pound cake.

"Don't forget," said Sue, "there are kids out there who poke kids in the eyes with sticks."

"I won't forget," I said.

"You get too dosed up, you won't know enough to run before the kid has blinded you."

I said, "I'll remember."

"Watch out for the fall," Sue said. "I'm just saying. High up as you must be, it's a long way down. I worry. You call, hear? You pay attention to your-self? Be good?"

"Is that an order?"

"Yes, sir," said Sue. "That is an order."

"Well, don't you worry, ma'am, I am General Homer Oney's boy. I'll watch out. I have a talent. I'll be back around to take you out for chili-cheese before you know it."

Mr. C drove into town to fetch me. I didn't weep. I thought it would be me to weep but it was Sue. And, hard to say because of his lenses, but I also think our Doctor Noggin. Harder to cure than to be cured, must be, some part of the nurse in us must need a boy to live forever in a needy zone of sickly.

Nurse Sue wheeled me out, hospital regs, and Mr. C went down to drive the car up to the curb, and whoever thought I would be good to see the Comet waiting there to ride me home was right. I would not have known it of myself. That's a lot of history, right? The Deathmobile? Too much life to see relived? Unso! She looked sweet to me, freshly waxed, said Mr. C, just ran her through the no-touch.

"Whose idea?" I asked Mr. C.

"Your Nurse Sue's," he said.

"Selfish, partly," Nurse Sue said. "I've heard so much about this car, I just had to see it. One thing strange, though, I never heard you call this car by name."

"But the Comet is the Comet," I said. "It's its name all by itself."

"Well, I'll tell you something greater," Nurse Sue said, "would be if you could name that car for me."

Nostalgia road, okay, sentimental alley. Still, no tears here. I was young, a pup, the Big Dog, after all, I had a lot of bark in me, a lot of life out there to leave my mark on. Nurse Sue gave me a kiss and a squeeze, and I sat down on the passenger side, asked Mr. C to put the top back up, keep the sun off, just as the General once had asked me; I've still got some skin to grow before we go convertible. I waved, what do you do, you wave and Sue waves back at you, so long, we'll see you in a couple months.

"She's a peach," said Mr. C. "I think she likes you."

"Lots of people like me," I said. "I'm lucky. I'm a likable kind of guy."

"Well, you look good," said Mr. C. "Whole lot better than I would have thought. I know a lot of those kids, they were afraid to come. It's a long way to get here, that's what they say, but you could see more that they were afraid."

"I wasn't pretty."

"No offense," said Mr. C, "but I wouldn't say you're all the way to pretty even now."

"Never was."

"No, I guess you weren't."

"But have I got a job?"

"Whenever you're ready."

I said, "Hey, Mr. C, I've got a big idea—can you spot me some money?"

"How much?"

"Don't know," I said. "Do you know that place called Gold's?"

We drove to Gold's and I went in while Mr. C sat out and waited. He gave me his credit card, said for Mr. Gold to step outside if there was any trouble, it's just that Mr. C could not go all the way quite in, said pawnshops gave him the bad-luck willies. Good luck though was that Mr. Gold was gone, had a long-haired, older guy at work for him who called me dude and knocked off twenty bucks from the price of a guitar. The sap's guitar. Shiny, heavy-metal-looking thing I thought the sap had likely outgrown anyway.

I dropped the guitar with Mr. C, spotted a pay phone and paged through the phone book, found the address, and directed Mr. C to drive us to the seedy side of town, across-the-tracksville, home to Tom and Mrs. Tom, another of those flat-roofed, gravel-topped affairs, kind of place you didn't need to go inside to see the wall stains and the figurines, to smell the mayo and the ketchup on the dishes in the sink, hear the bad reverberation of the fight the mom and pop fought over who said what and why the pop thought he should be entitled to his beer-league softball. I propped the guitar against the door, glad to find nobody was home. I wrote out a note, left my phone number for Mrs. Tom to call me just in case she thought Tom had stolen the guitar, or worse, paid for the guitar when lord knows they could ill afford it.

Mr. C said, "But if he plays, then wouldn't you think he already had a guitar?"

I said, "I don't think he does play. I just always thought he ought to."

That's a Good Sam move, we both agreed, kind of deed you'd like for folks to do you. I got a spiky high from it and then we drove out through the stray dogs and the cars on jacks and all that plastic kiddy stuff all thrown around with no sign of the kiddies, and then I felt the pull come from the bottom.

"So, Sue," I said. "Why not? So we'll call her Sue."

Mr. C ran up onto the interstate, got us up to cruising speed and said, "She feels like Sue. Sue sounds right by me."

We kept pretty quiet till we came upon that first range out of town, crested so you saw the water from the summit.

"Stillwater," I said. "You ever stop there, Mr. C?"

"Never have," he said.

I said, "I used to stop there, times I visited the General."

We passed in and out of sight of the water as we drove down through the pass, splashy silver glitters in our eyes of watered sunshine. Warmish, brackish water, stew of some surprising life. I got dizzy thinking of the birds that waded in that water and the birds that turned above it.

I said, "Want to?"

"Want to what?" said Mr. C.

"Pull off up here," I said. "Stillwater exit. You should see the birds."

Mr. C said, "Up to you, kid. I'll tell you though, you're looking pretty red-faced. Little worn-out. You maybe ought to take care not to overdo it."

I thanked Mr. C for his good-uncleness and told him not to worry. I'd been around here some before, was only just a little better than a year ago, though the thickness of the life that passed that year appeared to stretch out further in the past for me than all the other years I'd lived all run together. Seemed impossible, unreal. Being out there with the General appeared to me to be less real, in any case, than having hunted pill bugs in the weed lot with Mike, less real than the Orange Crate or Lemon Peeler, or our first year all together with Coach Jerry, running as a Husky. The birds were real enough. I watched the skinny-legged ones of them, and the ducks upturned and grazing off the bottom, heard the killdeers shriek and saw them through their broken-winged routine, saw their chicks had hatched, and that was real, all right; I watched the little birds and could remember them as eggs, though not with any hard, true feeling I had ever seen them with the General.

The General was dead. Could that be real? Yes, sir, he was dead. Cremated, according to my mother's wishes. According to the Reverend Marsh, my mother said she had to act, and certainly General Oney wasn't any Christian, didn't own up to the Christian rites, she said, so burn him. I looked out on the water, seeing whether anything was dead or not. I went back to Mr. C, who never did leave very far from Sue. I sat down on her fender, glad to see that much as I had lost, I was still a hefty, sighing presence to her springs.

I said, "You know, the F-4s fly this way sometimes and buzz these birds. Kills them."

"Phantoms?" Mr. C said. "No kidding. How?"

"Happened when I came here with the General. They say it's probably the sound, shock waves or something. But when they buzzed us we were thinking maybe more the sound just scared them."

I said, "I don't think he was a Christian, either. But I don't think that means you have to take and burn him. You would think there could be just a little love left over, or, what happens? I mean, you would think he should deserve a little more respect. A piece of ground, at least. A plaque that told you he made General."

Mr. C said, "Well, where is he?"

I said, "Ah, well, I guess I don't even know. I'm supposed to go ask Mrs. R."

Mr. C said, "We can go there. If he's in a box, or a can, you could bury him. It's what they did with that friend of his, Hal, isn't it? Or else you could strew him. Some folks like to strew the cremains, or you could buy an urn. He wasn't ruled a suicide, you know, bet you still could have a service with religion. Anything you want. I could take you there to Mrs. R's, if you want."

I said no, thanks, knowing the General himself would certainly have gone. Question of duty, I thought, but I was tired, on the downswing, drowsing there in Sue. I woke up at home, our shabby little ranch, its concrete slabs and pads, narrow patches here and there of dead and dying grasses. I thanked Mr. C, who carried in my kit, and kept on saying, *Anything at all, just anything you need, just call me.* We said our good-byes, and then I closed the door behind me in the house where I supposed I would be living.

Wasn't the house I thought it was. Sure it wasn't the kind of mess I wanted anyone to think I'd leave behind me. The way it looked in there was just how I imagined Tom's place looked. The yellowed, smoker's curtains, ashtray stink, and mayo and ketchup crusted on the unwashed dishes, a mean, green bloom of mold grown from the glass of milk I'd poured out for the General. The pecan sandies looked all right, and for that I said a thanks. I sprayed a disinfectant on the kitchen table and a chair, let it sit a bit, wiped it off, and set about the business of redressing my wounds. I could dress myself now. The one arm and my legs. Wasn't easy. But I did it. I said a thanks when I was done, and then I threw a clean sheet on my bed, said what I was calling to myself a prayer of thanks, and fell hard into sleep.

One day at a time. The recovering alcoholic's wisdom, bumper-sticker platitude that served just fine, I thought, for most recoveries in life—go to bed, sleep, don't dream, or if you dream don't fret too much about what happened through the night. Take instead the day. One day at a time, I told myself when I waked up again, look around your room, the old snack rack, did you greet it?

I said, "Good morning, snack rack."

I got up from my big queen, thinking maybe this would be the day I started drinking coffee. I brewed a pot. I poked around and found a couple bags of instant oatmeal. Box of raisins. Stuff I could eat that hadn't soured or expired. I sat down with my bowl and cup of joe, picked up one of the General's papers. I was young. I am young. I never lived with anyone who died before. I folded and refolded from the news from then, which I wagered to myself would not be too much different from the news from now. Statistics in divorce, murder, *hoo boy*, I thought, *we really kill each other, don't we?* Ethnic cleansing, suicide bombers, woman drove herself and her two kids into a lake in Texas. This kind of news could kill you.

Easy, I thought, slow down, lieutenant. Coffee was fine. Amazing how a hardened little raisin plumps up with some boiling water. And look there, it's a good thing anyway that we report. We tell on ourselves. The news to me right then looked like we all were looking for a pretty decent parent, some governance beyond ourselves. Not God, I thought, and opened to the sports page, big write-up in anticipation of the State game. No, I thought, not God, but something more like this right here, story of the underdog, a more local hero, a desert Husky's smiling prospect. We want ourselves, that part of ourselves we've lost beyond ourselves, returned to tell us, *This is what I've done, this is what I can be doing. My life,* the General said, *is pretty unbeliev-able. That anybody is alive at all and knows it, it's pretty unbelievable.*

I stood up to see about my dressings, started peeling and was far enough along and focused in my work so I was really sweating, pained and easy pick-ings for the first-rank fright that jumped through me when Mrs. R came ringing at the doorbell. I guess in retrospect I knew it was Mrs. R. Thing I had not known or would have guessed was that she did not have the Gen-eral. She had her bucket, and her mop, come to help me put the place in order.

I sat there in my underpants and burn goop, a real first-rank Boudreaux. "Mrs. R," I said.

"Child," said Mrs. R, and kissed me on the forehead.

Probably that kiss would be a good way to wind up. A nice conclusion to a new beginning. It sure hurt. That kiss, that *child*, it choked me through the chest and welled behind my eyeballs, another fine mimosa, another moment to have died for. But also there's another way, a little more, a word or two about the talk that goes with cleaning. Not that I was too much help in cleaning, or in talking really, either, but I listened, Mrs. R had news I think it helped me to hear. Good news, almost all of it. About the spring rains and an early jump on next year's Hearts of Gold, news about the rumor of a rib joint opening in the strip mall, and the building of a brand-new public pool, the closer news to me about the reverend who replaced the Reverend Marsh, the relief the congregation felt to see the Reverend Marsh depart for Texas.

"Oh, no, Lord no," said Mrs. R. "Nobody's mad at your old mother. We all saw it coming. I never heard a soul say anything except they wish your mother well."

Mrs. R was on her knees. She was up on stools, deep in cupboards, underneath the sofa. I wore out quick, sat, thankful for the way Mrs. R moved through those dishes and that moldy glass of milk and never quit her talk or showed a flicker of disgust. Not even with me, I thought, my legs or my arm, those broad, raw swaths of unskinned tissue.

"I'm sorry," I said. "We're a mess. Thank you."

"Nothing sorry to it, honey. Would you like for me to pull the curtains?"

"No," I said. "No, thanks, I don't think so. I think I'd like to take them down."

She didn't get to Mike until I asked her.

"He's been accepted, Adam. He got his scholarship," she said. "Come this June, we'll pack him off to the Academy."

I think we both expected more from me, Mrs. R and I; I know I was surprised to feel so mildly.

"The Academy," I said. "That's nice. That's fine. You all must be pretty happy."

Maybe I was tired. Could have been the meds. I would be tired. Expect it. Moody, napping, weak, they say, expect it.

I said, "Is he happy?"

"I believe he is," said Mrs. R. "You know, him and his daddy, they don't wear their happy where you see it."

"That's good," I said, drowsing, losing words from Mrs. R, her voice run in with sounds of bumping furniture and scrubbing. I think I hung around enough to hear the best of it, something of a soothing, constant confirmation. That Coach Krieg was a fraud. Hadn't known a soul at the Academy. Saw his chance with us, won his games, and then resigned to take a JC job in California. That Mike had earned his way by grades, was helped along by the strength of the General's letter. That he might play ball, Mike might, try out as a walk-on, he loved the game, no news to me, I said, "I knew it."

I had a nice long nap. Waked up to a clean house. A clean smell to the place, not like cleaner but an outside smell, like a breeze, a cool, dry breeze blown in from an open window. Seemed brighter, being cleaner, bigger where I saw Mrs. R had taken down the curtains. Quiet there, kind of quiet where you sense you are alone inside your house, though when I got up from the couch, and saw her bucket and her mop I figured Mrs. R must still be with me, a lady able somehow to be quieter than nobody at all. I found her in the back, not sitting in the Pitts, but looking like she'd like to.

She said, "What is this thing?"

I said, "It's called a Pitts."

"This?"

"Yes, ma'am, the General's airplane. Stunt plane. Before the crash."

"Good Lord," said Mrs. R. "I never would have guessed. You know, Michael used to talk about this plane. Made his daddy crazy when he came home all aflutter over how your daddy flew the loop-de-loos and such. Oh, yes, in those days it was General Oney, General Oney, General Oney."

"It was?" I said.

"Oh, yes," said Mrs. R. "Don't think he ever would have quit on talking up the General either, hadn't been his daddy told him to. Still, he said one day, you watch, he would fly that Pitts, said he'd be flying sons and daughters of that Phantom. How about you?"

"No," I said. "Never happen. I outgrew the cockpit."

I kind of toed around the crooked fuselage, showed Mrs. R the way the General worked the canopy for sunshine and for starlight. I felt the breeze pick up so you would call it something closer to a wind. The *move-along* wind. Only when I listened now, I didn't hear the *move-along* part. I walked the

General's concrete pads and mowing strips, stepped up on the concrete he had poured to seal my mother's planters, listening.

"So what are you going to do with it?" said Mrs. R. "This plane, what now?"

"Haul it," I said. "Find somebody with a truck and move it out of here. Then I'm going to tear out all this concrete. My idea is to plant."

I walked over to the Pitts, grabbed hold of the frame and rocked it. Wasn't really all that heavy. To get a bird into the air I guess you have to keep it light.

"I'm cold," I said. "It's surprising. Something with a burn, it gives you chills. I should go in anyway," I said, "time for the p.m. dressings."

We went in and I thought Mrs. R would say she had to leave but she did not and asked me could she help. I said sure, I'd like some help, she'd seen the worst when she walked in, I'd show her how, why not. I told her not to worry. I pulled the old wraps off myself. I opened up the Silvadene. I torched the General's Zippo and I sterilized the blade and scissors. Snip and scrape, cut away the dead stuff, that's the trick with skin to beat the scarring. Mrs. R decided on the blade to start. She had a good eye for seeing the sick stuff from the healthy. She had a steady hand. I was sweating almost sooner than she'd touched me, and I saw Mrs. R was sweating, too. She leaned toward my leg and scraped. She straightened up and looked at me and I could feel that with the sweat there on my face were tears.

She said, "Does it hurt?"

I said, "Hoo, boy, does it."

"Do you want me to stop?" she said.

"No, ma'am," I said. "I do not. Oh, I do," I said, "and I don't."

Mrs. R said, "So tell me, child, which is it?"

I reached and pulled my thumb across her sweating brow.

Funny, I thought, she felt so cool.

I said, "You've got a nice soft skin there, Mrs. R."

Mrs. R said thanks and kept on with the snip and scrape.

I said, "There was a game we played. Radio talk. Kind of pinch your nose and talk into your palm. Goes like this, like I say, 'Come in, Mrs. R, come in, please, do you read me?' And then you say, 'Roger, Adam. That's affirmative. I read you loud and clear,' like that."

My face streamed. Mrs. R handed me a clean white towel.

I said, "We could play it, if you want to."

I reached and wiped the sweat off from her forehead with the towel, wiped my face, and watched her work the dead stuff.

I said, "Want to?"

The author of *Under the Light,* a story collection, Sam Michel divides his time between Montana and Massa-chusetts where he writes and builds rock walls. He and his wife, the writer Noy Holland, are the parents of two children who accompany them on their many travels farther and farther south of the border.